Over the past five years, Amber Rose Gill has established herself as one the nation's favourite TV stars. With 4 million social media followers, she has since proven herself to be an influential entrepreneur and a firm favourite for global brands; she is the face of numerous campaigns. Her TV career continues to flourish as she works with Channel 4 to host *Josh Must Win* alongside Nick Grimshaw and with ITV to bring greater awareness of mental health to young people. Inspired by a lifelong passion for romantic fiction and an ambition to see better representation of ethnically diverse characters in the genre, Amber was the face of, and a judge for, the Mills & Boon Love to Write competition and published her debut novel, *Until I Met You*, in 2022.

Also by Amber Rose Gill

Until I Met You

One Summer in MIAMI

AMBER ROSE GILL

with NADINE GONZALEZ

MILLS & BOON

Mills & Boon
An imprint of HarperCollins*Publishers* Ltd
1 London Bridge Street
London SE1 9GF

www.harpercollins.co.uk

HarperCollins*Publishers*
Macken House, 39/40 Mayor Street Upper,
Dublin 1, D01 C9W8, Ireland

This edition 2024

2
First published in Great Britain by
Mills & Boon, an imprint of HarperCollins*Publishers* Ltd 2024

Copyright © Amber Rose Gill 2024

With thanks to Nadine Gonzalez

Amber Rose Gill asserts the moral right to be identified as the author of this work.
A catalogue record for this book is available from the British Library.

ISBN: 9780008614010

This book is set in 10.8/15.5 pt. Bembo by Type-it AS, Norway

Printed and Bound in the United States

I dedicate this book to the girls who have never seen themselves in a love story before. This one's for you.

CONTENTS

PROLOGUE

'Your attention, please! Guys and girls! Everyone! I've called you over to share big news! Pardon me if I'm a little hoarse. I've been screaming, cackling, bawling for one hour straight. Anyways, I'll get right to it. Your girl made history! I'm the first woman DJ to ever book Solstice main stage!'

'Hear, hear!'

'Cheers!'

'You go, girl!'

'That's what's up!'

'Next summer, I'll be performing at the Solstice Music Week alongside some of the best in the business. Tonight, though, we're going to party. Just don't trash my new place! The sofa is suede. Mess it up and I'll mess you up. Also, careful out there on the balcony. My plants are my babies. Please don't knock them over like last time. I love you all, but you're a rowdy bunch. Other than that, there are no rules. I'll be your DJ tonight. Get ready to dance until the sun comes up or my new neighbours call the cops, whichever comes first. Without further delay, let's get this party started!'

PART I

PITY PARTY

CHAPTER ONE

On the day she was fired, Kya woke up in the Miami Beach villa to the sound of tiny paws scratching at her bedroom door. Her brother, Adrian Reid, and his husband, Hugo Oliveira, had purchased the house, adopted a dachshund named Lucky who loved to nap but flat out refused to let anyone else sleep in, and promptly started inviting houseguests. Kya Reid was the first of a long line. She'd arrived from California the day before.

Groggy and jetlagged, Kya let Lucky in and ceded her bed. Since she was up, she decided to catch up on emails. This was an ambitious, some may say ridiculous, start to a weeklong Miami break, but they'd be wrong. Her work ethic was her superpower. Break or no break, it was better to stay on top of things.

On that bright summer morning full of promise she was as clueless as Lucky, curled up in a ball and snoring in the centre of her bed. Nothing could have tipped her off. The day before, she'd waved goodbye to her team, grabbed a handful of protein bars from the snack room, and left for the airport. She flew from cloudy Northern California to sunny South Florida without issues, streaming podcasts all the way. Adrian swung by to get her at MIA. Later, they met up with Hugo at an Italian restaurant. No calls from the office. No texts. No red flags of any kind. All quiet on the western front.

That was about to change.

After powering up her laptop, she logged into the company network ... or at least, she attempted to. ACCESS DENIED. Second attempt. ACCESS DENIED. She checked her password and even the wi-fi connection. ACCESS DENIED.

Kya called her office, but it was 3 a.m. in San Jose. She left a voicemail and went on to text her teammates: Seth, Alek, John Riley, Jon Yi. Night owls, they texted each other at all hours for far less serious reasons but her messages went unanswered.

Feeling uneasy, and with nothing to do but wait to hear from IT, she logged in to her LinkedIn account and tinkered with a post still lingering in her drafts folder.

LINKEDIN
GIRL DECODED

PRIVATE GROUP
15.3K MEMBERS
ADMINISTRATOR: KYA REID, SOFTWARE ENGINEER AT EX-CELL
MISSION: SHARING EVERYTHING I'VE LEARNED ABOUT THE TECH INDUSTRY

SEVEN DAYS IN MIAMI

Hi guys! It's Kya with another day in the life in big tech post.

I've got a busy day ahead. I'm traveling to Miami to visit family later this afternoon and comfort is key. OOTD: I'm wearing new trousers, a plain white tee, these old boots, and my fav leather jacket. (Pic 1)

At the office, I stash my luggage behind my desk (Pic 2) and swing by the cafeteria for coffee and a bowl of oats. The breakfast buffet has everything I love! (Pic 3) My heart could burst, but I'm steering clear of the pancakes.

I get a lot done before the 9AM stand-up meeting then keep on pushing until it's time to break for lunch. The team treats me to Thai as a nice sendoff. (Pic 4) It's been a while since I've taken a vacation and, honestly, I can't wait. For more on how I plan to stay connected with work while away, watch this space.

Bye for now!

She scheduled the post for later that night when traffic on the site was high. Then she responded to a few questions in the Q&A she'd posted the day before.

Q: **How did you get your start at Ex-Cell?**
A: I attended a college job fair and scored a paid internship. It offered minimum wage, which was a blessing considering that most interns don't get paid at all. As you can imagine, the money did not go very far in California. I took on odd jobs to make up the difference. It wasn't ideal. Thankfully, six months later, I got an offer. Full-time salary and benefits.

Q: **Were you always good with computers?**
A: Not really. In high school, I was the editor of a newspaper that no one bothered to read. Then I started a blog and my readership jumped. It was like magic. Online, a single post on the right platform can potentially go viral and reach millions.

Q: **Where are you from?**

A: Tampa, Florida, born and raised. My parents are from St. Lucia. We spent our summers there. It's been a while since I've been back, and I miss it.

Q: **Are you single? How is the dating scene in San Jose?**
A: I'm single, and the dating pool is too small. I'm ready to branch out.

Q: **I love your style. Where did you get that oversized leather jacket?**
A: It belonged to my ex-girlfriend. That war is long over, to the victor, the spoils!

All that busy work didn't help; Kya was growing anxious. She checked the time. A solid hour had passed. Seth, Alek, John, and Jon should have responded by now. Those were her people. They'd started at the company within weeks of each other, tasked to lead a new division. Trading information was their love language. They kept each other informed, always, through reams of text messages. Why hadn't any of them reached out?

Here, on the East Coast, life was unfolding at a leisurely pace. Her brother took off for work and Hugo set out for the gym. Kya refused to leave the house. 'I have to be here just in case,' she said. 'You understand, right?'

Her brother-in-law did not understand. 'No,' he replied. 'But you do you.' It was lunchtime when she finally got an answer. She was warming up leftover pasta when she got a call from the IT help desk. After confirming her name and ID number, the guy on the line confirmed something she already knew.

'You're locked out of the system.'

8

'For what reason?' she asked. 'Maintenance?'

'Nope.'

It was possible, though unlikely, the company had implemented new rules to keep employees from working while on paid time off. She'd never heard of such a rule, but it was possible.

'When will I get access back?' she asked.

'No time soon,' he replied. 'The account is suspended.'

'Until when?'

'Indefinitely.'

'I don't understand.'

'Check your inbox. You should've received an email explaining all this.'

'How can I check my inbox?' she snapped. 'I've been suspended … *indefinitely*.'

'Please hold.'

The call was transferred to HR. She confirmed her name and ID, and groaned when, once again, she was placed on hold. Kya came close to ripping out her hair when, finally, someone answered.

'Ms Reid, our standard practice is to cc the personal email account on file, the one linked to the job application. I would check there.'

'Check for what?'

'Sorry, I cannot assist you any further.'

Damn it!

Chest tight, Kya punched in the password to an Outlook account she rarely used anymore. She feverishly scrolled through newsletters, credit card offers, and coupon codes, until she found the message from corporate, timestamped 10 p.m. Pacific time. *In*

an effort to streamline the workforce ... Redundant ... Effective immedi-
ately ... Return all equipment ...

Kya dropped the phone. Stunned, she made her way back to the guestroom, Lucky trailing close by, and lowered herself onto the bed. Because the stylish Miami Beach villa wasn't home, she couldn't rage-scream as freely as she would have liked. Instead, she slipped on noise-cancelling headphones and blasted Eminem. When the tears came, she switched to Mariah.

Hours later, that's how Adrian found her. He'd returned home early looking forward to a fun afternoon at the pool with his baby sister. Instead, he found her in the foetal position, blubbering like a baby, crooning the lyrics of a sad girl's anthem for the hundred and fiftieth time through her massive headphones.

'Kya, what's wrong?' Adrian asked, alarmed. 'What happened?'

'I got fired, that's what!'

'Are you sure?'

'Yes! I'm sure. What kind of question is that?'

'How do you know?'

'ACCESS DENIED!'

'Why were you logging in? You're on vacation.'

'You're missing the point!'

Adrian climbed into bed with her and gathered her in his arms. 'Shh ... It's going to be okay.'

'I did not see this coming,' she babbled wetly. 'They were always going on about cutting dead weight, but I didn't think that was me.'

'Screw them,' Adrian said, raising a middle finger to the invisible powers that be. 'You're better than those greedy bastards.'

She sniffled. 'No, I'm not.'

'Yes, you are.'

'I have no idea what to do. I thought I'd work at Ex-Cell forever.'

'Oprah says when you don't know what to do, do nothing.'

'Unless Oprah has a job for me, please leave her out of this.'

Kya rested her head on her brother's shoulder. They were not close in age, but they'd had to band together out of necessity. Both queer, they fought for every scrap of approval their conservative parents could spare them. Their older, straight-laced brother was the golden child. Their childhood was a constant tug-of-war between him and them. Now that he was married with kids, the competition was over. She at least had the advantage of being the only girl and the baby of the bunch. Kya would always be the apple of her dad's eye. It was different with Adrian. As the middle child, he'd largely gone unnoticed. The medical degree, the honours, the brand-new house, all of it was to impress Don and Myriam who, for the most part, remained unimpressed.

'You'll find another job,' he said reassuringly. 'A better job.'

She was an MIT-trained software engineer. It was only a matter of time before headhunters came sniffing. But when you began your career at the top of the pyramid, with one of the world's leading tech companies, top tier in every respect, all other prospects looked dismal.

Hi guys! It's Kya, a twenty-six-year-old washout. Like and follow for more.

'You chose a cut-throat industry,' he continued. 'This is just how they do things; it's not personal. You're young and talented. You have your whole career ahead of you.'

'Thanks.' Kya planted a damp kiss on his cheek. 'Now go away, please. You're hogging the bed.'

She needed to be alone in the dark with her dangerous thoughts.

CHAPTER TWO

Watching others swirl down a drain of misery didn't bring Kya pleasure, but she had to admit it didn't hurt right now. The next night, from her seat in the back of the bar, Kya quietly witnessed the break-up of a couple huddled at a nearby table. 'I hate you!' the blonde woman screamed before jumping up and storming out through an emergency exit. The guy just sat there, dumbfounded, when really, he ought to have been rushing out to the parking lot and checking on his car in case she was smashing the headlights. Not that Kya blamed her. She'd been scorned, too, and the mix of rage and sorrow was unlike anything she'd ever felt.

'You were saying?' Hugo said.

Fifteen minutes ago, he'd abandoned her at their table to greet some DJ from the UK or wherever. He was back, casually picking up the conversation where he'd left off. She didn't blame him for ditching her, she was terrible company tonight. If only he hadn't insisted she come out. She was better off at home.

'I was saying,' she resumed, through clenched teeth, 'that none of this makes sense. What were they thinking? How could they possibly make me redundant? Do I look like dead weight to you? I'm a key player, the ace of spades. When I get back out there, I'm heading straight to HQ. I'll make those cowards tell it to my face. What? You think I won't? I'm not afraid of those men and their small—'

'Small what?' Hugo interrupted.

'*Ideas!*'

'Oh,' he said, disappointed. 'Go on.'

She carried on with her rant. 'I'll make them sorry. I'll cram their email down their throats! Do you hear me?'

'I hear you,' he assured her. 'And I love this energy. But that's assault, and if it lands you in jail don't call me. Or your brother. He works hard and doesn't need the stress.'

She slid him a side-eye. 'You two are useless!'

Hugo, an insufferable optimist, was fundamentally unable to grasp the gravity of her situation.

He shrugged. 'What can I say? We live a soft life. No riding, no dying.'

'Must be nice.'

He reached for her hand. 'This is a bump on a long road. You're strong. You'll survive this.'

Deep inside she did not feel strong. That was the problem.

Kya took a sip of her cocktail, which was unquestionably weak. She was determined to get drunk and this speakeasy-style bar, known for its speciality cocktails, had let her down. Two drinks and no buzz, just a constant ringing in her ear from the loud music, which was driving her insane.

'Do you want my advice?'

'Not really.'

'Chill out,' Hugo advised her anyway. 'Try to have a good time.'

'I *am* chill.' She could stab someone with an icicle, she was that chill.

'Dance!' he ordered. 'Shake it off!'

'Shut up before I assault *you*.'

'Look at where you are.'

She glanced around. The speakeasy was at the heart of artsy Wynwood. It was called Blood Orange due to its monochromatic décor. Everything, from the walls to the velvet chairs, the bold neon signs, even her mediocre cocktail, was in a homicidal hue.

'Looks like I'm in hell, if I'm being honest,' she said.

Hugo winked and ruffled her hair. 'Might as well enjoy it.'

He was a bad influence; that's what she liked most about him. Whenever she travelled to Miami to visit her brother, which wasn't often, she ended up spending most of her time with Hugo. Family lore had it that her sombre sibling had fallen under the Brazilian graphic artist's spell within seconds. It was easy to understand why. Hugo was life-affirming – and handsome, too. Thick black curls, amber skin, a wicked grin, he turned heads wherever they went. While Dr Adrian Reid performed rhinoplasty on the well-to-do, she and Hugo spent their days at the beach and hit the trendy spots at night.

Tonight's event was a private party. They were here at the invitation of one of Hugo's friends. Solstice Music Week was fast approaching and these sorts of events, showcasing electronic music and the genre's superstar DJs, were the norm. A nice change of pace. In the last six months, she hadn't attended any event that didn't involve a corporate logo tee. Normally, she'd be into it. Blood Orange was a cool venue. She'd locked eyes with a gorgeous girl in the ladies' room. When was the last time that had happened? She'd been single a while and eager to move on. Her eagerness lagged.

She'd been at the mirror, doing everything she could to look alive. Her reflection in the ladies' room mirror had shocked her.

Hugo had dragged her out of the house without much warning. Her face was gaunt and her deep brown complexion ashen. Kya did the best with what she had. With trembling hands, she applied lipstick as blush. She ran her fingers through her waist-length braids.

The girl at the next sink, who wasn't having a meltdown, confidently swiped on lip gloss and fluffed her hair. It was just the two of them in the dimly lit, narrow space that smelled heavily of lavender. The music's deep bass pounded at the door. The girl had deep bronze skin and thick curly hair tied back. She wore an oversized blazer, heels, and ... nothing else? She caught Kya staring. It wasn't full-on eye contact, a side glance at most, but there was fire there. And yet, even after all that, her deepest, most ardent desire was to escape, slip out the emergency exit like the angry blonde, hop in a ride home, and crawl back into bed – where Hugo had found her – and cry herself to sleep.

'How long have you known your DJ friend?' she asked Hugo.

He brought his straw to his lips. 'Which one?'

'The one who invited you ... the one from Scotland—'

'England,' he corrected her.

'Yeah, that one.'

'We go way back. Why?'

'Would they mind if we left early?'

Her question went unanswered. Hugo had many friends with whom he went way back, and a group had arrived. They crowded their small table, cackling over a joke that flew over Kya's head, knocking over her drink in the process. She had to get away from these clowns.

Kya got up and made her way to the bar. She needed something simpler and more substantial to survive the night. 'Tequila on ice!' she ordered.

The bar was social media central. A woman at the far end was vlogging, straight up talking to camera with a mini ring light illuminating her features. The guy in the seat next to hers was livestreaming the event. He wore jeans ripped to shreds and if Kya was in a better place, she would've asked him about his tattoos. But she was in a bad place and couldn't be bothered. She couldn't imagine the members of her private LinkedIn group taking an interest in the livestream of a DJ set, so her phone stayed firmly in the back pocket of her vintage Levi's. What would she even say?

Hi guys! It's Kya. Ten p.m. on a Saturday night in Miami and this is a nightmare day in the life of a girl who got laid off from big tech.

Kya scanned the room, looking for no one and somehow finding her, the girl from the ladies' room. Huddled with a group of guys by the stage, awash in red neon light, she glowed while the others faded into the shadows.

If there was anything worth Kya's neighbour photographing, it wasn't a cocktail glass, it was her. In this hellscape, she was an angel. Her light brown hair, now loose, spun to gold at the tips, creating a halo. She was beaming with joy, and when her little group erupted, her laugh bubbled to the surface, light and clear. Some people had made better life choices than her, that much was obvious to Kya. To be happy, what would that even feel like? God, she might die.

The music stopped abruptly to roaring cheers. Kya sighed and welcomed the relative quiet that followed. She wasn't a party girl at heart. Her phone held carefully curated playlists to suit her activities, mainly working, working out, and commuting to work. Power ballads and anthems — that's what she liked most. Anything to wake up the girl boss in her. She could use an anthem now. Hugo said she'd survive this ordeal, but she needed a little help to believe it.

Kya turned to the stage. Her rational thoughts were swimming for their lives, but somehow, she decided this was her chance. One DJ had wrapped their set and now another, the happy girl, was gearing up to replace them. She kept right on chatting with the others while a sound tech hooked her mic. It was a sign, from heaven or hell, that she should make a move.

Kya tossed back the tequila and made her way across the dance floor. Soon the music would pick up, the crowd would swell. It was now or never. The girl pushed up to the podium. Up close and in the light, she was more beautiful than Kya had thought. There was glitter in her hair and her eyelids, and somehow, she sparkled all over.

'Hey, DJ!' Kya cried. '*Heyyy!*'

Was she slurring? God! The tequila hadn't done her any good.

The girl glanced her way. Kya thought for sure she might dismiss her until one of the guys tried to and she blocked him.

'Don't!' she warned.

The single syllable was delivered in a pointed British accent. It took a minute, but Kya managed to connect some dots. 'Hey!' Kya shouted. 'Are you my friend's friend?'

The question sounded stupid even to her own ears.

The girl approached and hunched low to meet Kya's eyes. 'Maybe. I don't know. I've got a lot of friends,' she said. 'Do you need us to call someone to the stage?'

Why was she speaking to her this way? She wasn't a child lost in a mall. 'I'd like to request a song.'

The DJ smiled pleasantly. 'No.'

'No?'

'*No!*' she said. 'Which song, though?' she asked. 'Just curious.'

'"Survivor" by Destiny's Child,' Kya said, in hopes of persuading her. Already the chorus stirred inside her heart.

One of the guys on stage, having overheard, cried, 'This ain't karaoke night!'

Another jumped in, lightning-quick. 'Feeling emotional? Is it that time of the month?'

And yet another added, 'What else can we get you? A hot water bottle?'

Kya's enthusiastic face dropped and her bottom lip stuck out. It looked like she might burst into tears at any moment.

The DJ tried to intervene. 'Shut up! Can't you see that she's *not* okay?'

Her words were swept away in a torrent of laughter. They cackled and howled and congratulated one another on their quick wit. A minute ago, Kya had bragged about taking down her former employers, getting in their faces and telling them what's what. And now? She just stood there like the dead weight she was.

Let them laugh, Kya thought. *They have every right to. I'm not okay. I'm a joke.*

'Go and have a glass of water,' the DJ said. 'You'll be all right.'

The kindness cut deeper than any insult. Kya couldn't take it. She swivelled around and bolted. In her rush to get away, she bumped into a waiter. His loaded tray flipped out of his hands. A second later, Kya was covered in ridicule *and* bright and fruity cocktails.

If humiliation was a colour, it was blood orange.

CHAPTER THREE

Quinn sat on her balcony with her back to the sunrise. She scrolled through the Reddit thread her friend and publicist, Ivy, had sent along with a text which read, Don't let this ruin your day.

Quinn is booked and busy this Solstice Music Week. Here's why.

Below the headline were a couple of photos she'd taken with fans. The photos were cropped; everybody's smiling faces cut out. As a result, Quinn stood alone, smiling broadly, headphones slung around her neck, hair wild, fingers raised in a V, and always wearing some variation of a bikini top and a miniskirt. The subtext was clear: *Quinn coasts on her looks.*

The replies poured in. Coast to coast, guys had sharp opinions backed by blurry photos taken from the far end of crowds. They picked her apart, painted her as every DJ booker's wet dream. It was unanimous. Her appearance gave her an unfair advantage in an already rigged game. As if standing around looking pretty could get the job done. Drawing in a crowd wasn't enough, you had to thrill them, excite them, show them something new – a new song or a new spin on an old track. In a city overflowing with options, you could easily get ignored. Quinn did what she could to stand out, but it didn't stop there. She was an artist. She could deliver, no matter what she was wearing, a lace bra or a wool jumper.

Back to Ivy and her *'Don't let this ruin your day'* take on all this. As if Quinn hadn't worked her arse off to create a signature sound, grow a fan base, build a brand, and stand out in an industry dominated by MEN, only to let a mosquito of a man on Reddit come along and ruin it for her.

Nice try!

After years of playing at private parties in penthouses, mansions, and yachts, Quinn had Summer Solstice to look forward to. The music festival might as well be Oz, a gleaming city on the horizon. Nothing, certainly not some troll, was going to distract her.

Quinn finally looked up and took in the view. Moments like this sharpened her focus. She'd left a loving family behind, moved cities, moved continents, broke hearts, kissed friends goodbye, all to chase a dream. It had paid off. She'd made a name for herself. More than that, she'd made her dreams come true.

Quinn lived in a city that lived for fun, every day a party, which meant she was in her element. That was why she was booked, busy, and in her bag this Music Week.

She tossed her phone aside. Time to crack on with her Sunday routine. She got dressed and took off for bootcamp.

Bootcamp was not the sweet escape she'd counted on. Quinn arrived early and, as always, picked a spot, rolled out a mat, chose her weights, grabbed a towel, and slipped out to the adjoining room to stretch. It was usually quiet there, and Quinn enjoyed the downtime before her class filled up. Not this morning! A young Black woman with braids was giving the punching bag the beating of its life. It was enough to drive her away. She wanted peace and quiet, not whatever show of force this was. She returned to her mat, but the image of the girl lingered.

Why did she look so familiar? Quinn was sure she had never seen this person before. She was a stranger – a stranger who could pack a punch.

She chalked the odd feeling to a critical lack of sleep. She'd been working non-stop these past few weeks. Instead of lying in, like a sensible person, she stuck to her routines. A cup of tea on her balcony at dawn, an early workout, breakfast, and a studio session – that was the structure of her mornings. Her nights were chaotic. Her mornings brought her calm.

From squats to push-ups to planks, the feeling of déjà vu stayed with her. Then from nowhere, the memories came rushing back. The braids, the stride, the proud chin, the slurred words, the request. *Survivor!* This wasn't even their second encounter. Hadn't they bumped into each other, earlier last night, in the ladies' room? There was a moment when … Never mind that. Who was she? Why was she popping up everywhere? Where had she learned to throw punches like that? The better question was: why hadn't she swung at the guys last night? She'd folded so easily. It was heartbreaking to watch. Though, even in the ladies' room she'd seemed … off.

After class, Quinn poked around for her. She toured the weight room, Pilates room, and cardio floor, but she was nowhere to be found. She dropped the matter and decided to grab a smoothie at the snack bar. And there she was, standing alone and looking frazzled.

Quinn called out to her. 'Hey, you!'

She glanced over and instantly went pale. If Quinn weren't blocking the entrance, she suspected the woman would have bolted.

'Relax! I don't bite,' Quinn said. 'A little surprised to see you here. That's all.'

'I'm not stalking you,' she said, quickly.

'It's fine,' she said. 'Sorry about the guys taunting you like that. They're the worst.'

'Well, I'm sorry if I offended you.'

'You didn't,' Quinn said. 'I don't take requests. It's that simple. I'm not a wedding DJ. Imagine if I showed up at your job and told you what to do.'

For some reason, she flinched. 'You're right. I interrupted you at work and made a scene. It was your event, not my private pity party.'

'Next time you want to throw one of those, book me. I'll make it fun.'

'No, thanks,' she said. 'I'll pass.'

'My favourite people!'

Hugo Olivera, everybody's best mate, walked into the snack bar, radiant with a post-workout glow. He drew Survivor Girl into a one-arm hug and planted a kiss on her forehead. So, this was the friend they had in common.

'Quinn, you've finally met my favourite sister,' Hugo said.

Quinn looked from one to the other, not catching the resemblance.

'Sister-in-law,' Survivor Girl said, clearing up the confusion.

'Kya is Adrian's little sister, and what's his is mine,' Hugo explained. 'That's how marriage works.'

Kya … Quinn rolled the name around her mind like a pretty marble.

'This is Jade Quinn, my DJ friend,' Hugo continued. 'The one I told you about.'

They faced each other armed with this new information.

'Nice to meet you, Jade.'

How nice was it really when Kya sounded so sour? 'Call me Quinn or I don't answer,' she said. A silence passed between them.

Iced lavender matcha latte for Kya!

'That's me!' Kya slipped away to retrieve her order. She returned with the drink in hand and an excuse to justify her hasty retreat. 'I'm going to clear out my locker. See you later, H.'

'Take your time,' Hugo said. 'Adrian should be done with the HIIT class in ten.'

Kya nodded in Quinn's general direction and walked out, back straight, braids swinging.

'I didn't know Adrian had a sister.'

'Kya lives out west, Silicon Valley. She's a sweetheart.'

'That girl is no sweetheart, mate!'

He laughed good-naturedly. 'Okay! You got me. Kya is a killer. How did you meet?'

'She requested a song last night.'

'That doesn't sound like her,' Hugo said, frowning. 'Which song?'

'Never mind,' Quinn replied. That was between her and Kya. 'This was nice, but I've gotta run. I have a gig tonight.'

'Anything fun?'

'No … This is one of the dull ones to pay the bills.'

'Have you ever considered marrying rich?' he asked, teasing.

'I would, but I'm not the marrying kind!'

★

Quinn went home, had her breakfast, spent a couple hours in her studio working on a new set, played her gig, went straight to bed, and was up with the sun. Back at the fitness club, she picked a spot, rolled out a mat, chose her weights, grabbed a towel, and slipped out to the adjoining room. She wasn't seeking Kya out. She was going through the motions of her day. It just so happened it led her straight to Kya.

There she was, moving confidently around the bag. Each punch landed in staccato rhythm. She held her gloved hands close to her face, struck with force, and swayed out of the way. Her long braids, gathered loosely, whirled with each swing. It was not like Quinn to stare, but Kya had a way of commanding attention even as she kept to herself.

Like the day before, Quinn returned to her mat. After class, she did not have to search the fitness club for her. She knew exactly where she'd be, at the smoothie bar, ordering a lavender latte.

She did not panic this time around. She didn't react in any way. Her dark eyes were inscrutable. Yet overall, she looked more miserable than anyone had a right to be so early in the morning. She picked up her order at the counter and approached Quinn. 'I was a bitch yesterday,' she said.

'A little bit.'

Kya blinked back surprise. 'All right. See you around.'

She strode away, head high, spine stiff.

Wow. As it turned out, Kya could be a bitch two days in a row.

Quinn ordered a protein shake. On her way out of the snack bar, she encountered Hugo.

'Have you seen Kya?' he asked.

'I have.'

'Do you know where she went?'

'I'd be the last one to know.'

All that girl ever did was glare at Quinn, mumble a few words, and storm off.

Hugo tossed a towel over his shoulder. 'She's going through something.'

'Aren't we all?'

'Not you,' he said, grinning. 'You're winning, getting gigs, playing at Solstice …'

He was right. Quinn *was* winning. So, why was she letting this odd girl get under her skin?

'Kya is not herself.'

'You might be wrong there,' Quinn said. 'I think this is exactly who she is.'

'Even on her best days, she's withdrawn. She's not a people person,' he explained. 'You'd be better off messaging her on LinkedIn. That's where she hangs out.'

'You're joking?'

'She's super career-driven. That's part of the problem.'

Quinn had a long-abandoned LinkedIn account; the password was anyone's guess.

'Trust me. She's going through something right now. All I want is for her to have some fun.'

Kya did look quite miserable. 'Did she at least have fun Saturday night?'

'No,' Hugo said. 'Don't take it personally. It wasn't her scene.'

It was hard not to take it personally when it was your job. She was career-driven, too.

'Why not bring her to Golden Hour later?' Quinn asked. 'She might like it better. Moody speakeasies aren't for everyone.'

Hugo considered the suggestion. 'We'll see.'

CHAPTER FOUR

'Get up!' Hugo ordered. 'Let's go.'

'Go where?' Kya asked, eyes glued to her phone. She'd been scrolling all afternoon, curled up on the couch with Lucky at her feet. The guys had dragged her out of bed for what they'd called a mental health matinee. It started at the gym, the setting of the epic run-in with 'Call me Quinn', then brunch, followed by a quick stop at the farmers' market. That was enough for today. She wasn't leaving this house under any circumstances.

'Golden Hour,' Hugo replied.

'I need more information.'

'On the water. Chill vibes. Great drinks.'

Kya lowered the phone and locked eyes with Hugo. 'Is this another Quinn thing?'

'It is,' he said. 'Why? Is that a problem?'

Honestly, no. She owed 'Call me Quinn or I don't answer' yet another apology for having botched the first one this morning. Kya had been in a mood then. She'd spent her time at the gym shadowboxing with her own demons. She still hadn't heard from her actual friends and was much too sad to consider making new ones, but maybe she could get it together and apologize properly.

'Fine.' She swung her legs off the edge of the couch. 'Let's go.'

Golden Hour was a waterfront bar off the Venetian causeway. The main building's 1960s DNA was intact with its yellow, green, and icy blue colour palette extending to the pool deck. Some patrons came by boat left tethered to the dock. Kya and Hugo arrived just in time for happy hour. The featured cocktail was a spicy margarita. They both hated when a clever bartender dropped a couple of slices of jalapeño in a classic cocktail and labelled it 'spicy'. All the same, they ordered two.

The bar was crowded. Kya left Hugo to find someplace quiet to sit. There'd be time enough to catch up with Quinn. She found a lounge chair at a remote corner of the deck and immediately resumed doom-scrolling while contemplating her own fate.

**Massive Layoffs in Private Tech Companies in
Anticipation of an Economic Recession
Big Tech Loses Big!
A Timeline to the Tech Crunch
Startups Slash Jobs**

'Look who's here!'

Kya shivered at the sound of the familiar voice. Quinn had caught up with her. Dressed for the stage, her halo eclipsed the setting sun.

'Kya Reid, are you sure you're not stalking me?' she asked.

'This was Hugo's idea,' Kya said.

'Mine, actually,' Quinn said. 'I thought you might prefer this venue over the last. And I'm glad you came.'

Naturally, this only made Kya feel petty and small. 'Listen, I owe you an apology.'

'Another one?' Quinn asked, bewildered. 'What are you apologizing for now?'

'For being a bitch this morning.'

'Some things can't be helped,' she said with a shrug. 'We are who we are.'

There was little Kya could say in her defence. She'd never been in the running for Miss Congeniality but getting fired had made her extra bitchy, like a drop of jalapeño in an otherwise unremarkable drink.

'Come with me,' Quinn said.

'Where to?'

Kya was reluctant to leave the comfort of her lounge chair. She'd done what she'd set out to do and was ready to hang it up for the evening.

'Out of the sun, for one thing,' Quinn replied. 'Wouldn't that be nice?'

She took the tone of a professional nanny, skilled at handling difficult children.

'You don't have to babysit me,' Kya said, adopting the tone of an irritable toddler.

'Kya, I've got a set to play,' Quinn said. 'Are you coming or not?'

The answer was no; the single syllable was at the tip of her tongue. Then Quinn extended a hand and, without a second thought, Kya abandoned her lounge chair, her spicy margarita, and her will to fight.

At the DJ's podium, Quinn introduced her to the audio engineer, Mario, and with that introduction, Kya had a way into her world.

'Will you show me what you do?' Kya asked.

Mario furrowed his thin brows. 'Really?'

'Yes, really.'

He gave her a quick and dirty tour that left Kya with more questions. She unleashed her curiosity on Quinn. 'What's all this?' she asked, pointing to the decks covered in buttons, knobs, and levers.

'A standard two-deck console,' Quinn answered. 'That's the mixer in the middle.'

'Mario says the equipment belongs to the bar. Do you store your music on a portable drive?'

Quinn nodded as she slipped her headphones around her neck. 'That's how it works.'

'Sorry to annoy you with so many questions. The geek in me can't help it.'

'It's not annoying,' Quinn said. 'Most people don't care what I do up here so long as they have a good time down there.'

'Most people are stupid,' Kya said, just as a fresh spicy margarita appeared from nowhere.

Mario returned. 'Ready when you are.'

Quinn turned to Kya. 'The Q&A is over, babes.'

'All right.' Kya stepped back. 'Show me what all this equipment can do.'

'Is that a challenge?' Quinn asked.

Kya stirred her drink. 'If you're up for it.'

Quinn's eyes lit up. 'I'm down.'

For Kya, the only challenge was to hold it together until the evening was over and she counted herself safe from this girl's magnetic pull.

★

Yet, later that night, Kya still had a taste for danger. She'd crawled into bed with a loaner laptop from Adrian and spent a few minutes managing her LinkedIn group, scheduling posts from her drafts folder and vetting new members. Ten minutes in, she skipped all that and searched for Quinn, instead. It took only a few clicks.

J Quinn
Miami, Florida

An old page, most likely; the last post dated back years. The thumbnail photo was of a much younger Quinn with blue streaks in her curly hair. She had the same bright eyes and engaging smile. The outdated profile stated that she was a London-based DJ. Her genre was house/hip-hop. Music was her passion, life was a party, and on and on. Kya shut the laptop. The girl lived in a glitter-filled snow globe. In her world, a fun night out with friends counted as work. No one could make her redundant. No one could end her career via email. Was she aware of a looming recession? Was there a crunch in techno world? No! Life was a party!

Lucky scratched at her door. This time, Kya welcomed the distraction. It kept her from the sad truth. She was eager as Lucky to get into Quinn's world. Only a thin amount of pride kept her from scratching at Quinn's door.

CHAPTER FIVE

'Hello, love.' Quinn rolled out her mat alongside Hugo's. 'Where's our sunshine girl this morning?'

'In bed with the blackout drapes drawn,' he replied. 'She's sleeping off those spicy margs.' Hugo folded over and stretched his lower back. 'Plus, I'm giving her a break. She's in a dark place right now.'

'Why do you keep saying that? What's the crisis?'

'Didn't she tell you?' Hugo asked. 'You looked so cosy yesterday. I thought you'd be trading secrets by now.'

Quinn realized how little she and Kya knew about each other. They'd cracked jokes, exchanged barbs, but they hadn't exactly talked about anything deep.

'What is it? A bad break-up?'

'Kind of. She was fired.'

'Oh, no!'

'By email.'

'What?!'

'While on PTO.'

'What's that?'

'Paid time off.'

'You mean paid holiday?'

'I mean they waited until her plane reached cruising altitude before shooting off the email telling her never to come back.'

'You're joking, mate!'

'I wish.'

'So, Saturday night …'

'She was a mess,' Hugo said, confirming Quinn's suspicions. 'I probably shouldn't have forced her to leave the house. She only got the news the day before.'

'Jesus!'

Hugo rolled his shapely shoulders back. 'I know … Adrian is pissed.'

Over the years, Quinn had lost more jobs than she could remember. It wasn't easy, holding steady employment while juggling gigs. Back then the goal was to achieve financial freedom. She'd met that goal, and would never again apply, interview, and submit to a corporation. She sensed Kya was cut from a different cloth. She ran a LinkedIn group entirely dedicated to a desk job. It must have been a devastating blow.

'Will she be okay?'

'She'll survive.'

Survivor.

'She had a good time last night,' Hugo said. 'You hanging out with her made all the difference. Thanks for that.'

'Don't thank me,' Quinn said. 'I enjoyed it.'

Kya was sharp and funny. Quinn hadn't yet figured her out, and that kept things interesting.

'In that case, could you hang out with her today?' Hugo asked. 'Mondays are busy for Adrian and me; we won't be home until late. I hate to think of her alone.'

Quinn hesitated. Her Mondays were free, always. It was one of the perks of being her own boss. Even so, she had stuff to do, mainly laundry. Plus, Ivy was coming around for a mini jam session later in the day. It had been a while since they'd spent time together.

'We'll see,' Quinn said, keeping her tone noncommittal. But by the time they wrapped up the 7 a.m. power yoga class, she'd made up her mind.

Quinn stood outside the door of the white villa, phone in hand, finger hovering over the play button. She rang the bell. No answer. She knocked twice. From deep inside the house, Kya cried, 'Just a second!'

It took quite a few seconds. When the door finally swung open, Quinn was unprepared for those dark eyes boring into her. Bold, beautiful, deadly Kya. If she had to guess, she'd dressed hastily to answer the door. Her long braids spilled messily past her narrow waist. She wore a wrinkled white tee over a pair of cotton boxer shorts. Her clothes looked soft, but everything about her had a slight edge.

'Hi,' she said, hesitant. 'If you're here for Hugo, he's not home.'

Quinn hit play and raised her phone high above her head, in classic John Cusack fashion. The chorus of 'Survivor' poured out of the phone's speaker.

'What are you doing?' Kya cried, alarmed.

'Pardon?' Quinn shouted through laughter.

'I said—'

Quinn cut the music and lowered her arms. 'I heard you the first time.'

'Is this a prank?' she asked, eyes darting around to catch an accomplice hiding in the bushes.

'It's a joke, Kya. Can you take a joke?'

'Not before coffee. I just rolled out of bed.'

33

'Those signature drinks at Golden Hour are lethal. I never touch the stuff.'

'That was information I could have used last night.'

'Could you let me in? It's tough work standing in the sun with your arms held high. Remind me never to do it again.'

Kya moved aside. Quinn stepped into the hallway. The chilled air felt good on her warm skin. 'Next, you'll offer me a glass of water.'

'I have manners!' Kya protested. 'I'm surprised to see you, that's all.'

'Should I go?'

'No.' She swiftly shut the door. It seemed to Quinn that if she could barricade it, she would. 'It's a nice surprise.'

'I'm a nice person,' Quinn assured her. 'But listen, you need a coffee and I need a glass of water. Can we take this convo to the kitchen?'

'Follow me.'

Kya led her through the chicest living room, Palm Spring vibes for days. 'God! This place is stunning.'

Kya glanced over her shoulder. 'Is this your first time here?'

'I was at the housewarming party a few months back.' Quinn pointed to a bottle of gin displayed in a Lucite bar cart. 'That's my gift!'

Kya appraised the bottle. 'Good choice.'

Quinn took in the gauzy floor-to-ceiling curtains. 'It looked nothing like this back then. I love what they've done to it.'

'This is Hugo's handiwork,' Kya said. 'My brother had nothing to do with this.'

In the fresh, all-white kitchen, Kya poured her a glass of water. 'Ice?'

'No, thanks.'

'You sure?' Kya asked. 'Hugo makes the fancy kind, with fruit and edible flowers. It's his new thing.'

'Lovely. No all the same.'

'Will you have a coffee?'

'Never touch the stuff.'

'Of course. Tea? All we have is chamomile.'

'Water is fine. Thanks.'

Kya loaded a fancy espresso machine, working fast as if at gunpoint.

'Do I make you nervous?' Quinn asked.

She slammed a tin of coffee beans onto the immaculate counter. 'What do you think? You haven't told me why you're here.'

'Let me clear up the mystery. I'm here to take you out.'

Kya eyed her. 'Out where?'

'Outside.'

'What for?'

'Are you always like this?' Quinn asked. 'I'm not here to kidnap you. Hugo asked me to get you out of the house today, and here I am.'

'I don't need a babysitter.'

'Consider me your fairy godmother, here to lift your spirits, draw you out of the darkness.'

'I don't need one of those, either. I'm not afraid of the dark.'

Kya pressed a button and the espresso machine sputtered to life. She then moved on to froth milk, but the frother thing wasn't cooperating. The clamour didn't discourage Quinn. 'Have a coffee and get dressed. I don't have all day.'

'If you're so busy, don't let me keep you. I'm not leaving this house.'

'I'm not leaving this house without you, so it's up to you. Choose your own adventure.'

Kya dropped the frother in the sink. 'Why are you so committed to this? What's in it for you?'

Quinn shrugged. 'I owe Hugo a favour.'

Kya poured herself a messy cappuccino. 'He won't blame you. He knows me. I'll tell him you put up a good fight, but eventually gave up.'

'He knows *me*,' Quinn said. 'He knows I don't give up.'

Right then, a floppy-eared dachshund burst into the kitchen on stubby legs, pink tongue dangling from the side of its mouth. At the sight of it, Quinn could've burst with joy. 'What a cutie! Who's this?'

Kya reached down and scooped up the dog. 'This is Lucky,' she said, scratching behind her long, floppy ears.

'Named after the Britney Spears classic bop?' Quinn teased.

'Very funny,' Kya said. 'She's named after St Lucia, where our family is from. She's Adrian's baby, and my emotional support animal for the week.'

'She's adorable.'

Kya gulped her coffee. 'Want to hold her while I shower and change out of my pyjamas? Can't go out looking like this.'

'You're coming, then?' Quinn asked, startling.

'Yes, I'll come,' she said. 'Stop smiling like that. Just take the win.'

'I'll take the cute dog, instead.' Quinn held out her arms, eager to cradle her new little friend. 'Now hand her over.'

CHAPTER SIX

Waking up to Quinn banging on her door, enacting a scene from a 90s rom-com, was the stuff of late-night fantasies, and yet it happened. Kya was confused, at first, even sceptical. Her first instinct was to send her away, then she snapped out of it. Life sucked right now. She'd squeeze every bit of joy out of … whatever this was. But when they sped off in Quinn's sunshine yellow convertible, Kya's go-with-the-flow attitude dried up. She couldn't relax. They were three in the little car, if you counted the silence wedged between them. She gripped the armrest as they glided over the causeway. Only when Quinn took the exit leading downtown did Kya think to ask where they were headed.

'Where are we going?'

'My place, for a listening party. Some people are coming around for a studio session.'

'People!' Kya cried, alarmed. She could not be around *people* right now.

'One person,' Quinn said. 'She'll no doubt bring her boyfriend because that's how she rolls right now.'

Kya shifted in her seat. It was too late to do anything about it now. 'Where do you live, exactly?'

'Brickell,' she replied, her voice carrying over the wind that whipped her ponytail. 'Just over the bridge.'

'I figured you lived on the beach,' Kya said. 'In one of those shiny new buildings.'

'The beach is where I work, most of the time,' Quinn said. 'I need a little distance.'

'I get it.'

They crossed the bridge and were met with the white cityscape and glimpses of the bay.

'Did you know Adrian and Hugo lived on Brickell Key before they bought the house?' she asked, glad to have stumbled upon any topic of conversation. 'I loved their old place. It was small but cosy, and the views were incredible.'

They now lived closer to the beaches, but their only view was of the pool.

Quinn did not answer. At the light, she veered onto Brickell Key Drive.

Kya felt a tug at her heart. The secluded neighbourhood was located on a manmade island off the coast of the mainland. Every corner held a special memory. She'd jogged along these palm tree-lined sidewalks, read an entire book at the park, and loaded up on snacks at the overpriced gourmet market. She pointed out a great white building that scaled upward like a stairway to heaven. 'There! That's their building.'

'It's my building now,' Quinn informed her. 'Unit 510. Sound familiar?'

'Shut up! You bought Adrian's condo?'

'Snapped it up before they put it to market,' Quinn said. 'I got the best deal. Now do you understand why I owe Hugo a favour? He hooked me up.'

Quinn owed Hugo a kidney. This little outing could not make up for the perfect apartment.

'I think I love you,' Kya whispered.

'Ha!'

'I'm serious,' Kya said. 'You probably shouldn't have brought me here. I may never leave. Morning coffee on the balcony, sunset cocktails … Those were the good old days.'

'Just as good under new management,' Quinn said.

'I doubt it,' Kya said. 'My brother-in-law is the king of hospitality.'

'If he's the king, *I'm* the queen.' Quinn pulled into the building's garage, parked in Adrian's former spot, and cut the engine. She faced Kya. 'Now that you're on familiar ground, could you please relax?'

'How do you mean? I'm relaxed!'

'Don't lie to your queen. You've been nervous this whole time.'

'I don't relax easily,' Kya admitted, sheepishly.

Quinn's smile unravelled her. 'We'll work on that.'

It was the same apartment but different. Lighter, airier, and far less cluttered without her brother's extensive collection of movie memorabilia, now relegated to his new home office. A circular pink couch was the star of the show. A collection of vinyl records was on full display. The balcony was exactly as she remembered. The blue-and-white-striped outdoor furniture was likely included in the sale. There was one major difference: the second bedroom was now a recording studio. A state-of-the-art deck was where the queen-sized bed used to be.

'This was my room,' Kya pointed out. 'Hugo left mints on my pillow.'

'Most of my friends end up in my bed after a night out,' Quinn said. 'You know how it is.'

Kya had no idea. Seth, Alek, John, and Jon were welcome to crash on her couch if they were too drunk to drive home, but she would kick them out of bed if they ever tried to crawl in.

Silence spread through the room. Kya struggled with what to say next. She ran a finger along the decks. 'You're really committed to this.'

'It's no different than turning a spare bedroom into an office, is it?' she said.

Kya bit back a laugh. 'What about the future? Any concerns? Will you still be into this twenty years from now?'

Quinn tossed her a look. Kya retreated. 'I don't mean to sound like your judgemental dad or anything.'

'I've got news for you,' Quinn said. 'My dad is the least judgemental person in the world, the live and let live sort.'

'Lucky you,' Kya said, dryly. 'My dad is the type to judge and keep score.'

Quinn frowned. 'Sorry to hear that.'

'No, it's fine.' So what if Quinn's dad sounded like a character from a sitcom? Did she have to sound so petty? 'I don't know why I brought it up.'

'What do you say we leave our dads out of this?'

'Good idea.'

The doorbell chimed. It was her friends. According to Quinn, they were early. As far as Kya was concerned, they were right on time, saving her from inserting her foot further into her mouth.

Quinn's friends were a former beach club hostess turned PR professional and her boyfriend, an event promoter. To Kya, they would forever be the couple who split up at Blood Orange. They didn't recognize her, but she'd recognize them anywhere.

Her wispy blonde hair and his dumbstruck face were imprinted in her mind. Now they stood before her, hand in hand. Every so often she looked up at him adoringly, proving once and for all that love and hate were the opposite sides of the same coin. Quinn introduced them as Ivy Blake and Victor Ortiz, then ushered everyone into her studio. 'I'll play my new set. All I ask is a vibe check.'

'Is this for Summer Solstice?' Ivy asked.

'Only if it's good enough,' Quinn said.

'Stop it!' Ivy cried. 'You're going to blow them away.'

Quinn switched on a four-deck console. 'Ivy has great taste in music,' she said to Kya. 'We worked at a beach club one summer—'

'A while ago,' Ivy interrupted. 'I'm in PR now.'

'Got it,' Kya said.

'Quinn doesn't need my help,' Ivy said. 'She's going to be a star. Have you heard her play live before?'

'She has,' Quinn answered on Kya's behalf. 'She hated it.'

'I did not!' Kya cried.

'Hugo said so.'

Kya plopped into a chair. She was going to have a serious talk with Hugo tonight.

Ivy approached her. 'What type of music do you like, Kya?'

She shrugged. 'All kinds.'

'What's in your phone?' Ivy asked. 'Usually, that's a good place to start.'

'Good idea!' Quinn held out her hand. 'Let's have a look.'

'We're here to judge your music, not mine.'

She would have sooner jumped off the balcony than turned over her phone. Good thing Victor saved her life. 'We don't have all day, Ivy.'

'How long have you got?' Quinn asked, clearly put off.

'Don't mind him,' Ivy said. 'We're here now. Let's get started. I want to dance.'

Quinn slid a vinyl out of its sleeve and placed it on a turntable. Kya studied her gestures. Whereas behind the wheel of her car she'd been chaotic, here, in her element, she was focused, every move studied and controlled. She started them off with a steady, seductive bassline before mixing in a familiar melody. The latest from Doja Cat, if Kya had to guess. As the tempo picked up, Ivy swayed and Victor bobbed his head. Then all at once, in unison, Ivy, Quinn, and Victor belted out a chorus.

Kya startled. She was about to do what she always did, search for the lyrics online, when her phone rang. It was Alek. Her heart rate raced ahead of the beat of the music. She silenced her phone and signalled to Quinn that she would take the call outside. While she sprinted across the apartment, it occurred to her that she might have misread the entire situation. What if she and the guys were in the same boat? They hadn't reached out because, like her, they were all drowning in the same lake.

She took the call on the balcony. 'Alek! Hi!'

'Kya, girl, how's it going?'

'Not great.'

'I feel you.'

'What have you heard?' she asked. 'I'm way out in Florida. It's like I'm in exile.'

'Budget-cut bullshit.'

'Why would they do this to us?' she wailed. 'We delivered.'

'Uh … yeah.' He cleared his throat. 'We hate to lose you. It sucks.'

Kya closed her eyes. So they weren't in the same boat. She

was adrift, alone, just as she'd thought. Might as well get some questions answered. 'Who else did they let go?'

'No one else on our team,' Alek answered. 'But marketing got creamed.'

'If they wanted to trim down marketing, why did I have to lose my job?'

'It's not like that,' he said. 'Each development team had to lose a member.'

'Who decided this?'

'The order came from the top. There was a meeting.'

'A meeting? When?'

She hadn't missed any meetings, as far as she knew.

'Last month.'

'Last month!' Kya shrieked.

'They called a few of us in, and … Look, I know it sounds shitty, but they asked us to keep it quiet.'

'And what did you do at this meeting? Draw straws?'

'Hey,' Alek said, voice clipped. 'It's not like we had a real say in this. We're all just covering our asses.'

Kya's breath went shallow. They took her to lunch, waved goodbye to her when she took off for the airport, and all that time they knew.

'Why are you calling me now?' she asked.

'I wanted to check up on you. I feel bad.'

'Guess what, Alek?' Kya said. 'I feel bad, too.'

She ended the call. For a long while, she stared out at the view, which, in simpler times, always lifted her up. Not today. Her vision was blurred with the tears she refused to cry. Seth, Alek, John, and Jon had thrown her under the bus. Why did that surprise her? They were self-absorbed bastards who, at the end of the day, wouldn't have thought twice of sacrificing her to save their careers. What got to her was the fact that she hadn't been afforded the same privilege. It was a foregone conclusion that she would be the one to go. Her so-called friends, her 'team', thought her expendable. Well, she'd show them. She was going to find a better job at an even more prestigious company, with higher pay and better benefits. When she got that dream job, she would rub it in their smug little faces.

Kya swivelled away from the view and slammed straight into Victor.

He backed away, hands up. 'Woah!'

'How long have you been standing there?' she snapped.

'Long enough to know that you got screwed.'

'Nice.'

'Hey! It's not my fault. I was on my way to the kitchen to grab a bottle of water.'

'I'm going back inside,' Kya said.

She tried moving past him, but he filled the doorway.

'So, what's up?' he asked. 'Did you work for one of those tech companies?'

'Yes, I did.'

'I hear they round people up and fire them execution-style.'

'That's my experience.'

'A friend of mine heads a startup, in case you're looking for work.'

'I'm good. Thanks.'

'No, seriously. Things are picking up down here.'

That may be true, but down here was nowhere near where Kya wanted to be. She couldn't wait to head back to California. She needed to be on the West Coast.

'Thanks, Victor,' she said, with a slap to his back.

The door to the studio swung open, and Quinn and Ivy came stumbling out. If Kya had been paying attention, she would have noticed the music had died a moment ago.

'You just got here,' Quinn complained.

'It's work!' Ivy scoffed. 'You're not my only client, Quinn!'

'I never said I was.'

Kya looked from one to another. This was going to get messy unless someone intervened. She pushed Victor in the line of fire.

Dumbstruck, he looked from one to the other before regaining his composure. 'We'll come back soon,' he said to Quinn. 'Promise.'

The couple cleared out. As Ivy and Victor had failed Kya's personal vibe test, she was glad to see them go.

Quinn pushed the door shut. 'So much for that. You think I need new friends?'

'I'll stay,' Kya said.

Her taste in music might be decades-old, but she could offer encouragement, which was likely all Quinn needed.

'You sure?' Quinn said. 'I could take you home. This has been a bit of a disaster.'

'I want to stay.'

Quinn eyed her. 'It's not like you to be so … compliant. Everything okay?'

'Tough phone call.'

'Ah.'

Kya pocketed her phone and pushed her conversation with Alek to the back of her mind. Screw him.

'Not so fast,' Quinn said, brightening. 'Hand that over!'

'What?' Kya asked, confused.

'Your phone,' Quinn replied. 'Don't think I forgot. If you want to stay, the price of admission is a review of your playlists.'

Kya surrendered her phone without complaint. Now that Ivy and Victor were gone, she wasn't the least bit embarrassed or shy.

Quinn snatched the phone with glee. 'Let's see what we've got here.' A moment later, she was gasping with laughter. 'Kya, babes! There's nothing here but power ballads!'

'That's not true!'

'Fair enough,' Quinn said. 'You have an album labelled "Noise". What's that about?'

Kya explained the purpose of white noise and its variations. 'Green noise helps me focus. Brown noise helps me relax.'

Quinn went on scrolling. 'Some classic hip-hop. I can respect that.'

'I'm West Coast for life.'

She looked up and met her eyes. 'Is that right?'

'Absolutely.'

Quinn returned her phone. Kya pocketed it as quickly as possible.

'Does the noise stuff actually work?' she asked.

'It works for me, especially when I have trouble sleeping.'

'Have you ever tried tea?'

Kya dismissed the suggestion. 'Tea isn't the miracle cure you Brits think it is.'

'I could go for bubble tea right now, if you're into that?' she said in her teasing way.

Kya cracked a smile. 'From the place down the street?'

'Where else?'

'Let's go.'

CHAPTER SEVEN

At a wobbly pavement table, over bubble tea, Quinn confronted Kya. 'Tell me everything.'

Kya went very still. 'Regarding?'

'Please,' Quinn said. 'I wanted to spare your dignity earlier, but there's no point in that. Tell me the whole story.'

'What story?'

'You got sacked. Tell me about it.'

Kya looked around to make sure no one had overheard. 'How do you know that?'

'How do you think?'

'He *told* you?'

'Yes.'

'Is he telling everyone at the gym?'

'I promise you he's not,' Quinn said. 'Even if he were, what would it matter? Who cares what people think?'

'*I* care! I wouldn't expect you to understand. You live in a glitter-filled snow globe.'

'Do I?'

'No offence, but you kind of do. Parties at night, jam sessions all day, no normal person lives that way. No normal person looks like you.'

'What do I look like?'

'A goddess.'

It was hard to be cross when Kya was so earnest. 'Are you going to tell me what happened or what?'

'You want to hear about the job I lost?'

'Yes.'

'The job I spent years bragging about and built an online community around, only to get fired without notice then ghosted by all my work friends?'

'Is there another one?'

'Nope.'

'Then yes, tell me what happened.'

'That's it. That's what happened. I devoted myself to a job and the minute I stepped away from my desk they fired me in an email.'

Quinn tried to unpack her statements, one by one. 'First, it's okay to be proud of your work. It's not bragging.'

'Hugo says I couldn't shut up about it. He says I was obsessed.'

'Not obsessed. Passionate. But I'm not gonna lie, checking email while on holiday is rather obsessive.'

'I did it for content!'

'I can respect that.'

'I planned a series about staying connected while away. It was all mapped out.'

'That might've been your first mistake,' Quinn said. 'Why not a series about unplugging while away? Setting boundaries with your boss? Living life?'

Social media was integral to building Quinn's platform, but there were ways to go about it.

'That's my story. Could we drop this now?'

'It might help to vent.'

'Will it help me get my job back?'

The question shocked Quinn. 'You'd go back?'

Kya seemed equally shocked by her response. 'In a heartbeat!'

'Why?'

'It was my dream job.'

What dream chewed you up and spit you out? That sounded like a nightmare. 'What do they even do at this magical place that you don't want to leave?'

'E-commerce software. If you've bought or sold anything online, chances are you've used one of our platforms.'

Quinn shrugged. 'Chances are I don't care.'

'That's the point,' Kya said. 'You shouldn't have to care. It should be a seamless experience on the user end.'

'Fine,' Quinn conceded. 'I do shop online quite a lot.'

'Look us up. Ex-Cell is one of the top three tech companies to work for.'

'Not if they don't want you.' Who would tell her there was no more '*us*'? Ex-Cell had severed ties. Like after any brutal break-up, it was time for her to move on. 'Kya, it's over. There must be a small part of you that's happy to be free. Admit it.'

'No part of me wanted to be free,' Kya said, stubbornly.

'That's sad.'

Quinn watched her expression darken. She hadn't meant to make Kya even more miserable than she already was. Still, Quinn had one last question for her. 'Who called earlier? Why were you so upset?'

'It was one of the guys from work,' Kya replied. 'Turns out, they knew for some time I was about to get axed. They might've even offered me up as a sacrificial lamb to save their own sorry asses.'

'Repeat after me,' Quinn said, holding Kya's gaze. 'Those boys are trash, and I deserve better.'

'Those boys are trash,' Kya repeated, but stopped there.

Quinn had lost her. 'I want to hear you say it,' she said, wanting desperately to refuel Kya's rage with her own.

'I might have deserved it.'

'How?' Quinn cried, outraged. How could she possibly have deserved to be betrayed?

'Adrian says I chose a cut-throat industry,' she said. 'You'd think I could smell blood in the water, right?'

This was something Quinn could relate to. 'My industry is no better. You think it's a party, but you've met the people I work with. There are no darlings there. Say nothing of the trolls.'

Kya gave her cup a shake, rattling ice cubes and tapioca balls. 'You've got trolls?'

'Just one very active one at the moment. That's a record low for me.'

Already, Kya was reaching for her phone. 'Let's have a look.'

Quinn was quicker, snatching the phone before she got to it. 'Never mind that! Let's head back. You've done enough wallowing for today.'

'Don't fool yourself. I can wallow all day.'

'Consider wallowing in my recording studio, then. It's more comfortable.'

Back at her studio, Quinn eased Kya into her favourite chair, brushed her braids back, and slipped headphones over her ears.

'Play your Solstice set for me,' Kya said.

'You and your requests!' Quinn said. 'Could you just relax?'

'Play it!' she said. 'I won't be here for the concert.'

'It's new, and needs time to breathe,' Quinn explained.

'I shouldn't even have recruited Ivy. It's my sound. I'll know when it's ready.'

'Aw!!' Kya cried. 'I'm so proud of you. That's growth!'

'Shut up!' Quinn said. 'Now close your eyes. You don't have to listen to *noise* to relax. That's what music is for. Let me show you.'

CHAPTER EIGHT

They did not sail over the causeway on the drive home. Traffic was at a slow crawl. Even so, Kya had no complaints. Good vibes as far as the eye could see, all thanks to the person sitting beside her who, coincidently, was the same person featured on a major billboard rising in the distance. There she was, in her usual bikini top, flashing a smile, her golden brown hair around her face.

BLU WELCOMES QUINN at SUNSET SPLASH on JUNE 17

Kya screamed. 'My God! That's you!'

Quinn's jaw dropped. Next thing, she cut through lanes of traffic and veered onto the road shoulder, nearly swiping two cars in the process.

Kya clutched the door handle for dear life, her good vibes evaporated, gone. She turned to Quinn. 'A little notice next time you try to kill us wouldn't hurt.'

'Sorry.'

Quinn had gone pale; her breath came fast. Kya curled a hand around her wrist, felt her pulse leap under her fingertips. 'Aren't you feeling well?' she asked. 'My brother is a doctor. I can get him on the phone.'

She shook her head. 'I'm okay.'

'You don't look it,' Kya said. 'Asthma? Do you have an inhaler?'

'I don't have asthma.'

'What then?'

'That!'

Quinn pointed to the billboard in the distance, but the digital display now featured an ad for a new brand of vitamin water.

'The billboard?' Kya asked. 'What's wrong with it?'

'It's huge!'

'Most billboards are.'

'It's amazing!'

'Yes,' Kya said, laughing. 'It is.'

Quinn cupped her face and let out a soundless scream. Kya rested a hand on her shoulder and encouraged her to breathe. 'Deep breaths!'

Quinn tossed her arms around her and pulled her into a sloppy hug. It was Kya's turn to struggle for breath. She could feel Quinn's beating heart, and her pulse raced to keep up. Out on the causeway, traffic flowed more freely, and cars whizzed past. Kya was content to sit still with her.

Finally, Quinn straightened up. 'Sorry about that,' she said. 'I'll take you home now.'

'Wait,' she said, desperate to extend the moment. Quinn looked at her expectantly. Kya's mind went blank. 'Um ... Is this your first billboard?'

Oh, for the love of God! Did she have to sound like an idiot?

'Yes, Kya,' Quinn said. 'I've lost my billboard virginity ... with you.'

'I'm honoured, and don't take this the wrong way, but are you sure about that?' Kya asked. 'I thought in your line of work—'

'I've been doing this a while, but never on this level,' Quinn confessed. 'I mostly played private parties. And guess what? The bigger the party, the more discreet the client. I can't tell you how many NDAs I've signed. There were never any billboards or radio ads. This is all very new.'

'Is it stressful?' Kya asked.

'No, mate!' Quinn cried. 'I've manifested this!'

Kya didn't appreciate being called 'mate' and had no way to articulate this without coming across as peevish. Instead, she went for the low-hanging fruit. 'Manifested it? Don't tell me you believe in all that.'

'I believe,' Quinn said, one hand raised to the heavens. 'What do you think runs the world? JavaScript?'

It certainly wasn't the power of positive thinking, but Kya wasn't about to sit in this parked car and lay out her belief system, or lack thereof. 'Congratulations on manifesting your dreams.'

'Thanks.' Quinn let out a slow breath. 'It's thrilling … and nerve-wracking. I'll admit it.'

'Thank God! I was beginning to think you weren't human,' Kya teased. 'This is major. We should celebrate.'

Quinn lit up. 'We should!'

'Champagne?' Kya proposed, already plotting ways to raid Adrian and Hugo's premium stash.

'I didn't take you for a champagne/caviar girl,' Quinn said. 'How do you celebrate?'

'Me?' Kya wasn't high maintenance, then again, her face wasn't on a billboard. 'Greasy pizza. Cake for dessert.'

'That sounds delicious.'

'Then that's what we'll do.'

Kya searched for the nearest pizzeria, one without bells, whistles, or Instagram-worthy décor. What she wanted was a hole in the wall with a pizza oven. She found one with a few clicks. 'Take the exit and head north on Biscayne.'

Quinn had one request. 'First, let's get a picture of the billboard, for the content.'

'I got a better idea,' Kya said. 'Let's get a pic of you and the billboard. Get out of the car.'

'I like how you think.'

The photoshoot took ten minutes to pull off. A half-hour later, they ordered California-style pizzas at a takeout counter and hauled the boxes across the boulevard to the park. They found a bench where the bay lapped at their feet. A Ferris wheel spun lazily in the distance.

Kya raised a soda can in a toast. 'To your billboard! Cheers!'

'And to you!' Quinn chimed. 'To better days ahead!'

Kya shifted, uncomfortably. There might as well be storm clouds on the horizon because she couldn't see past tomorrow.

'Something good will come of this mess,' Quinn insisted. 'I promise.'

'Sure.' Kya opened her box and breathed in the classic pepperoni pizza.

'What did you dream of doing before you ever heard of Ex-Cell, Inc., or whatever that horrible place is called?' Quinn asked. 'Surely, you didn't dream of working in Silicon Valley at the tender age of ten – unless you were a very peculiar ten-year-old.'

'I was peculiar,' Kya admitted. 'Still am, but at ten I dreamed of ...'

Kya couldn't recall a single childhood dream. It was as if those memories were locked behind a screen, password protected. To buy time, she tore loose a slice of pizza and took a bite.

Quinn grabbed a napkin from the pile on her lap and dabbed at the corner of her mouth. 'Hold still. You've just got a little… There! Gone!'

The unexpected touch sent Kya reeling. Not just the touch… the care behind it.

'Well?' Quinn asked. 'What did you dream of as a child?'

'To be my own boss.'

Kya had dreamed of a future where she called the shots. Her mother, an executive assistant, had been at her supervisor's beck and call. A word from him and she'd abandon a family dinner, reunion, birthday party, or game night. 'It'll just take a second,' she promised repeatedly. 'Mommy has to work,' her dad would say. 'It's like that sometimes.'

Kya knew it didn't have to be like that. From what she'd gathered from clocking endless hours of TV, a person could live a life without answering to anyone. They could turn down meetings, refuse phone calls, ask a secretary in a pussy-bow blouse to block out hours on their calendar for the sole purpose of attending a basketball game.

'So maybe this is your chance,' Quinn said.

To do what? Kya thought. *Start a lemonade stand? Sell stuff on eBay?*

'I don't think so,' she said.

'Do you want to know what I think?' Quinn asked.

'If I said no, would that stop you?'

'No.'

'Fine. Go ahead.'

'You're hiding behind a major conglomerate,' she said. 'Their successes, their clout, are not your own. You've seen how easily it is for them to toss you out. You can't go running back to them, Kya. You can't look behind. Your future is ahead of you.'

'Damn,' Kya said. 'Who knew you were a sniper in disguise?'

Quinn's mouth was stuffed with four-cheese pizza, and her laugh was muffled. She was a dream.

'Are you done?' Kya asked.

'One more thing!'

'Oh, God! What is it?'

She dropped the crust in the box and set it aside. 'I believe in you.'

Kya thought she'd experienced every emotion known to man since the day had begun, and now a flow of affection. It was too much.

Quinn's phone chimed with a text. She plucked it out of her pocket and made a face as she scanned the message. 'It's Ivy,' she said. 'She and Victor and some others are headed to Smoke tonight.'

'Where's that?' Kya had never heard of it, and she and Hugo had been everywhere.

'A pop-up lounge in an old cigar shop on Washington,' she explained.

'Figures.'

'Skylar is playing a set. Victor's friend Nick is promoting.'

Was this the same friend who headed a startup? Kya wondered.

Quinn kept scrolling through the text. 'VIP. Open bar. They're sending a car. Hmm … I don't know about this. Hard not to feel like an afterthought. Why didn't they tell me any of this before now?'

'Who cares?' Kya said. 'You deserve a night out. Go to Smoke. Order top shelf. Run up a tab. That'll show them.'

'We should go together,' she said. 'Would you come?'

Kya hesitated. 'I don't think they had me in mind.'

'I won't go if you don't,' Quinn said, stubbornly.

'And miss the open bar? That's crazy.'

'It's been nice hanging out today, don't you think?'

'Very nice.'

Quinn pushed her unruly ringlets away from her face. 'Why should it end?'

Kya couldn't think of a single reason. 'Fine, I'll go. But I'm warning you, I'm not a VIP person. I won't fit in with the cool kids.'

'Funny,' Quinn said. 'You're the coolest girl I've met in a while.'

CHAPTER NINE

At the house, Kya swapped her loose T-shirt for a fitted one, and her faded blue jeans for a black pair. She added silver jewellery and stiletto heels so sharp they could double as weapons. Kya made no apology for her sartorial choices. She'd wear a variation of this outfit to the Met Gala, if ever invited. At the most, she'd throw on a blazer.

Quinn let out a low whistle when she came down the stairs. She was only teasing and Kya tried not to read too much into it. The guys weren't home. She sent them a quick text on the group chat, set the alarm, and locked the door on her way out.

Back at Quinn's, she disappeared into her bedroom and came out in a black minidress. Kya couldn't have whistled if she'd wanted to. Her throat was dry. Also, Quinn had caught her snooping. She returned a framed photograph of Quinn, Ivy, and an Asian girl their age with blue-streaked hair, onto the bookshelf.

'My girl gang,' Quinn said, with a nod to the photo. 'The one on the left is Amanda. She's British and Thai. We were best mates at school. Then she went off to uni and I moved around to get my career going. We lived together in London for a bit before I came over here. Then, my first year in Miami, she reached out and asked if she could spend a few weeks in the summer with me. She moved in with me and Ivy and ended up spending an entire year. We were so tight. I thought nothing would come between us.'

In the photo, the three women were smooshed together in the back seat of a car. Daylight couldn't come between them. While studying their smiling faces, Kya had felt a pinch of envy. She had no girlfriends to boast about. Throughout adolescence, there had always been some group of geeky guys willing to take her in. A geek herself, she felt right at home. Girls frightened her. She stuck to the same playbook through college; although by then, dread had been supplanted by desire.

Quinn sat on the arm of the sofa and fluffed her hair. 'They called us the Spice Girls.'

'What broke up the band?' Kya asked.

'Men.'

'Right. Sounds accurate. But Ivy's still here,' Kya pointed out.

'Ivy has Victor,' Quinn said.

'I wasn't going to mention this, but …' Kya hesitated. Should she mind her business?

'But what?' Quinn said. 'Out with it!'

'I'm pretty sure Ivy and Victor broke up at Blood Orange on Friday night.'

'Oh.' Quinn settled down. 'They break up all the time. You'll get used to it.'

'Good to know.'

'It's unfair to pin it all on Victor. Ivy and I have our own issues. She handles my publicity and does a stellar job, but it hasn't been the same between us since she took on this role. It's like mixing genres, it doesn't always work.' Quinn checked her phone. 'Oh God! They're here!'

She shot up and flew around the apartment, as if on a scavenger hunt. She gathered a card case, a set of keys, a compact, and a tube of lip gloss, then crammed the items into a tiny, sparkly handbag. 'That's it! Ready!' she announced.

Kya tucked her phone into her back pocket. 'Same.'

Kya's doubts were confirmed. Quinn's friends absolutely did not have her in mind.

'She's still here,' Ivy blurted as soon as the door to the black car swung open.

Quinn glared at her. 'What's the problem?'

'It's just … Nick will be there,' Ivy said, as if this explained everything.

'You mentioned,' Quinn said. 'He's promoting the event. What does that have to do with Kya?'

Kya instinctively backed away from the vehicle. 'I'll Uber home.'

'No!' Ivy cried. 'I wasn't expecting you; that's all. Come in. It'll be fun.'

'Are you sure?' Kya asked.

'She's sure,' Quinn said, flatly.

As Quinn touched Kya's lower back to ease her into the back of the car, Kya couldn't help but feel a spark.

At Smoke, Ivy and Victor kept Quinn on lockdown in the upper-level VIP area until Nick made his appearance a solid hour later. He was a good-looking guy, if you liked them tall and dark. Judging by the way she smiled at him, Quinn likely did.

Kya escaped the velvet-corded playpen and its free drinks and made her way to the bar to order a tequila – a move that was quickly becoming her MO.

A moment later, she was joined by none other than Ivy.

'Glad I caught up with you, girlfriend,' she said, sliding onto the vacant seat next to Kya's. Her silver sequined top caught the gold light over the bar. 'Didn't mean to be rude earlier.'

Didn't she, though? Kya wondered. And since when were they girlfriends? She gave Ivy a pass, for Quinn's sake.

'I get it,' Kya said. 'I wasn't on the list.'

'I can get anyone on any list,' Ivy boasted. 'I've worked as a hostess up and down the beach, and I know every doorman, every bouncer, and everyone who matters.'

'Impressive,' Kya said dryly.

Ivy bit her lower lip and gave her a look. 'You don't like me. Just say it. You can be real.'

'I don't know you,' Kya said. 'Real enough?'

'You barely know Quinn, and you like her.'

'Quinn came highly recommended by my brother-in-law,' Kya said coolly. 'I trust his opinion.'

Ivy shook her head. 'That's not it. Everyone likes Quinn. She's the nicest person you'll meet. Nick likes her, too. He's been hounding me to hook him up, but Quinn's schedule is tight. Tonight's the first time I've managed to get them together.'

'Does Quinn know?' Kya asked.

'I dropped hints.'

'Couldn't you have asked if she was interested?'

Ivy gave her that look again. 'You think I'm a crappy friend, don't you?'

Her standards were low. So long as a friend didn't cost Kya her livelihood, betray her, or make her feel like a fool, they stood a fighting chance. However, odds were that Ivy already knew she was a crappy friend to Quinn and didn't need Kya to hammer the point home.

'Does it matter what I think?' she asked.

'Nick knows people,' Ivy said. 'Who knows? Maybe someday he'll refer a client. I can't afford to piss him off.'

'Yeah,' Kya said, unconvinced. 'Who knows.'

'If you're wondering why I'm jumping through hoops for a "maybe someday situation", you should know that I lost a client last month.'

'One client?' Kya said. 'That's not so bad.'

'I only had two clients.'

'Including Quinn?'

Ivy nodded slowly.

The bartender came around and addressed Ivy. 'Can I get you something?'

'I'll have what she's having,' Ivy said, with a nod towards Kya.

'Tequila and lime?' he asked.

'God, no!' she cried. 'I'll have a cranberry vodka.' To Kya, she said, 'I don't know why I used that line. It sounds so cool in movies.'

Ivy wasn't the cool girl she was pretending to be. She was awkward, insecure, and covering all of that with blush and golden highlights. Kya was warming up to her.

'If it makes you feel any better, I was fired last week.'

'I know,' she said. 'Victor told me. And it doesn't make me feel better. It makes me feel terrible. Can a girl catch a break?'

The answer was no, but then Kya remembered Quinn and her billboard. Hope stirred within. Maybe someday her dreams could come true, whatever those dreams happened to be.

The bartender set Ivy's drink before her. She raised her glass. 'Let's drink to the struggle!'

Kya was done struggling, at least for today. While Ivy knocked back her cranberry vodka, she stole a glance at Quinn up in the highly visible VIP area. She and Nick seemed engrossed in conversation.

'Looks like they're getting along,' Kya said.

'Who?' Ivy asked.

Who did she think? 'Nick and Quinn.'

Ivy craned her neck to get a look at them. 'I don't know,' she said. 'That's not Quinn's happy face. Besides, she'd more likely go for a girl like you than a guy like him.'

'I call BS.' Kya had a good sense of these things, and that wasn't the vibe she was getting from Quinn.

'Yes, really!' Ivy cried. 'Why do you think I was thrown when I saw you? I figured she wouldn't want to spend any time with him if you were around. Unless I'm wrong about you?'

Was Kya wrong about Quinn? That was the more interesting question.

Ivy didn't wait around for an answer. 'I've got to find Victor,' she said. 'Next time we hang out, no boys allowed, okay? And I'll be the better version of myself. I'll work on my attitude, cleanse my aura, all of that. Sound good?'

'Sounds great.' Kya waved her off. 'Good luck!'

'Thanks! I need it.'

Kya waited until Ivy was far gone before she chanced a look at Quinn again, but she'd disappeared.

CHAPTER TEN

Quinn had tracked Kya on the move, turning away only when the crowd swallowed her up. She smiled blankly at Nick. What was he saying?

'If you're serious, Germany is where it's at!' he shouted over the music.

Ah … He wasn't saying much, only doling out the usual unsolicited advice.

'Miami works for me,' she said.

'But for how long?'

'For now.'

'I get it. You're hot, but you know what they say?'

Quinn stifled a yawn. 'Some like it hot?'

'Am I boring you?'

Oh, yes. She was bored at a visceral level, right down to the marrow. What was she doing making small talk with this guy when the one person she was interested in was somewhere off on her own? She scanned the room for Kya and spotted her at the bar, having a lovely chat with Ivy.

Quinn stared openly for a while until Nick cleared his throat. He was right about one thing: you had to strike while the iron was hot.

'Could you excuse me, Nick?'

'Where are you going?'

Quinn left him to figure it out on his own. She slipped under the velvet ropes, climbed down a flight of stairs, and cut a path through the dance floor. All the while, her heart kept time with the bass. When she made it to the bar, Kya was alone.

Quinn touched her shoulder.

Kya swivelled on the barstool to face her. 'What are you doing here among the commoners?'

Her humour was dry as stale bread. Quinn loved it. 'I escaped,' she said.

'They'll come looking for you.'

'You'll have to hide me. What are you drinking?'

Kya handed over her glass. Quinn took a small sip and winced. 'You don't play around.' She rested the glass on the cocktail napkin. 'Want to get out of here?'

Kya studied her through long lashes. 'What's wrong? Not having fun?'

Quinn moved closer. Her lips to Kya's ear, she whispered, 'I know a better place.'

'Better than a pop-up lounge in an old cigar shop?' Kya quipped. 'Get outta here.'

'It's quiet, low-key, and there shouldn't be a crowd. How does that sound?'

'Nice ... But isn't this your scene?'

'It is,' Quinn said. 'Just not tonight. Close the tab. We're leaving.'

★

The queue outside Smoke rounded the corner, but straight across the avenue was a quiet and welcoming pool hall. Just before the traffic lights turned from red to green, Quinn grabbed Kya's hand and, laughing, took off running across the street. Kya's screams only made her laugh harder. When they made it to the pavement, she screeched, 'Do you have a death wish?'

Quinn teased her. 'Cry baby!'

'A little notice before you try to kill us is all I ask,' Kya said.

Quinn pushed open the door to the pool hall. 'Come. I'll buy you a drink.'

At the bar, Quinn skipped to the jukebox while Kya ordered another tequila and lime for herself and something fruity for her. While Beyoncé belted out the first bars of a recent dance hit, they took their drinks over to a free pool table.

'Do you play?' Quinn asked.

'I do,' Kya answered. 'How's your game?'

'Not great,' Quinn admitted. 'I have an idea, though. Care to raise the stakes?'

Kya's lips twisted to control a smile. 'That's a bold move for someone with virtually no skills.'

Quinn circled the table, gathering the scattered balls into the triangle. 'Wait till you hear what I have in mind.'

'If it's a drinking game, don't bother. I can drink you under this table.'

'No worries, I'm a lightweight,' Quinn conceded. 'How about a round of truth or dare?'

Kya smiled outright. 'How did I not see that coming?'

'I want to get to know you,' Quinn said. 'This is a fun way to go about it.'

'If you say so.' Kya selected two cues off the wall-mounted rack and handed her one. 'Your play.'

'Where did you grow up?' Quinn asked.

'Tampa,' Kya said. 'My whole family is there.'

'Except for Adrian, right?'

'He was the first to fly the nest.'

'And you were next?'

'As fast and as far as I could.'

'Where did you go?'

'Boston.'

'Why did you want to leave so badly? Small-town syndrome?'

'Family drama.'

'Oh?'

'FYI: this is not how you play truth or dare – or pool.'

Quinn sat at the edge of the table. 'It's more fun this way. What was the drama?'

'My family has high expectations.'

'I'm pretty sure you met them.'

'Not all.'

'But you're so accomplished!'

Kya looked away. 'Your turn.'

'Shoot! What do you want to know?'

'You're far away from home.'

Quinn curled her fingers around the cue. 'You noticed.'

'How did you end up here?'

'I told you. I manifested it.'

'You're adorable, but that's nonsense.'

'You seriously think it's bollocks?'

'Does bollocks mean junk science?'

Quinn mulled it over. 'Depends on the context.'

'Well, yes. That's what I think.'

Quinn tugged gently at one of Kya's braids. 'I'm going to make you a vision board. You need clarity.'

'Before you start cutting up magazines, shouldn't I make my own board? It's my vision.'

She clapped. 'Very good!'

Kya rolled her eyes. 'Just answer my question, will you?'

'Fine!' Quinn relented. 'I landed a summer residency at Nikki Beach.'

'The club where you met the Spice Girls?'

'The same,' Quinn said, impressed. 'You've got a good memory.'

'I'm a good listener. It's a gift.'

Kya took away Quinn's cue and returned the pair to the rack, abandoning all pretence of playing pool tonight. It was just as well.

'Would you say you're living your dream life?' she asked.

Quinn considered her question. 'I never thought I'd make it this far. So, yes.'

'Most people keep moving the goal posts. The dream is always out of reach.'

'Most people don't have vision boards.'

'Screw it,' Kya said. 'I'm making one.'

Rihanna was playing on the jukebox. Quinn was genuinely having the time of her life, but it was time to switch it up. 'It's past midnight. Are we still celebrating my billboard or has the deadline passed?'

'There's no deadline,' Kya said. 'Anything you want, just say.'

'I want to dance,' Quinn said. 'I rarely get a chance to. When I'm at a club, I'm working, and even when I'm not, it's hard to relax. I'm focused on what the DJ is doing, listening for transitions, picking up tricks.'

'Where are we headed? Back to Smoke?'

'Why not?'

'Let's go.'

Quinn loved Kya's spontaneity. With her, plans turned at the drop of a dime with no drama, no fuss. She insisted on dictating when and where they crossed the street; that was all.

Back at Smoke, a new DJ had taken over. A former runway model from Senegal, he weaved Afrobeats into his set. The floor was packed. Quinn took Kya by the waist, and together they forged a path to the very centre. It was hot and thrilling, but nothing was hotter or more thrilling than Kya spinning, hands up, braids flying. This wasn't the sad person from earlier today, and that was reason enough to celebrate.

@LexyT

FOLLOWERS: 5.1K
FOLLOWING: 740

Life Hacks & Advice
She/Her

Audio Transcript:

Ready for some tech tea?

Tonight's topic is Girl Fraud! I know this is far from my usual content, but I must share.

Over on another platform, I joined a group run by Kya Reid, aka Girl Decoded. A software engineer at Ex-Cell, Kya gives stellar career advice for women trying to break into the industry. Don't ask me why I joined. I need tech support to unlock my iPhone. Ha! But here, in San Fran, we're so entrenched in tech culture, every other guy I've dated runs a startup out of his grandma's attic. It's ridiculous, at this point.

Anyway, I'm at an event Sunday night and I meet a guy who claims to work at Ex-Cell. He's hot and I want to impress him, so I drop Kya's name. Of course, he's heard of her. Know what else he's heard? Girlfriend was let go last week! Fired!

So much for impressing him!

As soon as I get home I get to sleuthing. First, I pull up the company's website. She was profiled on the Meet Our Team page. That's gone. There's no mention of her anywhere. Next, I log into the private group and Ms. Kya hasn't skipped a post. She's talking about staying connected with the office while on vacay. Like ... what is she on about? And is this a permanent vacay? Be honest!

What the hell is going on? I'm so confused! Is this Girl Decoded a fraud?

Has anything like this happened to you? Sound off in the comments below.

#StoryTime #KyaGirlCode #Fraud

CHAPTER ELEVEN

It wasn't the best night of her life, but it was way up there. Top five, at least. They shut down the club. On the ride home, reunited with Ivy and Victor, they rolled down the windows, blasted the car radio, and made up lyrics to songs they didn't know. But it was the quiet moments with Quinn that stood out in Kya's mind, every conversation, every look, every touch. The next day, to keep from reliving the experience obsessively, Kya kept busy. She took Lucky out on long walks, washed dishes, did laundry, all the while nursing a migraine. Finally, after dinner, she collapsed into her favourite chair in her bedroom for a check with the Girl Decoded community. She was met with a flurry of LinkedIn notifications. What could've happened since she'd checked in last? What had she missed?

A few clicks later, she had an answer: an accusation of fraud levied against her on TikTok. Obviously, a case of mistaken identity! She wasn't the only Kya Reid on the planet. She tapped the link to the video, ready for a good laugh.

Girlfriend was let go last week! FIRED!

TikTok user @LexyT blurted the words while touching up her make-up.

Kya had been fired from Ex-Cell and kept right on posting as if nothing had happened. That was the crux of the accusation. Her behaviour was sketchy, at best. To call her a fraud was outrageous!

Judging from the comments on her latest post, her community was eating it up.

Kya shrivelled inside. She hadn't meant to mislead anyone. Honestly, she hadn't given it much thought. The plan was to get a new job (a bigger, better job to rub in Alek's face) and make a grand announcement. Until then, the plan was to gloss it over, cover it up, pretend it never happened. So, yes, maybe, under those limited circumstances, she was a fraud.

Oh, Jesus.

Then, without warning, her mood flipped to rage. What was she supposed to do, post her termination email online the second she got it? Who was this Lexy T person to question her? No, really, who exactly was Lexy T? News travelled fast in her world, but this woman's story was too contrived to be true. When had she joined her group, anyway? Kya had an engaged community and could usually spot her followers by their handles or thumbnail photos.

She didn't have to do too much work to find out. She logged into her account, combed through her followers. Among the newest followers were Quinn, who'd joined as a joke, and Lexy Tanner. Kya had likely admitted her to the group in one of those intense moments while she waited to learn why she'd been locked out of her account. It was as if she'd joined simply to confirm the thing she already knew. But *how* had she found out? No one in their right mind would drop Kya's name to impress a hot guy – a hot girl, maybe – a guy, never.

Who was she, then? On LinkedIn, Lexy Tanner was a life coach in the Bay Area. On TikTok, @LexyT dispensed life advice and sold a four-part course on how to 'glow up and get the life you deserve'. On Instagram @LexxxxyT posted casual photos with friends at bars, at brunch, at karaoke, and one of her dear friends, a core member of her 'gang', was none other than quiet, unassuming, salt-of-the-earth John Riley. There he was in each photo, pink-faced – he could never handle his liquor – his toothy grin toothier than ever. John was indiscreet, a quality that she'd appreciated as he would keep their little group informed of all the office gossip. John had told Lexy the news. Or, more realistically, John had put her on blast on his group chat the instant he'd learned of her termination.

None of this made her feel any better.

Kya folded over, her head between her knees. And that's how her big brother found her, a moment later, when he popped his head through the doorway to ask if she was up for gelato for dessert.

'What's wrong? What happened?' Adrian cried. (This was becoming a habit.)

Kya handed him the phone with all the incriminating evidence. He thumbed through it, watched Lexy T's video, and combed through the comments section. Adrian was the type to sweat the small stuff, and she could not have loved him more for it.

Hugo came around for a follow-up. 'Gelato, yes or no? It's melting.'

'I'd love some.' Kya tried to sound upbeat, only her face was streaked with tears, and she failed miserably.

'Sweetheart, it's just dessert,' Hugo said, confused.

'Kya was called out for not telling her LinkedIn group that she got fired,' Adrian explained quietly.

'Called out by who?'

'A life coach in the Bay Area.'

'Sounds like they need to get a life,' Hugo said. 'Did they expect you to hold a press conference?'

'I scheduled out a few posts,' Kya said. 'So, on the surface, it looks like I'm still working and everything is fine.'

Hugo shook his head. 'You do too much, Kya.'

'I know!' she wailed. 'But now I don't know what to do.'

'Block the haters,' Hugo said. 'What else?'

Kya was considering the deceptively simple plan when Adrian spoke up. 'Address it head-on with a short video response,' he said. 'Confirm that your employment was terminated while you were away on a trip, and you planned to inform the community as soon as you got back.'

'I didn't, though,' Kya said. 'I never planned on telling them.'

'Yes, you did,' Hugo said, sharply.

Adrian sat at the corner of the bed. 'Kya, you're reeling now, but eventually you would have done the right thing. Don't beat yourself up. Besides, you're not the only person in this situation. People will relate.'

'And if they don't?' Kya asked.

'If they don't, you can tell them where to go,' Hugo said.

Kya looked from one to the other. They were both right.

Adrian recommended she post her response on TikTok. 'Hit them where they hit you. Show them that you're unafraid.'

'I'm not on TikTok,' Kya said.

'Are you serious?' Hugo asked, astounded. 'Not even for the guy who chops wood?'

'I'm not into guys,' Kya reminded them. There was no lumberjack exception.

'I'm on the app,' Adrian said. 'It's not all dance challenges and men chopping wood. My followers have questions about cosmetic surgery. I share the pros and cons.'

Hugo pulled up Adrian's profile on his phone. He had, to date, one million followers worldwide.

'Are you kidding me with this?' she cried. Adrian, a social media star? Kya was truly reeling now.

'You need to branch out,' Hugo advised.

'There'll be time enough for that,' Adrian said. 'Let's get to work on that response. I don't want this to fester overnight.'

'Okay.' Kya wiped her face with the back of her hand. 'Give me a chance to find my tripod.'

'I've got a studio set up in my office. Let's head over.'

Kya rolled her eyes. Of course he had.

'First, you need concealer,' Hugo added. 'Go take care of that. I'll put away the gelato for later.'

It took three takes before Kya came up with something halfway decent, which she scrapped. It was tough keeping her voice controlled, her emotions in check. Finally, she quit trying and just went for it. The result was raw but effective.

Audio Transcript: Response to Fraud Accusation

Hi guys. It's Kya, creator of Girl Decoded, a LinkedIn group dedicated to encourage young women to find success in tech. If you've followed me awhile, you'll know how hard I worked to get my foot in the door of one of the leading companies and how much pride I took in my job. Unfortunately, last Thursday I was let go.

Someone took the time to post a video on this app, calling me a fraud, because a few scheduled posts rolled out before I had a chance to process the news. This is to set the record straight.

I'm not a fraud – or a liar. I'm deeply embarrassed, that's all.

I dedicated years to a company that thought nothing of firing me the minute I stepped away from my desk.

Want the truth about a day in the life of a girl in big tech? It's gruelling, all-consuming. It's long hours, sometimes breakfast, lunch, and dinner at your desk. Weekends lost to deadlines. Projects scrapped with no explanation. Sparking with co-workers on ideas that never make it out of the email inbox. It's commuting home and already dreading the next day. But the next day could be the best yet. A new discovery, a smart collaboration, or a change in direction could be just the thing to get you over the slump. Working at Ex-Cell was exhilarating and maddening. Romanticizing my time there was one way to deal with the stress.

This was a terrible blow for me. I raged and cried. I had an epic pity party. Now it's time for me to get some perspective. A job isn't everything, and I need to figure out who I am without one.

I still don't know what the future holds. When I do, I'll check back in.

Bye for now.

PART II

PARTY CRASHER

CHAPTER TWELVE

LINKEDIN DM

QUINN: What on earth is going on in your comments section?!

KYA: Is this why you joined the group? To scroll my comments at night?

QUINN: What are they going on about? Who's this Lexy person?

KYA: A troll. Now we both have one. We're twinning!

QUINN: She's called you a liar.

KYA: I'm over it, and who cares what people think? Right?

QUINN: Wrong! This is not some random man on Reddit! This woman is casting aspersions on your character.

KYA: Casting what???

QUINN: I'm serious! You can't let this slide.

KYA: I made a video response on TikTok.

QUINN: TikTok? That's my wheelhouse. I'll check it out. Hold on …

QUINN: Found you! Kya, love, you've only three followers! Hugo, Adrian, and a bot!

KYA: I just signed up a minute ago!

QUINN: This video is 15 seconds long. Is there a part two?

KYA: It's direct, succinct!

QUINN: Okay. Watching now.

QUINN: Okay, done.

KYA: What do you think?

QUINN: Honestly? I don't think you went hard enough. It's too tame for a clap back.

KYA: I wasn't clapping back, just setting the record straight.

QUINN: We need to do more.

KYA: Track her down? Confront her?

QUINN: I'm up for it.

KYA: Hugo and Adrian won't let me. I'm in protective custody. ☹

QUINN: I'm free tonight. I'll break you out of lockdown. We'll go somewhere and talk.

KYA: No.

QUINN: No?

KYA: No. I don't want to talk. I'm done talking. I don't want to talk about that stupid job, losing it, losing sleep over it, debating whether I lied about it, all of it!

QUINN: ...

QUINN: Go change into a swimsuit. We're going to the pool. It's nice and quiet at night.

KYA: Your community pool? It's also closed at night, or have the rules changed?

QUINN: You're such a good girl. I bet you've never crashed a party.

KYA: Does an office party count?

QUINN: Grab a bikini. I'm coming to get you.

POOL HOURS: SUNUP TO SUNDOWN.

The sign was clear. However, the gate swung open freely when Quinn twisted the handle. Just as she'd promised, it was nice and quiet. They stripped off T-shirts, pushed down shorts, kicked off sandals, and dove into the waiting pool. The water was silky and warm. Kya swam a few laps. When finally she stopped for a breath, the knot in her chest had loosened.

Kya searched for Quinn and joined her at the deep end. Quinn was content to float about while keeping a tight grip on the pool's edge. Her bikini was copper. Moonlight turned her wet skin silver.

'Feeling good?' she asked.

'Yes,' Kya replied. 'Thanks for breaking me out of protective custody.'

'Anytime.' She released the edge and glided over. 'Speaking of time, how long are you here for?'

'I fly out on Saturday,' Kya answered. 'Adrian wants me to stay longer, or at least until his next houseguest arrives. Their new house is Miami's hottest Airbnb.'

'Will you take him up on the offer?' she asked.

'I don't think so.' Adrian was worried for her mental health, but if she didn't get back to her routines, her own gym, her bed, her favourite coffee shop, she might lose it. 'I miss home. Don't you ever miss the UK?'

'All the time,' Quinn said. 'I'm planning a trip home for Christmas. Miami in December cannot compare to London, but summer in Miami is special. You should stay. At least until the Summer Solstice Music Festival.'

'That's not likely,' Kya said. 'The houseguests would be here by then, and I'll have been evicted from the guestroom.'

A flicker of disappointment in Quinn's eyes nearly made Kya reconsider. Did Quinn want her to stay? Was that where this was headed?

'That's too bad,' she said, drifting away.

'Any gigs this week?' Kya asked. She wasn't one for FOMO,

the fear of missing out on something *truly* special, but it had its claws in her now.

'Just two,' she said. 'I'm pacing myself before things get wild.'

'I'll come out,' Kya said. 'Just tell me when and where. I'll show up.'

Quinn splashed water her way. 'Kya's coming out to party? Voluntarily? No force required?'

'For you, I will.'

Suddenly, there was nothing else to say. They fell into a static silence while Kya's emotions howled inside her. She recalled what Ivy had said about Quinn preferring her to Nick. Even if that were the case, what difference would it make? They were too different, she and Quinn, and they lived in different worlds. Was there really any room for a partner in Quinn's glitter-filled snow globe?

'It's getting chilly,' Quinn said. 'Let's head up, dry off and get warm. I've got wine.'

When they were dry and warm, and wine was poured in mismatched glasses, Quinn selected a newly issued vinyl of an old Corinne Bailey Rae album and opened a bag of caramel-coated popcorn.

Later, they moved to the balcony. Quinn proposed they play a game called 'Favourite Song, Favourite Line'. 'Let's start with your favourite song to sing in the shower.'

Kya had one condition. 'Not if you judge my choices!'

'I'm in no position to judge!' she cried. 'My favourite song to sing in the shower is Kylie Minogue's "Can't Get You Out of My Head". It's all just vibes.'

'That song is a classic, and Kylie is queen.'

'I agree,' Quinn said. 'Now what's yours?'

'Lady Gaga. "Bad Romance".'

'A fine choice,' she said. 'And your favourite line?'

'The one about friendship.'

'About not wanting it?'

'Exactly.'

'Sounds personal, Kya,' Quinn said. 'Who would trade your love for friendship? Is there a story behind that?'

'There used to be,' she said. 'It's over.'

'Bitter ending?' she asked.

'Bittersweet,' Kya admitted. 'Like most college girls, I fell stupidly in love my freshman year.'

'I didn't attend uni, so I escaped that fate,' Quinn said.

'Good for you. It's brutal.'

'Tell me about it.'

'Her name is Rosana. We met in Stats 101. We got along so well, same interests, same hobbies, same taste in clothes, even the same class schedule. We joined the same boxing club off campus. I thought we were perfect. Maybe a little too perfect, a little too comfortable. There were no highs and lows, no drama.'

'No excitement?'

'In the early days, yes,' Kya admitted. 'But it fizzled out. After graduation, I left for the West Coast. It should have ended there. We dragged it out with a long-distance thing. It was torture.'

'You wanted drama!' she exclaimed. 'You got it in spades.'

'I don't want drama,' Kya said, quietly. 'I want my heart to race when I hear her laugh, or her voice in another room. I want to meet her eyes in a crowd and know we have a connection. I want to matter to someone.'

Like Hugo mattered to Adrian. She did not have to be the star of a relationship. She'd be content to orbit the sun, as withdrawn and quiet as the moon.

Quinn stared at her. 'Kya … does anyone know how deeply you feel things?'

Kya laughed, wondering if she'd put too much of herself out there. 'You do, obviously.'

'I do now,' she said.

They kept the game going until, later still, they fell into Quinn's large bed.

CHAPTER THIRTEEN

Even before Quinn heard the soft click of the door, she knew that Kya was gone. She was alone in the flat, and the heavy silence pressed on her chest. She blinked her eyes open and stared at the ceiling, wondering what to make of this. Really, she was waiting for a knock on the door. Any minute, Kya could return with coffee and pastries, like in rom-coms. A fair amount of time passed before she trashed that theory. Kya had left without saying goodbye. That was all there was to it.

Did she leave a note?

Quinn got out of bed and walked about the flat, searching for clues to solve the mystery of Kya's sudden disappearance. She kept a pad and a mug stuffed with pens on the kitchen counter to scribble shopping lists, calendar reminders, addresses, or phone numbers. It was out there for everyone to see and would come in handy should an overnight guest decide to drop a note before sneaking out at dawn, but Kya hadn't made use of it.

Out of an abundance of caution, Quinn sent a text message to Hugo. He confirmed her suspicions. Yes, Kya was home. In fact, she'd just walked in! Did she want to leave a message? **Oh, for sure! Tell her I said good morning … and goodbye.**

Quinn tossed her phone onto the sofa. A set of keys bounced off the cushion and landed on the wooden floor with a clang.

They weren't hers; she'd never seen them before. They could only belong to Kya. Had she been in such a hurry to leave, to escape, that she'd left her keys behind? Was that what it came down to?

Keys in hand, Quinn roamed through the flat again, walking aimlessly from room to room. Her mood shifted from sadness to confusion to frustration to sadness again, finally settling on anger. It started as a tingling at her fingertips that rushed through her entire body, like a swarm of angry bees. Kya had left without saying goodbye, without so much as a note. Who does that?

Girl, bye!

After all Quinn had done for her, how could she do this? She'd been a true friend! No one could say different. She'd listened, offered sympathy, advice, and even bubble tea. She'd invited her to her home, to her music studio, spent her very precious free time with her. She'd talked the girl off an emotional ledge, and this was how she repaid her? Not that she was seeking repayment. She'd done it out of genuine caring, the kindness of her heart. At the end of the day, she was a good person and she treated people with respect. She would never run out on someone, not like this anyway. How rude! How bloody rude!

One question bothered Quinn: why had she done it? What could've triggered her? Last night had been … lovely. Stretched out on her bed, Kya had asked, 'Who broke your heart?'

'Who? Me?'

'Who else is in bed with us?'

'It's just …' Quinn stammered. 'What made you ask that?'

She shrugged. 'You're guarded.'

'With good reason! The world is messed up.'

'The world is a dark and awful place, but you somehow shine. I think it's to keep people away.'

'I blind them with my light?' Quinn asked.

'You blinded me.'

'But you see me now, don't you?'

'I see you, Quinn.'

'I see you, too, Kya.'

Soon after, they dozed off.

Quinn had stirred awake in the middle of the night and found Kya curled up beside her. The lamp on the bedside table was lit. In the soft glow, she looked like a sleeping angel. Quinn reached for the blanket at the foot of the bed, draped it over her bare legs, then went to the kitchen to check that she had coffee – because surely Kya would want coffee first thing. Back in the bedroom, she switched off the light. In the morning, Kya was gone.

Had she missed something? Quinn didn't think so. That was how it all went down.

Honestly? Screw it. She wasn't going to waste time mulling it over. At the end of the day, Kya was a smart and sensible human being. She must have had her reasons for behaving the way she did. Whatever those reasons might be, Quinn had zero interest. She was busy, anyway. She had a gig later today, one that paid very well. After breakfast, she would lock herself in her studio and work on her playlist. She'd put Kya out of her mind. Her triggers, her issues, her drama, her moods, her need for morning coffee, her smile, her laugh, musical in the night, her features soft with sleep, or any combination of the above, were none of Quinn's concern. She was over it. Done.

What about the keys, still in her tight fist?

She'd return them; it was only right. And *then* she was done.

CHAPTER FOURTEEN

Last night was too much.

Too quick, too easy, too much fun. Kya woke up in Quinn's bed with one idea: get gone.

Fifteen minutes later, she sat fidgeting in the back of an Uber moving at a snail's pace.

'Sir, can you go any faster?'

'It's six in the morning. I'm running on two sips of coffee. So… you tell me.'

Kya shut up and sat back. She couldn't outrun the scent of Quinn's sheets clinging to her hair, anyway. Just as she'd succeeded in putting her face out of her mind, there she was on a billboard. She was so pretty, it hurt to look at her. Or was it the glaring sunrise?

She looked away and resumed fidgeting.

When she got home, Adrian threw open the door and greeted her with a scowl, reviving her PTSD. She was sixteen again, creeping home at dawn.

'We were worried,' Adrian said.

She slipped past him. 'Worried? Really?'

Adrian followed her into the kitchen where Hugo, already dressed for the gym, was brewing coffee. 'He was going to send out a search party.'

'But why? You knew where I was.'

'Quinn didn't,' Adrian said. 'She messaged us, said you went missing.'

Kya gripped the edge of the kitchen island. 'When?'

'Just now,' Adrian said. 'I'll let her know you're okay.'

Before she could stop him, her ever responsible brother slipped his phone out of the pocket of his terry robe and sent a quick text to a group chat that Kya, obviously, did not belong to.

'Next time maybe say goodbye,' he said, sounding eerily like their dad.

Hugo passed her a cup of coffee. 'Don't worry. I'll tell her you can't party.'

'Please don't,' Kya said. 'You've told her enough.'

'What does that mean?'

'Forget it. I can't think.'

Kya sipped her coffee with new sympathy for her Uber driver. All she could think about was Quinn waking up alone, searching for her in the empty apartment.

'Do you know Quinn bought our old place?' Hugo asked.

'Do you know she turned the second bedroom into a music studio?' Kya replied. 'It's dope.'

'I don't know how dope it is,' Adrian said, fussily. 'Losing a bedroom hits resale value.'

Kya gave him a sharp look. 'Were you always like this?'

'Like what?'

'Never mind,' she said. 'I'm going to bed.'

Kya headed to her room. The plan was to text Quinn before a needle of guilt pierced straight through her heart. She would've got right to it if Adrian hadn't yelped like a puppy – only Lucky was napping in her designer doggy bed. She rushed back to the kitchen and took in the scene. Adrian had dropped the knife and the mango from the farmers' market. He held his hand to his chest, and his face was contorted in pain. Blood trickled down his arm and stained his white robe. To say that chaos ensued would be a lie. Hugo had gone pale, and mute, too. Of the two men, her brother's condition was more urgent. She went to him.

'Let me see,' she said.

He showed her the gash along the pad of his thumb. Even to the untrained eye, it required stitches. STAT.

'Let's get you to the ER.' Kya whipped around to Hugo. His colour hadn't returned, but he was still breathing. 'Hugo, honey, get the car!'

'Wait!' Adrian called out. 'We've got to get the bleeding under control.'

The surgeon had regained his composure and took charge of the makeshift operation room. He tasked Hugo with retrieving a first-aid kit and ordered Kya to grab a clean dish towel. They scattered to follow his orders. Adrian calmly walked them through the steps of rudimentary wound care. When Adrian was satisfied, Hugo helped him change out of his robe.

The nearest emergency room was only a fifteen-minute drive, a miracle in Miami Beach, but seeing its water views and a staff of attractive medical professionals, Kya wasn't convinced they were at the right place. She whipped out her phone.

'Guys, it says here Miami's top surgical centre is downtown,' she said once they were settled in the waiting room. 'Should we go?'

Adrian balked at the idea. 'A surgical centre for stitches I could've done myself?'

'If there's someplace better, we should go,' Hugo said, twitching nervously. 'Your hands are valuable.'

'This is an accredited facility with a solid reputation,' Adrian said. 'Could you two please relax.'

They could not. Thankfully, Adrian was offered professional courtesy and was not made to wait long. A doctor came over right away. An acquaintance of theirs, she reassured Hugo there would be no lingering disability. 'He's off dishwashing duty for now,' she joked.

The joke did not go over well.

Adrian winked at Hugo and walked off with his colleague.

'I suck in a crisis,' Hugo moaned when he and Kya were alone.

'Don't beat yourself up,' Kya said. 'At first, I thought you were going to pass out, but then you pulled it together.'

'I'm scared of blood,' he confessed. 'I hate to see it.'

'You're scared of blood, yet you married a surgeon,' she said. 'Make it make sense.'

'Opposites attract,' Hugo replied. 'Look it up.'

Instead, Kya looked up the hospital's credentials. 'Is this place even in your health insurance's network?' she asked. 'If not, the co-pay will be through the roof.'

'Who knows?' Hugo said.

Kya wanted to point out that he, the policy holder, should know, but then he brought up Quinn.

'Do you know healthcare is free in the UK? I don't know why Quinn ever left.'

Kya felt queasy just at the thought of her. She rested her head on Hugo's shoulder. *Notting Hill* was playing on a wall-mounted television. She envied Julia Roberts and Hugh Grant. Their happy ending was assured.

'How do you two do it?' she asked her brother-in-law.

He yawned. 'Do what?'

'Stay together,' she said. 'Make it work. You're very different. It sounds nice, but you're essentially incompatible.'

Kya put no credence in convenient theories advancing romantic delusions.

'I've dated my type of man, and I can tell you this: I never want to date someone like me again. *Eu sou louco.* I'm erratic, inconsistent. I party too much. I talk through movies.'

That was a gross understatement. 'You practically narrate the movie!'

'Exactly! I'm annoying AF.'

'You're lovable, and you've made Adrian so happy.'

'I give him what he needs to be happy,' Hugo said. 'He's not high maintenance, but he needs quiet time to read and study, watch documentaries, and the movies I'd talk through. He says he's distant, but he just needs to disconnect sometimes.'

When they were kids, Adrian preferred to spend time in his room, reading, playing video games, watching sci-fi marathons. His friends complained he never wanted to hang out. She hadn't thought this would carry over in his adult relationships. Maybe there was something to this theory. She and her ex, Rosana, couldn't make it work, despite being on the same page of the same book of every topic known to man. And yet, even with all that common ground, they'd sit down to dinner and not have a single thing to say to one another.

'I'm ready to start dating again,' Kya declared.

'As you should!' Hugo said. 'Don't take it so seriously this time. You're young and hot. Get out there and do some damage!'

'Calm down! I'm not starting today,' she said, even as she slipped an apology text to Quinn. 'I've got to find a job first. Once that's taken care of, I'll look into the apps.'

'Take your time,' he said. 'I'm happy for you, either way.'

It took a trip to the ER for Adrian to take a day off. Kya didn't judge; she was the same. Nothing short of a natural disaster could get her to skip work — a pattern she would like to break. It was only right they spend the day together.

They ended up at the new art museum. Adrian had long wanted to catch the digital art exhibit before it closed. Like nearly every venue in Miami, the museum sat on the waterfront with a set of stairs linking it to the bay where patrons sat and stared at distant cruise ships and the causeway, wheezing with traffic. Kya and Adrian sat with outstretched legs, the midday sun beating down on their shoulders. It was a perfect day, but it wouldn't be Miami if a storm cloud wasn't forming in the distance.

'H says you might want to start dating again?'

'H' stood for Hugo, husband, or honey. Why did they have to be so nauseatingly cute?

'When did he tell you this?' Kya asked, to dodge his question.

'As soon as he could,' Adrian said with a laugh. 'He's a lot of things, but discreet isn't one of them.'

'When things settle down, I'll hop on an app,' she said. 'Anyway, my expectations are low. I'm not looking for what you and Hugo have.'

'I hope not,' Adrian said. 'We nearly broke up last summer.'

'Don't be dramatic. You had a fight last summer.'

There'd been some bickering and mounting tension over when and where to buy a house, but that was the extent of it. The marriage was far from collapsing.

'It was more than that,' he said. 'We were stuck, and I couldn't get us unstuck. I spared you the details because I didn't want to burden you.'

Burden her? When he said things like that, Kya could easily forget their age gap wasn't all that great. Adrian had taken on many dad duties in recent years, their parents now devoted to their grandchildren. It was nice but unnecessary. Adrian took on too much.

'Thanks for staying together,' she said. 'For my sake.'

'Don't mention it.'

Kya kept her eyes on the ever-expanding black cloud, darkening the horizon. 'I'm never going to sacrifice my personal life for work again. It's not worth it. I lost the job and had no one—'

'You have us, Kya!' Adrian protested. 'You're not alone.'

'You know what I mean.'

She'd meant someone like Quinn, who'd listened and supported her and done everything she could think of to cheer her up, but definitely not Quinn because how was it her business dating a Miami DJ featured on billboards? How did that fit into a day in the life of a girl in tech? That's right. It didn't. She'd sent an apology message, but it would no doubt ring hollow. There was no making amends for what she'd done, and she knew it.

Kya pressed her hands to her face to hide her burning cheeks. There were no words to describe how badly she'd messed up.

Adrian folded her in a paternal embrace and whispered, 'You'll get over this.'

Her brother thought she was crying over her career yet again. Meanwhile, she hadn't thought of that stupid job for a while.

CHAPTER FIFTEEN

Just when the house was quiet and calm restored, Quinn's car pulled up to the kerb. Kya, who'd just come in from the pool, caught a glimpse of the yellow convertible through the kitchen window. In her swimsuit and soggy flip-flops, she rushed out to greet her, flinging the door wide open. The words that flew out of her mouth made no sense.

'Adrian needed stitches. We ended up at a hotel-type hospital. Then he took a day off, which never happens, so I hung out with him at the museum, that new modern art one. Anyway, forget it. I'm sorry, and I'm glad you stopped by because I meant to apologize properly, like face to face, and not on a dumb DM.'

Met with Quinn's stone-cold indifference, Kya abruptly shut up. Silence ballooned around them, taking the breath out of her lungs. She waited for any reaction on Quinn's part. When she finally spoke, it was a relief.

Quinn held out her hand. 'You forgot this.'

Kya gasped at the sight of Adrian's extra set of house keys. In her rush to escape, like a baby, she'd left them behind.

'Thank you!' she cried. 'I was in such a hurry, I forgot.'

'Cool,' Quinn said. 'Now take them. I'm in a hurry, too.'

Kya dutifully collected the keys, all the while rambling, 'I really am sorry, Quinn.'

Quinn spun on her platform heels and marched off. It struck Kya that she was dressed for work in her bodysuit and black miniskirt. Kya couldn't move, couldn't put one foot ahead of the other. She just stood on the porch, arms limp at her side, watching the most thrilling woman she'd ever met drive away.

You stupid girl …

Kya raced back into the house, the door slamming shut behind her. She wasted a good fifteen minutes searching the web for Quinn's event. Coming up short, she gave up and sought out a more reliable source of information than Google.

Hugo was in his art studio, a converted den bathed in natural light. An essential oil diffuser perfumed the air. He sat at his desk and appeared invested in his work. Kya was sorry to disturb him, but not so sorry she'd change course. The computer monitor displayed a colourful design. Although the concept was cutting-edge, the design app was ancient.

'There's better software out there,' she said. 'I'll hook you up.'

'Don't bother,' he said, pushing his mouse away. 'I'm over this. I might pivot to interiors.'

'You should,' she said. 'Look what you did with this house. I saw the before and after pics. Impressive. And Quinn loves it.'

'Quinn's a sweetheart.'

Kya felt a fresh rush of queasiness. She leaned on the desk for support. 'Quinn's pissed at me.'

'For what?'

It was no surprise to Kya that he'd forgotten. Everything that occurred before Adrian's injury was deleted from his mind.

'For leaving the way I did!'

'Right … What was that about?'

Well, in a nutshell, it was about Kya being chickenshit. She didn't have time to get into it. 'I have to apologize.'

'Okay. Do that.'

'She's working today, and I don't know where. Last time we spoke, she mentioned a private event. Could that be it?'

'Hold on.'

Hugo tapped into his network of friends and produced an answer within minutes. 'The Glass Lounge, a members-only club. I've been. It's boring.'

Boring or not, Kya had to go there and … do what? She'd figure it out in time.

'Where is it?' she asked. 'Can I borrow your car?'

'You can't just walk in there, Kya. It's a private party.'

'Haven't you ever crashed a party before?' she asked.

'A few … but who would turn me away?'

It clicked. Hugo was her diplomatic passport, her all-access pass. 'Come with me. Let's do it together.'

'Can't,' he said. 'I'm cooking tonight. I don't want Adrian anywhere near the kitchen.'

'Please,' she implored. 'We won't stay long. I'd feel more comfortable crashing a party with you.'

'One hour,' he granted. 'I really want A to relax tonight.'

'You and me both!'

Hugo locked his computer screen and rose from the desk. 'Let's get changed,' he said. 'If we're going to do this, it helps to look hot.'

The Glass Lounge was an atrium in a downtown office tower. They showed up looking a little too hot, judging by the expression on the elderly doorman's face. Hugo, in a white linen shirt and coordinating trousers, looked as if he were about to board a yacht.

Kya had unearthed her one little black dress, made of a square of Spandex. Just when she thought her all-access pass would be denied, Hugo said, 'We're with Quinn.'

'Yeah? Who's that?' the doorman asked.

'The DJ,' Hugo answered.

The doorman appeared unconvinced.

Kya patted her empty clutch purse. 'We have her music on a flash drive. If we don't get it to her fast, you won't have a party.'

'You hear that? I think we have a party now.'

'You'll hear the same ten songs all night, if that's what you want,' Hugo said.

'It's a cocktail party. Ten songs might be enough.'

'Why are you giving us a hard time?' Hugo asked. 'Does it look like we're here for the shrimp cocktail?'

'It's good shrimp,' he said with a wink. 'I wouldn't blame you.'

Kya threw up her hands. He was just toying with them at this point. Then some very important-looking men arrived, and he no longer had time for them. 'You've got ten minutes. Go.'

'Thanks, man,' Hugo said. 'That's all we need.'

He waved them through. Kya wanted to find Quinn straight away, but Hugo insisted they take a brief detour at the bar. 'You're tense,' he said. 'You've got to loosen up.'

'How can I?' Kya took in the crowd of men and women in various interpretations of the classic business suit. She couldn't imagine Quinn having fun performing for this stale crowd. 'Look at where we are. Someone is going to try to sell us crypto any minute.'

'It's a lawyer mixer.'

Kya shuddered. 'Why would Quinn take this gig?'

'It's a job.'

'True.'

How naïve of her to think anyone could escape the grind. Quinn had bills to pay, like everyone else. Tonight, her music served as a soft backdrop. No beat drops, no sudden races in tempo. It filled gaps in stalled conversations and pumped life into an otherwise lifeless room. And yet Quinn's sound was distinct, unmistakable.

Drinks secured, they rehashed the plan.

'We get this done and get out of here,' Hugo said. 'The clock is ticking. We wasted a quarter hour circling the block for parking.'

'Should we synchronize our watches?' Kya asked.

'You're stalling,' he said. 'Go say you're sorry and come find me. I'll be here, waiting. No, actually … I'll be over there.' He pointed in the direction of a woman waving at him from the far end of the bar. 'Catching up with an old client and seeing about new work.'

'I thought you were pivoting to interiors!'

'I'll pivot tomorrow.'

With no Quinn in sight, Kya followed the music. The sound was pumped in through hidden speakers, which were of no help. However, the atrium gave way to a courtyard where a smaller, more casual crowd was gathered. She spotted Quinn, on a podium.

Head down, headphones on, she rocked as she worked. Kya's lack of a plan was now a problem. Quinn was working. How could she disturb her? But she'd come all this way.

When a cocktail waiter bumped into her, Kya shook him down for a pen and a piece of paper. She scribbled a note and had him deliver it, all while hiding behind a potted palm to make sure

Quinn received it. Then she found Hugo and interrupted his meeting with his old client.

'That was quick,' he said. 'We're good?'

'I think so.'

All she had to go on was the half-smile that tugged at one corner of Quinn's mouth as she skimmed the note. Somehow that half-smile was the whole universe.

Q, I like you a little too much, and it scares me.

Forgive me?

K.

CHAPTER SIXTEEN

CALENDAR.GOOGLE.COM
FESTIVAL PHOTOSHOOT
8AM–9AM

It took two text messages from Ivy and a calendar alert to get Quinn out the door. She made the early call time despite monstrous traffic and a blooming migraine. She was running on little sleep, fuelled by strong black tea and a burning determination to forget Kya Reid. In the make-up chair, she blocked all intruding thoughts with earbuds. But a while later, when she caught sight of the glittery set, she couldn't hold back a bitter laugh.

'What's wrong?' Ivy asked, popping from out of nowhere. 'Don't you like it?'

Quinn had not expected Ivy to show up for the shoot, although marketing fell under her PR umbrella.

'My girlfriend said I lived in a glitter-filled snow globe,' Quinn said. 'Looks like she was right.'

'Excuse me,' Ivy said. 'Since when do you have a girlfriend?'

Quinn blamed the tea, picked up on the fly at Starbucks, and not nearly strong enough to get the job done. 'Sorry. I don't know why I said that. I meant a *girl friend of mine.*'

Ivy narrowed her blue eyes. 'Kya?'

'Yup.' Quinn looked away. 'She's going to roast me when I tell her about all this glitter.'

Kya would have roasted her, for sure, if they were on speaking terms, which they were *not*.

The crew rolled a DJ deck onto the set. Someone handed Quinn a pair of glittery headsets to use as a prop. The photographer, known only as EJ, greeted her with a twinkle in his eye. 'I once dated a DJ,' he said. No hello or good morning.

'Haven't we all?' Ivy replied on her behalf.

Quinn remained silent. Oh look! Another wanker she'd have to put up with.

'Ready to sparkle?' he asked.

'Ready as ever,' Ivy said.

Quinn did her best, but it was hard to sparkle when just the mention of Kya had her spiralling. She wasn't one to hold a grudge. Kya had apologized, repeatedly, profusely, orally and in writing. Apology accepted. No hard feelings. Yet … was there any excuse for what she'd done? To sneak out like that, no note, no goodbye … and for no reason at all? Who does that? If Kya couldn't deal, it was best to know this sooner than later. Anyway, she was headed back to California. There was no use dwelling on it.

When they took a break for an outfit change, Quinn retreated to the dressing room and rifled through her tote bag for the note stashed there. She read it carefully, for about the tenth time.

I like you a little too much, and it scares me.

'How's it going in there?' Ivy asked from behind the curtained partition.

Quinn shoved the note back into her bag. 'Tell EJ I'm not ready to sparkle yet.'

105

'You're good,' she said. 'He stepped out to take a call.'

Quinn drew back the curtain. She could use an extra pair of hands with her zippered corset.

'Come in.' Turning her back to Ivy, she brushed her hair out of the way. 'Help me out of this.'

'Couldn't help but notice you were struggling to sparkle earlier,' Ivy said, as she wrestled with the zipper.

Quinn shook her head. 'Who even says stuff like that?'

'Wannabes and posers,' Ivy quipped. 'EJ stands for Edward Jr. His daddy, Edward Senior, is a junior US senator from the great state of Florida. EJ went to Princeton.'

'I'm not surprised.'

'Seriously, though,' Ivy said. 'How are you feeling overall? Ready for Music Week?'

Freed from her latex corset, Quinn removed her second outfit from the garment bag. 'Absolutely.'

'Awesome!'

'It's just …'

'Just … what?'

'I'm curious what the competition is up to.'

'There's no competition!' Ivy cried, instantly in hype mode. 'You're the queen.'

'Thanks for saying that, but do you think they'll photograph the boys covered in glitter?'

'Probably not,' Ivy conceded. 'But who cares? You look good in glitter. Besides, the boys don't have what you have.'

'Which is what?'

'I hate to say this, but you really do sparkle. You're a star.'

'Sweet of you to say, but the competition has talent. I've been listening to Angelo's sets. He's good.'

Angelo was a newcomer, like Quinn. Unlike her, the Italian DJ had produced music.

'Want to hear him live?' Ivy asked.

'He's in town? When did he get here?'

'No idea,' Ivy replied. 'All I know is that he's playing later today on a yacht, a cocktail party hosted by Moët & Chandon.'

'Are you on the list?' Quinn asked.

'No.'

'Ivy, it's not a stag party. We can't just show up.'

'Why not?'

'Because I've got a reputation … And so do you.'

'Have you forgotten who I am?' Ivy asked. 'I know every bouncer, every doorman, every valet in Miami Beach.'

Quinn wiggled into a red dress. 'And I've heard this speech a million times.'

'What are you worried about? I promise I can get us in,' Ivy said. 'The question is: are you up for it?'

Quinn tugged the hem of her dress. 'Sure.'

Why not give it a go? For old times' sake, if nothing else. She longed for the days before they had reputations to protect. Life was simpler then.

How *not* to crash a party: show up dressed in black when the dress code called for white. With no chance of blending in, Quinn and Ivy shied away from the marina and sought refuge at a nearby raw bar.

Though they couldn't get in, nothing stopped the music from wafting out. Angelo's sound reached them at the table where they swapped stories and shared a basket of chips. Quinn preferred it this way. It was much better than lurking from a corner of a ballroom.

Angelo's choices of mellow tracks produced a sound far different from her own. He was good, but so was she. Quinn wondered what she'd been so worked up about.

I can do this, she thought.

What Quinn couldn't do was sit quietly through another Ivy and Victor break-up story. Her friend shared what had prompted the latest fall-out at Blood Orange. 'He thinks we should take a break.'

'So do I, frankly,' Quinn said.

'Quinn!' Ivy cried. 'He wants to see other people.'

'Let him,' Quinn said firmly. 'Aren't you tired of this, Ivy?'

'I am,' she said. 'But I was tired of being single before we met. I'm not sure I want to go back to that.'

Quinn reached out and touched her arm. 'That's not a reason, babes.'

'We can't all be you, Quinn.'

'What does that mean?'

'It means some of us get lonely sometimes!'

'I get lonely, too!'

'Yes, but …'

'But what?'

'Your music keeps you warm.'

Quinn rolled her eyes. Despite popular belief, her life wasn't an ongoing parade. She had hard times and disappointments. She'd known heartache. But as an innocent bystander of the Ivy/Victor slow-moving car crash, she feared no one would come out alive.

'That's enough about Vic,' Ivy said. 'We never get to see each other and I don't want to waste our time on him. I miss us. Hanging out, eating chips, talking crap. We used to do it all the time.'

'I miss us, too,' Quinn said. 'I'm off carbs, though.'

Quinn promptly reached for a chip. That bit about being off carbs was a joke, but Ivy didn't laugh.

'I've been a bad friend,' Ivy said.

Quinn shrugged. 'It cuts both ways. I've been busy, too.'

'There's more to it than that.'

'Doubt it.'

'There's something I need to tell you,' Ivy said, chin raised. 'You deserve to know the truth.'

What was she going on about?

'Christ, Ivy, come out with it,' Quinn said. 'You're freaking me out.'

'Nick Lambert.'

'What about him?'

'He's been pressuring me to hook him up.'

'Hook him up with what?'

'With *you*.'

'Ah.'

'The other night, all that confusion at Smoke, that's what that was all about.'

'This isn't exactly news,' Quinn said.

'Why?' Ivy asked sharply. 'What did Kya tell you?'

Quinn went still. 'What does Kya have to do with this?'

'We had a chat Monday night,' Ivy said. 'She picked up on what was going on. She's sharp.'

'She is.'

'And easy to talk to.'

'I think so.'

'And hot.'

Okay. That was enough. Quinn raised a hand. 'Kya didn't

tell me anything. She's not the type to gossip. I sized Nick up in seconds.'

They fell quiet for a while, then Ivy said. 'Well, I'm the type to gossip, and I want to know. Is she the one?'

Quinn reached for another chip. 'The one for what?'

'The one for *you*.'

'Absolutely not!' Quinn scoffed, even as Kya's note was burning a hole in her tote bag.

'You're not into her?' Ivy asked.

'No!' Quinn cried.

'No?'

'No!'

'Fine!' Ivy tossed back. 'No means no.'

'About Nick,' Quinn said. 'Next time just tell me. I would've handled it. We don't have to play these parlour games. We don't live in Victorian times.'

'I had my own dark motives for keeping quiet,' Ivy said.

'Which are?' Quinn asked, her brows arching with surprise.

'The man is connected.'

'The man is a joke,' Quinn said, dismissing this take on Nick Lambert.

'True, but he has lots of influential friends. I didn't want to piss him off.'

Ivy looked deflated, slumped in her seat, her shoulders rolled forward. Quinn couldn't stomach it. 'What's the point of putting all this work in building businesses and reputations if we can't piss off a random guy or two? Forget Nick! He's a bore. In the short time we talked, I wasn't sure if he wanted to date me or manage my career. I'm not interested in either option. And for the record, he's not the only one with connections. Guess who else has loads of friends?'

'Who?' Ivy asked.

'*You*, you stupid idiot!' Quinn cried. 'You know every bouncer, every doorman—'

'Shut up! I couldn't even get you into this stupid party!'

Quinn piled more chips on her plate. 'Trust. I'm *never* going to let you live this down.'

'If it got you over your jitters, it will be worth it.'

'What jitters?' Quinn asked. 'I wasn't jittery. I was curious. It's not wrong to scope out the competition.'

'If you say so,' Ivy said, unconvinced.

'Okay! Fine!' Quinn cried. 'I had jitters. Happy?'

'Why would that make me happy?'

'I don't know what got into me,' Quinn went on. 'I'm not that girl.'

'Jitters are normal,' Ivy said reassuringly. 'You're going to be fine.'

'I don't want to be fine. I want to be unforgettable.'

'You already are,' Ivy said. 'If it took crashing a party for you to figure it out, I'm glad to do it. Anything for my only client.'

'Wait … What?' Did she hear that right? She couldn't be Ivy's *only* client.

Ivy averted her eyes, looking jittery herself. 'It's a long story. We're going to need another round of drinks.'

'No time,' Quinn said. 'It's late. I've got to get going. You can tell me all about it on the ride home.'

'Late?' Ivy checked her gold watch. 'It's six thirty.'

That was late. Quinn ought to be in bed by now.

Then Ivy caught the date displayed on her watch. 'Oh, my God! Tomorrow! I totally forgot. Big day for you. What's the plan?'

'I've got a sunrise set at Space.'

'That's it?'

'That's enough,' Quinn said. 'Let's go.'

CHAPTER SEVENTEEN

Kya spent the day floating on an inflated doughnut raft all while drowning in misery. It was her last full day in Miami and Quinn hadn't reached out. She'd added her number to the note, hoping for a call, a text, anything at all, but it was obvious Quinn was freezing her out. Could she blame her? She'd been kind, and Kya had met her kindness with cowardice. Her remorse was mixed with something else. She missed Quinn. Not in a romantic way – she wasn't delusional. Quinn would likely end up with Nick, or a Nick equivalent. Kya, a medallist in the 'will she, won't she' games, would never participate in that sport again. It was a waste of time. So, why had she let her feelings bleed into that note?

What was wrong with her? Couldn't she keep it together?

After dinner, Kya packed her bags then joined Adrian and Hugo on the deck for the last time. She collapsed onto the seat opposite theirs. Lucky immediately leaped from Adrian's lap onto hers. She cuddled her close. 'I'm going to miss this little one.'

'Why are you rushing back to California?' Adrian asked. 'Stay another week or two.'

'Or maybe just one,' Hugo suggested. 'We've got guests the week after next.'

'Is this an Airbnb?' Kya asked. 'Are you going to charge my AmEx?'

'Our rates are reasonable,' Hugo assured her.

'Who's coming?' Kya asked.

'Sam and Roman,' Adrian replied.

The names sounded familiar. 'They got married in Tobago, right?'

'That was Naomi and Anthony,' Hugo said.

'I can't keep up with all your friends,' Kya said flatly. 'Anyway, it doesn't matter. I'm leaving tomorrow. I've got stuff to do.'

'Like what?' Adrian asked.

'Update my resumé!' she cried, exasperated.

'After college, I postponed grad school for six months,' Adrian said.

'Your point?' she asked.

'I wanted to be one hundred per cent sure about medical school.'

'Can anyone be one hundred per cent sure about anything?' Kya asked.

'If anyone can, it's your brother,' Hugo replied.

'If you let me, I'll cover your rent for a few months,' Adrian said. 'That way you can afford to take a break and reimagine your future.'

What would she do with all that free time? 'Hard pass,' she said. 'I need to hustle. That's just who I am.'

Lucky scurried off her lap and rejoined the couple. The highly sensitive animal likely preferred their chill vibes to hers. It was time to go home. She could not be around happy, well-adjusted people or pets.

'In that case, what time is your flight?' Hugo asked. 'If I can't convince you to stay, let me take you to the airport.'

That was an offer she'd gladly accept. 'Thanks,' she said. 'I fly out at five.'

'In the morning?' Hugo asked, scandalized.

'No, man!' she cried. 'Are you nuts? Nothing gets me out of bed before dawn.'

Meet me at Club Space for a sunrise set. I'll leave your name at the door.

If Kya hadn't been awake, riddled with doubt, second-guessing her decision to travel home, she might have missed the text. As it was, she was awake, staring at the ceiling, wondering if maybe she should extend her stay by a couple of days – if only to placate her brother who was genuinely worried about her. Then the text came through, and Kya was out of bed, kicking off boxer shorts, rifling through her suitcase for her favourite jeans. A shot of bottled cold brew coffee, a quick text to Adrian and Hugo via the 'A.K.H.' group chat, and before the break of dawn, she was in a ride on her way to a rave.

She made it to Space with no problems and, as promised, her name was on a list. However, making her way through the club took effort. The doorman pointed the way, but it did not make navigating the dense crowd any easier. To say nothing of the dancers with tin foil for hair or the green-eyed alien balloon volleyed about. Kya was undeterred. She moved with purpose through the smoke-filled room, her eyes on the girl on stage in a silver bomber jacket. She was so sexy, so freakishly confident. With a push of a button or the twist of a knob, she controlled the pulse of the crowd. With a simple text message, she'd got Kya out of bed before dawn, a miracle, and at a club downtown. Kya had no regrets. To see her again was a thrill no smoke show, no laser lights, no giant disco ball could intensify.

A man grabbed her arm.

That man nearly got decked, but then Kya recognized Nick Lambert. Bleary-eyed and dishevelled, yet somehow still handsome after what looked like a long night.

'Hey!' he shouted in her ear.

'Hey!' she shouted back.

'It's you again,' he said.

Again? They'd briefly met at Smoke, and Kya had quickly dipped, leaving him alone with Quinn. She was anything but a third wheel.

'You look lost,' he said. 'Where are you headed?'

'To the stage,' she answered.

'Need help?'

What was he going to do? Plough a route through the crowd? 'I'm good. Thanks.'

'Mind if I ask you a question?' Nick said.

'Shoot.'

'Are you gay?'

Kya pushed away from him, only to have the crowd around them react and bounce her onto his chest. He grabbed her arm again, this time to steady her. 'Settle down!' he said, laughing. 'I'm just curious.'

She was curious about him, too. Like, for example, she was dying to know who he thought he was.

'Why are you asking?' she said. 'Is this a Pride event?'

Nick looked away and raked his knuckles against his stubbled chin. 'I'll just come out with it,' he said. 'I think we're going for the same girl. Am I wrong?'

'You're wrong,' she said bluntly. 'I'm going to meet my friend who is performing tonight, or today, really. I don't know where you're going or what you're looking for.'

'Kya … don't be like that,' he said with a sheepish expression that might work on some, but not her. 'I'm just sizing up my competition. Can you blame me?'

Kya didn't bother to answer. She turned and went on her mission to reach the stage. Nothing, not even a tool like Nick, would distract her.

CHAPTER EIGHTEEN

There you are!

It was a rare thing for Quinn to spot anyone from behind the decks; her focus was on her work. Her mother could enter the club, and she wouldn't know it. Somehow, she spotted Kya from the moment she walked in – tight black tank, loose jeans, long braids spilling down her back. Hit with relief and a rush of excitement, Quinn tracked her moves as she sliced through the crowd right up until Nick blocked her.

Earlier, he'd come around to say hi. 'Things were awkward last time,' he'd conceded. 'I'd like a second chance to make a first impression.'

Since Quinn wasn't the type to hold a grudge, she said yes.

Nick was nice enough, but also a nuisance. He had a knack for robbing Quinn of her time. Kya would be leaving for San Jose soon and Quinn feared she'd waited too long to reach out. In a moment of weakness, 4.45 a.m. to be exact, she sent the text and hoped for the best.

For now, Nick and Kya were banging on about something in the middle of a hyped-up dance floor, of all places. In the time it took for Quinn to blend one track with another, the exchange was over, and Kya was moving towards the stage. She motioned to the security guard to let her through the ropes and got back to work. Just knowing she was there made Quinn's night. Her day, actually! It was six in the morning. Time to get to work and give these people what they came for.

As soon as the set was over, with the crowd still chanting her name, Quinn grabbed Kya by the hand and dragged her off stage, down a hall, out the first door she encountered, which, as luck would have it, opened to a deserted back alley. It wasn't the ideal spot for reconciliation. On the outside, the club was a nondescript concrete block dropped on a busy downtown corner. The noise from the highway overpass was as loud as the music inside. The morning sun was punishing on the eyes. When the door slammed shut, locking them out, Quinn wished she'd thought this through, but no matter. They were together again.

'Did you bring me out here to kill me?'

'I brought you out here to clear the air.'

'You know what they say: nothing like car exhaust to clear the air,' Kya quipped.

Quinn added Kya's unfailing sense of humour to the long list of things she liked about her. 'I don't want you dead,' she said. 'If anything, you'll need your last breath to apologize properly.'

'I've apologized twice!' Kya cried.

'Yes, well … now I'm ready to hear it.' Quinn waited. 'Go on. I'm listening.'

'I really am sorry,' she said. 'Though, to be honest, I'm a flight risk. When things get intense, I get lost. I'm not proud of it, and maybe I need therapy. Scratch that. I absolutely need therapy. You've every right to be angry. Really, you shouldn't speak to me again. Although, I'm glad you reached out. I wouldn't want to leave things like this. You've been so good to me and—'

'Kya!'

'Yes?'

'Shut up and kiss me!'

That was all it took. Kya had her back against the chain-link fence and locked in a hungry kiss. Although she'd asked for it, Quinn wasn't prepared. She gripped the steel wire for support, which came in handy when Kya abruptly pulled away. She stared at her, wide-eyed, lips parted. She was so lush, so insanely beautiful, Quinn just wanted more and more and more of her.

Kya stepped away from her. 'That can't happen again!'

'Why?'

The door swung open. A security guard poked out his round head. 'You two shouldn't be out here. It's not safe.'

'Sorry, officer,' Kya said. 'We'll abide by Space rules.'

The guard didn't so much as crack a smile. He didn't budge, either. They dutifully filed back into the club. There was time enough for Kya to figure out that Quinn didn't follow rules.

PART III

BIRTHDAY PARTY

PART III

BIRTHDAY PARTY

CHAPTER NINETEEN

Around the corner from the club was an all-day diner. They slid into a booth and ordered coffee, tea, and stacks of pancakes. Kya was cutting into her homestyle stack when a response from her group text came through. Her brother was notoriously bad with text messages, and it was no surprise that Hugo replied first. His reply, though, was surprising.

She stared at her phone.

'What?' Quinn asked.

'A message from Hugo,' Kya replied.

'Say hi.'

'Sure,' Kya said coolly. 'He says happy birthday.'

'Oh.'

Oh? Was that all she was going to say?

Quinn buried her nose in her big, steaming cup of English breakfast tea.

'Why would he say that?' Kya prodded.

Quinn lowered the cup onto the saucer with a clatter. 'Maybe because it's my birthday.'

'Quinn!' Kya cried. 'When were you going to tell me?'

'Likely never,' she admitted. 'It's not a big deal.'

Kya wasn't buying it. 'Who doesn't celebrate their birthday?'

'I celebrated with a sunrise set,' Quinn explained. 'I could have played at Space any time. I picked today.'

'I mean celebrate with friends and family,' Kya said. 'And a real cake, not a pancake stack!'

'My friends are scattered all over the world,' she said. 'It's not reasonable to think they'll fly in for a party. Plus, this is nice, pancakes with you.'

'That's sweet, but it's not enough,' Kya said. 'I want to give you a gift. What would you like for your birthday?'

'Time. Stay longer.'

'I wish I could,' Kya said, while quietly wishing the opposite. There was no way she was staying in Miami a second longer than necessary. Although she wasn't proud of the way she'd skipped out on Quinn the other day, she recognized the wisdom of her actions. Getting far away from Quinn was a good idea. Her career was off the rails. She had to focus and strategize to get it back on track. The last thing she needed was to lose her head over this girl.

Kya's phone buzzed with another text, another bombshell that took her out. 'You've got to be kidding me!'

'What is it this time?' Quinn asked.

'My flight's been cancelled!'

'No way!'

'Due to weather conditions?'

Kya looked up from her phone in disbelief. A radiant blue sky mocked her through the diner window. What weather conditions? she wondered. Quinn, meanwhile, was in stitches. She bumped her shoulder. 'Don't laugh! This is serious!'

'I agree. It's a sign, and signs are very serious.'

'A sign to call the airline and book the next available flight?'

'Or extend your stay.'

'Quinn …'

'Music Week starts Monday! You won't want to miss it.'

It was such a simple request. Time … more time together. Her stomach dropped at the thought. The day she met Quinn, she'd boarded a rollercoaster and there was no getting off. But how could Kya say no?

She picked her phone off the table and called Hugo. 'Guess what? My flight is cancelled.'

'Does that mean you'll stay?' he asked.

The entire world wanted her to stay in Miami. Who was she to fight the world?

'I'll stay a week,' she said. 'Happy now? You win!'

'I always do,' Hugo said.

Judging by the look on Quinn's face, she'd won, too.

'Your brother will be happy,' Hugo said. 'Let's celebrate. What would you like for dinner?'

'We should celebrate Quinn's birthday, too,' Kya said.

Quinn flicked her with a napkin.

Hugo was game. 'Should I get a cake?'

'You should,' Kya said. 'What's a birthday without cake?'

'Maybe invite a few friends?' Hugo suggested.

'Knock yourself out.'

Kya ended the call.

'What did you do?' Quinn asked.

'I got Hugo to throw you a party. Invite Ivy and Victor and whoever else you'd like.'

'Will you let me contribute something?'

'Please don't. Let Hugo be Hugo.'

'Fine! As long as you're staying for Music Week.'

'Is this a fair exchange?' Kya wondered aloud. 'It's your party and your big concert. What's in all this for me?'

Quinn smiled as if the answer was obvious. 'Me, of course.'

'A party ain't a party until a couple breaks up!'

Kya didn't know the redhead who'd dropped that gem, but she was wiser beyond her twenty-odd years. When Ivy and Victor broke up, once again, and with their usual flourish, those thoughtful words put it all in perspective.

The shouting match erupted just as soon as Quinn blew out her candles. Victor stormed out this time, leaving Ivy in tears by the edge of the pool. Quinn handed her a tissue and reminded her of her inherent greatness. 'You are a badass babe. Don't you dare let that man take you down!'

Ivy took a few deep breaths and wiped her eyes. A round of vodka shots later, the party resumed. Some didn't budge from the terrace, which was the de facto dance floor. Others stretched out on the lounge chairs and stared up at the moon. It was a warm night and a few stripped down to their underwear and jumped into the pool. Kya took Quinn to her bedroom to search for swimsuits.

'Do you think this is the end for Ivy and Victor?' Kya asked.

'No,' Quinn said flatly. 'I don't think that.'

'I hope the drama didn't ruin your birthday,' Kya said soberly.

'No! Never!' Quinn exclaimed. 'Your brother might not recover. The good doctor looked stricken!'

'He hates conflict.'

'Will he be all right?'

'He'll be fine.'

Kya switched on the light, only to wish she hadn't. Her bedroom was a mess, crammed with her luggage and computer equipment.

Quinn didn't seem to notice. She circled Kya and shut the door. Leaning against it, hair fanned over the bleached wooden slats. 'I had a great birthday. Thank you.'

Kya's heart melted. Was a birthday even a birthday without a kiss? No. Never. She stepped forward and brushed Quinn's lips with her own. Quinn wrapped her arms around her neck and dragged her into a deeper kiss. When Kya pulled away, only slightly, the air around them was electric.

Quinn smiled cheekily. 'Guess it happened again.'

CHAPTER TWENTY

REDDIT
u/Nite Light

Miami's Reigning Queen of House Music Stumbles and Falls Hard

Ivy sent her the Reddit post sometime after midnight, but Quinn hadn't caught it until her alarm rang at six — just in time to ruin her morning mantras. Along with the post, Ivy shared some wisdom. 'All press is good press.'

Quinn loved Ivy, but the girl could use a day off. A profile in *The Sunday Times*, even a scathing one, was press. This was the work of a troll, which made it trash.

'Nite Lite' posted a blurry photo of Quinn and Kya at Smoke, seated at the bar, practically melting into each other's eyes. The caption read:

Is Quinn falling for this queen? Seen here at Smoke with Kya Reid, a failed tech blogger and former Ex-Cell employee recently accused of misleading her social media followers.

She couldn't read past that. It was enough they'd invaded her privacy. Why go out of their way to paint Kya in such a negative light? Why drag in the drama of her former job, or even her private LinkedIn group? She'd made such an effort to put all that behind her.

The photo gave her chills, but in a good way. It was beautiful.

Quinn got Ivy on the phone. She rarely slept, spending her nights doom-scrolling until dawn. Predictably, she answered on the first ring. 'Hey there,' she said, stifling a yawn.

'One day or another, this man is going to reveal himself – they always do. When he crawls out of the woodwork, I'm going to stomp him like the roach he is.'

'It's not that bad,' Ivy said, yawning still. 'Think of the buzz! With all this talk, your events will draw even bigger crowds.'

Quinn wanted to scream, to hurl the phone across the room. 'I'm not using Kya for buzz!'

'You're not, but someone out there is. Accept the benefit.'

'If you think—'

'Give me a second to run the blender, will you? I'm making a smoothie.'

Quinn took a few deep breaths while Ivy's monster blender whirled. Her career wasn't built on hype. She didn't need scandal to draw a crowd. If there was a way to put that message on a billboard, she'd pay for it.

Ivy got back on the phone and mumbled an apology. 'That was bitchy of me. I'm in a dark place.'

'And so is Kya,' Quinn insisted. 'She doesn't deserve this.'

'Neither do you,' Ivy pointed out.

Not really. She'd signed up for this, but Kya hadn't. 'She's a private person,' Quinn explained. 'This is going to wreck her.'

'Let's not tell her,' Ivy suggested.

'That's not how relationships work,' Quinn snapped.

'Are you in a relationship? Is that what's happening?'

Quinn studied the photo more closely now. It certainly looked like it. 'I'm in something, and I don't want to ruin it.'

'I'm going to take off my promoter hat and talk to you like a friend,' Ivy said. 'Or even a therapist.'

'Please do.'

She was this close to firing Ivy the publicist, but she could use a friend.

'That pic melts my heart,' Ivy said. 'You two are so obviously into each other, no one is going to read the stupid caption. And the stuff about her job is old news, anyway.'

'Not that old. It happened last week.'

'It'll blow over,' Ivy assured her. 'Isn't she leaving for Cali soon? That would solve things.'

'She's staying the week because I asked her to. She's staying for me.'

'Damn.'

'I'm going to need more feedback than that,' Quinn said.

'Here's what you're going to do,' Ivy said. 'Send Kya the post. Give her a moment to process it. Then lovingly explain what will likely happen next time you're out together. As the hot new couple on everyone's radar, you'll get lots more attention than she's likely used to. Can she handle it?'

Could Kya handle it? Would she run?

Quinn would soon find out.

Quinn's message turned Kya's phone radioactive. Kya stuffed it into the gym locker and spent thirty minutes attacking a punching bag with blind rage. It felt as though she'd been outed once again, and this time they'd targeted her personal life. The timing was terrible: just days before Music Week. Quinn didn't need this. Now her name was linked to a fraud, a faker, and a failed blogger. Could it get any more humiliating than that? Yes, it likely could. Her life was on a downward spiral, hooking anyone on its path.

With each jab and punch, Kya thought of the post. Although the caption was a hit job, the photo was a work of art. Under any other circumstances, she would have thanked the photographer, would have made it her screensaver, or even framed it. She and Quinn weren't touching, hugging, or kissing in the back alley of a club. They were simply gazing into each other's eyes. It was sweet, but not really. The intensity of the look they shared had Kya at her throat.

After their respective workouts, they'd agreed to meet at the smoothie bar to talk. What was there to talk about? Kya's life was a blazing dumpster fire. She had to extinguish it before it spread and killed them all.

Quinn was waiting, a strawberry smoothie in one hand and Kya's favourite, an iced lavender matcha latte, in another. She looked nervous. Kya had never seen her this way, and she wanted to kiss her berry-stained lips.

Quinn handed her one of the drinks. 'I'm sorry.'

'What about?' Kya asked, startled.

'My troll is now your problem. He dragged you into this, trashed your reputation, just to get at me.'

'My reputation is already trash, so ...'

'Don't say that!'

'It's true. I'm making peace with it.'

'Well don't,' Quinn snapped. 'You're getting a new job. That's the plan. Will this hurt your chances?'

It shouldn't, but it would. Silicon Valley wasn't the land of saints and do-gooders. It was a boys' club. Most of her former colleagues were notorious for their bad behaviour, but Kya wasn't one of the boys. The same rules didn't apply.

'Don't worry about it.'

'I'll worry if I want,' Quinn said. 'You can't stop me.' She reached for Kya, who adeptly turned away and reached for the latte. Quinn shot her a look, then motioned for Kya to follow her out of the gym. They went to her car to speak privately, far from the eyes of the barista, who hadn't been paying attention to them anyway. Kya felt a little foolish for overreacting, but really all she wanted was to keep Quinn from getting burned.

'They got one thing wrong,' she said. 'If anyone is falling for anyone, it's me.'

Quinn smiled at her for the first time that morning. 'Is that right? I'm curious. Who are you falling for?'

'The bartender at Smoke, obviously.'

'The one behind the bar, with the muscle tee and the tats?'

'That one.'

'I didn't think he was your type.'

'He had a tattoo of a dagger on his forearm. That's hot.'

'Hotter than me?'

No one was hotter than Jade Quinn.

Kya set her cup in the holder and took her hand. The yellow convertible was parked in the shade of an oak tree that shed its leaves all over the parking lot. Quinn let down the top and they pushed back the seats. Quinn stared up at the clear sky. Kya's gaze followed a gaggle of ducks crossing the lot. It struck her as odd, considering there was no pond or lake within walking distance.

'How do you really feel about all this?' Quinn asked quietly.

'Everyone who sees that picture is going to think I roped you into my queer agenda,' Kya said.

Quinn laughed. 'Anyone who knows me knows I have a queer agenda of my own.'

'Have you been with a girl before?'

'Yes.'

'In a real way – or just bi-curious?'

'I don't label things, Kya,' Quinn said. 'Let's just say you're not the first girl I've fancied. What does it matter, anyway?'

It didn't matter. Kya was looking for an easy way out, some excuse to pull the plug on all this. 'I'm wondering if it's worth it for me to stick around. You've got a job to do this week and can't afford any distractions.'

That Reddit post was a smear campaign in the making. It might not work, or it might mess with Quinn's big moment. Why chance it?

Quinn looked at her, the way she'd looked at her in the photo, with longing and feeling. Wasn't that how they'd got into this mess in the first place?

'Don't look at me like that!'

'Like what?'

'You know like what.'

'Like I *like* you, maybe?' Quinn asked, those brown eyes ever brighter.

Kya turned away and sought out the ducks. They were nowhere to be found.

'For some reason, my booking Solstice got some people in their feelings,' Quinn explained. 'They're trying to tear me down. They've made it about my looks, my clothes, and now the girl I'm with.'

Kya understood their motivation all too well. Haters were going to hate; that was a given. But the ones who'd vilified her for losing her job were the ones who thought she hadn't deserved it in the first place.

'I know I asked you to stay, but—'

'But what?' Kya interrupted.

'I don't want them dragging you through mud just to get dirt on me. Maybe the smart move is for you to go home.'

The suggestion left Kya cold. As Quinn had pointed out, the world didn't run on logic and JavaScript. It ran on the very human impulse to make dumb choices, and Kya was only human. 'I'm not going anywhere.'

'Don't be stubborn, Kya.'

'I'll be stubborn if I want. You can't stop me.'

Quinn rolled her eyes. 'You're impossible.'

'I'm not going home. I'm all in.'

'"All in"?' Quinn said. 'I'm not asking you to commit crimes. We're going to have a little fun while telling some very nasty people to fuck off. That's all. Nothing crazy.'

'I don't care if things get crazy,' Kya replied. 'I'm here for the ride.'

Quinn brightened. 'Let's take a ride to the beach. I haven't been for a while.'

'South Beach is a short walk away, at most a bike ride.'

'If we stay here, I'll never relax,' Quinn said. 'I booked a concert on the beach to wrap up Music Week. It'll be all I can think about.'

Kya rested her hand, palm up, on Quinn's lap, beckoning for hers. Quinn obliged her.

'We could just spend the day at the pool.'

'It has to be the beach. I have a fantasy.'

'Let's hear it.'

'I want to fall asleep on the sand.'

'Tell me more. What else would we do?'

'I'll tell you what we won't do,' Quinn replied. 'We won't give any energy to those trolls.'

'Agreed,' Kya said. 'And we won't talk about my job, not one word.'

'Or Music Week. I'm sick and tired of it, and it hasn't even begun.'

'We won't take any calls from my brother or my brother-in-law,' Kya said. 'I love them, but … you know. They're a lot.'

'We won't take calls from anyone. We'll unplug!'

'We're off-the-grid girls!'

'I love this for us!' Quinn exclaimed.

Kya loved it, too. Maybe a little too much? She drew a breath and collected herself. 'Where would we go?'

'Key Largo. It's not that far of a drive. I've never been.'

'I've been, but I was six. I don't remember much.'

'It's settled,' Quinn said. 'What do we need for the trip?'

'We need a plan,' Kya replied. 'An American road trip is not like a drive along the British countryside, Quinn. There's tradition to uphold.'

'Like what? We Brits are big on tradition.'

'A karaoke playlist, for one thing,' Kya said. 'We have to commit, hit notes higher than Ariana Grande ever could.'

'That's simple enough,' Quinn said. 'I've got a playlist for that.'

'We must have snacks,' Kya said.

'Of course we'll have snacks! Who do you take me for?'

'I don't mean apples and trail mix.'

'What do you mean?'

'Chips.'

'Crisps?'

'Yes. Not the low-cal kind.'

Quinn rolled her eyes. 'We'll get bags of greasy crisps. Happy?'

'Yes.'

'Good. Are you ready to get out of this car park? We've been here a long time.'

'It's a parking lot, but whatever. I'm ready.'

Quinn started the engine and put up the rag top to give the A/C a fighting chance. 'I wonder where the ducks went,' she murmured.

'You'd noticed them?' Kya asked, surprised.

'How could I not? The little one with the wobble was adorable.'

Quinn backed out of the *car park* – as she'd called it.

Kya closed her eyes, feeling dizzy. *I'm worried I'm falling for this girl.*

CHAPTER TWENTY-ONE

An hour later, driving south on the interstate, Quinn's sat nav pointing the way, Kya caught a glimpse in the rearview mirror of the person she could be if she only got out of her own way. She'd always wanted to be a carefree girl, the kind of person who took off at a moment's notice, instead of planning a trip for weeks only to postpone it for months. She dreamed of having someone, not a clan or a crew, just one special person to make life an adventure.

Was this the summer her dream came true? Okay ... no. This was a one-off thing, and she didn't believe in dreams. Now was not the time to start.

They arrived at Key Largo in good time. The island was at its core a fishermen's town, nothing inherently glamorous about it. They were far from South Beach with its parade of luxury cars. Bait shops outnumbered coffee shops and designer boutiques. The resort was appropriately named The Blue Wave. A fresh coat of seafoam green paint and conch shell accents drove the point home.

Quinn pushed open the door to the lobby. 'I like it. It's cheeky.'

The woman at the front desk waved them in. She wore a sea-foam uniform. Her name tag read Paula. 'Ladies, welcome.'

'We booked a resort pass,' Kya said. 'The website says we get two lounge chairs and an umbrella.'

'It's Sunday,' Paula said. 'Most of our guests are checking out. You'll get the whole resort to yourselves.'

'Lucky us!' Quinn said.

Once a credit card was swiped and the paperwork was out of the way, Paula gave them the lay of the land. 'We've got snorkelling, kayaking, and free bikes for you to use. Instead of two lounge chairs, how about a sunbed?'

Quinn was overjoyed. 'Nice!'

'Just so you know, it's a rocky beach,' Paula cautioned. 'Most people come here expecting sand, but this ain't the Bahamas.'

Quinn plummeted from her high. 'Oh.'

Kya wished she could give her the Bahamas, anything to get her to smile again.

'The water is clear, though,' Paula added. 'You can see the fish. It's great.'

That was enough to lift Quinn's spirits. 'Sounds like paradise,' she said.

Paula was right. There wasn't a square inch of sand to stretch out on. However, the water was exceptionally clear.

'Napping on the sand is out of the question. Are you disappointed?' Kya asked.

'No!' Quinn reached down and picked up a crushed shell. 'If I can't be happy in paradise, please have my head examined.'

'It is stunning.'

'Paula mentioned kayaking and snorkelling. Which do you fancy?'

'Do we have to choose?' Kya said.

'We can do whatever we want.'

As it turned out, they had to choose. According to Paula,

kayaking wasn't available on Sundays, but they could snorkel to their hearts' content, which they did.

In the unreasonably warm waters, they discovered coral reefs, colourful schools of fish, a sunken iPhone, and each other. They locked eyes through thick goggles. Quinn swam around her like a mermaid. Touching her glistening skin underwater felt like a luxury Kya did not deserve. She would never forget this day.

At one, they abandoned the beach to search for lunch. They didn't have to go far. The hotel's patio restaurant offered grilled fish tacos and free refills on lemonade. Quinn told her how she got her start playing DJ sets for free at her friends' birthday parties. Soon, she was in high demand, the most coveted DJ in her little suburb.

'The first time, I was terribly nervous. I spilled beer all over the decks, which is why I don't drink while I work. I need a clear head. And to make matters worse, I played the wrong song. Our friend Owen requested "Changes" by Bowie. I played Tupac.'

'Which is why you don't take requests anymore?'

'You're still cross about that?'

'I'm not! I swear!'

'You are, too. Did I scar you, Kya? Will you ever get over it?'

'I'm not cross. It's your job and I respect it.'

'How did you get started with computer programming? Were you into coding early on?'

Despite what Kya had shared in her blog Q&A, she didn't really have an origin story. A product of her times, she'd grown up online. Computers were everywhere. What else was there to do? But then, it hit her. 'When I was twelve, my friend Elena built a computer with used parts.'

'Impressive.'

'It was the coolest thing anyone in my school had ever done. I was so impressed; I blogged about it.'

'You were on LinkedIn at twelve?' Quinn teased.

Kya laughed. 'Shut up!'

'You didn't try to build one yourself?'

'God, no.'

The waiter arrived to clear away the plates and refill their glasses. Kya was grateful for the interruption. Unlike Quinn, she had never truly known what she'd wanted to do with her life. She had no clear vision of a future to run towards now. Did she really want to return to the tech industry, after the way they'd spat her out? What else could she do? What else was she even qualified to do? A feeling of unease spread inside her, but she sipped her lemonade and kept quiet about it. This getaway was going to be a relaxing break from her problems. She wanted to have fun. The waiter was young enough, with freckles and shady brown hair. She asked him for a recommendation. 'Hey, where should we hang out later?'

'On a Sunday?' he said. 'Let's see. Ted's Tiki Bar is always a good time. There's a live band. The happy hour is lit. Dollar shots at seven. Don't miss that.'

Kya frowned at Quinn. 'We'll have to miss it, if we're hitting the road by five.'

'Six,' Quinn said. 'What's the rush?'

There was no rush, no curfew. They were free.

★

Ted's Tiki Bar lived up to its name – a concrete dance floor under a straw roof and bamboo everything. The band played raucous salsa music. Quinn rested a hand on Kya's hip, as if to keep her from drifting away. But Kya wasn't going anywhere. Quinn's light touch anchored her. Although not the best salsa dancers, they were enthusiastic. They twisted and turned and spun around. They clapped in time to the beat. When a guy asked to cut in, Quinn said, 'Not on your life!' When another offered to buy them drinks, Kya politely turned him down.

The band took a break. Quinn and Kya lingered on the dance floor as the others flowed to the bar. 'If we'd only said yes to the free drinks, we wouldn't have to fight for one now,' Quinn said.

Kya agreed. 'It's a madhouse.'

Quinn checked the time. 'Kya … it's dollar-shots o'clock.'

'What? It's seven! Already?'

'Time flies when you're dancing tipsily to salsa music!'

How had she not noticed the setting sun, the sky turning purple? 'We have to hit the road.'

Quinn cocked her head. 'Do we, though?'

'We can't stay here.'

'Why not?' Quinn asked. 'You heard Paula. Everyone's left. There should be plenty of vacancies.'

Vacancies. Plural. Okay. She could do that. They'd each get a room, rest, and hit the road in the morning. 'All right. Let's find Paula.'

Paula was behind the desk like earlier, flipping through a magazine. 'Ladies! Ready to take off?'

'Actually, we'd like to stay the night. Could we have two rooms?'

'Sorry. No rooms. Just bungalows.' Paula opened a colourful map of the property. 'Our most popular ones have water views. The sunrise is incredible.'

'We'll take one of those,' Quinn said.

'Bungalow 1 or 2, take your pick.'

'Lucky number 2, please,' Quinn said.

Paula grabbed a key off a hook. 'Down the path toward the beach but hang a right. You won't miss it.'

They left the lobby, grabbed their beach bags stored in the trunk of the car, and giddily made their way to the bungalows. The day's heat had not relented, but the breeze made it bearable. They slipped off their sandals and kicked up rocks as they went. Kya slowed her pace and took in the deep beauty of the night. A quarter moon peeked out between the tufts of clouds. The sea roared just feet away. The palm trees ruffled their crowns. Kya was no romantic, but if she didn't kiss Quinn this very instant, she would never forgive herself. What else was a night like this for?

Quinn turned around to face her. 'What are you thinking about?'

'This.'

Kya took her hand, pulled her close. She felt Quinn's heartbeat and every breath winding through her chest.

Quinn looked up at her, eyes sparkling. 'What took you so long? I've been waiting all day.'

Their first kiss in the alley was rough. Their second, in Kya's bedroom, was sweet. This one, under the stars with the wind in their hair, was a dream, but it felt just right.

*

The robes and towels stacked in the seafoam green bungalow smelled of the sea. Kya slipped the Do Not Disturb sign on the doorknob, only to remove it minutes later in anticipation of the pizza delivery. They opened windows, lit a citronella candle, and ate on the floor. Quinn said California-style pizza would forever remind her of Kya, who was sure that was the most romantic thing anyone had ever said to her.

After dinner, they played cards, a game of poker with rules made up on the fly, until Quinn rose to her feet and, extending a hand to Kya, said, 'It's time for bed.'

Kya wasn't so sure. She took her hand and pulled her back down to the floor.

Quinn let out a playful cry. 'Is there something you want? Another round of poker?'

Everything Kya wanted was in her arms. 'I want to see you, all of you.'

'In other words, you want me naked?'

Kya rolled her head back. This woman would be the end of her. 'Are you always this bold?'

'Always.'

Quinn rose to her feet again, towered over her. 'Take my clothes off.'

Kya laughed, nervous. 'Is that an order?'

'Yes.'

'I don't take orders,' Kya said with a shrug.

Quinn held her gaze. Could she see straight through Kya's bluff? Of course she'd take orders from Quinn. She'd let her do anything to her she wanted.

'You've put me on a pedestal,' she said. 'You think I'm a queen or a goddess. I'm not. Take my clothes off and *look* at me.'

Kya was on her knees now, gazing up at her admiringly. She *had* put Quinn on a pedestal and despite her request, as touching as it was, she would remain there. She was Kya's high priestess, better than mere mortals, *regal*, divinely beautiful, perfect in every way.

Kya would walk two steps behind her, worship her on her knees, shield her from harm. If Quinn had something against that, well, too bad. That was how it was going to be.

'You're doing it again.'

'Doing *what*?'

'You're looking at me like I'm outer worldly. I'm just a girl.'

Just a girl, looking at another girl, asking her to … what? What a joke!

'Sorry, Quinn, you're not,' she said. 'You're a star. You're a dream. You're an angel. You can't change that.'

Kya unfastened the buckle of Quinn's shorts and worked the hard denim over her hips and down her legs. Then she untied the string bikini; the triangles fell to reveal the sharp tan lines that had intensified over the day and the beautiful V between her thighs. She was so beautiful, Kya found it hard to breathe. Her words faltered. Yet, she rose to her feet and, heart pounding, stripped Quinn of her T-shirt. She tugged at the strings of her bikini top. The knots came undone quickly and there she was. Kya took in her slender neck, full breasts, honey brown nipples, nipped waist. How was she to believe Quinn was just an ordinary person? Kya was clever and a shrewd poker player. Her brothers had taught her the card game on rainy nights at home. Later, in college, she cleaned up on poker nights. She recognized a winning hand when it was dealt. Yet tonight, she would lose it all.

She inched close and breathed in Quinn's sunbaked skin. 'May I touch you?'

'Yes.'

'Where?'

'Wherever you like.'

Quinn stared at her with a look of defiance. Then all at once, they pounced at each other. They stumbled backwards onto the bed, knocking over a cosmetic case in the process. Laughing, they pushed aside Quinn's headphones and portable speaker. But when Quinn yanked a tie out of her hair and let her curls fan across the pillow, Kya's laughter died.

'Quit worshipping me, and touch me,' Quinn insisted.

'I'll worship you if I want,' Kya whispered. 'You can't stop me.'

'Fine! Do what you like! Just use your hands!'

Kya climbed over her. 'You little—'

'Don't you dare!'

Kya undressed and climbed over Quinn. She pinned her between her knees. 'Hi, beautiful.'

'Hello.'

Those were the last words they would exchange that night. The air turned to smoke between them. Kya knew instinctively that what would happen next wouldn't be sweet, pretty, or lovely. Quinn was impatient, and she was hungry. They were going to devour each other. She wouldn't be satisfied until she had Quinn's skin under her fingernails or bruised the smooth bronze skin with her teeth. But when Quinn reached out for her and pulled her onto her soft body, it was like sinking into honey. Kya's mouth sought hers. She slipped a hand between her thighs and sank her fingers into her warmth and her wetness. When the citronella candle burned out, Quinn opened for her, and Kya licked and tasted her until she cried out her name and begged her to stop.

CHAPTER TWENTY-TWO

Quinn would rather die than admit it, but she was slightly panicked to wake up to an empty bed. As her eyes grew accustomed to the light, she made out Kya's silhouette through the window. Kya was on the porch, in the chair she'd claimed as her own, her braids on her bare back, her feet on the rail. She hadn't run off.

Quinn grabbed a sarong off a bench at the foot of the bed and turned it into a dress by fastening the ties around her neck, then joined Kya outside. She caught the cloudy look on her face but tried her best to ignore it. 'Hey, love.'

'Hey you.'

Quinn ran her fingers through Kya's braids, freeing the tangles. 'Have you been out here long?'

Kya closed her eyes. 'Not too long,' she said quietly. 'I wanted to catch the sunrise. Paula was right. It was spectacular.'

More than her quick wit, Quinn appreciated her silences. This was who she was at her core, always deep in thought even when pretending not to be. She lived in her head; nothing would change that. Not that Quinn would ever want her to change. She liked her as she was. Quinn's world was filled with noise, music, laughter, chatter. Kya managed to live in the eye of the storm, kept safe in a bubble of silence, although never quite at peace.

'I have a question,' Kya said.

'Let's hear it.'

'Do I still have to call you Quinn after last night?'

Quinn laughed. 'Call me what you like.'

'Jade ...' Kya said tentatively. 'No ... You're my Quinn.'

The way Quinn beamed! She shouldn't like it as much.

She kissed her forehead. 'In the mood for what passes as continental breakfast in the dining room?'

'I'd rather die.'

'Room service then?'

'Yes, please.'

'I'll get the menu.'

Quinn ordered all their favourites, fruit, pancakes, buttered toast, a pot of coffee, and a cup of tea. They ate on the balcony to the sounds of surf and seagulls. Check-out was at noon. After breakfast, they'd have to shower, pack, toss their bags in the boot of her car, drive back to Miami before traffic picked up. Quinn didn't want to think about it, but their days, their hours, were numbered. She took another sip of tea and tried to clear her head. Kya was telling a story, something funny Hugo, ever the clown, had done or said – she wasn't sure. There was so much more at stake. She set her cup down and reached for Kya, drew her close, licked maple syrup off her lips. 'I wish we could stay longer,' she whispered.

'Me, too,' she whispered back.

'I have a fitting later today—'

'Don't worry about it,' Kya said, interrupting. 'I should spend time with Adrian and Hugo tonight.'

Quinn left her seat and slipped onto her lap. She wrapped her arms around Kya's neck. 'Tomorrow night is the first gig at LAB. It's kind of a big deal. DJ Angelo is performing, too. He's a rising star. You're coming, right?'

'I'll be at every gig, big or small. That's the only reason I'm having dinner with the guys tonight, to let them know not to count on me for the next few days.'

Quinn went still. The relief was overwhelming. This entire time she'd been convinced Kya was pulling away. She was not one to worry about such things. What had got into her?

Kya stroked her back. 'Are you all right?'

'I was just thinking …'

'About?'

'Wouldn't it be easier if you just stayed at my place, instead of commuting back and forth?'

'It might, if only you hadn't turned your guest bedroom into a music studio.'

'There's always the sofa.'

'Isn't it suede?'

'*Italian* suede.'

'I'd drool all over it.'

'I'd kill you.'

'I very much want to get out of this alive,' Kya said.

'I reckon you'll have to sleep with me.'

'Hmm …'

'BLU is putting me up for the pool party. It's a suite, so there may be an extra bed. At the very least a pull-out sofa situation.'

'You had me at hotel suite. I'll sleep on the floor for five-star accommodations.'

'What do you have against our little bungalow?'

'Nothing.' Kya brought her hand to her lips. 'Conch shells will always remind me of you.'

CHAPTER TWENTY-THREE

Kya got home in time to catch Hugo and Adrian on their way out. She dropped her waterlogged tote bag on the floor and took in their sharply tailored suits. 'Where are you guys off to looking so smart?'

'To the Biltmore,' Hugo answered. 'Your brother is being honoured tonight.'

'And you didn't tell me?' she protested.

'You weren't supposed to be here,' Hugo reminded her.

'Trust me, it's no big deal,' Adrian said. 'Every so often a medical board or another throws a gala, for fundraising, if anything. This one was scheduled months in advance. We thought you'd be back in California by now.'

It looked like a big deal to Kya. They were wearing Tom Ford.

'Don't worry about it,' Hugo said. 'He wins an award every few months.'

'Well, I'm never here to see it. Can I tag along?'

'Only if you really want to,' Adrian said. 'It's not all that exciting.'

'Actually, I could use the company,' Hugo said. 'There's always an open bar at these things.'

'Give me one sec!'

Kya took off down the hall. Lucky, springing out of nowhere, was hot at her heels. In her bedroom, her suitcase was open on the floor, the way she'd left it when she last rifled through it, right before her rapid getaway with Quinn. She rifled through it now for her go-to little black minidress and capped-toe stiletto pumps. The outfit might be too edgy for the Biltmore, one of Miami's most prestigious hotels, but she had no other options. A swipe of lipstick and she was done. She and Lucky joined the guys who were waiting in the living room. Hugo was adjusting Adrian's tie. He was certainly making a fuss for something that wasn't a big deal.

'Why haven't I ever heard about these awards?' Kya asked in the car, on their way to Coral Gables.

'You don't follow me on TikTok,' Adrian replied.

'I'm a blogger at heart,' Kya said. 'I can't help it. I may start a Substack.'

'Ever heard of vlogging?' Hugo asked. 'Get into it.'

At the Biltmore, she and Hugo got into the open bar. Meanwhile, Adrian was taken into custody by the hosting committee. They marched him off to a reserved area where the honourees rubbed shoulders and enjoyed 'small bites' while they waited for their trophies and honours.

The Spanish-style hotel, built in the 1920s, was the home of a country club. The guests were elegant and mature. Kya felt wholly out of place. She fidgeted, smoothed down her dress. The stretchy fabric was forgiving, but the thing had been crumpled up in the bottom of her suitcase for days now. She didn't want to embarrass her brother.

'Do I look okay?' she asked Hugo. Kya spoke over the rim of her martini glass, to avoid anyone picking up on her discomfort and reporting her to the fashion police.

'You're glowing!' Hugo exclaimed. 'You've never looked so good.'

'Oh, come on!'

'I'm serious,' he said. 'All thanks to Quinn.'

Just the mention of Quinn had Kya's pulse racing. From a gilded mirror on a far wall, she watched as colour spread from her neck to her cheeks. She was instantly back in their little bungalow in Key Largo, enveloped in the scent of the citronella candle and Quinn's coconut-scented body oil. She could feel Quinn's skin rough with sea salt and taste her on her tongue.

'I owe her one. I should send her a bottle of wine or something.'

'What do you mean by that?' Kya asked.

'Don't you know?'

She shook her head. What didn't she know?

'I asked her to take care of you and she did an amazing job. She deserves an award.'

'About that, I can't believe you asked her to take care of me!'

Kya's voice bounced off the panelled walls. Hugo took her by the elbow and marched her to a remote corner of the ballroom.

'I asked her to hang out with you, get you out of the house when we were busy with work. You may not remember this, but you were really down.'

'You make it sound like I needed a babysitter.'

'My friends and I take care of each other when in crisis. We show up with food, do laundry, take them to the bar, do wingman stuff – all of it. It's just what we do.'

Hugo was far from home. He and his friends had formed a community. They looked out for each other. What did Kya know about community and friendship? Her friends had thrown her under the bus at the first opportunity.

Hugo finished his drink and returned to the bar for another round. Kya stood alone in a corner among the potted palm trees until an older man approached and asked where she'd gone to medical school. Once she wriggled her way out of that conversation, she stepped out to a nearby balcony for air.

She *was* upset. Quinn had been tasked to look out for her, like a problem child, an unruly kid needing supervision. It cast a different light on their relationship. She hated the idea of Quinn spending time with her out of obligation or duty. However, deep inside, she knew better. It might've started that way, as a favour to a friend, but it quickly evolved. She was sure of it. A favour was a coffee date, or a quick text message to check in. Quinn had made space for her in her life, had forgiven her when she'd acted like a jerk, and showed her true kindness and friendship. In return, there was something Kya could do for her. Quinn would never admit it, but the troll thing got to her. Chasing down trolls was busy work, like playing whack-a-mole online, but this one had left a trail that she could easily follow. Kya wasn't much of a vlogger and shied away from most social media platforms. However, she did have a singular set of skills that she could put to use here. She could pull the thorn out of Quinn's side.

A stylish woman joined her on the balcony, looking somewhat flustered. Patting the pockets of her elegant jumpsuit, she asked, 'Do you have a light?'

'No. Sorry.'

'That's all right,' she said. 'They should be starting any minute now.' Her gaze swept over Kya. 'Who are you married to?'

Funny question. Was this a first wives' club?

'Do you have to be married to someone?' Kya asked. 'I didn't know.'

'Married or related in some way,' she replied. 'You wouldn't come here on a Monday night voluntarily, would you?'

She had a point. She also had keen green eyes that sparkled with good humour and salt-and-pepper hair styled in a bob. Kya decided she liked her.

'My brother is getting an award tonight.'

'Who's your brother?'

'Dr Adrian Reid.'

'I know Dr Reid!' she exclaimed. 'Excellent plastic surgeon.'

'That's what they say. Who are you related to?'

'My husband is the chairman of the board. Carl Miller, Dr Carl Miller.'

'Are you a doctor, too?'

'God, no. I'm in biotech.'

'Nice!' Kya knew she liked her for a reason. 'I'm a software engineer.'

'Very nice! Where do you work?'

Suddenly, this exchange wasn't quite so nice anymore. Kya would rather leap off the balcony than go down this path. The perceptive woman might have picked up on it and quickly changed course.

'What am I doing, grilling you about work?' she said. 'Forget I asked.'

Somehow, her kindness made it worse. This question was going to come up often and what was she going to do? She couldn't run from it forever.

'I used to work for Ex-Cell until I got laid off. I'm just hanging out with my brother until I figure things out.'

'Ex-Cell ... That's impressive.'

Didn't she hear the part about them laying her off? Or had Kya been too subtle?

She opened her pocketbook, removed a pack of cigarettes, a wallet, then a slim leather card case. She handed Kya a thick business card with embossed black lettering. Kya hesitated before taking the card. What did she need it for? She had one week left in Miami. Then she'd head back to California, the true seat of innovation. It only took a fraction of a second for her to acknowledge how wrong that line of thinking was, not to mention elitist. She took the card. Corinne Miller, the wife of Dr Carl Miller, was also the CEO of BioFlow Enterprises.

'What's your focus?' Kya asked.

'Lab automation.'

She knew nothing of lab automation. It sounded impressive, though. 'I won't be in Miami long.'

'That's all right,' Corinne said. 'If you have the time, give me a call. I'd like to show you what we do.'

Hugo, fresh martini in hand, found them on the balcony. To no one's surprise, not Kya's, anyway, he and Corinne embraced like old friends.

'Hugo designed my logo,' Corinne explained, although no explanation was necessary.

'He's looking into interior design now,' Kya said. 'He's very talented.'

Hugo shot her a look. As outspoken as he was, he was oddly shy about this. For once, he was the one who needed a nudge. Kya had no qualms about it.

'In that case, we need to talk, honey bunny,' Corinne said to Hugo. 'Carl and I are downsizing to a condo.'

'I'd like that,' he said.

Corinne glanced at her bejewelled watch. 'We should go inside now. It's time.'

'It was nice meeting you,' Kya said.

Corinne looked just as flustered as earlier. 'Could I hang out with you guys?' she asked. 'If one more person asks me where I went to medical school, I'm going to lose it.'

'Of course, darling,' Hugo said. 'Us laypeople have to stick together to survive the night.'

Ten minutes into the ceremony, Kya realized that Adrian wasn't being honoured for his contributions to medicine, but 'technology, public outreach and education'. In short, Adrian now had an award-winning TikTok account. She thought of her own account, which had earned five hundred followers based on that one pathetic video. She would delete it. She didn't want to start a new chapter based on old news and past mistakes. As the master of ceremonies was saying, 'One has to look to the future for solutions.' Maybe she could do more with video, something fun, like document Music Week. It promised to be chaotic, parties stacked on parties. Quinn would perform almost every night. Having a goal, like documenting the behind-the-scenes action, would give her something to do, aside from following Quinn around – although following Quinn around was all she wanted to do.

The idea was still swimming in her head when they made it home later that night and gathered at the dining room table with pints of ice cream, their favourite gourmet caramel sauce, and mismatched spoons.

'Feel free to rent out my bedroom,' Kya said. 'I'll be staying at Quinn's for the next few days to tag along at her performances.'

Adrian dropped his spoon in his empty bowl with a clang. 'Excellent news!'

This was rich. Hadn't he begged her to stay? 'Don't sound so excited to be rid of me.'

'Don't be offended,' Hugo said. 'We're just happy you're getting out without anyone having to drag you by the hair.'

Kya was offended nonetheless. 'I thought the point of my staying was for us to have more quality time together.'

'You missed the point,' Hugo said flatly. 'We didn't want you to rush back to California, curl up in a ball in your apartment, eat chocolate and cry your eyes out.'

Kya scoffed. As if anyone could keep her from eating chocolate and crying her eyes out.

'I have a heavy workload this week,' Adrian explained. 'Last week's injury wrecked my schedule.'

'You took one day off, bro!' Kya cried. 'One day!'

'That's all it takes,' Adrian said. 'You'll come by for dinner, right? You have to eat.'

'I'll do laundry and stock up on your snacks, too.'

'Do what you like. This is home, Kya.'

Hugo stood to clear the table. 'I'll come out to support Quinn. We'll hang out like old times. Do you have her schedule?'

'Nice! I'll look it up.'

Kya unlocked her phone and a flurry of delayed alerts popped onto the screen. Going off the grid was great until you got back to dozens of missed calls and messages. It was even more frightening when they were all from one person: Jon Yi.

Kya dropped her phone, irrational anger bubbling up inside her.

'What's wrong?' Adrian asked. 'No wi-fi?'

No shame was more like it! How dare Jon reach out now, after days of silence. In the wake of what happened, her so-called office bestie hadn't so much as sent a 'hang in there' cat meme. The text read: I know you hate us but …

Leave it to Jon to figure that out. He'd always been the most perceptive of the bunch, which was why she'd liked him. He was wrong on one thing, though. There was no 'but'; she hated them, full stop.

At the office, Jon's desk was steps away from hers. On slow days, they spent hours chatting about their favourite TV shows, anything with dragons and magic, conducting deep dives into pilot episodes, dissecting character arcs, crying over disappointing series finales. Often, they'd slip away from the others to have lunch on their own. After a quick tour of the cafeteria, piling food on their plates, they'd head to the deck and catch up on each other's personal lives, which was easy enough since neither of them had one. Jon once said he could fall in love with her if he tried. He was bi, so it wouldn't be too much of a hassle. 'It would solve all our problems,' he said. He often proposed thoughtful solutions in that same tone of voice at their daily morning meetings. They'd been the only single people at the last corporate dinner. That was no reason to get together. Jon was a romantic, looking for love, and she'd never settle. Kya did not want a dull, dreary man. She wanted a woman with sparkle.

Her bubbling anger fizzled now and made way for sadness.

'It's fine if you can't find the schedule,' Hugo said. 'Don't get worked up about it.'

Kya stared at him blankly. She had no idea what he was talking about.

Adrian zeroed in on her with concern. 'Are you okay?'

'I missed a few calls from a work friend and it brought all that stuff back.'

'Block them all,' Hugo said. 'If they were real friends, they wouldn't have done you dirty.'

She set aside her phone. 'I agree.'

'You don't know that,' Adrian said. 'People have reasons for doing what they do. That office was toxic for everyone. It might do you good to hear them out. It's therapeutic.'

'Block them,' Hugo insisted. 'You can reach out when you're back in California. This week, you party.'

Again, Kya sided with Hugo. A party was the cheapest and most efficient form of therapy.

PART IV

THROWBACK PARTY

CHAPTER TWENTY-FOUR

Voicemail 1: Birthday girl, I've got a surprise for you! Call me!

Voicemail 2: Quinn! My God, where are you? Call me back! Now!

Voicemail 3: Either you're dead or you've blocked my number. Either way, I'll find out soon enough and you'll have to answer for yourself.

Quinn had been off-grid for not very long, maybe twenty-four hours. Why was her voicemail clogged with increasingly unhinged messages from Amanda Kaur, her childhood friend and former flatmate? Say nothing of the texts she didn't have time to read.

After dropping Kya at home with the promise to pick her up the very next day, Quinn had dashed across town for her fitting. An hour later, done with the tailor, she finally unearthed her phone, dead in the bottom of the swamp lake that was her carry-all bag. She plugged it into the car charger and, after a moment, the screen lit up like Piccadilly Circus. So many people had been trying to reach her. The most persistent of them all was Amanda. Alarmed, Quinn got her on the phone. Her friend answered straight away.

'Finally!' Amanda cried, her familiar voice roaring through the car speakers. 'Where the hell were you?'

'Why? What's the emergency?' Quinn asked. 'Are you in trouble? Do you need bail money? If so, how much?'

'Put away your chequebook,' Amanda replied. 'There's no emergency. I'm camping out in your lobby, or don't you live here anymore? The doorman is committed to protecting your privacy. He won't confirm or deny.'

'It depends. Are you in Brickell or the beach?'

'Brickell.'

'You're in the right place.'

'Okay, so, where are you? I've been trying to reach you forever!'

'I went dark for a day. It's good to unplug every now and then.'

'Lovely! A little social media detox?'

'Exactly.'

'Good for you! Meanwhile, I've spent my time stalking you on social, trying to figure out where you'd disappeared to.'

'Sorry, sweetie!'

'Sorry isn't going to cut it, love,' Amanda said. 'I was worried, and so was Ivy. Something to do with a Reddit post? I don't know. She said you might've gone into hiding to save your reputation.'

For a Reddit post? Please! Then Quinn thought of Kya and something inside her snapped. She was still angry about the whole situation. 'Well, I haven't gone into hiding. I assure you.'

'Assure me in person,' Amanda said. 'When are you coming home?'

Quinn veered onto Brickell Key Drive. 'I'm five minutes away!'

'Five actual minutes or are you running on Quinn time?'

Amanda had every right to be sceptical. Back when they lived together, in the small, dreary flat in London, and again, here in

Miami for a year, 'five minutes' meant anything from a quarter to a full hour. A lot had changed since then. Quinn was an adult now with proven time management skills. 'Five minutes Eastern Standard Time,' she said. 'I'm pulling into the car park as we speak. Hold still and please don't harass poor Benny.'

Benny was her sweet doorman who should've retired ages ago, but who'd stayed on for the love of the job – he was a self-proclaimed people person – and the very real need for a steady income. 'Times are hard,' he'd said.

'I can't promise that,' Amanda said. 'He looks like Father Christmas.'

'I'll be right there!'

Quinn parked and jumped out of the car. She didn't trust Amanda to behave, but more than that, she was truly excited to see her friend again. It had been years since Amanda had returned to England, to the arms of her boyfriend, Brian, and a job at a financial firm. Life had worked out well for her, but she was back in Miami now and together they'd turn back time, shred every inch of progress. Quinn couldn't wait.

When Quinn burst through the door, Amanda scrambled off the leather-upholstered bench and cheered, as if she were the last to cross the finish line at the London Marathon.

'Benny! I'm here to rid you of this pest!' Quinn announced.

Benny laughed. 'Nah, she was good company.'

Quinn rushed past Benny straight into Amanda's open arms. They collided and nearly toppled onto the polished marble floor.

Quinn caught her breath. 'Next time, a little notice, some advance warning, wouldn't hurt!'

'Where's the fun in that?' Amanda asked. 'It would ruin the surprise.'

Nothing could ruin this surprise, she thought.

Funnily enough, she and Amanda had not been particularly close as kids. The former ballerina, star of the local dance school, had led a separate life. She was forever on stage. A recital, a play, a Christmas special, Amanda lived to dance. That ended when they hit their mid-teens. Amanda aged out of the local school. Rather than join a company, she retired, hanging up her ballerina slippers for the last time and taking to the dance floor instead. That's when their friendship truly flourished. After secondary school, they left the suburbs for London, Amanda for uni, and Quinn for the close proximity to the underground clubs, splitting rent on a two-bedroom ground-floor flat. Good times.

With Benny's help, they loaded Amanda's luggage into the lift. Amanda leaned heavily on the far wall. Her inky black hair was gathered in a messy plait. Her even brown skin ashen. 'Sweetie, you must be exhausted,' Quinn said.

'It was worth it,' Amanda said. 'I'm ready for sunshine.'

'If you're here to escape London weather, I've got news for you. It rains here, too. Quite a bit.'

'I'm here for *you*, silly girl. I won't miss your big festival debut. You've never done anything like this, have you?'

Quinn's throat tightened with anxious anticipation. 'No. Never.'

'I'm so proud I could cry.'

'Had I known you were coming, I would've waited outside the airport with a sign and balloons.'

'It was all very last minute, I promise you,' she said. 'I had some free time and booked a cheap flight, hoping to make your birthday. I didn't overthink any of it, but that was my first mistake. The flight was cancelled, and I couldn't book another until days later.'

'I love you for this,' Quinn said. 'Don't ever do it again.'

'Oh, I won't.'

They wheeled her luggage to Quinn's door. 'How long are you staying for, exactly?'

The last time Amanda had showed up, she'd stayed a year.

'A week. I grabbed everything I own and shoved it into the suitcases. Prepared for anything, you know.'

Judging by the weight of the suitcases, she'd come prepared for battle.

'I'm going all out this week,' Amanda explained. 'If you see me out there, losing my mind, tend to your business.'

'I promise.'

Quinn unlocked her door and Amanda rushed in. 'Oh, my God! Quinn!' she cried. 'This is *amazing*! Well done!'

'It's nothing you haven't seen before,' Quinn said, rolling the largest piece of luggage into the hallway. 'I sent you pics, didn't I?'

'You did, but you suck at photography.'

She did a pirouette in the living room, her long black plait whipping around as she twirled. She was still very much a ballerina, dressed in black leggings and classic flats.

'That's fair,' Quinn said, struggling, alone, with Amanda's overstuffed weekend bag.

'You didn't catch this view! It's perfect!'

Quinn dropped the bag. 'Will you come here and help? You're not checking into the Waldorf.'

'Leave it alone. I'm not checking into the Quinn Estates, either. Ivy is giving me my old room back.'

'For real?' Quinn asked, letting the last piece of luggage topple onto the floor in the hallway and leaving it there.

'We're teaming up for Music Week. I'm her plus-one now that Vic is out of the picture. But is he *truly* out of the picture?'

Quinn hid her relief the best she could. As happy as she was to see her friend, this week was for Kya. If Amanda hadn't thrown her plans, she would've spent the evening tidying up, stocking the fridge, and filling the flat with flowers and candles in anticipation of her arrival. She wanted to make everything pretty for her.

Quinn stepped over Amanda's overturned suitcase and flopped onto her sofa. 'Honestly? I have no idea.'

'If she dumps me, I'm crawling back to you.'

'Absolutely. I won't let you down.'

'You know what I think of all the Ivy and Victor drama? I think they truly care for each other, but are too scared to admit it.'

It was an interesting theory. Although Quinn didn't think it applied to Ivy and Vic, it likely applied to her situation. Kya had a head full of excuses for why they wouldn't work out. On the ride back from the Keys, she'd suggested they keep PDA at a minimum while out in public this week. 'I want the focus to be on you,' she'd repeated. 'I think it's better that way.'

'Better for you or for me?' Quinn had asked.

'For both of us.'

It was bullshit, but at the time Quinn had preferred not to call her on it. Kya's intentions might be good, but it didn't matter, in the end, not when she was pulling away.

'Wait.' Amanda retrieved her travel bag and flung it open. 'Look what I've got for you. A little taste of home.'

She produced the familiar red and gold package of Quinn's favourite ready salted crisps.

Quinn raced over and snatched it from her. 'Thank you!!!'

she cried. 'I have to order these online whenever I'm homesick. You can't just get them at the corner store.'

'I've saved you the trouble because I've brought all your favourite flavours.'

'You spoil me!'

'It was no trouble. I grabbed them at Heathrow.'

'Still, I appreciate it.'

Quinn plopped back onto the sofa and ripped open the bag. 'Should I make you some tea?'

'In a minute.' Amanda twirled again. 'This place is everything! Quinn, you've come so far.'

'Please don't remind me.'

She went trotting down memory lane anyway. 'Remember that first time you played at Nikki Beach? The DJ ate a bad oyster or something and got violently ill? And then, like, Ivy did her thing and got Oscar to put you on. Remember that? Remember Oscar, the notorious grouch?'

'I remember Oscar!'

'I remember that night! You blew the roof off that place.'

'There was no roof to blow off, but okay.'

'I knew you were going to be a star then. I was sure of it.'

'Settle down. I'm not a star!'

Quinn had been sure of nothing back then, only that she wanted to play her music. She still hadn't 'made it'. The road to stardom was long and treacherous.

'I drove past a huge billboard of you on the highway just now. If that doesn't make you a star, what does?'

'You saw that?'

'I did.'

'I looked good, didn't I?'

'You looked amazing!'

Laughing, Quinn went to the kitchen and put on a kettle. Amanda followed, leaning on the counter. 'I never told you this, but that first night you took the stage was a turning point for Ivy and me.'

'A turning point? How?'

'It was obvious that you were where you belonged … and we weren't.'

'Stop! That was the point, wasn't it?'

They'd called it the 'lost summer'. They'd agreed not to resist their aimlessness. Just let life take them wherever it wanted. That summer was the best of Quinn's life. She'd made no money, but gained two best friends.

'We stayed up late on the roof that night, talking,' Amanda continued. 'We knew serving drinks and hosting drunk tourists at a beach club wasn't going to take us anywhere. That was when I decided to return home.'

'You never told me.'

'It was your moment. I didn't want to rain on your parade.'

Quinn pulled a tin of sugar from a cupboard. 'What parade?'

'The parade your life has become. It's well-deserved. Relax and enjoy it.'

'I can't enjoy it if everyone I care about can't relate, runs away, and keeps secrets.'

'Everyone? It was just Ivy and me. You know how stupid we were back then.'

It wasn't just Ivy and Amanda. Quinn didn't want to bring up Kya now, but her snow globe theory was proving to be right. Her success had put her in a bubble, out of reach from everyone.

'I want to know what's going on with you lot. I want to know what you're going through and how you feel about things. No more of this fake shit.'

'Fine.'

'No more talk about billboards and stardom. Let's talk about real life.'

'Sounds good. How are your parents?'

'They're well. Yours?'

'Never better.'

An awkward silence hovered for a while, then Amanda cleared her throat. 'I applied for a promotion at work. There's a good chance I'll get it.'

Now they were getting somewhere. 'Tell me everything. What's the title? Does it come with a huge office?'

Amanda did not settle for crumbs. Quinn was certain she'd run that firm someday.

'I applied for a senior buyer position. It comes with a tiny office, and an assistant.'

'What are you buying?' Quinn asked. 'Startups? Whole companies?'

'Women's shoes and accessories.'

'Is that a thing your firm is into?'

'I'm not at the firm. I'm at Harrods.'

'Are you kidding me right now?'

'No.'

'You're a buyer? At Harrods?'

'Yes.'

'And not a junior associate at a VC firm?'

'That's right.'

'Since when?'

'Since last year.'

'What?'

'I quit,' she admitted. 'It wasn't for me. I hated every minute of it.'

Quinn didn't know what to say.

'Is it really so surprising?' Amanda tried to make light of it. 'You know I love to shop.'

'We talked. We texted. I sent you pics of my new flat, bad pics but still. You never once mentioned leaving the firm.'

'I know ...'

'Please don't say you didn't want to rain on my parade. I'll lose it.'

No reply.

'Does Ivy know?'

Amanda delivered her answer in a shaky voice. 'I'm here to tell you both ... in person. Too much time had gone by and I kept deleting the texts.'

Changing careers wasn't unusual. Her silence around it definitely was. 'It's obviously working out if you're in line for a promotion.'

Amanda brightened. 'If I get it, I'll have to hit the ground running. There won't be any time to travel. That's why I have to make the most of this trip.'

'What does Brian have to say about all this?' Quinn asked.

'He thinks it's stupid.'

'Ouch.'

Naturally. Brainy Brian, as they liked to call him when he wasn't around, was the quintessential finance bro. He loved his job. Still, one might expect a little more support from their fiancé.

'That's why Brian and I are no longer together.'

'Excuse me?'

'We broke up.'

'When?'

Amanda pressed her lips together as if to keep the answer from spilling out.

Quinn shook her head in disbelief. 'Let me guess: last year?'

'Sort of.'

Quinn stared at her, jaw ajar. Was this even Amanda, or her evil twin?

'Are you all right?' Amanda asked in a small voice.

'I'm okay,' she said. 'It's a lot to take on an empty stomach.'

'Should we head over to Ivy's now and get her to set up a charcuterie board or something?'

That seemed like a good idea, considering Quinn's refrigerator held only a few bottles of Gatorade. 'Let's do that.'

'Okay. Let's go.'

CHAPTER TWENTY-FIVE

Ivy owned the flat on Michigan Avenue. For a while, she rented out the spare bedrooms for extra income, which was how first Quinn then Amanda ended up living and working with her. Although the location was perfect, the building was old and the narrow windows didn't let in much light. The rooftop terrace more than made up for it. It was their spot for late nights and lazy Sunday afternoons. They'd gather at one of the umbrella-topped tables with snacks, or what passed for charcuterie, to complain about work or recap a bad date. Those days, there hadn't been much to celebrate. Ivy was looking for love. Her dating life was chaotic, and she'd never had a steady boyfriend in her life. Amanda was looking to escape her fate. An alternative life was waiting for her back home. Her dad had found her a job, and her mum was busy planning her wedding to Brian. Amanda's future had been set in stone. As for Quinn, she was looking to make her mark. Success in the UK didn't easily translate in the US; she had to work for it.

After Ivy's first date with Victor, she called an emergency rooftop meeting the following day.

'Tell us everything,' Amanda said. 'Where did you go? What did you do?'

They hadn't gone anywhere. They'd spent the night in,

watching movies and eating wings. Already, Ivy thought he was 'the one'.

'The one what?' Amanda asked bluntly.

'The one for me,' Ivy explained.

Amanda's raised eyebrows nearly touched her hairline. 'Are you for real?'

'I'm no expert,' Quinn said. 'But doesn't finding "the one" require a little more legwork?'

'She means in bed, love,' Amanda said.

Ivy spat out her white wine.

'That's *not* what I meant!' Quinn cried.

'What then?' Amanda asked.

'They could go on a few more dates,' Quinn suggested. 'Get to know each other better.'

Ivy didn't want to hear it. She was smitten. It was the last night they'd seen her so happy.

They'd gathered at the roof to celebrate Quinn's first set at Nikki Beach, the one that made her a fixture on the South Beach scene. She'd started at the club as a waitress. After that first set, she'd never waited a table again. By Ivy's account, she'd single-handedly orchestrated the whole thing. One afternoon, their manager, Oscar, had approached her in a panic. Their scheduled DJ had cancelled due to food poisoning. They needed a replacement, fast.

'Quinn can do it.'

'Who's that?' he asked.

'The new girl.'

'With the curly hair and the accent?'

'That's the one.'

Oscar scoffed. 'This isn't amateur hour.'

'She's no amateur,' Ivy said. 'Quinn plays at Harry's on Fridays. Any day now they'll poach her.'

At the mention of the trendy wine bar, Oscar paid attention. 'Harry's, huh?'

'Among other spots,' Ivy said. 'Give her a try. You won't be sorry.'

'Send her to my office.'

'Yes, sir.'

Ivy cornered Quinn. 'Oscar wants to see you.'

Quinn recalled freezing. Under any other circumstances, that line was the kiss of death. Oscar seldom pulled a staffer off the floor to hand out employee of the month medals. She passed her orders to the next available waiter and followed Ivy to the back office.

'Is this about the guy who grabbed my bum last night?' she asked.

'No, he had it coming.'

'What then?'

'Patience,' Ivy said. 'If this works out you owe me big time.'

'Okay.'

'Fluff your hair. He only knows you as the girl with the curls.'

Quinn slowed to a stop. 'I don't like the sound of this.'

'You will,' Ivy said. 'He's going to ask you to play Tyler's set.'

'Where's Tyler?'

'At the ER.'

'Is he okay?'

'He'll live, but never mind him,' Ivy said. 'You play his set. I flood our social media channels with clips. We go from there. Are you ready?'

'Of course I'm ready.'

Ivy pointed at the closed door. 'Good. Now go convince Oscar that you can do it.'

Quinn shook out her curls and marched up to the door. The rest was history.

Tonight, Ivy wiped a table still wet from the morning's downpour and set out colourful bowls. The snacks were the same ones they'd stocked up on back in the day, except the crisps were 'premium'. The jar of salsa was their favourite grocery store brand, and so was the bargain white wine.

'Like old times!' Amanda said with a sigh. 'You don't know how much I needed this.'

They took their usual seats. Ivy got down to business. 'You're a buyer at Harrods. How good is your employee discount?'

Amanda piled salsa onto a chip. 'Pretty decent.'

'And you kept that from us?' Quinn said. She had a cart filled with studded leather harnesses from a British designer, and had yet to pull the trigger.

'I'll make it up to you.'

'You better,' Ivy said. 'Now, let's move on to Quinn. She dropped off the face of the earth this weekend, and I'm not ready to let that go.'

Amanda rose to her defence. 'She needed some alone time before things got crazy. Isn't that right, babes?'

Ivy wasn't buying it. She eyed Quinn. 'Alone time? Really?'

'No,' Quinn admitted. 'Not really.'

'When you said you went off-grid, you mean you ran off with someone?' Amanda asked.

'You didn't think I'd take off by myself, did you? I'd go mental.'

Solo retreats did not appeal to Quinn. Too much quiet was unsettling.

'This makes so much more sense now,' Amanda said. 'What's he like?'

'*He* is a *she*,' Ivy said.

'Woah!' Amanda cried. 'You weren't going to mention it?'

'You would've heard about it eventually,' Ivy said. 'It's trending on Reddit and some other apps.'

'Trending?' Amanda reached for her phone.

'Please, don't!' Quinn pleaded.

'Sorry, sweetie! I have to find out what the drama's about, or else I won't sleep tonight.'

Quinn could simply tell her and save her the trouble. It was about people who couldn't mind their own business.

Amanda found the post quickly enough. 'My God,' she whispered.

Like Ivy had said, the story hadn't died down. Quite the contrary, it had strengthened and doubled in size, moving from Reddit to Instagram, and the comments were in the thousands.

Amanda ignored the caption and zoomed in on the photo. She let out a silent scream. 'Quinn! This is so freaking romantic! The way she looks at you! I'm getting chills.'

Quinn would have buried her face in her hands, if her hands weren't greasy from the crisps she'd consumed.

'Don't be embarrassed,' Ivy said. 'It's trending for a reason. All the comments are overwhelmingly positive.'

Amanda shared a few of those comments. It warmed Quinn's heart that so many of her fans were speaking up for Kya, even though they had no clue who she was.

'So, what's she like, then?' Amanda asked.

'One of those smart types,' Ivy said. 'Into tech.'

Amanda approved. 'Very cool! I do like them brainy.'

'Speaking of brains, how's Brian?' Ivy asked. 'Why didn't he come with you? We would've showed him a good time.'

'Brian's gone,' Amanda said flatly.

'Gone?' Ivy filled her wine glass. 'Where'd he go?'

'Where do broken hearts go? Did anyone figure that one out?'

'Stop it!' Ivy cried. 'You broke off your engagement?'

'Yep.'

Ivy was stunned. They'd informed her straight away of Amanda's move from finance to fashion, but hadn't yet filled her in on the Brian stuff. Quinn could finally relax. Having to sit quietly while her friends analysed the girl she liked was a form of torture. She was ready to move on.

'I bought a dress that's perfect for an English country wedding,' Ivy lamented.

'That's presumptuous of you,' Amanda said. 'We'd never set a date, plus I'm a Londoner.'

'We're from the suburbs,' Quinn reminded her.

'Go ahead and sell the dress on Depop,' Amanda continued. 'There's no wedding. I'd rather stay single forever than marry Brian.'

'What went wrong?' Quinn asked.

'When I quit my job, he went absolutely bonkers,' Amanda said. 'The timing wasn't ideal; I'll give him that. We were saving up for the wedding, and eventually to buy a place. He called me unstable, unreliable. I let him talk. It was clear to me that he didn't know me or even like me very much.'

Kya's words floated back to Quinn. *I like you a little too much …* To be liked for who you were was everything.

'I had no future at the firm. They were going to fire me sooner or later,' Amanda continued. 'They sensed a lack of motivation. I spent my lunch breaks browsing the shops, checking the displays, observing how they moved merchandise. So, after a disastrous performance evaluation, I took the initiative, quit, and decided to use the money I'd saved to try to break into retail, a field I truly love. I didn't expect Brian to understand, but I didn't anticipate a scolding, either. Even my parents were more chill about it.'

'Screw Brian!' Quinn said.

'I've never met him, but screw him,' Ivy chimed.

'In conclusion,' Amanda said. 'I'm single for the first time in a long time. I have a career I love for the first time ever. I'm in a good place, but like everything it's scary.'

Quinn took in her friends' worried faces. If life had brought them together, it was likely because they needed each other. They'd pulled themselves out of tough times back in the day, and now, reunited, they could do it again.

Amanda turned to Ivy and said, 'What about you, love bug? How are you getting on?'

'I'm not,' Ivy admitted. 'I'm in this strange on-and-off thing with Victor, and I'm in a career that sounds cool, but isn't. Sorry, Quinn, but I need to get out of PR. It's not working out.'

'Don't apologize to me,' Quinn said. 'Do what you love. I'm less interested in managing my reputation and just putting good work out there.'

If Ivy dropped her as a client, Quinn wouldn't bother finding another publicist. People either loved her or they didn't. End of story.

'I might join my father's company. He's going to retire soon and will need someone to carry it on.'

Ivy's father owned a real estate agency, which explained why Ivy owned her apartment.

'That sounds reasonable enough,' Quinn said.

'Right? I've only been rebelling against it my whole life.'

'Sometimes what we're searching for is under our noses the whole time,' Amanda said, bursting with newfound wisdom.

'Maybe,' Ivy said.

'Could you give me some real estate advice?' Quinn asked.

'What do you want to know?' Ivy replied. 'I'm not licensed but don't let that stop you.'

'Should I sell the flat?'

'Why? Do you regret buying it?' Amanda asked.

'Sort of.'

Quinn might've jumped the gun when it came to buying property. Investing, rather than renting, had seemed smart at the time. With Kya leaving, she wondered if she'd traded in her freedom. The old Quinn would've hopped on a plane and picked up a few gigs in LA. New Quinn had a mortgage.

'Buying property is never a mistake,' Ivy said. 'How do you think my family made all their money, so at twenty-five I can waste time reinventing myself yet again?'

'You're not wasting time,' Amanda assured her. 'Can we normalize a little chaos. Not everyone has to be a boss babe at twenty-one.'

'Start over as many times as you like,' Quinn said. 'No one is keeping score.'

Ivy groaned. 'My mother is.'

'That can't be helped.'

'Guys, I'm starving. Crisps and salsa are not going to cut it. Can we go out to eat? We could go to that dive bar on Fourteenth Street? I loved their burgers.'

'That bar is closed,' Ivy said. 'You weren't here long enough to keep them in business.'

'Oh, no! How about that other place? We used to hang out and play pool. They had a jukebox and pictures of Madonna on the wall. Is that still open?'

'I don't remember that place,' Ivy said. 'Where's it located?'

'On Washington,' Quinn replied. She knew exactly the place. She and Kya had played the jukebox, but never got around to playing pool. 'Across from Smoke.'

'What's Smoke?' Amanda asked.

'A pop-up club,' Ivy said. 'It's already shut down.'

'Was Miami always like this?' Amanda wondered aloud.

'Always,' Ivy said, checking her phone. 'And the pool hall is closed on Monday nights.'

'Damn it!' Amanda started eating straight from the bag of crisps. 'We have to hang out tonight, guys. I don't care where we go. Quinn, maybe your girlfriend could join us. I want to meet her.'

'First, she's not my girlfriend. She leaves for California at the end of the week. Second, you'll meet her tomorrow. Tonight, she's with her family, and I'm with my friends.'

Amanda stared at her in awe. 'Is this what healthy boundaries look like?'

'Pretty much.'

'I know where we can go,' Ivy said. 'Come with me.'

They ended up in Ivy's kitchen. She cooked spaghetti olio. Quinn ran through the playlist of their summer parties, and Amanda danced barefoot on the tiled floor.

PART V

PARTY GIRL

Babes! It's finally Music Week!!! Can you believe it? I'm excited to share my official itinerary. Starting off strong with a pool party at BLU. Anything can change, so follow my socials for updates! Link in bio.

SOLSTICE MUSIC WEEK

Tuesday, June 17
BLU
SUNSET SPLASH
4PM–9PM
Featuring: Quinn

*

Thursday, June 19
ON THE HOUSE
HAPPY HOUR
5PM–10PM
Featuring: Venus Retrograde & Quinn
*

Friday, June 20
LAB
9PM
Quinn & DJ Angelo

Sunday, June 21
SUMMER SOLSTICE MUSIC FESTIVAL
Bayfront Park
Artists: Amy Pike, Nico, Quinn, Skylar … and more

BONUS TRACK
Tuesday, June 23
Lummus Park Beach
3PM–7PM

CHAPTER TWENTY-SIX

POOL PARTY

To get into the spirit of things, Kya did it all. She shaped her brows and extended her lashes. She waxed anything that could be waxed. She went shopping with Hugo for party clothes – a new little black dress, a similar style in white, two miniskirts and an assortment of tank tops. Instead of waiting around for Quinn to pick her up, she showed up at her door with a box of California-style pizza, a gag gift with sentimental value. She kissed Quinn in the back of the black car taking them to the storied beach resort, for luck but also for fun. The one thing she would not do was hold her hand when they pulled up to the hotel's crammed entrance.

'You go first,' she said. 'I'll follow in a minute.'

Quinn slipped off her ultra-glam sunglasses and eyed her. 'Are you serious?'

She looked so betrayed; Kya felt like the villain in her fairy tale. 'We talked about this.'

'You said no PDA. You said nothing about walking two steps behind me. I think you're taking this way too far.'

Kya pointed out the window. 'Every single person out there has a phone. Every phone has a camera.'

'I know how technology works, Kya.'

'I'm just saying—'

'All you're saying is that you don't want to be photographed with me.'

'It's day one. Let's pace ourselves. We can go viral some other day.'

'How do you know we went viral?'

'Because I looked it up!'

'We said we wouldn't give energy to trolls!'

'While we were away, sure,' Kya said. 'But we're back in the real world, where trolls can cause real damage.'

The driver got their bags out of the trunk then came around to open the door. 'Sorry, ladies. They're asking me to move out of the way. It's crazy busy here.'

It was, as he'd described, crazy busy. Was it so unreasonable to play it cool?

Quinn slipped out of the car and climbed the steps to the hotel lobby – alone.

Past the glass doors at the hotel was a different world, opulent, over the top, overflowing with giddiness. Emotional baggage left behind on the back seats of cabs, BLU was the place for fun. At the customer service desk, champagne was offered and turned down. Quinn was scheduled to play in a few short hours; she would need a clear head. The suite wasn't ready yet. The clerk apologized for the delay, but the hotel's social media coordinator had a suggestion. She had arranged for interviews with prominent outlets.

'They're waiting,' she said. 'You could meet with them now, if you like?'

Quinn agreed. 'Let's do it.'

They led her to a seating area where she answered questions on music but also topics as far-ranging as travel, hobbies, favourite foods, and celebrity crushes.

This was the way to play it, Kya thought, watching from a safe distance. It was easy enough to blend in with Quinn's entourage. As far as anyone knew, she could've been her assistant. She just wished the pit in her stomach would dissolve.

The interviews did not last long, either that or Quinn put an end to the whole thing by rising to her feet. She came over to Kya and, avoiding her eyes, said, 'Sorry about that.'

'No, it's fine.'

An attendant approached with their keycards in neat little envelopes. 'Your suite is ready. Joseph will escort you.'

On the ride up to the twentieth floor, Joseph entertained them with tales of the hotel's illustrious past, the list of famous guests who'd stayed at the very suite assigned to Quinn, and epic parties. 'There's a lot of excitement around your event,' he said. 'Is this your first time playing here?'

'It is,' she said. 'I'm excited, too.'

Kya was grateful for Joseph. All that talk served as a buffer. She only had to listen, and Quinn could go on avoiding her eyes, as hostilities strengthened, and a sort of cold war had begun.

A box of British chocolates and a handwritten note were waiting at the suite. The pillowcases were embroidered with Quinn's initials. But what really had Kya were the premium toiletries that she would be taking with her. With a press of a button, Quinn drew back the drapes to take in the vast ocean view. It was perfect except for the menacing clouds rolling forward.

She frowned. 'The party is outdoors, poolside.'

'Are you worried you'll get rained out?' Kya asked, already checking an app for weather predictions.

Quinn refused to even consider this. Turning her back to the window, she said, 'Let's unpack.'

Quinn took her garment bag into the bathroom and looked around for a steamer. Kya had packed light and her simple outfit didn't require any special care. She could take it easy for a while, rest up before the big event, but the tension was such that she couldn't relax. Quinn was upset with her. Nothing would be right until she smiled at Kya again.

Unsure of what to do with herself, Kya placed the vlogging camera borrowed from Adrian on its charger and went out onto the balcony. The wind was picking up. At the pool below, guests were packing and heading indoors. Kya caught the flash of lightning that ushered in the storm. The sudden downpour had everyone scurrying. Heavy sheets of rain completely obstructed the view. Raindrops needled Kya's face and arms, prompting her to rush back inside.

Inside the darkened suite, Quinn was in the bedroom, searching for the light switches Joseph had pointed out a moment earlier. Someone knocked on the door. Kya answered. It was the event coordinator. She showed up with a bottle of champagne, as if the sparkling wine could make up for the weather.

'Hi, I'm Jenna,' she said. 'I'm so sorry the weather isn't cooperating! We've been on storm watch all day, and we think it's wise to postpone the event for a couple hours. The skies should clear up around seven. If you agree, we'll post the change in schedule.'

Quinn nodded, biting into her lower lip. What choice did she have? Kya felt for her. This wasn't the smooth start she'd hoped for, and Kya hated the part she was playing in it.

'In the meantime, we invite you to visit our spa. I highly recommend the hot and cold experience. By the time you're done,

you'll be nice and relaxed and ready for a great night! How does that sound?'

'Sounds wonderful,' Quinn said.

She had a good attitude; Kya would give her that.

Jenna rattled a few more benefits of the unplanned delay. 'Plus, it'll be a lot cooler. Less humid. The sun doesn't set until seven forty-five, so we'll catch that golden hour. The photos will be gorgeous.'

'It'll be fine,' Quinn assured her.

'Great,' Jenna said. 'I'll get the ball rolling.'

Quinn's mask fell away as soon as they were alone. 'Is this a bad sign?' she asked.

'It's not a sign, it's a storm.' Kya hoped this was the one time her pragmatic mind and logical thinking could be of some use. 'You heard Jenna. The skies will clear. The heat and humidity will let up, and you won't miss golden hour.'

Quinn again nodded. Although, she did not look convinced. 'We have the afternoon free. What should we do? Are you up for the spa?'

'I won't turn down a massage,' Kya said.

'All right,' she said. 'I'll make the call.'

Considering the state of their relationship, a cryo-chamber was ideal. In the suite, there'd been nothing but cold air between them, anyway. The icy fog fit their mood perfectly. But when they progressed to the sauna, Kya, fully thawed, couldn't take it anymore. She wished she could rewind the clock, start again, from the day they first met.

'Do you think we'd be hanging out together if Hugo hadn't asked you for a favour?' Kya asked.

'I *wanted* to spend time with you.'

That was nice of her to say, but Kya couldn't imagine anyone wanting to spend time with her in those early days. She hadn't wanted to spend time with herself. 'I'm just surprised at how far we've come, considering how it started. It was so random.'

'It didn't start as a favour to Hugo,' Quinn insisted. 'It started in the ladies' room at Blood Orange. We were at the sinks, our eyes met in the mirror. Don't you remember any of this?'

Kya was in such a state that night, but her encounter with Quinn in the ladies' room had stopped time. The memory, still vivid, set her mind aflame. 'I remember,' she said quietly.

'There's nothing random about us.'

'I know that.' What she didn't know, or fully understand, was why Quinn was still in such a mood. Seated across from her on a teak bench, wrapped in a thick white towel, arms folded, hair piled on top of her head, she seemed angrier than earlier. How was that even possible? 'Why are you so mad?'

'You should know.'

'Well, I don't.'

Quinn let out a breath. 'I can't deal in half measures, Kya. As basic as this sounds, it's all or nothing for me.'

The heat fuelled Kya's exasperation. All or nothing? They were only going to be in each other's lives for another week. What was she expecting from her? 'Don't you think you're overreacting a little?'

'I don't,' she said stubbornly.

Her stubborn streak had always infuriated Kya, but in a good way. Now she was no longer sure. 'Is it so much to ask to fly under the radar for a while?'

'A while is all we have.'

'Exactly! There's no need to blow up the internet. Don't you care about all those things they said about you … about us?'

'If I'm with somebody, I'm *with* them. I don't care what anyone has to say. I don't care how many photos they post. I don't care if they shred me to pieces in their comment sections. I simply don't care. That's who I am, Kya. I'm just wondering who you are.'

'That's not fair.'

'Maybe, but here's the thing. A week, a month, a year, it makes no difference to me. I'm here with you now, and I'm going to give it everything I've got.'

'Quinn …' Kya's voice cracked, which was fine since she couldn't think of a single thing to say. All her arguments were melting in the suffocating heat.

'I know all this started because some idiot took a photo of us and posted it on the internet and said some pretty shitty things, but guess what? I love that photo, and I'm grateful to the wanker who took it. It says everything you won't … The way you look at me … Had I not seen it, I would have never known how you feel. So now it's up to you to decide how this week will go. I'm telling you right now, I'm not one to walk on eggshells.'

Someone opened the door to the sauna, looked from Kya to Quinn, and made the smart choice to walk away, leaving them to roast alone in their private hell.

CHAPTER TWENTY-SEVEN

Quinn was worried she'd gone too far. Would Kya walk away? She took that mixtape of emotions to the scheduled sound check but could not focus. The growing tension between her and Kya was unbearable. They hadn't exchanged a word since returning from the spa. At their suite Quinn had showered, dressed for the night, and left to set up. Now she felt terrible. She hadn't asked Kya to stay in Miami only to quarrel the whole time.

More than anything, she was angry with herself. Yesterday, her friends had marvelled at her ability to respect healthy boundaries. Today, after Kya had essentially drawn a map, outlining territory she would and would not cross, what had she done? Stomped on it like a big baby! To top it off, Quinn felt like a fool. She'd considered renting out her home and booking gigs in Los Angeles, all to be close to a woman who would not be photographed with her. Had she made this out to be more than it was?

Quinn had fallen in love twice in her life. Her first love, Jason, was eighteen when they met through mutual friends. He'd serenaded her at a birthday party, grabbing the karaoke mic and belting out Prince's 'Kiss'. For the six months they were together, they were known in their circle as Jade & Jason. It ended soon after she'd left home for London. Jason wanted way more than her extra time, he wanted a lifelong commitment. Quinn couldn't do it, her future was calling. After that relationship went bust, she never allowed anyone to call her Jade again.

Two years later, she was living and working in Ibiza. Billy was a Brit on perpetual holiday. He'd hired her to play a yacht party for him and his friends. He was not seeking a commitment, which she rather liked. No pressure. No expectations. No regrets if things ended badly. He was unpredictable, disappearing for long stretches and reappearing out of the blue. He missed her birthday. He never called and never answered the phone. He never answered a direct question, either.

'It's time for dinner. What are you in the mood for?'

'Whatever. I'm not picky.'

'What club should we go to on Saturday?'

'Hmm … not sure about Saturday. I'll circle back to you.'

'Where's this relationship going?'

It was a legitimate question. They'd been dating for close to a year.

'I didn't take you for a girl who'd ask that.'

'Just curious. What kind of girl do you take me for?'

'You know, like me.'

Like him? No commitment, no strings attached, no answers to any questions, no opinion on anything, no definite plans. She was nothing like him. She didn't like to waste her time. Work in Ibiza was fizzling out. Quinn was considering an opportunity in Miami. She couldn't afford to live like he did. His carefree existence was sponsored in part by his father who owned the yacht he threw parties in. She ended things right then.

Each time she fell in love, Quinn was aware it was happening. She didn't enter that tunnel blindly, never allowed herself to get trapped. She always had an escape route planned. It was different with Kya. Mainly because Quinn had never fallen for a complicated woman with ideas and opinions and ambitions and emotions that raged like a storm. Things were messy and they hadn't even started yet. There was no exit in sight, not for Quinn, anyway. But if Kya buckled so easily under pressure, if she couldn't take even the mildest heat, it was best to deal with it now. Quinn was not going to turn into Ivy, wishing the person she was with could be different, show up differently, or just show up at all. It would hurt, but if Kya walked away, she wouldn't chase after her.

'Quinn, we're good to go.'

Those words drew her out of her thoughts. It was showtime. Jenna had been right about one thing: the heat let up. Unfortunately, the low-hanging clouds stayed put. Not even a ray of golden sunshine broke through. The crowd below was rowdy and agitated at having to wait so long. Quinn burned with the same energy. She tapped the mic.

'Hey, beautiful people! Listen up!' she cried. 'I don't care if the skies open up. I don't care if it pours. We're here and we're going to have the party we sorely deserve. My name is Quinn. I will be your DJ tonight. Let go of your worries and focus on having a good time. I'll take care of the rest. If you've come to sit pretty, you're in the wrong place. Get up! Get a drink, if you need it. Forget your job. Ditch your boyfriend, if you have to. Turn off your phones. Mute that group chat. This is our time. Got that? It's summer. We're young and free, and so very much alive. Let's make the most of it. All I ask is one thing in return, a small favour really, if you're up to it, I'd love to hear your voices. If this sounds good to you, scream my name!'

CHAPTER TWENTY-EIGHT

By the time Kya made it to the party, Quinn had already kicked things off. But she hadn't missed a beat. Quinn's voice, raw with emotion, had floated over the hotel grounds as Kya raced across the garden towards the pool deck. At the guarded gates, she flashed her neon green bracelet and was granted access. Kya stumbled forward, out of breath, searching for the stage. Finally, there she was. Arms outstretched, conducting the crowd as only she could. They were chanting her name. Kya couldn't breathe, let alone speak.

That was how Ivy found her, moments later, motionless, in awe. She grabbed Kya's arm and pulled her away from the entrance. Apparently, she'd been blocking the flow of traffic. The security guards had been trying to get her attention for a while.

'Are you okay?' Ivy asked.

'I'm fine,' Kya replied, trying to hide her turmoil. 'Nice to see you again.'

'Yeah, same.' She turned to a tall, lanky Asian woman next to her. 'This is Amanda, Quinn's friend since childhood.'

'Actually, we despised one another as children, but I'll let Quinn tell you that story,' Amanda said. Her accent echoed Quinn's.

Kya recognized Amanda from the framed photograph on Quinn's bookcase, the third member of the so-called Spice Girls. In the photo, her smile took over her face and she winked at the camera. Here now, her fine features were composed as she studied Kya carefully.

'Nice to meet you,' Kya said.

'Likewise. I've heard so much about you.'

'All good things, I promise,' Ivy said. 'Did you just get here? Come hang with us.'

No sooner than the offer was made, it was rescinded. 'Actually, I'll catch up with you guys later. You'll be okay with Amanda, right?'

'What kind of question is that?' Amanda asked, offended. 'Of course she'll be okay. Where are you off to?'

'Anywhere but here.'

Ivy turned and walked briskly away. Kya and Amanda watched her go until the crowd swallowed her slim figure.

'Any idea what got into her?' Amanda asked, bewildered.

The answer was obvious when Victor, trailed by Nick, approached.

'Amanda?' Victor said. 'Is that you? Long time no see, girl!'

Amanda shook her head. 'Vic, if you're going to spoil my night, have the decency to come up with something more original than that.'

Victor raised his hands, defenceless. 'I'm not here to spoil anything. I've been looking forward to Quinn performing at BLU for a minute. This is the perfect venue for her.'

'We'll pass on the message,' Amanda said.

Vic's handsome face crumbled. 'Why the attitude?' he asked. 'We used to be cool.'

'Are you certain?'

'No matter what Ivy's told you, I'm not the bad guy,' he said. 'Things are complicated; that's all.'

Amanda shrugged. 'You don't have to explain yourself to me. No one can fully understand what goes down between a man and a woman; I get that. But if you're not the bad guy, why did Ivy turn and run the instant she spotted you?'

Victor looked around as if just now noticing Ivy's absence. 'Like I said, it's complicated.'

Amanda sighed. 'Uh-huh.'

Oddly enough, Kya's sympathies were with Vic. No one could fully understand what went down between a man and a woman, or a woman and a woman, for that matter. Things could get complicated fairly easily. There was no better explanation.

'Hey, Kya,' Victor said. 'You look good tonight. I got something for you.'

That was a surprise. 'Yeah? What've you got?'

'Hold on. Give me one sec.'

While Victor rifled through his wallet for whatever fun surprise he had in store for Kya, Nick nudged him aside and introduced himself.

'Amanda,' she replied. She draped an arm over Kya's shoulders. 'This is my new friend Kya.'

'Kya's everyone's new friend,' Nick mumbled.

'What was that?' Amanda asked.

'We've run into each other a few times. That's all.'

'All we do is run into each other,' Kya confirmed.

'All right, then,' Amanda said, putting an end to the awkward exchange.

Victor produced a business card. 'Remember I told you I'd hook you up?'

'Not really, no.'

'The day we were all at Quinn's—'

'What day was that?' Nick interrupted.

'Give me a break. I can't remember what I had for breakfast this morning. Anyway, you were on the phone, crying—'

It was Kya's turn to interrupt. 'I wasn't crying!'

She remembered that much.

He handed over the card. 'Anyway, I told you I'd hook you up with a friend.'

Kya ran her fingertip over the familiar embossed lettering.

BioFlow Enterprises
Corinne Miller, CEO

If Kya believed in signs, she'd count this as one.

'Corinne does some really impressive things,' Victor said. 'I don't know too much about it, but her company was featured in *Forbes* last year. She's a family friend, and a cool lady. You'll like her.'

'I met Corinne at an event last night,' Kya said. 'You're right, she is cool.'

'See? What did I tell you?' he gloated. 'Give her a call.'

'Thanks,' Kya said. 'I might do that.'

When the guys left to antagonize another group of unsuspecting women, Kya slipped the card in her back pocket and put it out of her mind. She'd missed ten per cent of Quinn's opening set. For some, the music was background noise or a beat to jump around to. To Kya, it was personal.

'That Nick is kind of hot,' Amanda said.

Kya whipped around and studied her face. Was she serious? 'I wouldn't know about that,' she said cautiously.

'His attitude is rubbish, though.'

'Pure trash,' Kya agreed.

'Let's move closer to the stage. Ivy will find us, eventually.'

There was nothing Kya wanted more than to get closer to Quinn. On stage, surrounded by a sea of people, she was beyond her reach. With a twist of a knob, she stripped the melody of a popular song leaving only the heartbeat of the baseline. With the spotlight framing her face, she was once again the enigmatic angel who'd so intimidated Kya at the start. She travelled back in time, revisiting the key beats of their story in an effort to re-thread their feeble connection. The moody ladies' room of a speakeasy, the bright smoothie bar of a fitness club, Adrian's kitchen, the pool, the pool hall, the park, her parked car, her music studio, the back alley of a club, bungalow number 2. Each encounter had tightened the ring around them, drawing them closer.

Did they have a future? No. Would this last past this one week? No. Would Kya draw the wrong kind of attention and get dragged online? Yes. Would it be worth it? Absolutely.

'Are you sure you're okay?' Amanda asked. 'You've been staring into space for a bit now.'

'I'm fine.' Though truthfully, she felt light-headed. 'It's just I can't believe how much time I've wasted.'

'No, we're good,' Amanda said. 'The night is young. For now, we're taking in the lie of the land. But things will get wild in a second.'

'I mean with Quinn!' Kya cried. 'We don't have much time and I wasted a whole day.'

Amanda's eyes widened with understanding. 'Oh! I see!' She motioned for Kya to carry on. 'What happened today?'

'We had a fight.'

That wasn't exactly true, Kya thought. She'd laid out her

conditions, then Quinn had done the same, and now they were no longer speaking to each other.

'I wouldn't worry too much about it. She'll never admit it, but she gets nervous before gigs. Look at her now. She's in her element, having fun. That row will be old news before the night is over.'

Kya wasn't convinced. 'She's an angel, and I'm blowing it.'

Amanda took her hand in hers and patted it like a concerned grandma. 'Sweetie, are you a little drunk?'

'I haven't had a drink all day!'

'This is just you?'

'Just me … falling to pieces.'

'Or falling in love. Whatever. What do I know?'

Kya hastily withdrew her hand. Amanda laughed. 'Relax, darling!' she said. 'Quinn fancies you, and she doesn't hold grudges. I promise you, it's all going to work out.'

'You're right.'

'I know I'm right,' Amanda said. 'How about we get you a drink?'

Kya shook her head. No more delays or detours. 'Get me to the stage.'

CHAPTER TWENTY-NINE

Quinn stripped the last song of its melody, leaving only the thrum of the base to flicker out. High on adrenaline, she thanked the crowd through raucous applause. 'Thank you for the love and the energy! This was a dream! Enjoy your night! Be safe!'

The set had drained her. She was hot, sweaty, hungry, and spent, but she'd never felt better. To make it perfect, Kya was waiting at the bottom of the stage. Then it all came crashing back, and Quinn's own heartbeat thinned to a thread. Three short steps unfolded between them. Yet she hesitated as if at the edge of a cliff. Kya extended a hand. Delirious with relief, Quinn grabbed it and let Kya guide her down the steps and across the cluttered landscape of cups abandoned on cocktail tables, overturned chairs, confetti on shimmering glass. Every so often, someone stopped them to ask for a photo. Kya stepped away but did not hide, waiting patiently until Quinn could return to her. Finally, they made it as far as the hotel lobby then sought refuge in a lift. Even there, they weren't alone and were forced to stand side by side, but hand in hand.

At the suite, Kya locked the door behind them. 'I'm sorry I let you down today,' she said.

Quinn took her pretty face in her hands. 'Don't say that. I'm sorry I said those things. I appreciate that you're here at all.'

'Are you crazy? I'm the lucky one.'

Kya closed her eyes, as if she couldn't make sense of her good fortune. She clearly didn't get it. So often, after playing an amazing set, Quinn returned to an empty and quiet room to come down from a high all alone. To have Kya here this week was such a gift. But just because she wanted this, it didn't mean Kya was ready to handle all that would come her way.

'Let's talk,' she said.

'We're done talking,' Kya said. 'I'm here. I'm all in. There's nothing more to say.'

'I need you to know that this is scary for me too, babe. I don't mean to push you. If you're not ready—'

'I'll never be ready for this. Never.'

Okay. That was … brutal. 'Am I such a pill?'

Kya leaned close and kissed her ear. 'I don't care. I'd swallow it.'

Quinn was shivering already. They could talk later, she decided, just as Kya changed her mind.

'Actually, I do have something to say. You are one stubborn b—'

'Babe, watch what you say!' Quinn cried.

'It's true!' Kya exclaimed.

'Well, yeah, I am! Sorry it took you so long to figure it out. Can we move on now?'

'No, we can't. You're uncompromising. I thought I was being reasonable earlier. Didn't you get where I was coming from?'

'Did you miss my heartfelt apology just now?'

'After you dragged me through hell!'

'I didn't *drag* you through anything, Kya.'

'I had a mental breakdown!'

'You're a little drama queen. That's not my fault.'

'This week is going to wreck me.' Kya sighed with resignation.

'Probably,' Quinn said. 'Now that you've got all that off your chest, kindly shut up and kiss me.'

Kya kissed her slowly and Quinn's world spiralled. She pinned Kya to the door and slipped her hands beneath her soft cotton shirt. She loved the feel of her skin, always warm to the touch. She loved her breasts, small yet lush and full. Her hardened nipples drilled into Quinn's palms, sending a thrill through her body. She was ready to rip Kya's clothes off when a knock and a tentative call of 'Housekeeping!' sent them scrambling away from the door.

'No, thanks!'

'We're good!'

'Extra towels?'

'Actually … yes,' Quinn replied. She opened the door and accepted a pile of white towels. 'We'll need these for the ritual,' she said to Kya.

'What ritual?' Kya asked, distractedly. She was slipping off her clothes.

'I have a post-performance ritual. It involves a hot shower and a chilled glass of wine. Will you join me?'

'That's funny,' Kya said. 'I have a post-performance ritual, too. It involves a chilled glass of wine and a cigarette.'

Quinn dropped the pile of towels and went to her. 'My ritual can wait.'

'We'll get to it,' Kya assured her. 'In time.'

They were back in each other's arms, gripping at each other. The bed was too far away. Quinn pushed Kya onto a corner chair and straddled her. Kya held her still with one hand, fingers digging into her waist. The fingers of her free hand slid up her inner thigh, leaving a trail of goosebumps. Her thumb found and brushed against her clitoris, over and over, until the emotions of the day flooded through her, leaving her weak but happy, in Kya's arms.

In the morning, when Quinn threw open the bedroom curtains to a pristine view, an immaculate sky, not a whisper of a cloud anywhere, she couldn't believe her eyes. Of course, it would turn out like this, rain on game day and nothing but golden sunshine the day after.

'Are you seeing this?' she asked Kya, who was still curled up in bed.

She covered her face with a pillow and moaned. 'I'd rather not.'

'It's a beautiful day.'

'I trust you.'

Quinn yanked the sheets off her long, toned, but listless body. They had the room until noon, maybe a little longer if Quinn requested a later check-out. They had to take advantage while they could. She ran the tip of a finger down the length of Kya's thigh. 'Come on,' she said. 'It's like Key Largo, but with sand.'

Kya tossed the pillow aside and met her eyes. 'That sounds nice.'

'If there's a better way to start the day, I don't know it.'

'There's a better way,' Kya said. 'But it is very pretty outside.'

Quinn let her gaze wash over the curves of Kya's body. 'Very pretty.'

'Don't look at me like that if you hope to get anywhere near the beach,' Kya warned. She swung her long legs over the edge of the bed. 'Let's go!'

They scrambled around, pulling on swimsuits and slathering on sun cream. They raced each other down the hall to catch the lift just before the doors slid shut. This time they were blissfully alone. Kya drew her close and kissed her full on the mouth. Her skin was warm and she tasted like mint toothpaste. Quinn wondered if a lazy morning in bed might've been the way to go. Then they reached the ground floor, the doors parted, and Kya sprang out ahead. Quinn chased after her, across the garden and out a back gate to the boardwalk where they nearly crashed into a cyclist, down a flight of wooden steps on which Kya's sandals came loose, and finally onto the beach. They arranged for a sunlounger and an umbrella. Napping in the sand, as she'd once fantasized of doing, was overrated. Getting sand out of her curly hair was more trouble than it was worth. Besides, real life was dreamy enough. Kya rushed into the rolling waves for a swim. A while later, she walked out of the sea and stretched out next to her in the shade of the umbrella. What more could she want?

Kya reached for a towel and patted her arms dry. 'Last night's performance was fantastic. You were amazing. Did I tell you?'

'No,' Quinn said. 'You told me I was a stubborn B, and then you made love to me in the shower.'

'That's right,' Kya said. 'I have no regrets.'

'Me, too. And you're right. Last night was special.'

'I met Amanda.'

'Did you?' Quinn sat up. 'I didn't even get a chance to say hi. I'll have to make it up to her tomorrow. Did you two get on?'

'She's great. I like her a lot,' Kya said.

'I love that girl. She brought me my favourite snacks from England. I promise to share them with you when we get home.'

'She says you two despised each other when you were kids.'

'We belonged to rival gangs,' Quinn deadpanned. 'She was ballet core and I was dark and goth.'

'You? Dark and goth? I can't picture it. You're my glitter-bomb angel.'

'That's sweet of you to say, but you ought to know better by now.'

'On your birthday you said your friends wouldn't travel halfway around the world to celebrate you. It seems like you were wrong.'

'I was,' Quinn admitted. She and her friends lived wildly different lives. They were spread out around the globe. They didn't meet for regular Sunday brunches but would show up for each other.

'You're lucky. I've been feeling friendless lately. That's the toughest part of all this.'

'What about me? I'm the best friend you've ever had.'

'So humble and modest, too.'

'The wing beneath your wings, babe.'

'I've made another friend,' Kya said. 'You'll never guess. It's Victor.'

'Seriously?'

'He hooked me up with a local entrepreneur for a job opportunity. I already had the hook-up, but that was still nice of him.'

'Very nice. Will you consider it?'

'The job?' Kya asked. 'No way. It's not in a field I'm remotely interested in. I will follow up, though. Seems like it's meant to be. First, I run into this woman at my brother's award ceremony the other night, then Victor hands me her card. You're the expert. Is this a sign?'

'It's a sign you should start believing in signs,' Quinn said coolly. Anything to hide her searing disappointment.

CHAPTER THIRTY

The following morning, Kya reached for her stash of Corinne Miller business cards. Next thing, she was joining the tech CEO for lunch at a Korean restaurant with a Michelin star.

'Thanks for meeting with me today,' Kya said, once they were seated.

'Please,' Corinne said, perusing the cocktail menu. 'I've been dying to try this place, no one is ever available, and as a bonus, I get to expense it.'

'Do you have to worry about that? You're the boss.'

'I imagine my CFO might have something to say about that. I know how to make money and how to spend it. She's the one that knows about managing it.'

'A female-led company,' Kya noted, low-key impressed.

'I insist on it,' Corinne said. 'Maybe it's different for you, but the tech industry was just one giant man cave back when I started.'

'It hasn't changed much,' Kya said. 'They let women in, but it's still a cave.'

Corinne folded the menu and set it aside. 'A damn shame.'

'Speaking of men,' Kya said, 'I wasn't sure whether to get in touch but Victor Ortiz passed me your card and I figured I had to act on it.'

'Little Vic Ortiz? His grandfather was my father's accountant for decades. I've known him his entire life.'

'I think it's safe to say he's grown up now.'

'Either way, it's smart of you to reach out,' Corinne said. 'Always take the meeting. You never know what may come of it.'

They were on the same page, at least. Kya recognized opportunity when it knocked. Something could come out of this meeting. She didn't see a future for herself in lab automation, but she was open to freelancing if only for an excuse to stay in Miami a while longer. If she stayed, she and Quinn could take their eyes off the clock. They'd have months to explore this thing between them, rather than burn through it in a few short days.

'I'll get straight to it,' Corinne continued. 'We weren't looking to hire right now but considering your experience at Ex-Cell, we might grant an exception. I'm sure you'd be an asset to us. Tell me more about your time there. Together we could figure out how best to use your skillset.'

Kya's cheeks burned. She reached for a glass of water then stopped herself. Embarrassing or not, she had to get it out. No stalling. 'My time at Ex-Cell didn't end well.'

'Even so,' Corinne said. 'It's impressive.'

'It was all very impressive until they fired me,' Kya said bitterly.

'You kids take things so personally,' Corinne said. 'You know what they say, right? Your career hasn't begun until you get axed.'

No one said that. And Kya wasn't a kid. Up until recently, she earned a six-figure salary while balancing a successful blog and day-trading stocks – although any clever kid could do any combination of those things from their home computers.

'Next time it won't sting as much,' Corinne promised.

'No,' Kya said. 'I won't go through this another time.'

'You will if you want to make waves.'

Her brother managed to make waves all while being treated with respect. His contributions were valued. Was that too much to ask?

'Maybe you don't need a job as much as you need a little advice,' Corinne said.

'I'll take the advice, but I do need a job,' Kya said. 'I don't know what to do with myself when I'm not working.'

'Have you considered working for yourself?'

'No.' She was a lot of things, but a boss babe wasn't one of them.

'You should.'

The waiter came around for the drink order. Corinne went for a classic martini, and Kya stuck with tap water, asking only for a wedge of lime.

'Please don't hold back on my account,' Corinne said. 'I hatched the plan for my company over drinks with my friend, Joanne. We were at one of those networking events, bored to tears. She's now my CFO.'

'I have a long night ahead,' Kya explained. 'It's Music Week, and my girlfriend is playing an event later.'

Had she really called Quinn her girlfriend? How would she have reacted if she'd overheard? Would she blush, or turn away?

'What instrument does she play?' Corinne asked.

'She's a DJ.'

'Will she be playing at that concert downtown, the one that draws people from all over the world, blocking traffic and causing chaos?'

'Yes! We're so excited!'

Kya was shocked by just how excited she truly was. Everything had been building up to the week, and this one major performance. She couldn't wait to see Quinn on the main stage.

Corinne topped up her water glass from the carafe on the table. 'In that case, you really should stay hydrated.'

'I'd like to hear more about the networking event that started it all. How did that brainstorm session go? Did you draw an org chart on cocktail napkins?'

'I'll never forget that day. We were miserable, just moaning over our awful jobs. At the time, my employer was demanding I relocate to San Francisco, even though I was hired to work remotely. It was just a ploy to get rid of me. They knew I wouldn't do it. I'd have no choice but to quit. Joanne had been passed over for one too many promotions. So, we're at the bar, ordering another round of Cosmopolitans – we thought we were so cool – and Joanne says, "We should branch out on our own." I'm so glad we did. Our company is small and nimble. We love what we do, and we don't have to answer to anyone. Well, I have to answer to Joanne and vice versa, but I'm fine with that.'

Kya picked up her phone and opened an app. 'Do you mind if I take notes?'

'If you like.'

'I blog about this stuff, the ups and downs of working in tech. My subscribers would love this story. I mean … if it's okay with you?'

'Certainly. We need all the exposure we can get.'

'I'm not *Forbes* or anything.'

'Nobody reads *Forbes*, but I'm willing to bet your subscribers read your blogs.'

They used to, anyway, Kya thought. She'd built an engaged community and she missed them. This could be the way back, writing about others who'd struggled in the industry, taking the focus off herself.

'All I ask is that you use a flattering photo of me,' Corinne added.

Kya laughed. 'That shouldn't be difficult.'

Lunch was delicious. By the time they left the restaurant, Kya had enough material for a series of blog posts – but still no job.

CHAPTER THIRTY-ONE

Quinn: Glam day tomorrow! Are you in?

Amanda: Same spot?

Quinn: Absolutely.

Amanda: Say less. I'm in!

Despite her precautions, Quinn's hair was stiff with sand and her nails were a mess. She could not show up for her happy hour set looking like a mermaid ejected from the seas. So she had recruited Amanda, her partner in all things glam, and booked the appointments.

The next morning, Amanda was waiting on the pavement outside Ivy's building. She raised an arm, as if hailing a taxi. Quinn pulled up to the kerb and slipped into the passenger seat.

'You're alone! Where's Kya?'

'Networking. Power lunch.'

'How very serious of her.'

Kya had scheduled the meeting at the very last minute. She said nothing would come of it, but a girl could hope.

'It's just you and me today. Is that all right with you?'

'Perfect.'

They drove to a modest salon in Miami's lower east side, the same one they'd discovered together all those years ago. Quinn was loyal, and if she liked a business, no matter how small, no matter what picky reviewers had to say online, they had in her a customer for life.

Their hair washed and faces slathered with a conditioning mask, they sat side by side for pedicures.

'You killed it on Tuesday,' Amanda said. 'The weather was horrible. The whole event could have gone bust, but you showed those people what you can do.'

'Thanks, babe!'

Quinn no longer felt the pressure to show anyone anything except a good time. People had come out in spite of the weather and she owed it to them to make the night memorable. Although she was happy her friend liked her performance, she'd be even happier if she liked her girl. She wanted Kya to feel supported and welcomed in her world.

'Kya says you two got along okay,' she said tentatively. Why was she so nervous?

'Once she loosened up, we had a blast.'

'What do you mean?'

Kya was serious. It didn't mean she was uptight.

'She was having a mini–mental health crisis. We talked through it.'

'Don't exaggerate!'

'It's the truth! You know what else is true? I think she's caught feelings for you. Like, for real feelings. She's down bad.'

'I'm not sure we're talking about the same person. Kya keeps her emotions locked in a vault.'

'Well now she's let them *all* out. She was convinced you were cross with her over something or another, I don't even know. She fell to pieces.'

To pieces?!

The salon owner approached them. 'Ladies? Bottled water?'

'Yes, thanks,' they replied in unison.

Quinn sipped her water, trying to make sense of what she'd learned. She couldn't imagine Kya falling apart in front of anyone let alone someone she'd just met. Then again, her words echoed in Quinn's head. *You dragged me through hell.* She hadn't taken that accusation seriously. Perhaps she should have.

'I met Victor's friend Nick,' Amanda said. 'He was flirty in a dark, unappealing way.'

'I don't know about him,' Quinn said.

'Seems like no one does.'

'We'll find you someone better.'

'Please do, and soon. Remember, I don't have much time. I fly home on Monday.'

'Don't worry. I got you.'

A good guy was hard to find, but surely Amanda could do better.

'On second thought, forget it,' Amanda said. 'Don't trouble yourself.'

'No trouble,' Quinn assured her. 'I'll check my roster.'

'I've changed my mind. I don't need a man to have fun.'

'True! You're a vibe unto yourself.'

'Plus, I've got you lot.'

'We're way more fun than any guy.'

'It's settled. This holiday is for the girls.'

While Amanda's nail technician showed her an array of nude

colours, all the same shade of ballet slipper pink, Quinn took a call. It was Jenna, the event coordinator at BLU.

'Calling to tell you how pleased we were with your performance at Splash.'

'My pleasure.'

'You handled the setbacks professionally. That's exactly what we're looking for on team BLU. I'm calling to extend an invitation for you to return later this summer.'

'I'd love that. Get in touch with my booking agent and we'll set a date.'

'We're looking for more than just one booking. That's why I'm calling, to see how you might feel about a residency.'

'Pardon?'

Had she heard right? Headlining at BLU would be a dream! The venue attracted the biggest talent from all over the world. Quinn had avoided all long-term commitments since wrapping her Nikki Beach residency. The gig had dragged on far too long. She had turned down several since then, preferring short-term commitments that allowed her to work as much or as little as she wanted. But the right residency would do two things: 1) put her squarely on the map; 2) provide stable income. She could quit a myriad of other gigs. She wouldn't have to play for lawyers, accountants, and bankers at their annual reunions. She could test her new music to live audiences in real time. A residency would offer stability until she figured out her next move. She was keen on making music of her own and the extra income would make that transition a lot smoother. In a matter of seconds, Quinn saw her future clearly. A pristine sky, not one cloud, not a single blemish. This was it! The missing element that would fuse everything together.

Of course, she could not let Jenna in on this.

'A residency is quite a commitment,' Quinn said coolly. 'How long did you have in mind?'

'One year,' she replied. 'I realize you're very much in demand. My goal is to get the conversation started. Talk to your people, and when you're ready for a discussion, please get in touch.'

That sounded reasonable.

'Will do.'

'I'm glad you're open to it. Talk soon.'

When she got off the phone, Amanda asked, 'What was that about?'

'A potential residency at BLU for one full year.'

'Is that, like, a residency in Vegas? Would that make you the Céline Dion of house music?'

'I think so!'

'Brilliant! Things are looking good for us.'

Quinn leaned back in the padded recliner and closed her eyes.

Quinn returned home to find Kya on her back on the sitting room floor, feet propped up on the sofa, braids fanned out on the rug. Don't you look comfortable, she was tempted to say, only Kya didn't look all that comfortable. She clutched her phone with a tight grip. Her brows were drawn tight as her gaze skimmed the screen.

'Hey, babe,' she said.

'Hi,' Kya replied thinly.

Something was wrong.

Quinn kicked off her shoes and sank down on the floor next to her. Kya smiled and clutched her phone tighter, angling the screen away.

'I'm not an insecure person,' Quinn said. 'If I were, I'd say you're acting shady, maybe texting an ex.'

'My ex is blocked,' Kya said. 'I block them all.'

'Ruthless,' Quinn said. 'You'd block me?'

'Never,' Kya replied. 'While you're on tour, taking over the world, I'll be curled in bed, watching your performances on YouTube.'

'Will you cry yourself to sleep?' Quinn asked, just to complete the picture.

'I'll put together a sad girl playlist and everything.'

'Could you add some Bonnie Tyler to the mix, for good measure?'

'Anything you like.'

'For the moment, we're still very much together.' Quinn joined her on the floor. 'Maybe hit pause on those plans?'

'Maybe.' Kya's gaze fanned her face. 'You look pretty.'

'I was going for stunning.'

'You're always stunning.'

'Please tell me what's going on,' Quinn whispered. 'You looked so stressed just now. Was it lunch? Was it terrible?'

'Lunch was great. I got an idea for a new series for Girl Decoded.'

'Sounds exciting.' Quinn leaned close and touched the tip of her nose to hers then pulled away. 'Why aren't *you* excited?'

'Because I logged into my account just now and it's a dumpster fire.'

'Is it?'

'The comments, the DMs … Everyone wants to know why I was let go and what my plans are. I don't have an answer to either of those questions.'

'You don't owe them any answers,' Quinn said.

'It's not that simple,' Kya said. 'I created this community. I owe them transparency.'

'You told them the truth. You don't owe them any more than that,' Quinn said hotly. 'If they truly cared about you, they'd give you time. They wouldn't pressure you like this.'

She was sceptical of this so-called community. Hadn't one of them turned on Kya? Gone out of their way to humiliate her? Hadn't they readily believed the lies?

'Want my advice?'

'I want you. Not sure about the advice.'

Kya was already more relaxed than when Quinn had found her a moment ago. The phone tossed aside, abandoned, she sat upright. 'You're getting it anyway,' she said. 'Post your blog, the whole bloody series. If anyone has anything negative to say, activate your inner bitch and block *them*.'

Kya reached up and cupped Quinn's face. 'Say that again.'

'You flirt.'

Quinn was laughing when it struck her. She owed Kya transparency.

'Jenna called today with an offer.'

'I'm not a confident woman, so I'll just say it: this makes me nervous.'

'It's a job offer, babe,' Quinn said. 'A year-long residency at BLU.'

'That's amazing! Does it come with the suite?' Kya asked.

'Hmm ... I don't think so.'

'Still amazing!'

'She was impressed by the way I handled the rain and all the setbacks,' Quinn explained.

'Did you tell her you were also handling a personal crisis at the time?' Kya asked.

'Right … I'll call her back, tell her my girlfriend was driving me mad. She'll be properly impressed.'

Kya stared up at her blankly and then turned away, her cheeks flaming red.

'What is it?' Quinn asked.

'Nothing,' she said quickly.

It was not 'nothing'. Quinn played back the track and found the glitch. GIRLFRIEND. Now she was as perplexed as Kya looked. What was she thinking? That word was loaded. You couldn't toss it out like that mid-conversation!

'I'm proud of you,' Kya said, breaking the awkward silence. 'Congrats, Quinn.'

'Thanks.' She sensed there was something more, but didn't press it. 'We should celebrate. I've got just the thing. Prawn cocktail crisps straight from home.'

Kya sat up and crossed her legs. 'Prawn what?'

'Crisps!' Quinn hollered from the kitchen. She reached into the cupboard for the familiar pink bag.

'I had shrimp salad with lunch!' Kya hollered back.

'Forget your salad!' Quinn balked. 'You claim to be a snack connoisseur. Well, you haven't lived until you've tried these.'

'I doubt that very much.'

Quinn returned to the sitting room and sat on the rug, facing Kya. She ripped open the package. 'Open your mouth and close your eyes.'

Kya did as she was told. Quinn slowly lowered the bag to the floor, quickly losing interest. This woman … so trusting, so open.

The idea that she could someday be blocked from her life made Quinn queasy.

'Open your eyes,' Quinn whispered.

Kya blinked her eyes open, uncertain as to why the rules had changed. Quinn crushed away her confusion with a kiss.

CHAPTER THIRTY-TWO

HAPPY HOUR

Depending on who you asked, happy hour took on a different meaning. For some, the appeal was the specials: ten-dollar cocktails, two-dollar oysters, five shots for five dollars. For others, it scratched the itch for escapism and play after a long day's work. For Kya, specifically, the appeal was the girl who'd brought her to the rooftop venue that soared forty-eight floors over the city centre. There were no water views to speak of, only a jungle of buildings of various heights and the string of street traffic below. At sunset, the headlights and streetlamps flared and the city glowed.

Kya ran into Hugo in the unisex bathroom. They caught up on family matters as they touched up their make-up.

'I heard Quinn killed it at BLU,' he said. 'Wish I could've been there. Your brother and I had plans.'

'Keep this to yourself, but you may get a chance to catch her again before summer ends. They've reached out with an offer.'

Hugo let out a low whistle. 'Quinn is in her bag!'

'Looks like it.'

'How about you, *minha irmã*?' Hugo asked. 'Are you doing, okay?'

'I'm getting back into blogging.'

'As you should,' he said. 'Don't let anyone bully you out of anything, not even me.'

Kya laughed. 'You'll be happy to know that I'm posting BTS clips on TikTok during Music Week.'

'That does make me happy. I'll check out your posts.'

'How's Lucky?'

'She misses her favourite aunt, naturally.'

'I miss her, too!'

'She'll get new houseguests to spoil her soon. Sam and Roman arrive tomorrow.'

Kya capped her tube of lip gloss. 'Already?'

'They had to shuffle some things around. They'll only be in Miami for the weekend.'

'Do you think they'll make it to Solstice?'

'Doubt it. We're taking them out to brunch on Sunday. You and Quinn should join us if you are not too exhausted from the concert.'

'I can't speak for Quinn, but I'll try to make it,' Kya said.

'Perfect,' he said. 'We look gorgeous, let's get out there.'

As soon as she got out there, Amanda caught up with her and dragged her away. 'Tonight, we cut loose!' she declared.

'Is that right?' Kya said.

'Oh, yes,' she said. 'Quinn's set doesn't start until eight. That gives us exactly seventeen minutes. Tequila shots?'

'Lady, that's probably a bad idea.'

'All my good ideas are bad at the core,' Amanda said. 'Somehow it works out.'

'In that case, the first round is on me.'

The bartender lined up the glasses. Kya brought a wedge of

lime to her lips. It had been a long day, month, year. Tonight, she would learn what it meant to cut loose. As it turned out, it meant cheering your girl so loudly you went hoarse within an hour. It meant climbing on a bench to get a better view, only a glass partition saving you from plummeting forty-eight floors to certain death. It meant making fast friends with a group of women you'd never meet again under any circumstances, and trying jalapeño poppers that set your gut on fire while the music pulsed through you. Finally, the DJ shouts you out and the whole world is magic.

Quinn wrapped up her set and, as planned, they met by the elevators. Kya arrived first. She came around eventually, light on her feet, as if walking on air. 'Hey you! Waiting for me?'

'Who else?'

'Any number of people,' Quinn teased. 'I saw you tonight, party girl. You were having a blast.'

'You noticed? I'm shocked.'

'Oh, I had my eyes on you.'

'I'm flattered. You weren't too busy on stage being worshipped?'

'Not at all.'

They agreed to keep the party going. In the back seat of the car taking her and Quinn to Location B, a popular spot, Kya pulled her onto her lap and kissed her bare shoulder. She wanted a chance to worship her privately, without a frenzied audience. Quinn kissed her hungrily until every square inch of Kya's body sparked with want. When they arrived at the bar, Kya was breathless.

Cutting loose meant helping your date climb out of the car, in a miniskirt that showed off her long, glossy legs. It meant ducking into the dark space and straight onto the dance floor where they joined the others. They danced freely. Quinn's hands were on her body, slowing her down, even as the music picked up. That's when Kya knew it was time to go.

An hour later they were home at last, not on the balcony or in the bedroom, but in Quinn's generous closet. Kya struggled with the zip of Quinn's bustier. Getting her in and out of her stage clothes was always an ordeal, but so worth it. When Quinn finally broke free from the latex trap, she sank onto the carpeted floor. 'I can breathe!' she cried.

Kya kneeled onto the floor next to her. 'Hi,' she said. 'I'm Kya. I'll be your DJ tonight.'

Quinn bit back a smile. 'Is that right? I love that for me!'

'I only play eighties pop.'

She stretched out on her back and covered her eyes with her arm. 'I spoke too soon.'

'Nineties power anthems.'

'God no!'

'And every boy band hit of the aughts.'

'Look,' she said. 'If you want to end this, just say so.'

'I don't want this ever to end.'

Her words ushered a ghostly silence that spread from the closet throughout the apartment. Kya could die. What was going on in her head? Was she just spewing out words without forethought or logic? From calling Quinn her girlfriend earlier today and professing undying devotion now, something was seriously wrong. Whatever the glitch, she had to get it fixed.

You can't do this, she told herself. Whatever 'this' was, she couldn't do it. It had to stop.

Quinn extended her arms. 'Come to me.'

To hide her turmoil, Kya buried her face in the softness of her breasts and breathed in Quinn's scent. Once the feeling had passed, she sank her teeth into the tender flesh, hoping to leave a mark that would outlast the night.

CHAPTER THIRTY-THREE

The buzzing phone drilled through her sleep. Kya blindly reached out and brought it to her ear without checking the caller ID. She trusted that whoever was calling this early had a legit reason. 'Hello?'

'Hey!' It was Adrian. 'H saw you last night, and now I'm a little jealous.'

That was *not* a legit reason.

'Bro ...' she moaned.

'How you doing?' he asked. 'I miss you.'

Okay, that was sweet.

Kya slipped off her sleep mask, climbed out of bed and tiptoed out of the room so as to not disturb Quinn. She imagined Adrian at the clinic, seated at his desk, ready to receive the first patient of the day.

'What time is it?' she asked.

'It's seven. I never get to call you in the morning when you're out west.'

Kya flopped onto the couch, resigned. If this was a privilege for him, she wouldn't take it away. 'I miss you, too.'

'Are you having fun?'

'I'm having a blast.'

'Good. That's all that matters.'

'I met with Corinne Miller for lunch the other day,' Kya added quickly. She wouldn't want her overachieving brother to think she was a slacker.

'Do you mean Carl's wife?'

'She's more than that!'

'I know,' he said. 'I'm just trying to put her in context.'

'Put her in the context as CEO of her own company.'

'I forgot how cranky you are when you don't get enough sleep.'

'I'll get off my soapbox now.'

'What did you two discuss at lunch? World domination?'

'Naturally,' Kya said. 'We also talked about how she launched her company. She thinks I should start my own business.'

'What do you think?' he asked.

'It's a crazy idea. Can you imagine?'

'Easily. That's what I did.'

'It's not the same.'

'How so?'

Adrian studied medicine, got the requisite training and passed the board exams, and opened his own clinic. Essentially, he'd started his own company. Kya had never thought of it that way before. Adrian was a small-business owner. He owned his practice.

'I'm sure with your skills and background you could do something similar. You're not bound to Silicon Valley, you know.'

'Hmm …'

'And if you need seed money—'

'I don't want your money.'

'Good, because I'm not offering it,' he said. 'I could help you raise it. We know people who do that sort of thing. Roman, for one. He finances tech projects all over the world. You could ask him about it this weekend. Are you joining us for brunch on Sunday?'

'I'll be there.'

She would definitely join them now that she had this added incentive, no matter how exhausted she was from the night before.

'The first rule of business is never to put in your own money, or your relatives' money, if you can help it.'

'Got it.'

'Are you comfortable over there at Quinn's? You can always come home.'

'I'm fine.'

She could not tell him that Quinn's place was starting to feel like a second home. That might signal, if only to herself, that she was moving way too fast.

'Time to meet with my office manager. Before I go, I've started following you on TikTok.'

'You and ten others.'

'More like ten thousand.'

'Are you kidding?'

'Okay. Talk soon.'

The line went dead. Kya had forgotten her brother's infuriatingly abrupt way of ending calls. Just out of curiosity, she checked her follower count on TikTok and it was almost as many as she had on LinkedIn, which was outrageous considering she'd been blogging for years. Kya reviewed her TikTok profile. She'd deleted that first teary-eyed hostage-style video. Her posts of Quinn and last night's sound engineer were doing extremely well. She liked this new direction, and was eager to apply it to blogging. There was no time like the present. Since she was up, she might as well be productive, too.

LINKEDIN
GIRL DECODED

– LUNCH WITH THE CEO –

Hi guys! It's Kya.

A clever woman told me over Korean barbecue: "Your career hasn't started until you get axed." I believe it. As you might have heard, I lost my job at Ex-Cell recently. Until you get caught in the grinding wheels of the machine, and left to take stock of your scattered pieces, you can't begin to know your true worth.

I had the pleasure of sitting with Corinne Miller, CEO and founder of BioFlow Enterprises, a tech firm with a focus on laboratory automation. With her founding partner and CFO Joanne Owen, Corinne hatched the plan for her innovative company over cocktails. Here, at Girl Decoded, we love an enterprising boss babe...

Kya hit POST just when Quinn stepped out of the bedroom, looking sleepy and disoriented. She set aside her phone on which she'd typed, edited, and posted the blog.

Yawning, Quinn asked, 'Did someone call, like, at four a.m., or was that a dream?'

'Sorry, that was no dream,' Kya replied. 'That was my brother. He's one of those five a.m. types. He actually called at seven. It only felt like four because last night was one for the books.'

'It was,' she said with a private little grin.

'We have ten hours until we do it all again. What should we do with our time?'

'Waste it,' Quinn said. 'Lounge by the pool. Get Ivy and Amanda to join us. Order lunch.'

'Aren't we two productive bright young women!' Kya exclaimed.

'We are who we are. It can't be helped.' She came around and dropped a kiss on Kya's forehead. 'Tea?'

'Never.'

It was coffee or nothing. You could take the girl out of Silicon Valley, but you could never take the Valley out of the girl.

CHAPTER THIRTY-FOUR

LAB on Collins Avenue was a proper nightclub, standing three storeys high under a mirrored domed ceiling. It was the type of club that people stood in line for, in any weather, and subjected themselves to humiliation at the hands of a ruthless doorman, in hopes of gaining access to the world behind the yellow rope. Others reserved tables and spent thousands on bottle service just to avoid that fate. Those with access to the VIP skybox did not have to bother with any of that; these palaces were built for them.

They arrived before the club opened its doors. Quinn was dressed in silver and Kya in black. Together, they made a striking couple, commanding loads of attention, which was exactly what Kya did not want, although, she didn't seem to mind. She asked the 'talent liaison', a handsome Black man with a slight Caribbean accent named Trevor, about the sound system. Quinn loved how her mind worked. She asked sharp questions, was endlessly curious, and absorbed information quickly.

'We have a room for you and your people,' Trevor said. 'Don't get too excited. It's no bigger than a closet, but there's plenty of snacks.'

The snacks were not insignificant. Bacon wrapped dates, chicken salad wraps, carrots and hummus, and a bottle of champagne on ice. Quinn would make a meal of all this at the end of the night.

'If you'd like anything else, please ask.'

'Water?'

'The mini-fridge is to the left and fully stocked.'

Kya helped herself to a water. Quinn reviewed her guest list to make sure Amanda and Ivy, and whoever they were rolling with tonight, would not have a hard time at the door.

'Angelo is across the hall, if you'd like to say hello before the madness begins. I'll introduce you.'

Quinn had been looking forward to meeting Angelo ever since she'd tried crashing his event on the yacht. She turned to Kya. 'I'll be right back. Will you be okay?'

Kya froze a beat, then stammered, 'I'll be fine.'

Quinn had noticed that even the tiniest bit of consideration threw her off. The poor baby, had she been surviving on crumbs? The thought broke her heart. When this week was finally over, and her schedule less hectic, Quinn intended to lavish her with attention – if she'd let her. Maybe they could go away again, take a trip somewhere far, and forget about time. She was planning this ideal trip in her mind when Trevor knocked on Angelo's door.

The guy who opened the door was about Quinn's age, but that's where the similarities ended. He was tall, thin, pale, and dressed in the style of the late Steve Jobs. In her silver minidress and with her eyelids speckled with silver glitter, it was reasonable to assume they'd be playing at two very different venues.

'I'm Quinn. Nice to meet you.'

Angelo mumbled a response. 'Hi' or 'Hey,' Quinn wasn't sure. She waited for more, but he seemed to be done with the conversation.

232

Trevor cleared his throat. 'If neither of you has any questions, I'll be on my way.'

Quinn was already heading back to basecamp. 'Thanks, Trevor! I think we're done.'

What a waste of her time. Outward appearances aside, she and Angelo had a lot in common. They were basically on the same career track, and it would have been nice to talk about their shared experiences. But she scrapped that idea. He wasn't interested.

Kya brightened when she walked back in. Quinn put Angelo out of her mind. How could she think of anyone when Kya was looking at her like that?

'That was fast,' she said.

'He wasn't all that interesting,' Quinn replied.

'They never are.'

Trevor returned, this time with Amanda and Ivy. 'Quinn, your people are here,' he said. 'Ladies, enjoy your night.'

Amanda and Ivy, flirty and happy a second ago, were soon at each other's throats, prepared to duel at dawn over Trevor.

'Ladies!' Kya said. 'Calm down. The night is young. There are enough Trevor types out there for both of you.'

'You swore off men,' Quinn reminded Amanda.

'Oh, right,' she said, contrite. 'I did say that.'

Ivy pulled the champagne bottle out of the ice. 'Should we pop this open?'

Even though Quinn would not drink a drop, she agreed. 'We absolutely should.'

It was past eleven, and LAB was open for business. She could feel the excitement crackling through the building. There was nothing like a club late at night with your friends. Most people gave this up when they got older and took jobs at evil corporations, like Ex-Cell. But this was the life Quinn had signed up for. There would be no end until she pulled the plug. Some people, like Angelo, brought their insecurities into it, making a competition of it, rather than what it was: a celebration. She would not be dragged into that poisonous well.

Ivy filled plastic cups. They were just about to toast the night ahead when a knock on the door interrupted them. Ivy answered, champagne bottle in hand. Outside the door stood a very pale, very thin man with a striking resemblance to Angelo. He was most likely a younger brother.

'Hello,' he said. 'Angelo says he's sorry if you were offended earlier. He's not much of a talker and prefers to be left alone before gigs. He's looking forward to tonight, and thanks you for opening for him.'

He was sorry if Quinn was offended, but not sorry for offending her. Classic! And what was this about opening for him? Just because she was playing first, that didn't mean she was an opening act.

Ivy set down the sweaty bottle and grabbed one of the flyers piled on the table. 'Quinn *alongside* DJ Angelo. That's what it says here. Quinn is not your opening act. Please get your facts straight.'

He shrugged. 'Same thing, right?'

It was not the same. Angelo knew this. If he was under the impression that her role was to warm up the room for his triumphant rise to the stage, he was more delusional than she'd thought.

'Thanks for stopping by,' Ivy said, and shut the door firmly in mini-Angelo's face.

Everyone broke out laughing – everyone except for Kya. Her inner light had dimmed and her glossy lips were pulled into a pout.

'Hey, girls, could you give me a minute?' Quinn asked. 'I need to settle in before going out there.'

'No worries,' Amanda said. 'Let's find our table.'

Ivy topped up her cup. 'Let's find Trevor.'

'Leave that poor man alone,' Quinn pleaded.

'Sorry. There's no chance of that.'

Kya followed Ivy and Amanda out the door. Quinn caught her by the waist and drew her back in. 'Not you!' She slammed the door shut and pressed Kya against it. 'Stay with me. I'm really frustrated right now.'

'I get it,' Kya said. 'This is a lot.'

'Could you help me?' she asked.

'Of course. What do you need?'

'Oh, I don't know … Let's think of something.' Quinn nudged aside the drape of Kya's halter top, exposing the black lace of her bra. Kya stirred at her touch. 'Is this okay?' Quinn asked.

'Only if you lock the door,' she said.

Quinn reached for the lock and twisted it shut. She then killed the overhead light. A single lamp made the room glow. 'Better?'

'So much better.'

Kya attempted to drag her onto the floor. Quinn laughed and pulled her up. 'No, babe! We have options!'

Although the options were slim. There were the few stiff chairs, an ottoman, and the table which, though solid, could not hold their combined weight.

'But we don't have time!' Kya exclaimed.

A second later, she had Quinn on a windowsill with her skirt hiked up around her hips. 'Do me a favour, please?' Kya asked.

'Anything.'

'Forget that man. If you must obsess over someone, obsess over me.'

'I'll do my best.'

'One more thing?'

'What?'

'Call me your girlfriend again.'

Quinn screamed and caught Kya's face between her hands. 'I knew it! You tried to play it off, but I knew it!'

'Knew what?' Kya asked. 'That I liked it?'

'No. How would I have known that? You looked so confused.'

'You just sprang it at me!' Kya fired back. 'I didn't know we were official. We never talked about it.'

'I'm sorry. I'm British. We don't make a fuss. What do you need, a formal request with your HR department?'

'I'm American,' Kya said. 'Making simple things complicated is our love language. The more red tape, the better.'

'You're my girlfriend for now,' Quinn said. 'We're practically living together! I'm not going to date other people while you're here. Are you?'

'Maybe Trevor. Who knows?'

'Shut up and get to work, girlfriend!'

Kya let out a quiet laugh. 'Close your eyes.' Quinn did as she was told, and shivered as Kya's hands skimmed up the length of her legs and reached up for her panties. Outside the locked door, the club's pulse quickened. Excitement crackled through the walls. A strong bass made the floors jump. The club would be full to capacity tonight. Hundreds of people would fill the space. In this room, however, it was just the two of them. Kya called her kitten and she absolutely lost it when she bit her inner thigh.

'Does my girlfriend like that?' Kya asked with a low and wicked laugh.

Quinn was ready to fire back when Kya kissed the spot she bit then licked it and bit it again before moving to what she really wanted. With every lick of her tongue that followed, there was no room for logical thought. Within minutes, Quinn bit back a cry and blindly reached out for something to steady her. When she gripped the curtain, it was too late. She was crashing. The curtain rod crashed down, too.

'Are you okay?' Kya cried.

'I'm fine!'

'Stay here. I'll take care of it.'

She hopped to her feet. Quinn watched as she expertly snapped the curtain rod in place.

'Leave it,' Quinn said, breathless. 'The boys have done far worse; I'm sure of it.'

'The boys don't know how to cover their tracks.'

No boy was as clever as Kya.

'Thanks for this,' Quinn said. 'I needed to let out steam.'

Kya kneeled beside her and kissed her. 'Don't thank me. I wouldn't be a good girlfriend if I didn't.'

Something about the way she hesitated to use the word 'girl-friend' caught Quinn's attention.

'Kya, is that why you blushed so hard yesterday?' she asked.

'I don't know what you're talking about,' she replied.

Quinn would have believed her if she weren't blushing now. 'I called you my girlfriend and your cheeks flared up. You don't remember? We were on the floor … kind of like now.'

'I was confused!'

Quinn stroked Kya's hair. 'Better?'

'Much. Listen, I've worked with guys like Angelo. He just wanted to mess with your head. It's a power move to knock you off your game.'

Quinn truly didn't get people like that. 'It's a party, a good time! We're at a club, for Christ's sake.'

'It's business, babe. There's money involved, big money. No one messes around when it comes to that.'

Quinn shook her head. She refused to play that game.

'Are you going to be okay?' Kya asked.

'Of course! The day I let a guy like Angelo mess with my head—'

'It's fine if you're upset.'

'I'm not upset. Look at me! I'm fine!'

'You look beautiful,' Kya whispered.

'I wish we could just stay here.'

'We can't. You better get out there and slay.'

'Sure, but I should put my knickers on first; don't you think?'

'Maybe. If you can find them!'

Quinn did not kill it; not like she'd hoped. By the end of the night, it was clear Angelo had won the strange competition they'd engaged in. She'd done well, but he'd had the packed club going from the start. By every measure, he'd beat her. She was mature enough to realize it, but not enough to accept it. When Nick cornered her with his usual mix of insight and patronizing rubbish, Quinn went blind with rage.

'It was an off night,' he said. 'It's not like he's better than you or anything like that. His sound is new; people ate it up. That's all. In the end, this was a good experience for you. With these larger venues, you'll have to learn to read the room.'

Read the room? Really?

'Thanks for that insight,' she said, bitingly. 'I don't know how I manage without you.'

Thank goodness for Kya who, with a hand pressed to the small of Quinn's back, steered her away from the man. 'Don't waste your breath,' she said. As it turned out, she'd worked with guys like Nick, too.

Quinn did some post-match analysis on the ride home. What had gone wrong? She'd shared billings with other DJs before and always held her own. Something was off tonight.

What was it? Was she tired? Distracted? Had there been too much going on with Kya, Amanda, Ivy? Were her girls a little too much fun? There was a time for everything. Shouldn't she focus on her music for the moment? Quinn had worked hard to get to this so-called next level. She couldn't afford an 'off night'. She couldn't blow it.

Kya reached for her, hugged her, kissed her, did her best to cheer her up. Quinn melted into her arms. It was easier than talking, than sharing her feelings. Her head was in a fog. There were only two days left before Solstice. She had to get her shit together.

'I'm going straight to bed,' she informed Kya on the lift ride up.

'No post-performance ritual?' Kya teased.

'Not tonight,' Quinn said. 'It's so late. I'm fried.'

'Me, too,' she said.

Quinn let them into the flat, went straight into her wardrobe and shut the door.

The next morning, Kya brought her tea in bed. It was just right, a minor miracle considering how fussy Quinn was about her tea.

'Thanks,' Quinn said.

Kya sat at the edge of the bed. She was most beautiful in the morning, with her braids swept to one side and her face scrubbed clean and soft. 'I'll take care of everything today,' she said. 'All the meals, any errands, anything you need.'

Quinn's heart split open with gratitude. All night, she wondered how she'd ask Kya for some space, and was worried she might not understand. 'I'm likely going to spend the day locked up in the studio. I need to work on my set.'

'I understand.'

'I may be in there for hours.'

'Got it. It's crunch time.'

'Yes, exactly that. I won't need much. I'll eat my weight in toast and tea. Don't worry. I'll be fine on my own.'

Kya's beautiful, scrubbed clean face clouded. She was clever and had figured out what was being requested of her. Quinn felt awful about it, but she really needed her to go away for a while.

'No worries,' she said. 'I have to finish the blog series, do some research on Corinne's company. I don't know too much about it.'

'Good idea,' Quinn said. She was only half-listening, her attention was already on the work ahead. She was going to start from scratch, review each song on her playlist.

Kya got up and went into the en suite bathroom. Quinn took her tea into the kitchen. She dropped a slice of bread into the toaster and rummaged in the cupboard for a new jar of jam. She listened to the sounds of Kya in the shower, then the bedroom, getting ready for the day. Kya emerged wearing jeans and a white T-shirt, her leather hobo bag slung over her shoulder. 'I'm heading out,' she said.

'Already?'

Quinn checked the time. It wasn't too early, but they'd been out late last night. She hadn't meant to rush her out the door.

'I'm going to write at the coffee shop down the block. You know it, right? Next to the boba shop?'

She knew of it, but she'd never gone. 'You don't have to go just this second.'

'It's best to start writing early.'

'Hold on.' Quinn reached for a spare key off a hook on the kitchen wall. 'Take this.'

Long after Kya had left, Quinn leaned against the door, uneasy in the silence. Now that she had what she'd asked for, space, she had to make the most of it. She silenced her phone, turned off notifications, and left it sitting on the charger in her bedroom. Then she took her tea and toast into her studio and got straight to work. She reviewed each song on her playlist, replaced a few, shuffled them around, experimented with new transitions, then started the process over and over again.

The hours slipped by. Lunch was a frozen pizza and the last of the crisps from home. By the time she slipped off her headphones, a headache was forming at her temples. She couldn't go on a second longer. Kya had called this crunch time, but Quinn wasn't an accountant. There was nothing to crunch. She'd always been the go-with-the-flow type of girl. And she had the sinking feeling that nothing was wrong with her original set. All she'd done was tinker with it and make some minor improvements, nothing more. A big part of her performance had always been her personality. It drove the trolls mad, but that was the truth. Honestly, last night she'd played small, intimidated by the venue itself. She'd had an off night. So what? It happened. She'd learned something – not to 'read the room', she wasn't a newbie, but to take the loss like a big girl.

Before she'd allowed Angelo to mess with her head, she was having the best time with Kya. Then Ivy and Amanda arrived and all four of them were poised to have a great night. In short, she'd let an outsider pop her bubble, the glitter-filled snow globe that kept her happy, safe, and secure. Never again.

Quinn tossed her headphones aside and stretched. She'd lost track of time. The sun was setting. All she wanted was to check in with her girl. She desperately needed a shower and a chilled glass of wine. Had Kya spent the whole day at that coffee shop? Had she wrapped up the series? Getting back to blogging was important to her, it was her creative outlet. She'd been nervous about it and Quinn had offered nothing this morning, not a hug, not a kiss, not even a scrap of encouragement. She was a crap girlfriend, and Quinn wouldn't blame Kya if she never came back.

Panicked, Quinn sprang to her feet. She hadn't checked her messages all day. What if Kya had tried to reach her and got nothing in response? She yanked the door open and, shocked, came to an abrupt stop. Kya wasn't out there, somewhere, brooding, and holding a grudge. She was in the kitchen, carefully opening takeaway containers. The table was cleared of the clutter Quinn had piled on it over the last few days. A lit candle flickered in the waning sunlight. She looked lovely. The food smelled delicious. Where had she found that candle? More importantly, how was this woman so wonderful?

'Kya,' she said shyly.

'I know you said you wouldn't eat, but I was hoping to tempt you with pasta. This is from A & H's favourite restaurant, the best in the city according to them. I've had better in LA, but I'm an elitist California girl.'

Quinn approached her, tentatively, as if Kya were a mermaid who might plunge back into the sea if she made any sudden moves. 'I'm so happy you're here. I missed you.'

'I won't be here long,' she said. 'I'm going to spend the night at Adrian's to let you work in peace.'

'Don't go. What about all this food?'

'I'll leave the tray in the oven.'

'Okay, but what about the candle?'

She looked up, fighting a smile. 'I'll blow it out.'

'Don't. I'm done working. I want to be with you.'

'Do you feel ready for tomorrow?' Kya asked.

'I don't care, honestly.'

'I don't believe that.'

'It's true,' she said. 'I'm hungry and exhausted. I want a shower and a glass of wine. I want to sit with you on the balcony, watch the sunset, and talk. I hate how dismissive I was this morning. You're so good to me, and—'

'Quinn!'

'Yes?'

'Go take that shower.'

Quinn nodded. 'And you won't go anywhere?'

'Hey! This was your idea. You wanted me to go—'

'And now I want you to stay. I never said this would be easy. I'm fickle AF.'

'Fine! I'll stay!' Kya said, laughing. 'I'll take all this out on the balcony, open a bottle, put on a record, even. We'll eat, watch the sunset, and talk. You'll tell me about your day, and I'll tell you about mine. Does that sound okay?'

'That sounds perfect.'

'Okay, well … Go!'

Quinn retreated, walking backwards. 'I did miss you, babe. Very much.'

Kya blew out the candle. 'Hurry. You'll miss the sunset.'

CHAPTER THIRTY-FIVE

Getting kicked out of Quinn's world was traumatic and it hurt more than Kya was willing to admit. What had gone wrong last night? Her posts on Quinn's set had garnered thousands of likes. One video in particular, of Quinn dancing behind the decks, lost in her own world, was just shy of going viral. The short clip captured her beauty, talent, and something impossible to define, something otherworldly. Whatever it was, it held everyone's attention. Too bad Quinn was blind to all this.

She compared her performance to that of Angelo, which wasn't fair. The other DJ had an unusual sound and drew something different from the crowd. He started out mellow then gradually gained muscle. Angelo was no genius, however. He relied heavily on all the old tricks, plunging beat drops and familiar hooks. Quinn's set had an easy flow that moved through everyone. Kya had felt it, first-hand, on the dance floor. She, Ivy, and Amanda, a little buzzed from champagne, had the time of their lives. Kya was a little distracted, her phone held high, trying to record Quinn at all angles. She was focused on her mission of getting as much footage as possible, not solely to post on social media, but to fill her personal archives. When she returned to California, reviewing these videos would instantly take her back to Quinn. Even with all that going on, Kya had a blast. Ivy and Amanda were feral, spinning wildly, hands in the air, releasing inner demons. By the end of the night, they were pink in the face, but at peace. Quinn, though, was miserable.

Nick was partially to blame. Kya ran into him twice last night. The first time was during the interim, Quinn had wrapped her set and Angelo had not yet taken the stage. Amanda and Ivy had left for the bar with the promise to return with a drink for Kya; she was waiting on Quinn at their reserved table. Nick had a girl on his arm and made sure she'd noticed. He pinned the petite brunette to his chest, but he didn't bother to introduce her. Instead, he asked about Quinn.

'How's our favourite DJ? I heard she got into it with Angelo earlier.'

'Did she? I wouldn't know.'

'Yeah, you would,' he smirked.

Nick had his faults, too many to list, but he was exceptionally good looking. Last night, he wore his chestnut hair slicked back. His deep tan made his blue eyes pop.

'Sorry,' Kya said flatly. 'I don't.'

'She should be more careful,' he said. 'Angelo's star is on the rise. He could have been useful for future collaborations. In this business, you can't afford to toss people aside. He has a production deal. Did you know that?'

What did Nick actually know about this business? Was he an underground producer or something? And who cared what deals Angelo had? 'Quinn doesn't have to take bullshit from anyone to secure a deal,' she said.

Nick's eyes flashed as if she'd unwittingly confirmed something. Kya was grateful the brunette dragged him off.

When she ran into him a second time, his date was gone, but

Quinn was by Kya's side. Nick jumped straight into it, doling out his unsolicited advice. His tone very different from earlier. He was trying for sincere but coming off as a creep. Quinn was having none of it. Kya caught the exact moment a spark ignited in her eyes. She was about to go off on this man, right here, in front of everyone. Someone would likely record it, and that clip would make the rounds just in time for Solstice. Nick wasn't worth it.

She'd placed her hand on the small of Quinn's back and steered her towards the exit. It had been a long night, and their ride was waiting. It was time to go home. Kya sighed heavily. That had been the last time she'd felt connected to Quinn. After that, she'd folded within herself. Back at her building, she'd made their disconnection official by declaring, in the elevator, there would be no post-performance ritual. This translated simply into: 'Please leave me alone.' Kya was happy to do it. She understood the concept of giving someone space. She would be the first to ask for it whenever confronted with a deadline or burdened by work. She would have offered it freely, but Quinn had wanted more than space. She'd wanted Kya gone.

She wandered around the neighbourhood before finally sliding into a booth at the coffee shop. Writing in a public space required, at the minimum, a laptop, as to appear legit. Kya was locked out of the one computer she'd travelled with, which left her with only her phone. Annoyed, she called the most cheerful person she knew.

'Hey, Hugo!'

'Sweetie!' he answered. 'Glad you called, but do me a favour: don't tell your brother. He gets so jealous!'

'What is up with that?' Kya asked, bewildered. 'The other day he called me super early just to say hi, and it was all because we ran into each other at happy hour.'

'I don't think he understands that you and I have our own thing,' Hugo said.

'After all this time?' Kya said. 'Nothing can come between us.'

Hugo's laughter was high-pitched and musical. 'One day he'll figure it out.'

Kya cracked a smile for the first time that day.

'I was going to call you, regardless,' Hugo said. 'I've got a bone to pick with you, as they say.'

'Wait. We're at the bone-picking stage of an issue?' she asked. How did she not know this?

'You and Quinn.'

That was all he said, and it was more than enough. Kya's hand trembled as she stirred sugar into her cappuccino. 'What about us?'

'You tell me.'

'There's nothing to tell.'

'I can't believe I didn't see what was in front of my very eyes,' he continued.

'See what?'

'Don't you dare play that game with me!'

There was no use playing any game with Hugo. He would beat her, fair and square. But she wasn't about to give her cards away. He would have to produce receipts.

'Could you be more specific?' she said.

'Okay,' he said. 'I was texting with Sam—'

'Your old friend Sam? The one who's visiting soon?'

'You know exactly which Sam.'

'Just checking!'

'She said, casually, that she hoped to meet you and your girlfriend during her trip.'

That was weak sauce, as far as Kya was concerned. 'Just because your friend said a thing, doesn't make it so.'

'I told her you two were just friends. She was like, "No, mate, they're definitely more than that."'

'Is that all you've got, *mate*?' Kya asked. 'Quinn and I are friends. We hang out. We have fun. This is not news to you.'

'Sam follows your TikTok.'

'It's a bunch of BTS stuff. You know that.'

'I keep up, but I don't have time to scroll through comments. Sam is a blogger and gets off on all that. She says the girlies are gushing over you and Quinn and what a cute couple you make. They've posted BTS of their own.'

Were the girlies gushing? Kya hadn't checked. 'Okay, so … maybe we're more than just friends.'

'You sneaky—'

'Settle down, hear me out,' Kya said. 'Quinn and I sort of bloomed from nothing. I'm as surprised as anyone. Before you get excited, please remember I'm leaving as soon as Music Week is over. Nothing will come of this.'

'Not if you've already decided that it won't,' he said.

Kya was sorry, but no amount of positive thinking was going to solve this dilemma. She and Quinn lived parallel lives, on opposite coasts. Quinn lived by night. Kya wasn't necessarily a morning girl, but her nightlife was within the safe confines of her apartment. Today had made it all the clearer. The first bump in the road had exposed their cracks.

'Anyway, I agree with the girls,' Hugo said. 'You make a cute couple. It doesn't have to last. Not every story ends the way we'd like, but it can still end well.'

When he wasn't clowning around, this man had an astonishing

degree of emotional intelligence. Her brother was lucky to have him.

'I can't believe I didn't see it! It was so obvious!' he exclaimed.

'Right? You're sharper than this!'

'No wonder you fell apart because she was a little mad at you, and crashed a party just to say you're sorry when you could've texted.'

'I did not fall apart, and Quinn was more than a little mad. A text message wasn't going to cut it.'

'Apparently it worked,' he said. 'Come to think of it, I deserve the credit for putting you two together.'

'Probably best you don't think about it.'

'For now,' he said. 'I'm telling your brother tonight!'

Great. She could expect another wake-up call.

'All right, *irmãzinha*. I've got a client call in five minutes. Gotta run.'

'Cool. I've got some writing to do. Have a good day.'

'Love you!' Hugo said before hanging up.

Kya felt a pinch to the heart. She considered spending the night at her brother's place so Quinn could work uninterrupted. She would pick up dinner first. No matter what Quinn had said, she had to eat.

Kya spent the rest of the day working on the BioFlow series. She researched the company and drafted the next two posts to round up the series. When she was done, she killed time scrolling social media and could confirm the girlies were indeed gushing. #K&Q #couplegoals #girllove and countless rainbow emojis. It warmed Kya from the inside out. She should have stayed in that soft world. Instead, she somehow ended up on Reddit.

Quinn vs. Angelo

A first-round knockout!

If you were at LAB last night, you would have witnessed the undoing of Quinn. Her set was off. The vibe was flat. Good thing Angelo came to deliver.

Quiet and withdrawn in real life, Angelo shows up on stage. He wears plain clothes and rolls with a small crew. Unlike Quinn, who pulls up in a party caravan, covered in glitter, new girlfriend at the hip.

We hear Quinn spoke with Angelo early in the night. He must've rubbed her the wrong way. Who knows? Even so, that's no excuse. It just goes to show she's not quite ready for the big time. She does okay at a happy hour or by the pool, but LAB is for the pros. You've got to bring the big guns.

Who did she have to thank for this scorching hot take? Some idiot who went by 'Night Lite', Quinn's most persistent troll.

This time she hadn't been namechecked; she was simply the 'new girlfriend'. And there she was, in the attached photo, at Quinn's hip. They had just arrived at LAB. Trevor was expertly pointing out all the bells and whistles that made the club come alive once they opened its doors. Quinn had draped her arm around Kya's waist. They were staring up in awe at the mirrored dome ceiling. Whoever was taking these pictures truly had talent and was wasting it trolling them. They could've easily earned money as a portrait photographer, taking engagement photos and the like.

Though biased, Kya was convinced Quinn had done an amazing job at LAB. She'd read the room accurately. The night had just begun; most people weren't as drunk or loose as they were when Angelo took the stage. He'd been handed the better slot by the luck of the draw or, more likely, the power of the patriarchy. Whatever the case may be, Quinn had nothing to be ashamed of. Kya wasn't the only one who thought so. The comments from the people who'd actually been at the club were strongly in Quinn's favour.

I don't know what you're on, man, but Quinn slapped.

Quinn served. Period.

Angelo was all right, but Quinn is the Queen. Don't mess with her.

What fresh hell of sexism is this?

Kya shut the app in disgust. Quinn would see this, Kya thought. Ivy would send it to her. She might've quit PR, but doom-scrolling was her favourite pastime. Quinn was already so upset; she didn't need this.

'Who is this fucker?'

She'd mumbled the words, but the waiter who'd come to clear the table had caught it and gave her a quizzical look. 'Excuse me?' he said.

'Sorry!' Kya held up her phone. 'I'm dealing with a troll.'

'Good for you,' he said. 'Don't let them get away with it, the cowards.'

'Thanks.'

That was just the boost Kya needed. She would expose this man for the coward he was, hiding behind an anonymous account to tear people down. Kya ordered yet another coffee and began combing through his profile, his friends' profiles, and anyone who commented too frequently. She then cross-referenced those profiles on TikTok, Instagram, and good old-fashioned Facebook. It was a tedious task and by the time she looked up, the afternoon was gone. Her neck was stiff. Her eyes stung. She wanted nothing more than to go home.

She ordered dinner from one of Adrian and Hugo's favourite restaurants then walked to the building and waited in the lobby for the delivery. She rode the elevator with a couple locked in a kiss, which made her feel even lonelier. Quinn was still in her studio when Kya let herself in. She set the food on the counter and cleared the table. She found a plain white candle deep in one of the kitchen drawers and lit it. Frowning, she took in the set-up. She should've bought flowers. When Quinn came stumbling out of the studio a moment later, flowers were the last thing on her mind. Her brown eyes mirrored Kya's own deep longing.

Nothing mattered. She was back in Quinn's world.

It wasn't until Quinn fell asleep later that night that Kya resumed her search. She slipped out of bed and locked herself in the bathroom with her phone and the last of the bottle of wine. Where had she left off? Oh, right. Facebook, cross-referencing Night Lite's impressive group of friends. One had attended the University of Miami and proudly displayed her class reunion photos in an album made available to the public, which wasn't very smart. Kya skimmed the comments of each photo, until she spotted the same stupid thumbnail that Night Lite used on Reddit, an oversaturated photo of the Miami skyline. The comment: **Good times.**☺

The reply: **Always a good time with you!** ❤✨🎀

Kya studied the photo, a group of ten young men and women in their best business casual outfits, champagne flutes in hand, smiling broadly. The second to the left had dark hair, a deep tan, and blue eyes that popped. *I knew it!*

Kya smacked the phone down and took a swig from the wine bottle. God, she loved being right!

CHAPTER THIRTY-SIX

Summer Solstice marked the longest day of the season; there was something ominous about that. Quinn wondered why she hadn't picked up on this, as intuitive as she was. This long day, predicted to be the warmest on record, would either make or break her, physically and emotionally. She was going to play at the biggest venue of her life. According to the trolls, one in particular, whom she would not name, she wasn't up for the task. Quinn had caught the viral Reddit post, all on her own, like a grown-up. Ivy hadn't sent it her way. Amanda hadn't mentioned it. Kya hadn't brought it up. She suspected all three were hiding it from her. They wouldn't want anything to mess with her head this close to the main event. Unfortunately, a bunch of losers had found it necessary to share the post on multiple sites and tag her over and over again. Her phone had lit up with notifications. Quinn had read the words and let them wash over her. She figured it was best to get it out of the way, learn in advance what the haters were thinking, and let that knowledge fuel her determination and drive. She was not going to let anyone get into her head again. That was done. She'd cured that vulnerability, and she was ready to push forward.

Those thoughts floated to the surface even before Quinn had opened her eyes. Trapped in her thoughts, thinking, overthinking, this was not how she wanted to start the longest day of her short life. She wanted to *feel* something. Then she remembered that she wasn't alone, and didn't have to go through any of this by herself.

Quinn opened her eyes and there was Kya. Tucked away at the far side of the bed, eyes glued to her phone, and a crease between her shapely brows. 'You and that phone,' she murmured. 'Put it down! Come snuggle with me.'

She smiled without looking up. 'I've been awake and waiting for a while now, Queen Quinn.'

'The wait is over. Come.'

Kya set the phone on the bedside table and sank deeper under the blanket. Quinn shared her pillow and they lay facing each other, noses touching. She reached up and smoothed the crease that was still there, stitching her brows together. 'What's the matter, babe?'

'Nothing.'

'That's not true. It's so early, and something is troubling you. What is it?'

'Today is the day,' Kya replied. 'Maybe I'm nervous for you. Is that allowed?'

'Anything is allowed except for these worry lines. It's not that serious.'

'We both know it is,' she whispered.

'I think we need some stress relief. What do you say?'

She kissed the tip of Quinn's nose. 'What do you have in mind?'

Quinn offered some suggestions. 'A quick trip to the gym? A run around the block? A swim?'

Kya slid a hand down Quinn's thigh. 'No, babe. Any other ideas?'

'Kiss me. We'll figure it out.'

'Kiss you where?' she asked.

'Lady's choice.'

Kya sank deeper beneath the sheets. Quinn offered herself up, dissolving like sugar at her touch. Kya knew her body well enough, and should not have been surprised when, reaching between her legs, she found her hot and wet. Her breath grew sharp. Quinn tightened around her fingers. Stars burst behind Quinn's shut eyelids and just when it was getting good, the bloody phone rang, shrill, imperious, tearing into the sultry silence of her bedroom. Only it was Quinn's phone, not Kya's.

'Ignore it,' Kya said, speaking into the tender skin of her neck.

'I can't, not today ...'

With a sigh, she withdrew and fell onto her back, leaving a void so deep Quinn could cry.

'Answer it,' she said, encouragingly. 'It might be important.'

'Hold on. Let's see who it is. For all we know it's a cold call from a used car salesman.'

It wasn't a car salesman. It was Frankie, the publicist who'd coordinated that insufferable photoshoot, no doubt calling with another stunt for her to participate in. Unfortunately, she was contractually obligated to take the call.

Grabbing her phone, Kya slipped out of bed before Quinn could catch her. She mouthed the word 'coffee' before leaving the room.

Quinn cried, 'Tea!' and answered the call.

Frankie extended an invitation to a concert pre-party hosted by a record label executive at his penthouse overlooking the concert site. 'You won't want to miss it,' he said. 'Everybody will be there.'

'All right. I'll be there, too.'

'Great. I'll text you the address.'

Quinn pulled on a pair of boxer shorts and joined Kya in the kitchen. This was likely the last few hours they would have to themselves. She'd booked hair and make-up at noon. Then it would be off to the penthouse party. From there, they'd head straight to the festival grounds. She laid all this out to Kya.

'That's a lot,' she said.

'None of this spells fun for you, I suppose,' Quinn mused.

'Don't worry about me. I'll have fun with Ivy and Amanda. Scrambled eggs?'

'Okay,' Quinn said, watching her closely. A moment ago, she'd caught Kya frowning at her phone again while she filled the kettle. Something was on her mind and she was keeping it from her. If it wasn't the Reddit post, maybe it was some development on her own blog? Either way, Quinn decided to clear the air.

'I saw it,' she said.

'Saw what?' Kya asked, her head in the fridge, rummaging for eggs, butter, and bread. Truthfully, Quinn wasn't sure she had any of those items in stock.

'The Reddit post,' she replied. 'I was tagged, like, a million times.'

Kya shut the fridge and faced her. 'Oh, babe. I'm sorry.'

Quinn went to her. 'Don't be sorry! Nothing is going to ruin this day for me. I've worked hard to get here. The boys are in their feelings, but I can't help that. You'd think I stole their spot in the sun or something. They're going to write their hot takes and try to strip me of my confidence. It's not going to work. I won't let anyone rattle me. If tonight doesn't go well then at least I'll learn something. Maybe I'm not a big venue performer. Happy hours and pool parties may be where it's at for me. Maybe that's my niche, who knows? I don't have to slay every venue and my career doesn't have to look like all these other guys' careers. I can take it in another direction.'

Kya was nodding, taking all this in, but she still looked as if she were keeping a secret.

'Are you going to tell me what's wrong, finally?' Quinn asked.

'No,' she said, firmly.

'Why?'

'We'll talk tonight, after the concert, or tomorrow,' she said. 'I promise it's no big deal.'

'If it's no big deal, why do you look like that?'

She laughed off the question. 'Like what?'

'Stressed out!'

'I'm fine,' she said. 'I need coffee, and we're out of eggs.'

'I thought so.'

Later, they took their cups out to the balcony. Standing side by side, they breathed in the fresh air and took in the view. The bay was a clear green in the morning light.

'The week went by so fast,' Quinn said.

Kya kept quiet. She sipped her coffee, her eyes on the distant horizon.

'When do you think you'll be heading back?'

'To California?' she asked.

Quinn nodded, afraid to speak. This question had been low-key haunting her all week.

'I haven't had a chance to book a flight,' she said. 'With so much going on.'

'I get it,' Quinn said quickly. 'There's no rush, right?'

Kya answered with a tilt of the head, a gesture that could mean anything. Quinn felt as though she was drowning in the ambiguity of it all. She wanted to tell Kya how much she cared, how much she cherished every last minute they had left together. She wanted Kya to feel all the things she'd felt these past weeks: desired, cherished, supported, protected, pampered, spoiled … She could go on forever. What if the experience had been wholly one-sided? What had Kya gained from following her around? If she was keen on returning home, to her own life and busy schedules, Quinn would not blame her.

'I forgot to tell you. Adrian and Hugo know about us.'

'You told them?'

'No, Hugo's best friend clued him in. She follows us on social and … apparently people love us online.'

'Oh, I know,' Quinn said. It was #K&Q all over the place. 'I love us, too.'

'Me, too.'

'Really? You don't mind?'

'Why would I mind?'

She sounded offended, but Quinn could think of ten reasons straight off the top of her head. 'For all the unwanted attention, for one thing.'

'I think we're past that.'

'Are we?' Quinn asked. 'Where are we at, exactly?'

She turned to face Quinn. 'Do you really want to have this conversation now?'

'When should we have it?' Quinn replied. 'When you're boarding the plane back to LA?'

'San Jose.'

'Same difference.'

Kya cradled the coffee mug to her chest, as if drawing courage from its warmth. 'I don't have the logistics sorted out. All I know is how I feel. This *is* nice, and I don't want to lose it. At the same time, I know how complicated it will be. Do you understand?'

'I do,' Quinn replied, warmth spreading throughout her chest.

'Babe, can't we talk about all this tomorrow? You shouldn't get worked up today.'

Unfortunately, Quinn wasn't the type to let things fester. If something was eating at her, she would confront it in real time. 'I'm not worked up,' she said. 'I'm actually really happy.'

'So am I,' Kya said.

'The lads are going to tease me to death when I get back to the fitness club. I'm surprised they hadn't figured it out already. Hugo seems to know everything.'

'Now that they know, they're likely planning our wedding,' Kya said.

Marriage ... She and Kya hadn't talked about it. Not surprising, it was far too early for that conversation. However, Quinn generally liked to warn potential partners on her position on the institution as a whole.

'I'm not into it,' she said.

'Into what?' Kya asked.

She was confused and rightly so. Quinn was having trouble putting her feelings into words this morning. She tried again, using a familiar formula.

'I'm not interested in marriage.'

This was what she said to anyone she was involved with. It was only right for them to have this information up front in order to proceed accordingly. She sipped her tea, too cool for her taste now, anxiously waiting for Kya to respond.

'I don't see what people get out of it,' Kya said, finally.

'Me too!'

'Hugo and Adrian are happily married, but they would have been happy regardless, I think.'

'I just don't understand the concept of being legally bound to love, honour, and cherish someone until death. If you love someone, you should want to do it anyway.'

'There are legal benefits,' Kya said. 'I get it, but there are ways around it.'

'Maybe I'll change my mind down the road. For now, though, I don't see it.'

'Me, neither,' Kya said.

'You just don't want a conventional title, wife or wifey,' Quinn teased. 'It would drive you mad.'

Kya laughed, knowingly. 'It would drive me insane.'

Every time Quinn had initiated this conversation before, it had never gone so well. Somehow, it always resulted in conflict, and the tension lasted for days. Even the guys who hadn't wanted to commit to a relationship had bristled at the idea of her not wanting to jump through hoops to win their ring. As if a ring were the ultimate prize. Last she checked, she wasn't in the NFL or NBA.

'Everything is so easy with you,' Quinn said.

Kya shook her head. 'Have you forgotten about the time I snuck out of here while you were sleeping?'

Quinn balked. 'Water under the bridge, babe.'

'London Bridge or the Golden Gate?'

Quinn lit up. 'We should go to London!'

'Now?'

'Not now, but someday!' she said. 'I'd love to show you *my* London, my favourite pubs and all my old haunts.'

'I'd love that,' Kya said, quietly.

'Good. We'll do it.'

Quinn looked straight ahead. The sun had risen higher, and the bay glistened. She was glistening, too, on the inside. As much as possible, they had cleared the air. Plus, they had a plan, something to look forward to. She could hold onto that.

CHAPTER THIRTY-SEVEN

PRE-PARTY

'From out here you get a full view of the main stage. Enjoy!'

There were two parties in one. An open house on the penthouse's main level, and a private event in an adjoining room exclusively for the music producers, DJs, and other industry insiders, packaged as a 'meet and greet'. Kya was not an insider. When Quinn was led away at the request of their host, his girlfriend, a stern redhead, steered Kya to the balcony and left her there to enjoy the view of the bayfront park turned festival grounds. Although, you didn't need a penthouse view to see the stage. It was a beast, likely visible from outer space, and crowned with a gigantic neon sun that tossed wavy rays of yellow and orange light in every direction. There were four stages in all, Kya learned, but only one truly mattered.

The gates did not open until four; however, the frenzy had begun. Kya better understood Corinne's concerns but didn't share them. She was into it. Who didn't like a circus? Downtown Miami was overrun by festival-goers dressed in a rainbow of colours or hardly dressed at all, ripped jeans and T-shirts hanging on by a thread. They'd made this pilgrimage from the ends of the earth for the soul-liberating experience of partying inebriated in the crushing Miami heat. You had to respect that.

Kya left her post on the balcony in search of something to eat.

All the usual suspects were gathered at this one address. A quick glance around confirmed it. Everyone looked vaguely familiar. She'd likely bonded with one or the other in a nightclub restroom, shared drinks at a bar, or danced until closing with the whole lot of them over the course of the week. Ivy and Amanda had both made it, too. Ivy was at one end of the room, chatting with a pair of identical twins in matching pink wigs, and pointedly ignoring Amanda, huddled on the couch with … Trevor?! Kya couldn't believe it. Her money had been on Ivy.

At the buffet table, Kya recognized a woman she'd met at happy hour. Her name was Bree, if she remembered correctly. Bree wore an acid green minidress and her eyelids were painted a complementary shade of blue. She greeted Kya like a long-lost friend. 'Are you here alone?' she asked over the music.

'My girlfriend is meeting with … whichever billionaire owns this place.'

She gave Kya a thumbs-up. 'That would be my dad, and he can talk for hours. Follow me. The good stuff is upstairs.'

Kya happily followed her up a flight of stairs to a loft with a second, smaller buffet, and a bartender set up in a corner. This was a cosy offshoot of the rowdy open house. Downstairs, a dance battle had broken out on the living room floor. Up here, a small group of friends was spread out on the low sofas, talking quietly, sharing a laugh, and among them was Nick.

Nope! Not worth it! Kya thought. She wasn't all that hungry.

She mumbled an excuse to Bree, before heading downstairs and returning to her spot on the balcony. She preferred the chill vibe out here.

It was no surprise to find him here. After she'd discovered his identity, Kya spent every free minute combing through his posts.

His takes on the local entertainment industry had earned him an impressive following. Sadly, he used that platform to uplift what he called the 'players', the men, and dismiss any contribution made by women. Quinn was his favourite, but not his only target. He had a pattern. The bold, unapologetically sexy types triggered him. A while back, he became obsessed with a Miami dancer. Her performance in a viral pop video pushed her to stardom. Months later, she performed on stage at the MTV music awards. That was enough to set him off. He shared her photo and called her classless for having worn clear heels on the red carpet. In her defence, the heels were from an Italian design house and fresh off the runway.

Why would he do it? This was *his* world. Why fly above it, like a bird migrating south, and dump all over it? She would never understand guys like him. He needed access to these people, right?

Eventually, Kya would have to tell Quinn, but definitely not before her performance, and not afterwards, either. This was her big special day. Everyone deserved one, not just brides. She'd put a lot of effort into her set and her look. Her hair and make-up were professionally done. She wore a loose T-shirt over a pair of brushed gold denim shorts to the party, and stashed the matching halter top in her tote bag for later. She would look stunning in the custom-made set. Kya only wished that she had something more powerful than her iPhone to take photos. Maybe she could borrow Nick's paparazzi camera or telescopic lens?

'Hey, you! Are you hiding from me?'

It was no surprise he'd followed her outside, too. He cosied up to her, his back to the view.

'Nicolas Lambert,' she said.

'We're old friends now,' he said, with a foolish grin. 'Call me Nick.'

'How about I call you Night Lite?'

Watching the colour drain from his face was immensely satisfying. Kya hadn't meant to draw blood. She hadn't come here with the intention of attacking him today. In fact, she'd done her best to avoid it. However, the damage was done, and there was nothing to do about it except revel in it.

'I don't know what you're talking about,' he said, finally.

'I think you do,' she said. 'Look, I totally get why you chose that handle. Nick Lambert. Night Lite. NL. All the best artists preserve their initials. It's just … Night Lite is a little childish, don't you think? Sort of exposes you as the big baby that you are. Any kid can figure out what's going on here. You have a crush on Quinn. She doesn't feel the same. Your little heart is broken. You take to the internet to troll her. Quinn is totally fine with it, by the way. She doesn't care what sad, insecure men have to say about her on social media, but I do. I care a lot. You and I are not so different, and you called it from the start. We have feelings for the same woman. Unlike you, my ego isn't involved. I'd never intentionally hurt her, but I'd take down anyone who does.'

Before her eyes, Nick turned to stone. His jaw tightened and his mouth thinned to a straight line. His eyes were vacant and did not meet hers. They were fixed on something or someone behind her. Kya glanced over her shoulder, and her gaze collided with Quinn's. She stumbled backwards and gripped the steel handrail for support. She was vaguely aware of Ivy hovering at the doorway, looking downright furious. For the moment, she could only focus on her person.

'Listen. I can explain.'

What was there even to explain? By the look on her face, Quinn had heard everything. It was so unfair. Kya had taken every precaution to keep her out of this. To be thrown into this mess hours before taking the stage wasn't cool. Kya resented Nick and herself, too. Why couldn't she have held it together for just a while longer?

'Is this what you were keeping from me?' Quinn asked.

Kya nodded. Funny, she seemed more interested in this point than the revelation itself.

Nick spoke up. 'You can't believe a word she says. She's a fraud; you know that.'

'You're the fraud, Nick. I knew it the day we met,' Quinn said, coolly. 'And don't worry. It's not like you've betrayed my trust, or anything. We were never friends. I won't cry over this or lose any sleep. Enjoy your life, and I wish you success with your hateful little posts. Kya, let's go.'

Hateful little posts … In the end, that was all he had. Kya would have felt sorry for Nick, but Quinn was pulling her away, and escaping with Quinn was all she wanted.

Ivy wasn't as generous. She tore into him. 'You talked a lot of trash under your stupid alias and made a lot of people miserable. The only silver lining is that I don't have to pretend to like you anymore.'

Kya and Quinn made a quick getaway, ducking into the elevator without thanking the host or saying goodbye. Once they were alone, Quinn turned on her.

'When did you find out?'

'Late last night. I did a little digging—'

'A little digging? Are you some kind of genius? It's like you're MI6!'

Kya shrugged. 'Anyone could do it.'

'Shut up. You're too modest,' she said. 'You must've been freaking out.'

'Not at first,' Kya admitted. She had taken a fair amount of time to gloat. 'Once I had him, it felt effing fabulous.'

'And you let me sleep through all this?' she cried. 'You should have woken me up.'

'You're hours away from—'

'Okay, fine. Why not tell me this morning?'

'I'm sorry. Maybe I should have told you, but I felt it was a distraction you didn't need.'

'Please, don't ever be sorry,' she said. 'You were fearless back there. I just wanted to grab you and kiss you.'

'You can grab me now,' Kya said. 'It's not too late.'

Except, it was too late. The elevator doors slid open and a large group, more party guests, no doubt, were waiting to get in. Each looked as though they were going to very different events. Some in denim cut-offs and cowboy boots, others in silver disco glam, and a couple more in flowy boho frocks. Quinn took her hand and, together, they dashed out of the building and across the busy boulevard. Six rows of cars racing towards them. Kya wailed all the way.

'I won't get us killed. When will you trust me?'

'Where are we going?' Kya asked.

It was too early to head to the venue, and if the plan was to return home, the car was still in the building's garage.

'Over there!' Quinn pointed to the observation wheel spinning in the distance, not far from the quiet corner of the park where they'd celebrated her billboard with pizza that first day they'd truly got to know each other. 'I've always wanted to ride it. Okay with you?'

Kya nodded. Anything Quinn wanted was okay with her.

They made their way to the ticket booth. The attendant informed them that the ride was sold out. Tickets were only available online and booked in advance. Quinn presented him her phone. He scanned a code and produced two tickets.

Kya watched this transaction carefully. 'When did you book the ride?'

'A minute ago.'

'A minute ago, you were meeting the billionaire music producer.'

'He isn't a billionaire,' Quinn said. 'But he is a bore. I booked the ride on my phone while pretending to take notes.'

'Clever girl!'

'Standing there, listening to him, it hit me: there was no reason to meet this so-called industry giant. He needed us. We're doing the work, babe. We're the innovators. They're using us for profit. And I realized something else, even more important.'

'What's that?' Kya asked, hanging onto her words. This gorgeous woman was a force of nature; no one was ever going to pull anything on her.

Quinn looked up at her. 'I hated leaving you alone, and I had to find you.'

Before Kya could respond in any way, the attendant hollered, 'Move aside! Next!'

They moved aside and got in line. When it was their turn, Kya took Quinn's hand and guided her into the pod. They had it to themselves, a little cocoon in the sky. They sat on the same side with their legs propped up on the opposite bench.

'Please don't worry about me,' Kya said. 'I get that you're busy, and I'm fine on my own.'

Quinn straightened up to confront her. 'I'll worry if I want!'

Okay. This conversation was taking a turn. 'Let's not fight,' Kya said. 'This is supposed to be romantic.'

'Kya, a large part of romance is caring and worrying about one another.'

The wheel lurched into motion. Quinn fell back into Kya's arms, and that put an end to any quarrel. Their little pod rose higher and higher, offering them a far superior view of the festival than the penthouse balcony. The crowd before the gates had swelled, and the police patrol was active, sirens swirling, directing the flow of traffic and the stream of people. It was one big colourful and chaotic mess.

'I could switch out of my top up here, couldn't I?' Quinn said, looking around. 'I had hoped to do it at the party.'

'I'll help.'

She pulled the golden halter top out of her bag and it caught the sun. She was going to look stunning on stage and Kya couldn't wait. For now, though, she was happy to help her slip the soft T-shirt she wore over her head. Quinn moved onto Kya's lap as she fastened the ties at the nape of her neck. Then Kya closed her eyes and pressed her forehead to the velvet smooth skin of Quinn's back. A large part of romance was simply knowing how good you had it.

Quinn leaned into her. 'Look at all those people,' she whispered. For the first time today, she sounded unsure.

'Are you nervous?' Kya asked.

'I'm not.'

'It's all right if you are.'

'Okay, but I'm not,' she said with a familiar uptilt of the head. Kya wasn't buying it.

'If you get overwhelmed, keep your head down and focus on your sound. Do what comes naturally to you. At some point it will all flow. The nerves will pass, and you'll blow their minds.'

'And if I don't?' Quinn asked, quietly.

Kya hadn't considered the worst-case scenarios. This colourful group of people were dance music experts, festival aficionados. What if she were heckled or booed off stage? Kya would fight them all.

'I'll be waiting,' Kya replied. 'We'll get out of here, find an all-night diner and get pancakes, or tea and toast – whatever works for you.'

'That sounds good,' she said.

'It won't come to that. You're ready, you *will* blow them away, and we'll be celebrating at the end of the night. I promise you.'

Kya felt the moment the tension left Quinn's body. She twisted and took Kya's face between her hands. 'Seal that promise with a kiss.'

'I don't want to ruin your make-up.'

Her lips were expertly lined and glossy. The make-up artist had done an amazing job. She couldn't mess with that.

'That's fair,' Quinn said, and pointed to the side of her neck. 'How about here?' She tugged at the bodice of the halter, dragging it low. 'Or here?'

Kya followed the trail of her fingertips with her lips, as they spun round and round, forgetting the world and all that waited for them.

CHAPTER THIRTY-EIGHT

Amanda and Ivy sent Kya a text with their exact location: **4th in line, ready to rush the gates. Come find us.** There were no special VIP privileges, no friendly bouncer to wave them through, no list Quinn could put them on. They would have to queue up, like everyone else. This was a first; this past week, they hadn't stood in line for anything, except the ladies' room.

The girls would have to wait. Kya was in no hurry to leave Quinn. She hugged her for as long as she could, right until the moment they were forced to part ways. Even then, she could not bring herself to walk away. Kya stood watching until she disappeared through a heavily guarded entrance reserved for talent. For a while longer, she just stood there, staring at the locked gate. One of the guards smirked at her ungraciously.

A follow-up text got her moving: **Girl, where are you???**

Kya raced to the general entrance and found Ivy and Amanda in the midst of an argument.

'It's fine,' Ivy was saying, her tone clipped. 'I've only been single a couple of weeks. I have no business dating, anyway.'

'As long as you're cool with it,' Amanda said, eyes bright with mischief. 'You're my girl, and I don't want things to get awkward between us.'

'I'm cool,' Ivy said.

Although, to Kya, she looked pretty heated.

'Where is Trevor now?' she asked. 'Is he joining us?'

'No,' Amanda said. 'He stayed at the penthouse to watch from the balcony. His partner hates crowds.'

Ivy blinked rapidly. 'His ... what?'

'*Partner*,' Amanda replied, lengthening out the word. 'You might have heard of him. Jess Katz, of Katz Food Group. They own every trendy restaurant in Miami. He might take issue with us fighting over his man.'

Kya cheered. 'I knew I liked Trevor!'

'He's very sweet,' Amanda said before turning to Ivy. 'But you're not. You owe me an apology. What kind of friend do you think I am?'

Ivy pressed her hands to her flaming red cheeks. 'Sorry! It's just ... you two looked so into each other.'

'I thought so, too,' Kya admitted. 'You were very cosy on the couch.'

'Yes, but if only you two fools knew what we were talking about,' Amanda said with a cheeky little smile.

'If only you'd tell us, instead of playing guessing games,' Ivy retorted.

'There's still hope for you and Trevor. He's interested in you.'

Ivy took a step back. 'In what twisted way?'

'Professionally.'

'Interesting,' Kya said.

'I need more information,' Ivy said, shaking her head.

'You're right about one thing: we did hit it off, but not like you think. We talked about careers. I told him I'm a buyer and up for a promotion. He's been managing LAB for over five years, and he's looking to scale back. He could use an extra pair of hands;

do you follow? Someone to assist him in daily management tasks, someone he can trust and train, someone eager to break into the entertainment industry. It's how he got his start, and he's eager to pay it forward. It would be an outstanding opportunity for one lucky candidate. If you didn't know, LAB is one of the premier nightclubs in the world.'

'I know,' Ivy said.

'Everybody knows,' Kya added.

'Great!' Amanda exclaimed. 'I gave him your number. Expect his call.'

'Me?' Kya asked, confused.

'Not you, sweetie! I forgot you need a job, too. Next time.'

'Wait. You gave him my number?' Ivy sounded even more confused than Kya was a second ago.

'Yes, and you're welcome,' Amanda said. 'This is a way for you to spend your nights at the club without getting side-eye from your parents at Sunday dinner.'

'I can't believe I never considered this,' Ivy whispered. 'It's genius.'

'Sometimes, you need a friend to point the way,' Amanda said.

'Hey, congrats,' Kya said. 'This is exciting news.'

'Let's not get ahead of ourselves,' Amanda cautioned. 'It's not a done deal.'

'I get it,' Ivy said. 'And if Trevor doesn't call, I'll call everyone I know. I'll crack into the industry.'

'That's right. Put those contacts to work,' Amanda said. 'One of those hot doormen must have moved up by now.'

Ivy rolled her eyes. 'I don't *only* know hot doormen!'

'But you do know your fair share,' Amanda said.

'True,' Ivy admitted.

'Never mind hot doormen!' Kya balked. 'You'll be hiring them some day.'

'Holy shit!' Ivy cried. 'I'm going to run this town.'

Amanda grabbed Ivy's shoulders and shook her. 'Yes, girl!'

Kya laughed so hard she dropped her water bottle. It rolled out of reach and as she chased after it, a guy standing in line just a few feet back caught her eye. He looked a little familiar, but hadn't everyone today? She snatched up the bottle and rejoined the girls. She was about to ask Amanda for professional advice when a shiver ran down her back. The shaggy black hair, sharp cheekbones, creamy skin … The heat and the emotions of the day had clouded her vision and clogged her brain. She knew this man.

'Give me a minute,' Kya said to the others. 'I'll be right back.'

'Don't go too far!' Ivy cautioned. 'We have to stick together. It's the wild west out here.'

'This won't take long,' she assured her. 'I have to tell somebody off.'

'Don't let us keep you, then,' Amanda said. 'God speed.'

Kya marched down the line with a soldier's determination until she reached her target. He was deep in conversation with another guy. They were both in tie-dye T-shirts and cargo shorts. He wore the same Air Force Ones that he wore to the office every Friday.

'Jon! What are you doing here?'

Jon Yi startled. 'Kya?'

'You little pr—'

'Kya!' he cried, drowning out her tirade. 'I can't believe it!'

The man had the nerve to smile, as if they were not at the bone-picking stage of a serious issue.

'Don't you Kya me,' she retorted.

'Hold on! *You're* mad? You ghosted me.'

Ghosting? Ha! This wasn't a simple matter of a few missed calls, or a date gone wrong. This man had stabbed her in the back.

'Jon, I thought you were my friend.'

'I *am* your friend, Kya! Your only friend.'

'That's not true. I've got friends now.'

'Is that why you never answered my calls?'

Kya advanced, hands on her hips. 'I didn't answer your calls because I don't speak to traitors who attend secret meetings and vote to get me fired!'

'Kya …'

He looked hurt, but so was she. 'You sided with the boys. That's unforgivable.'

'What are you talking about?' Jon took her arm and moved her away from the line before adding anything else. Everyone within earshot, including his tie-dye twin, were listening in. In a hushed voice, he asked, 'You think I got you fired?'

'Didn't you?'

'No!'

'Weren't you at the meeting?'

'What meeting?'

'Alek said—'

'You'd believe Alek over me?' he pushed back, indignant.

'He said there was a meeting, and you all decided I should be the one to go,' Kya continued, undeterred. 'Then you took me out for Thai food and wished me safe travels, knowing very well I was about to get sacked.'

'That would be pretty shitty, if it were true,' Jon said. 'May I tell you my side of the story now?'

'Fine. Let's hear it.'

'It's simple,' he said. 'Alek lied to you. If there was a meeting,

I didn't get the invite. Soon after you left for your trip, I got called into HR and was fired on the spot.'

The news hit Kya on the head. She felt instantly dizzy. 'For real?'

'Yes, for real,' he said. 'At least you didn't have to sit across from Jeff in HR, or clear your desk while a security guard watches your every move, or carry boxes filled with *Game of Thrones* memorabilia to the elevator while everyone stares and no one, including Alek, can look you in the eye. That Thai lunch was my last supper, too.'

'Jesus …' Kya muttered. 'They did us dirty.'

'Yup.'

'Why didn't you call me?'

'I was a mess,' he said. 'I locked my phone in my car. I couldn't talk to anyone for days.'

'Jon, I'm so sorry!'

'That's okay. I can't imagine how you felt, opening that email.'

Kya couldn't recall the feeling. It felt like ages ago. She felt nothing now.

'I wish I'd known,' he said.

'Never mind that.'

Kya got locked out of a computer; that was all. She shuddered at the thought of meeting with Jeff Green, the sleazy HR director. Come to think of it, she'd got the better end of the stick. She returned to her first question. 'What are you doing in Miami?'

'A friend had an extra concert ticket and dragged me out of my apartment,' he explained. 'You would know that if you answered my calls.'

Kya rubbed the back of her neck. 'I was busy.'

'I know,' he said. 'I follow you on TikTok. You're busy dating one of my favourite DJs.'

'How is she your favourite?' Kya asked. 'I hadn't heard of her until I got here.'

'You were always behind the times, Kya,' he said. 'For someone so progressive, it's a little weird.'

'And she's not really my girlfriend. It's way more complicated than it looks online.'

'What? No hashtag K&Q?'

'Yes ... for now.'

'Gotcha,' he said. 'I'm really happy to see you, crazy girl. I was hoping we could talk. I've got some ideas, you know.'

Kya was no longer listening. She threw her arms around Jon's neck and squeezed him tight. 'I'm so glad I don't have to hate you anymore!' she cried.

'Me, too!' he said, laughing. 'You scared me back there. Remind me never to cross you.'

'Don't ever,' she said. 'I'll kill you.'

'I've been warned.'

'Is it just the two of you?' she asked, glancing at his friend, who was glancing at them.

'Yeah, just us.'

'Do you want to join my friends, Ivy and Amanda? They're lots of fun. We could hang out together. I've missed you so much.'

'Hell, yeah. Are you kidding?' he asked. 'It's a miracle I found you. I'm not letting you go.'

'*I* found you, Jon.'

Typical man, taking all the credit.

CHAPTER THIRTY-NINE

The first order of business was to secure the merch, T-shirts, banners, and commemorative glowsticks. Ivy took on the leadership role, delegating tasks to Amanda and Jon's friend, whose name Kya hadn't yet caught. Jon asked Kya to stay behind. He wanted to steal a few minutes to catch up. Only, like children, they had to swear they would not budge from the spot where Ivy left them.

'We have to stick together,' she repeated. 'I've heard horror stories of girls having to walk home alone after losing their friend group.'

Amanda snapped open a fan. 'Ivy, you drove us here. If anyone walks home, it won't be you.'

'Quinn and I left the car at the garage,' Kya added. 'We have it all worked out.'

'So, you'll wait for us here?' Ivy asked.

'We might head over to the frozen lemonade stand, but no further.'

'No frozen lemonade!' Ivy cried, exasperated. 'No random sugary drinks. It's plain water, sparkling water, vodka, or nothing.'

'Plain water, sparkling water, vodka,' Kya repeated. 'Got it.'

'Your anxiety is through the roof today,' Amanda observed, dryly.

'We won't budge,' Jon promised.

That promise was enough to reassure Ivy. It did nothing to calm Jon's friend who tossed him an anxious look. Still, he went with the plan and left with the others.

Jon nudged her. 'We're getting that sugary drink, right?'

'For sure,' Kya replied. 'She can't tell us what to do.'

In line at the lemonade stand, Jon nudged her again. 'So, you and Quinn have it all worked out?'

'Don't twist my words,' she said. 'It's just a ride home.'

'That's not what it sounds like to me. How did you meet her?'

'My brother-in-law dragged me out the night after I got the news. She was playing a set. The moment I saw her, I forgot all my problems. She was so beautiful. It's anyone's guess what she sees in me.'

'I'd guess she thinks you're sexy, smart, genuine, and cool.'

'Thanks, but she's unreal. Can we agree on that?'

'Agreed, but so are you.'

Kya reached out and ruffled his hair. 'This line isn't moving. Should we skip the lemonade?'

'Definitely.'

They returned to the designated spot. 'Who's this guy you're with?' she asked. 'What's his name? Why do I feel he low-key hates me?'

'Shit! I didn't introduce you?'

'No, you didn't. Now he probably thinks I'm your ex or something. Please clear that up.'

Jon laughed. 'His name is Liam. He doesn't hate you. He might be scared of you. If anything, he's worried you'll murder me.'

'Is this the same Liam you met on the app?'

'The same.'

'That was a month ago. You're taking trips together?'

'A lot can happen in a month, Kya.'

'Apparently.'

'It's good to see you,' he said, quietly.

What he must've gone through, she wondered. And all alone, too. Jon's family was in the Midwest. 'How did you cope?' she asked. 'At least I had my brothers.'

'I thought only one of your brothers lived in Miami.'

'I got another one free when he got married,' she replied.

'I wouldn't have wanted to see my family, to be honest,' he said. 'I needed to be alone. I locked myself in the apartment, and watched *The Office* on repeat.'

'The UK version or ours?'

'Both. Theirs then ours.'

'That's the only way to do it.'

'I felt like crap, but I learned something,' he said. 'It matters who you work with.'

Kya agreed. 'Absolutely.'

'The worst was knowing I'd never get to work with you again.'

'I feel the same. The others can kick rocks.'

'Next time, I'll be more selective,' he continued. 'I'll vet the people I associate with.'

Kya didn't think that was possible. 'How?' she asked. 'Everyone I've talked to says tech is rotten to the core. All we can do is deal, sleep with one eye open, and expect to get knifed in the back at some point or another.'

'I reject that,' he said, firmly.

'What can we do? We don't live in Wakanda.'

'You haven't seen the movie, so please don't.'

'I haven't seen it *yet*. I will, eventually.'

'Well, eventually, the culture will change but we have to change it.'

Kya took a swig from her water bottle. 'How do we go about that?'

'Start our own company.'

'Not you, too!' she cried. Had everyone caught the entrepreneurial bug?

'Why do you say that? Who else reached out to you?'

'No one is checking for me,' Kya assured him. 'You make it sound like I'm some hot commodity. I'm not.'

Even Corinne, for all her enthusiasm, hadn't made her an offer.

'I think you should consider it,' he said.

'Consider what? I don't have a single idea. What could I possibly offer that isn't already out there?'

'Girl Decoded.'

'It's just a blog, Jon.'

'It's a media startup.'

'You're not serious.'

'You've got proof of concept, and you've got reach.'

'Haven't you been paying attention?' Kya asked. 'When they found out I got fired, they dragged me through hot coals. I'm trying something new, but who knows how that will go?'

Her readers were interested in the life of a twenty-something in a niche industry. That eagerness would wane the more time passed. She hadn't dared to check the level of engagement of the Corinne Miller profile.

'I've been paying attention,' he said. 'You got dragged, for sure. Then you told them where to go, got a hot girl, and partied your ass off in Miami.'

'Hold on!' Kya said with a start. 'That's not how it went down.'

'But that's how it played out, and that's all that matters.'

The group returned with the T-shirts, flags, and glowsticks, and any discussion of turning her blog into a multimedia empire was parked.

Liam approached them with caution, as if Jon were petting a wild animal, a killer who would kill again. He was handsome, though, with light eyes and freckles on the bridge of his nose. Jon looped an arm around Liam's neck. 'This is Kya,' he said. 'When she's not blocking my calls, she's pretty cool.'

'I really am,' Kya said, knowing she'd made a terrible first impression. 'Maybe we can all hang out sometime.'

'We're staying at The Standard for a couple more days,' Jon said. 'Come through. We'll talk over my idea.'

Kya gave him a kiss on the cheek. 'I will. I promise.'

A second later, the promise was forgotten. Music erupted and the ground started rumbling under their feet. Amanda unfolded a printout of the schedule. The plan was to hop from stage to stage and catch the best DJs from each line-up. She'd circled the names of her favourites and mapped out an itinerary. No one objected.

They made their way across the field. Kya and Ivy fell in step. Ivy sprayed SPF on her face as they walked. 'That Nick, right?!'

'Right,' Kya cried over the music. Conversation was getting increasingly difficult the closer they got to the action.

'What do you think?' Ivy asked.

She was still trying to puzzle him out. Kya had given up. She'd rather forget Nick, altogether.

'That man blew up my phone, begging me to introduce him to Quinn. And when it doesn't work out, what does he do? He trashes her online! Who does that?'

'Guys with no ideas of their own.'

That's what she thought of Alek and the others, back at Ex-Cell

HQ, secure in their jobs. For once, she was glad not to count herself among them.

Amanda shushed them. 'Not one more word about that man!'

She was right. It was time to delete Nick from their minds. The sun was setting in a veil of soft colours, and something electric was moving in the air. Smoke machines pushed out great tufts of purple haze. They were close enough to one of the stages to feel the music. The only thing left to do was dance.

Kya had spent countless hours hanging out at bars and coffee shops with Jon. They'd gone hiking and bowling. They'd watched movies and played video games. They'd never gone dancing, not to a club, a rave, or a house party. Here they were, together, feeling high, getting down. They had the best time, until the lights of the main stage sparked, signalling that the headline acts would begin soon. Quinn was third in line to perform, the only woman on schedule. Which explained why the boys had got so worked up. It wasn't easy to be the first at anything, let alone the first woman, a woman of colour, a woman of colour who was unapologetically queer. But Quinn was going to show them all. Nick would have to eat his words.

Amanda let out a cry. 'It's starting!'

Ivy rallied the troops. 'We're done here! Let's move!'

This time, Kya led the way, forging a path through the crowd until they made it to the main stage.

Smoke gave way to fire. Long flames burst out of cannons and faded into the darkening sky. It hit Kya all at once. Her girl was about to take the stage. Her best friend was here to witness it. New friends would share the experience. They would never forget this night. How had she gone from crying in her brother's spare bedroom to this in a matter of weeks? It was all going by so fast, but now wasn't the time to look back in wonder. It was time to get messy.

Ivy made sure they were all accounted for. Liam was recording a vlog. Amanda was laughing at something a stranger had said. Jon got Kya to climb onto his shoulders. They bounced about, risking serious injury to themselves and everyone around them until Ivy ordered her to get down. The first act took to the stage, then the second, then finally, *finally*, it was time.

In the crackling silence between sets, Quinn was escorted onto the stage. She took position behind the decks. Kya took in her hair, her skin, the flash of gold of her outfit, but also a hesitancy in her walk that maybe no one else saw. While the sound technicians buzzed around her, she took a moment to scan the crowd. In her heart, Kya knew that she was looking for her. Also, deep in her heart of hearts, Kya knew she loved this woman. She loved Quinn with everything she had inside. It had happened so fast, in a matter of weeks, she'd gone from *I like you* to *I can't live without you.*

Everything had been leading her to this. There was nothing she could have done to stop it. From the day they'd first met and instantly clashed, Kya was head over heels, madly, deeply, irrationally in love. It was the only reason she'd stayed in Miami, reached for every possible excuse not to return to her life in California – a life that no longer held any appeal. It was as if that life belonged to someone else. Some other girl had set the alarm clock at six every morning, not her. She'd dressed in office-appropriate outfits and commuted to work, ordered the same latte day after day after day, eaten breakfast at her desk, taken meetings, laughed at the stale jokes, nodded, pretended to listen, hung out with the guys, ordered takeout, slept in on Saturdays, folded laundry on Sundays, run a mile or two, and got up to do it all again on Monday. Could she ever be that girl again?

'Don't just stand there!' Amanda cried, shaking Kya out of her love-induced stupor. 'Get onto Jon's shoulders. Wave this banner. Maybe she'll see us.'

Kya did as she was instructed. She raised the banner, which was identical to every other banner raised. The crowd began to cheer. In the frenzy, it was a miracle Quinn spotted her at all. Her beautiful face lit up. She waved, blew kisses, and brought her hands together in the shape of a heart. Kya could do none of those things. She was hopelessly in love. Her only hope was that Quinn could feel it, and that feeling would carry her through.

CHAPTER FORTY

SOLSTICE

All the clichés are true. When the time comes, you grow numb. You feel disoriented. Blood rushes at your temples. Your heartbeat is all you can hear. There is a tingle in your fingertips, a strange rumbling in your belly. You break into a cold sweat. Tears sting your eyes. Your whole body shivers. You don't respond to your own name, and someone has to touch your elbow and guide you onto the stage. He whispers, 'You'll be all right.' You're not sure. The stage is larger than any you've been on, and you feel as small and powerless as a doll.

The sea of people rises and roars. A tsunami of cheers rolls forward, but you're no fool. You know how easily those same people can turn against you. The cheers can turn to sneers at any moment. They love you. They hate you. In truth, they couldn't care less about you, your wellbeing, your ambitions, your silly hopes, and dreams. If you can't deliver, give them their money's worth, you are worthless to them.

What are you doing up here, anyway? If you turn and run, who could blame you? Who would question it? They'd discuss it on Reddit, or wherever, and conclude you simply weren't ready. You were not up to par. They'd call you an amateur, and for once they'd be right. You don't belong on this huge stage, have no business facing this sea of people. You scan the crowd now, mulling this over. Turn and run? Yes. Just as soon as you can breathe again.

That's when you spot her, as close to the stage as she can possibly get. She's on the shoulders of some guy you've never seen before, waving a flag. In a crowd of faces, you would always spot hers. You manage to smile, wave, blow her a kiss, acknowledge her in some way. The last thing she said to you was to focus. Put your head down and focus. Tune out the world and focus. Breathe and focus. You'd stupidly tried to ignore her advice, had refused to admit that you were … scared. But she's the wisest person you've ever met. Her words come rushing back now. She promised that if you followed those easy steps, it would all flow.

Over the stage, a neon sign flickers on and flashes your name. The sea rages now and she is taken under. You don't know where she's gone, but you know she's there. And knowing it, feeling it, gives you everything you need. The numbness, the tingling, the rumble in your belly, all subside. You remember why you're here. It's not to prove your worth, and not to stick it to the haters. You're here to play. Music is your joy. Sharing that joy is the one thing you do well. It's a singular talent; you were born with it. You play. It's what you do. It's who you are.

They hand you the mic. You skip your carefully crafted pre-amble and just speak your mind.

'Everybody, listen! It's the longest, hottest, most gruelling day on record, but it will not bring us down! My name is Quinn. I'm your DJ, just one of many tonight, but you will remember me. Now before we get started, if you love me, show me the love, and say my name!'

★

Quinn didn't remember anything after that. Never had a set gone by so fast. Never had she felt such a connection with a crowd and so much love in return. The feeling would stay with her forever, but everything else would fade. She had no complaints. That was exactly how it should be.

Quinn was guided off stage, just as she'd been guided on, and led to the white tent reserved for the DJs and MCs. It was crowded with the ones who'd gone before her and those still waiting their turn. They all cheered her arrival, surrounded her, congratulated her, promised to reach out to her in the coming weeks 'for collabs and stuff'. The validation of her peers was priceless. However, nothing was better than celebrating with her friends and the woman her heart belonged to. They'd agreed to meet at the parking garage after the concert. What would she do until then? Hang out here, talking about future collaborations? There would be time for that down the line. But finding her friends wasn't as easy as that; they might as well be in a foreign country with so many gates and guards between them. It was worth a try.

Quinn sent Kya a text. I'm done here. Where are you?

A moment later, a text bubble popped up and disappeared. She was trying to puzzle it out. However, trapped in a pit of people, there wasn't much she could do. Quinn approached one of the security guards outside the tent and asked if she could smuggle in her friends. The answer was no. 'If we say yes to you, we'll have to say yes to everyone.'

That made sense.

'How can I get to the other side?' she asked.

'Why would you want to? It's a madhouse out there.'

'That's where my people are,' she replied.

He nodded. 'There's a gate for the crew, just to the side of the stage. I'll take you there. Have your people meet you.'

Quinn quickly texted all this information to Kya then set off on the perilous journey of crossing the border.

'Are you sure about this?' the guard asked, when they reached the fence. 'Once you're out, it's over for you. I can't let you back in. No one can.'

'I'm sure,' she answered, even though she hadn't heard from Kya or anyone.

He unlocked the gate. 'Tight set, by the way,' he said, and stepped aside to let her through.

'Thanks.' Quinn slipped out to a sort of deserted holding pen. It was dark, and no one was waiting there. She checked her phone. The battery life was down to ten per cent, and still no word from Kya. As romantic as this had seemed a minute ago, she wondered if she had made a stupid mistake.

At last, she heard them even before she saw them charging at her. Ivy, Amanda, two guys she didn't know, and beautiful Kya. They were laughing, screaming, running wildly, flags flapping overhead.

'There she is!' one guy cried.

'There you are!' the other echoed.

'You killed it! You killed it! You killed it!' Ivy screamed.

Amanda looked as though she were crying. 'You were amazing!'

And Kya said nothing at all. She crashed into Quinn, threw her arms around her, and together they tumbled onto the grass, laughing, screaming, crying, hearts pounding, their joy lighting up the night.

PART VI

GIRLS' NIGHT OUT

GIRL_DECODED
DRAFT 4:05AM

If, like me, you've been viewing life through a computer screen, using apps to connect with faceless strangers, logging countless hours online, your screentime a disgrace, respectfully, you need to get out more. The answer is not in the algorithm. Get out of the house, out of your routines, out of your head, clock out, log off, toss out the smart watch or smart phone, and anything else preventing you to unplug. Go for a walk, a hike, or—like me—go to a world-renowned music festival. Grab some friends, lace up your sneakers or your boots, and don't forget to hydrate. You're too young to let your life grow stale. You're too old to waste your time. I get it; we're all scared. That's normal, I believe. How are you supposed to feel standing at the edge of a cliff with your future stretched out below, and no one to catch you? But that fear is fuel, it's the energy you'll need to take the leap.

CHAPTER FORTY-ONE

It took everything she had, every scrap of energy, for her to crawl out of bed, shower, dress, and book a ride to the restaurant. Kya had promised her brother that she would join him and his friends at brunch, and was intent on keeping that promise. Even though, she realized how foolish it was to commit to a brunch the morning after a music festival. What was she thinking? She was exhausted, and that word didn't fully paint the picture, didn't account for her aching muscles, pounding headache, and the pinch in her lower back. Kya was young by all measures, but the age of hopping on friends' shoulders was long gone. Never again!

Last night, after they were reunited with Quinn, they headed to the far edges of the crowd to enjoy the rest of the concert. They didn't leave until the last DJ shut it down with a solid performance. And then there was a long line to file out at the park, and the even longer line of cars to file out of the parking garage. Hungry and still a little rowdy, the group decided to meet at the all-night diner where Kya and Quinn had first had pancakes after the sunrise set at Space. They slipped into a corner booth and ordered stacks of waffles and pancakes, plates of sausage and eggs, hash browns, and whatever else was on the menu – they'd ordered it all. While they feasted like kings, they relived the night, swapping stories, photos, anecdotes, and any bit of gossip they'd picked up. Quinn told them all about the tent where she'd been held up until it was her time to take the stage, who she'd hung out with, and among them, which were utter arses whom she would never speak to again. They parted with the others around four in the morning. Kya and Quinn kept right on talking as they brushed their teeth, filling each other in on every minute they'd been apart. Then, they collapsed into bed, quickly stripping off the pyjamas they'd only just put on. Now, five short hours later, Kya was off to brunch?

She wasn't hungry.

She was all talked out.

All she wanted was to curl up next to her girl and sink into the warmth of her body, but she'd promised her brother and she'd keep that promise.

Kya left Quinn a few notes scattered around the apartment. They all said the same thing: **Meeting Adrian for brunch. Back soon!** She left yet another note stuck to the front door: **Seriously, it's not like last time. I'm coming home straight after.** In the ride, she followed up with a text message, saying pretty much the same things, adding, **Miss you already.**

Quinn replied a moment later with a simple heart emoji that set Kya's heart on fire. She imagined her reaching for the phone, typing the one-symbol response before slipping back to sleep. Kya dreamed of coming home to her, every day, forever.

The restaurant was at a nearby hotel with umbrella-topped tables scattered around the pool. She should've known Hugo would pick a stunning location. As she walked past the buffet, with a spread of everything anyone could crave, ever, her mood lifted, and her appetite returned. The hostess led her to the table where Adrian, Hugo, Samantha, and Roman were gathered, mimosas already in hand.

'Girlie, you had a rough night!' Hugo exclaimed. 'I want to hear all about it.'

Kya lowered her eyes. She was a hot mess! She'd picked her clothes up off a chair in the corner of Quinn's room. The outfit had looked nice on her a couple days ago, and still looked nice, although wrinkled. She'd swiped on make-up – mascara and lipstick – on the ride over. She'd added dark sunglasses for a moody rockstar vibe. By sharp contrast, Adrian, Hugo, Samantha, and Roman looked as fresh as the Sunday morning.

It was too much. Kya wanted to turn and leave.

Thank God for big brothers! Adrian stood to hug her, pulled out her chair, and set a cup of coffee before her. 'Kya, this is Roman and Samantha,' he said.

'Good to meet you,' Roman said.

'Yeah, same!' She slid off her sunglasses, smiled, and tried her best to look friendly.

Roman, with his chestnut brown skin and dark features, was more handsome than she'd imagined. Samantha was so pretty. Her tawny brown skin soaked up the sun and her brown hair fell in soft ringlets past her shoulders. As pretty as she was, Kya thought Quinn even more so, with the sort of face you could hold in your hands and stare at endlessly and always find something new and surprising – a dimple, a freckle, a gleam in her eye.

'Okay, that's out of the way,' Hugo said. 'Tell us how Quinn did last night.'

'Don't harass her!' Samantha said to Hugo. 'She just got here!'

Despite this, four pairs of eyes were pinned on her, waiting expectantly.

'She played the set of her life, I think.'

Hugo hammered the table with his fists. 'Good for her!'

The waiter came to take her order. 'You can have anything you want,' Adrian said, as if she were a child he had to coax to eat. Kya ordered a poached egg topped with caviar, fresh berries, more coffee, and a mimosa just for fun. When the food arrived, she dug into it, like a child, as if she hadn't eaten for days.

'I hear you're interested in founding a startup,' Roman said.

The man didn't waste time, did he?

'Where did you hear that?' Kya asked.

'I told him,' Adrian said.

'I'd like to hear your ideas,' Roman said.

Kya had zero ideas, so she presented Jon's. 'Is a media startup a thing?'

'Definitely.'

Roman shot out a list of every mainstream media outlet that had started out as a feed, a blog, or just a series of photos on now forgotten social media platforms. 'The important thing is to have a message,' he said. 'A message, and a target population who needs that information.'

Arguably, she had those two things. Could it be that simple? Maybe the problem was that she didn't see herself as an entrepreneur, a founding father, a visionary of that sort. Besides, didn't you have to start in your parents' garage, tinkering with something or the other, labouring in silence, for *ages*, before you sought financing and brought that thing to market?

Samantha intervened. 'Can't you see you're freaking her out?'

Kya loved her for it.

'Kya doesn't freak out easily,' Hugo said.

She loved him for the vote of confidence, but he was dead wrong. She freaked out all the freaking time.

Samantha turned to Kya. 'Unlike the men here, I'm the only

one who's sort of done what you're thinking of doing, and I can tell you it's not easy. It takes time. I was finally able to quit my job last year.'

'That's impressive.'

Admittedly, Kya didn't know much about Samantha, the sort of content she created, how she got her curls to curl like that, or anything outside the fact that she'd met Roman at an epic wedding in Tobago. The memory of that trip had Hugo in a chokehold, and for a while it was all he could talk about. That aside, she was the only person at the table making sense right now.

'What is it you do, again?' Kya asked.

'I'm a travel vlogger, and I've written two travel guides.'

'Nice.'

'My point is you do not have to quit your job or get bankers involved. You can start slow.'

'Kya doesn't have a job to quit,' Hugo said. 'So, she's fine.'

Kya pivoted to Quinn in a desperate attempt to change the subject. 'Do you guys want to see the video I took of Quinn on stage?'

It worked like a charm. She handed over her phone and went back to enjoying her brunch without having to contemplate her future. Funny, just this morning, 5 a.m. to be exact, she felt differently. So much so, she wrote a draft post all about the thrill of diving off the deep end into the unknown. She might've welcomed this conversation then. Right now, she just wanted to sip her mimosa in peace.

When the meal was done, the guys left the table to gaze longingly at the hotel's golf course. Even Hugo, who only loved soccer, and only cheered for Brazil, tagged along, hand in hand with Adrian, leaving Kya alone with Samantha.

'Hey,' Samantha said, edging closer.

Her British accent was different from Quinn's. In what way, Kya wasn't sure. But everything about Quinn was just different. No matter how lovely Samantha was, no matter how phenomenal this brunch had been, Kya wished she was home with her.

'How's Miami so far, Samantha?' Kya asked.

'Call me Sam.'

Naturally. The similarities with Quinn didn't stop at the accent. 'All right, Sam. Are you having fun?'

'Miami is great, but spending time with Hugo is the best.'

'I feel the same.'

'I've been watching your TikToks,' she said.

'Have you? That was just for fun.'

'How can I get in on that?' Sam asked.

'In on what?'

'The fun!'

'I don't know what you mean.'

'This is my last night in Miami.'

'Okay ...'

'I want to have fun.'

'And by fun you mean ...'

'I want to party.'

'I see.'

'I don't care where we go. A club, a lounge, a dive bar, it doesn't matter to me.'

Kya saw Sam clearly for the first time today. Underneath the lovely exterior was steel. She was on a mission, determined to get her way. Now that she knew what this was, Kya got into it. 'Let's coordinate with the guys—'

'No guys.'

'None?'

'I want a classic girls' night out.'

'But—'

'I have my reasons,' she said. 'I can't get into it right now. I promise to tell you later. Trust me. I wouldn't ask if it wasn't important. I really, really need this.'

'Well, if you really, really need this, I'll see what I can do.'

Kya reached for her phone. It was sitting in the middle of the table where the others had dropped it after watching the clip of Quinn's performance. She pulled up the group chat.

British Blogger Samantha Roberts in desperate need of a girls' night out. Can you help?

The responses poured in, all overwhelmingly positive.

Amanda: I'm exhausted, but I'm in! Anything for a UK girl!

Quinn: Anything for you, babe.♥

Ivy: Just bring her to Blood Orange. We're all going, anyway.

Quinn: We are?

Amanda: That's news to me … and I'm sitting right across from you.

Ivy: Didn't I tell you? Solstice afterparty. Get into it!

Kya shared the news with Sam. 'Looks like we're all going to an afterparty at a Wynwood speakeasy. Sound good to you?'

'Which speakeasy? Blood Orange?'

'You've heard of it?'

'Yes, I've heard of it! Stalking Quinn online is my favourite thing to do. I'm a huge fan.'

'You're in luck. Quinn will be there, and you can tell her yourself.'

'You make such a cute couple,' she said. 'If you don't mind my saying.'

'I don't mind.'

'One more thing,' Sam said. 'Hugo is my plus-one; he's one of the girls, always.'

Kya didn't mind that, either. 'No problem. Everybody loves Hugo.'

'Wonderful.'

Sam picked up her phone and dispatched a few texts to her own group chat.

Kya slipped her sunglasses back on and sipped her mimosa. They were heading back to Blood Orange, where it all began.

After brunch, Adrian insisted on driving Kya back to Quinn's. They piled into the SUV and when they veered onto the familiar road Sam looked around, confused. 'Quinn lives in your old neighbourhood?'

'She lives in our old place,' Hugo answered. 'She bought it from us.'

Sam lost it. 'I love that for her! That flat is lovely. We never wanted them to leave.'

'Not this again,' Adrian mumbled. 'It's small. There's no room to grow.'

'There's room to dream,' Sam said. She went on to share her favourite memories of the tiny apartment. Sunset cocktails on the balcony. A holiday party that nearly got them evicted from the building. A kitchen fire Kya hadn't heard about. The time Sam had slept over before that now famous trip to Tobago.

'Good times,' Hugo said with a forlorn sigh.

'It's a special place,' Kya said. 'I love it, too.'

They'd pulled up to the building's entrance. Kya had a grip on the door handle, ready to take her leave, when her brother hit her with that question.

'What's tomorrow?' she asked. Had she missed something?

'You get your room back,' Roman answered. 'We're clearing out. Sorry we displaced you.'

'No worries,' Kya replied, still unclear on how to best to handle her brother's initial question. What had made him think she was coming back at all? The short time she had left in Miami, she intended on spending with Quinn. Except now, with her foot out the door, didn't seem like the right time to make such a dramatic declaration.

'Quinn is gracious,' Adrian went on to say. 'But it's been a while, and I'm sure she'd like her privacy.'

She nearly laughed in his face. What privacy? She and Quinn shared everything and kept nothing from each other. How did he not know this? She turned to Hugo for an explanation. Hadn't he told Adrian like he'd said? Hugo averted his eyes. As did Sam. Only Adrian was looking at her expectantly, waiting for an answer, and a vehicle that had pulled up behind them flashed its headlights, urging them to get a move on.

'I don't think Quinn has a problem with my staying.'

'Even so,' Adrian said. 'I'd like to have you back. You said you'd come home for dinner this week and never did.'

'Things got hectic,' Kya said. 'You know how it is.'

And if he didn't know how it was, somebody should have told him. Someone like his husband who was staring out the window, not contributing a word to this conversation. Or someone like her. She should have just told her brother what was going on. They could have had a nice sunrise phone chat about it.

Adrian made his best pitch. 'I'll order our favourite foods. We'll watch a movie and eat on the couch, like old times.'

There was no time to answer. The waiting car blared its horn.

Kya hopped out and, before shutting the door, she said, 'I'll call you!'

As they pulled away, she stood on the kerb wondering if her brother had always been so ... overbearing. No, this was new. He was likely still worried about her. If that were the case, she'd have to talk to him. In the meantime, she made a mental note never to fall apart at his house again.

She and Adrian were close, but cool about it. Sometimes, they'd go weeks without talking. From an early age, they understood each other. When he first met Hugo and worried that a 'smoke show' like that – his words, not hers – wouldn't fall for a boring doctor like him, he'd sent her a screenshot of his profile with the briefest of messages: **Smash or—?**

To which she'd replied: **Smash, for sure!!!**

Guys like that don't go for guys like me, he texted back.

Hold on. I'll get the manual ... Looks like you're wrong, bro. Says here they absolutely do.

Kya might've had a sixth sense about Hugo. Although she hadn't predicted marriage, she knew he and Adrian would hit it off. How had Adrian not known about Quinn? Did he really need a third party to clue him in? Hadn't he picked up on her emotional turmoil?

In the elevator, Kya shot Hugo a message. **Hey! Didn't you tell him???**

Hugo replied straight away. He had no doubt expected to hear from her. **Nope. Sam and I talked it over. We think it's your news to tell.**

The one time she'd counted on her brother-in-law's indiscretion, he let her down! It would have saved her an awkward conversation with Adrian. He would be happy for her, of course he would. A little too happy, maybe. He'd see this new relationship as a quick fix to all her problems. Plus, he'd have heaps of brotherly advice. So much advice, she wouldn't know what to do with it. Much of it wouldn't apply, anyway. She and Quinn were too new; they weren't at the meet-the-family stage of things.

Kya: Blood Orange tonight?

Hugo: Definitely.

She pocketed her phone and put Adrian, Hugo, Sam, Roman, and the whole affair out of her mind. She was home.

The apartment was quiet when Kya let herself in. She slipped off her sandals and placed them neatly beside Quinn's in the entryway and took the takeaway bag into the kitchen and set it on the counter. The note she'd stuck to the refrigerator, as well as the one on the front door, were missing, which meant Quinn had found them.

From the bedroom, Quinn called out, 'Is that you, K?'

Kya went to her. She was curled in bed, the sheets down to her hips, her arms wrapped tight around a pillow.

'Who were you expecting?' she asked from the doorway.

Quinn stirred and raised her head off the pillow. 'Cute outfit, babe.'

She considered the outfit she'd slapped together with little thought or care. 'Thanks.'

'Now take it off.'

'Excuse me?'

She lifted the blanket, as if opening a portal to her warmth and love. 'That's the price of admission.'

'No fair,' Kya mumbled, even as she tore at her clothes. 'You're still dressed.'

'Hardly! Besides, I know you love a challenge.'

Kya slipped under the blanket as soon as her bra hit the floor. Quinn drew her close, but it took some work to strip off her cotton top and get to silky skin. She told Kya where to put her hands and how to touch her. Kya would have done anything to please her, but she had her own ideas; things she'd thought about all through brunch. What resulted was the sweetest battle of wills. It was torture. It was fun. It was one climax after another until they fell, panting, on their backs.

'That was amazing,' Kya said, breathless.

'*You're* amazing.'

'No, you are.'

'I said it first.'

'I take it back,' Kya said. 'You're a brat.'

'Stop arguing,' Quinn said. 'Kiss me. I missed you this morning.'

Kya didn't resist. She kissed her and whispered, 'Thanks for agreeing to go out tonight. That was sweet of you.'

'Actually, the timing is perfect,' Quinn said. 'I just heard from Amanda and she got the job. We likely would have gone out anyway to celebrate.'

Kya gasped. 'Amanda got the promotion?'

'Yes! She called me a minute ago in tears. She's very teary lately; have you noticed? Turns out they reached out to her on Friday via email. And the message was sitting in her inbox all weekend long. Can you imagine? Ignoring your work emails and simply enjoying your holiday?'

'I can't imagine,' Kya said, flatly. 'What kind of freaks are you?'

'The kind you like?' Quinn suggested.

'So, we're back at Blood Orange,' Kya said. 'Full circle.'

Quinn slipped a hand under her T-shirt. 'It's always a good time.'

Kya sank deeper into the pillows. The scent of lavender washed over her. 'What did you make of me when I requested that song?'

'Honestly?' Quinn asked.

Kya nodded, bracing herself for the absolute worst.

'I thought you were bold for asking for what you wanted,' she replied.

'Bold?' Kya couldn't believe it. Could she not see how nervous she was at the time?

'Yes, bold!' Quinn said. 'I don't expect others to read my mind, but I don't often ask for anything. I wait and see how things unfold.'

'You might wait forever.'

'It's not the best strategy,' she conceded. 'I'm trying to get better at asking for the things I want, but I'm patient.'

What did Quinn want that she didn't already have? And what did she want from her? Kya would not ask; she would wait and see. 'How do you feel this morning?' she asked, instead.

'Like death. Like I've been run over by a truck or trampled by wild horses.'

Kya turned to her, alarmed. 'That bad?'

'It's part of the job,' Quinn said. 'I love it. I could do it over again if they asked.'

Kya shifted uncomfortably. This might be the thing she was most envious of in the entire world, this love for the life you had, this knowing you were doing what you were put on earth to do. Would she ever have that?

'I brought you brunch.'

'You're always bringing me food!'

'Should I stop?'

'Don't you dare stop!' Quinn warned. 'I feel so pampered.'

'That's the goal.'

She nuzzled closer, caught Kya's earlobe between her teeth and tugged. 'I got your notes, silly girl,' she whispered. 'Don't be so paranoid. I knew you'd be back. Nothing is like last time.'

'I'm still so sorry for putting you through that,' Kya said. 'I'll never stop apologizing.'

'I beg you to stop!' Quinn cried. 'You've apologized and apologized. I still have that first note to prove it.'

'Do you?'

She nodded, then did the sweetest thing and recited the note by heart only with a twist. 'I like you a little too much, and it doesn't scare me.'

Kya took her face between her hands. There was that gleam in her eyes, diamond bright. 'Not even a little scared?' she asked.

'No,' Quinn answered. 'Now, what did you bring me to eat?'

CHAPTER FORTY-TWO

The speakeasy was tucked away in the back room of a tattoo parlour. A special code was required to access it, and it was best to wait for your entire party to arrive before making your way to the door. Conveniently enough, they'd arrived within seconds of each other and, with introductions out of the way, Ivy had something to say. 'This may be our last night out together. We have to make the most of it.'

'Jesus, Ivy, don't be so dramatic,' Amanda said.

'It's true,' Ivy insisted. 'Kya will be gone soon. Who knows when you'll be back. Quinn and I are workaholics at heart. And you, Hugo, have been nesting these last few months.'

'Hunting down vintage furniture is a full-time job,' Hugo said in his defence.

'It feels like I'm witnessing the end of an era that I missed out on,' Sam said, frowning. 'Hugo, remember that time—'

'No,' Ivy interrupted her bluntly. 'This is not the time for reminiscing. We're making memories tonight, not reliving old ones.'

'Hear, hear!' Amanda cried, ready to go.

Quinn reached for Kya's hand. 'I like this energy; keep it up. But Kya isn't going anywhere anytime soon. So, chill on that.'

Kya didn't know what to say, and was grateful when Sam, nervous, stepped forward. 'In that case, I've got news,' she said. 'My boyfriend is going to propose ... soon.'

Amanda, standing next to her, pulled her into a one-arm hug. 'Congrats! Exciting news!'

Ivy was more cautious. 'Hold on. He's *going* to propose? He hasn't yet?'

Kya sided with Ivy. Wasn't this announcement premature?

'No, but I'm onto him. He's not that clever. There was a very small, very luxe-looking package delivered to our flat which he signed for and hid away.'

'Are you sure that wasn't the latest iPhone?' Amanda asked, concerned. 'Men are precious about things like that.'

'She has a point,' Kya said. 'An iPhone, a drone, a Nintendo Switch ...'

Sam dismissed the argument. 'It wasn't a gadget! You don't go to Hatton Garden for a Nintendo.'

'Right,' Ivy said, although she, like Kya and Hugo, had no idea where that was.

'We're on our way to Tobago tomorrow,' Sam continued. 'He planned the trip. He never plans trips.'

'But he's from Tobago,' Hugo pointed out. 'I plan our trips to Brazil. It's easier that way.'

Sam was losing patience with all of them. 'That's where we met and that's where he'll do it. He bought a ring. He booked a flight. He's going to propose. I know it.'

Quinn flew to her defence. 'When you know, you know.'

Sam shot her a thankful look.

'Do you think he'll do it in the sacred waters?' Hugo asked.

'What sacred waters?' Amanda asked.

'Never mind,' Sam said. 'It's a long story, and it won't matter where he does it. Tobago is magical.'

'Will you say yes?' Ivy asked.

'Yes, I'll say yes! And this will be the first of many hen do parties. I'm harnessing girl power to get me down the aisle.'

Amanda offered a translation for all the non-UK girls. 'That's a bachelorette party.'

'Before I'm a fussy married lady, I want to party in Miami.'

'You can party in Miami, regardless,' Quinn said. 'Married or not. What difference does it make?'

'This is what I needed to hear,' she said, looking nervously from one to the other. 'And why I wanted to hang out with you lot tonight. I'm not going to turn into my mum just because I'm getting married.'

It wasn't a question, but her uncertainty was obvious. Sam, though she loved Roman, though she wanted nothing more than to marry him and spend the rest of her life with him, was freaking out. Funny how that worked out, Kya thought. The thing you wanted most terrified you.

'I don't know your mum, but no,' Amanda assured her. 'We don't turn into our mothers. We turn into ourselves.'

And with that bit of wisdom, they entered the speakeasy through the tattoo parlour.

Kya was struck with nostalgia as soon as she entered the venue. It was familiar, yet not. The dance floor was smaller than she remembered, and so was the stage. There was the bar where she'd ordered a tequila and sat feeling miserable and out of place. Down the hall, to the left, was the dark and moody restroom where she'd first locked eyes with Quinn. To the right was the lounge where she'd nursed those god-awful cocktails. It was filling up fast. A couple was kissing at the table where Ivy and Victor had broken up. Kya remembered the scene vividly, Ivy rushing out the nearest exit in tears. Yet tonight, when Victor showed up, Ivy did not run or hide, like last time. She nodded and managed a half-smile. That was growth.

Amanda located the props set aside for karaoke night and found everything she needed to turn Sam into a blushing bachelorette: a veil, a blue garter to slip on over the leg of her jeans, and a sash with the words KISS THE BRIDE in sparkling pink.

Sam was game, but she had one request. 'No photos, please! Roman will think I've lost my mind.'

'You heard the bride!' Amanda cried. 'Put away those phones!'

Then there was nothing left to do but order a round of shots, followed by another, then storm the dance floor and dance like mad. Other women wished Sam well or stuffed dollar bills down her halter top. It was her every dream come true.

After midnight, they took a break on the back patio. There, Kya would soon learn more congratulations were in order. An interior design magazine had contacted Hugo seeking to feature the new home in a future publication. Kya was floored. Hugo in glossy print? How had his head not yet exploded?

'A magazine credit or two is enough to get started,' he said.

'Yes, of course.' This was way more than a vanity trip. He needed the exposure to pivot into home design. 'What good timing!'

'It's going to be insane getting the house ready.'

'More like you're going to drive everyone insane,' Kya said.

'But don't worry. I'll be out of your way. Adrian must be so proud!'

'It was his idea to buy the house, so he's very pleased with himself.'

'Adrian is the smartest person I know, and he's always right.'

He clinked his glass to hers. '*Saúde!*'

Kya tried sharing the news with Quinn, but more and more people were crowding her and congratulating her on her Solstice set. They insisted that she was one of the best performers of the night. Kya moved aside and watched the scene unfold. It was as if a cosmic piñata had been smacked open and goodies were raining down: dream jobs, promotions, media exposure, engagement rings. And Kya, like an idiot, had somehow come up empty-handed. She had nothing to boast about except a TikTok account with a few thousand followers, the popularity of which was based on her girlfriend's work. She knew she shouldn't feel this way, petty and small. She should be happy for everyone. She *was* happy for everyone. She wholeheartedly wanted Hugo to break into his dream industry. She was relieved Ivy had got over Victor and was turning towards her future. She was overjoyed for Amanda for clinching that promotion. Finally, she was proud of Quinn, so proud her heart could burst. Why then was a whiny little voice in her mind repeating: *What about me?*

The mob cleared and their little group joined them.

'What's next?' Amanda asked them.

'For us? London!' Quinn replied.

'I meant what's next for tonight, but yay! London!' Amanda cried. 'The things we'll do! The places we'll go! The damage we'll do! London is not ready!'

Forget London, Kya wasn't ready.

'Don't get too excited,' she said. 'It's just something we talked about.'

'We agreed,' Quinn said. 'We're going.'

Sam offered to set up their itinerary. 'I'll give you a list of the new hot spots to hit.'

'Thanks, Sam,' Kya said. 'Those spots may not be so new by the time we get there, but I appreciate it.'

'Hold on!' Quinn said. 'Are you trying to get out of this?'

There wasn't anything to get out of. They'd discussed a trip on the balcony the other morning over coffee and tea. Discussion wasn't even the right word, far from it. Quinn had brought it up, and Kya had liked the idea. They hadn't crossed out dates, or checked flights, or anything like that.

Sensing trouble, the others dispersed just as quickly as they'd arrived. Sam went to return her borrowed bachelorette accessories. Hugo thought he saw someone he knew at the far side of the patio. Ivy and Amanda left to check out the view.

There was no view.

Quinn confronted her, but with such tenderness, Kya was instantly disarmed. 'What is it? You don't want to come away with me, anymore?'

Kya's heart tanked. 'Of course I do. It's just—'

'Sorry to interrupt.' Two girls in their twenties, full make-up and minidresses, approached tentatively. 'Just wanted to say that we're obsessed with you. Pretty sure we started the K&Q hashtag. You're everything we want to be.'

Somehow, Kya and Quinn managed to return bright smiles. 'That's so sweet,' Quinn said. 'Thanks.'

'Can we get a picture with you?' one asked.

'Yeah, sure,' Kya said.

The girls recruited a third friend to take the photo. Kya and Quinn shuffled around and posed as the perfect couple for two strangers who didn't know any better.

CHAPTER FORTY-THREE

Sometime later, Kya ran into Ivy in the ladies' room. Over a shared box of breath mints, they got to talking.

'What's up with you?' Ivy asked. 'Are you leaving? Are you staying? Are you going to London?'

'You got it right the first time. I'm leaving soon.'

'Then Quinn got it wrong,' Ivy said. 'Did you tell her?'

'She knows.'

It wasn't as if she was blindsiding Quinn. She had to go home at some point. The food rotting away in her refrigerator wasn't going to clear itself out.

Ivy fluffed her hair in the smoky mirror. 'It's the lunar eclipse, forcing us to make tough choices.'

Kya hadn't taken the lunar eclipse into account, but she didn't really have a choice. She had to resume her life already in progress.

'Maybe it's this club,' Kya said. 'It's strange being back here. Do you know this is where I saw you for the first time? I was in the lounge with Hugo, and you were at the next table, breaking up with Victor.'

'Oh my God!' Ivy cried, horrified. 'That was your first impression of me? I was at my worst. That was a rock-bottom moment.'

'For me, too,' Kya admitted. 'I was sulky, whiny, and all-around miserable. I hate to say it, but your ordeal made me feel a little less tragic.'

'Misery loves company,' Ivy said. 'Look at us now, thriving!'

Kya didn't know about that. Tonight, she felt as though she were floundering.

The door swung open, and Amanda poked her head in. 'Come on, ladies. We're getting out of here.'

'Where are we going?' Ivy asked. As the ringleader, those decisions usually went through her.

'To a bar on the beach, Ocean Drive.'

Ivy made a face. 'Those bars are tourist traps!'

'Sam is a tourist,' Amanda pointed out. 'She'll love it. Come on. It'll be fun.'

Amanda and Kya were also tourists, although they would never admit it.

'All right. Let's go,' Ivy said.

So much for an early night.

The bar on Ocean Drive was loud. They overcharged for watered-down cocktails served in novelty glasses by a team of gorgeous waitresses who flirted shamelessly as they collected their tips. Sam and Amanda loved it, and it was fun. Ivy loosened up. Quinn was greeted like a star. Only, Kya couldn't get into it. Not even when a few celebrities showed up, and ordered watered-down drinks for everyone to show off. Not even when Sam, Ivy, Amanda, and Quinn hopped onto the bar and started singing along to yet another song Kya had never heard. Since Hugo knew the lead bartender, it wasn't a problem. The scene was caught on camera, anyway, and likely going viral, generating free publicity for all parties involved.

She wanted to join the fun. She wanted to make memories, like Ivy had ordered them to. But the girls were celebrating, and she was sulking. These were parallel paths that would never cross.

The adjoining space was a quieter game room with a dartboard and a pool table. Kya decided to hide there. She approached a stranger and proposed a round of pool. Although she was readily handing him his ass, she took no joy in it.

'Okay, you got me,' her opponent said. 'You won fair and square.'

He was a guy – a standard bloke, as Quinn would say. He didn't take too kindly to losing.

'Beginner's luck,' she said to appease him. 'Another round? Maybe you'll do better.'

'No, thanks.'

He set down the cue and backed away slowly. Kya gathered the balls and set them one by one in the triangular rack. This was peak avoidance, she realized. She didn't know what to do with herself. She should join the others.

'*Minha irmã*,' Hugo said. 'What are you doing in here by yourself?'

'It's quiet in here. That's all.'

'Is that all?'

Kya didn't bother to lie; he could see right through her. 'What have you got there?' she asked, eyeing the silver platter in his hands.

'Onion rings. The best in the city.'

They sat leaning against the edge of the pool table, munching on onion rings in thoughtful silence. Then Hugo had to ruin it by asking, 'Now tell me. Why are you hiding?'

'You won't judge me?'

'I'll judge you, but so what? We're family.'

She leaned on his shoulder. 'True.'

'Go on. What's troubling you this time?'

'This time! You make it sound like it's a recurring thing.'

'It's been a rough month for you. What we won't do is pretend that it wasn't.'

'Everyone has something to celebrate tonight.'

'Everyone except you?'

She nodded and helped herself to another onion ring.

'Good things are coming, he said. 'You'll see.'

'I had a good thing,' Kya said. 'It wasn't great; I know. It was actually pretty awful, but it was mine. I've lost it. Everyone thinks I should have gotten over it by now. Like it's easy to turn the page. It's not easy.'

'Everyone?' he asked, sceptical. 'I don't know a single person who expects that from you.'

'Maybe it's just Quinn, then?'

Even as she said it, she realized it was unfair to Quinn. She had never pushed her, but she did have certain expectations that Kya could not meet right now. Hopping on a plane to the UK, for one.

'She wants to see you happy,' he said. 'We all do, but you're going to have good days and bad days.'

'I'm going back, soon. This week. No more delays.'

Hugo looked at her steadily. 'Just promise you won't go begging for your old job back. It was awful, and you deserve better.'

'I won't!' she promised. 'Maybe something with remote work. Sam loves being a digital nomad.'

'Yeah, but you have to figure out what *you* love.'

She loved being here with Quinn and her family. She just

didn't love feeling like a failure all the time. She could not shake off that feeling.

'I want you to know that I get it,' Hugo said. 'I was in the exact same position as you last year.'

'No, you weren't!'

She didn't mean to minimize his experience, but she couldn't recall a time when he'd been fired or cancelled or publicly shamed. Hugo was loved and cherished by all.

He gave her one of his dazzling smiles. 'You don't think so? My career is in the can. Meanwhile, your brother wins award after award.'

'Ugh! He does win an awful lot of trophies.' She thought of the mantel in their family home, riddled with Adrian's plaques and awards. So, Hugo did understand how horrible it felt to be proud of your partner while drowning in self-pity. 'I feel your pain.'

'And I feel yours,' he said. 'And if you ever need to talk, I'm here with onion rings.'

'They're pretty good,' she said. 'But I'm going to need water now.'

'I got you.'

He kissed her on the cheek, and left for the bar. Only it was Quinn who returned with her water. Tonight, she looked ethereal, in a delicate minidress in a pale pink with thin straps. She could go her whole life and never know anyone as beautiful as Quinn.

'Here you go,' she said.

'Thanks.' Kya took the glass from her, took a sip, and set it on the table.

'I think Sam had the night of her life,' she said. 'What do you think?'

'Well, if it turns out this hen do was for nothing, at least she had a good time.'

Quinn shook her head. 'So cynical,' she said. 'I think you've had enough. Let me take you home.'

PART VII

BONUS TRACK

CHAPTER FORTY-FOUR

It was just the two of them in the back seat of the car, and the ride was tense. Quinn stared out the window. The city was a glossy black, its vivid colours muted. She glanced at Kya who sat staring straight ahead, arms folded across her chest. The last time they'd gone through this, after her so-so performance at LAB, Quinn had been the silent partner, short-tempered and in no mood to talk. Therefore, she was in no position to harass Kya now. Really, she should just let her be, but she couldn't just sit here. She was jumping out of her skin. How had they got to this point? Just this morning they were so happy.

'Kya, you are killing me. Say *something*.'

'I'm sorry,' she said.

The problem was that Kya was feeling sorry for herself; that much Quinn had figured out.

'Never mind that,' she said. 'Just tell me what's wrong. Don't you want to go to London anymore?'

'That's not it.'

'It doesn't have to be London. It could be anywhere. You decide.'

She said this knowing full well a change in destination wasn't the solution. The problem was bigger than that.

Kya turned to her with an open, honest, heartbreaking gaze.

'I thought we were planning a trip sometime down the line, a few months in the future.'

'I just thought, since we're both free.'

'I'm *not* free!' she said, incredulous. 'I have to get my life in order. I promised you a week, and the week is over.'

'But you'll come back, won't you?'

Kya shrugged. 'I have no idea when that will be.'

'You don't have to stay in California to find work.'

'Yes, I do! That's where the jobs are. That's where my life is, Quinn. There are some businesses here, but all the major players are out west.'

'So, you're going to pick up where you left off?'

'Yes, that was the plan all along.'

'What about all this talk about starting your own company, becoming independent, even freelancing?' Quinn wasn't making any sense with these questions, but a cloud of panic had fogged her brain.

'Did I say anything about freelancing?' she asked.

'Maybe. I don't remember.'

All this talk and she couldn't say what was in her heart: *I don't want you to go. Stay. Stay with me. This doesn't have to end.*

'Jade, I'm not like you. I don't get paid to party. I need a stable income.'

Those words stomped out the silent plea of Quinn's heart. She wasn't sure if it was her use of her first name, which instantly put space between them, or the oversimplification of her career that caused her to flinch.

'If that's what you think I'm doing, Kya, getting paid to party, then I think we're done,' she replied, sharply. She was sick of defending her career and explaining herself. Kya could join the lot of critics if she liked.

'That's not what I think!' Kya cried in frustration. 'Look, I'm trying to tell you how I feel and doing a poor job. I can't do this tonight. My head is swimming.'

'I don't understand,' Quinn said. 'After everything you've been through, you're going to run back and join another corporate entity?'

Kya laughed. 'You make it sound like I'm joining a cult.'

'I may not be a computer specialist, but I know this: if you think success is working at some big company, you're going to be disappointed. You can get another job, of course you can. But they'll toss you out when they're done with you.'

'What are you talking about?' Kya wailed. 'It's a *job*. Every day, all over the world, people start new ones. It's not that big of a deal. You were happy for Amanda when she got her promotion. Can't you be happy for me?'

'It's not the same!'

How could she compare the two? Last she'd checked, Amanda and her friends hadn't been humiliated by Harrods.

'It's the building to the left, right?' their driver asked.

His booming voice startled them both. They'd forgotten where they were. Quinn offered more accurate directions, pointed out the building, even a free spot where he could let them out – anything to keep from arguing with Kya.

They were silent in the lobby. They were silent in the lift. Once they made it to the flat, Quinn went straight to the walk-in closet to change out of her dress. When she came out, wrapped in a dressing gown, Kya was busy shoving clothes into her bag.

'What are you doing?'

'Packing.'

'Seriously? You're running away again?'

'No, I'm not. I'm hanging out with Adrian tomorrow night, and I might as well do laundry while I'm there. They always have the good stuff.'

'You're hanging out?'

'Movie night. He wants to catch up.'

'You never mentioned it.'

Oh, God! Quinn hated to nag, and yet she couldn't stop the interrogation.

'It came up after brunch. I forgot to tell you. He's so concerned about me. It's a little over the top. Anyway, I should spend some time with him before heading home.'

Home …

'And when will that be, if you don't mind my asking?'

'Soon. As soon as possible.' She zipped the bag shut and finally faced her. 'Don't look at me like that.'

'Like what?'

'Like you don't understand, because I know you do,' she said, a crack running through her voice. 'Please don't make it difficult.'

Quinn wanted it to be difficult. Why should it be easy for her to walk away?

She went over to the bedside table and found the note Kya had stuck to her door this morning. She'd smiled and even laughed a little when she found it, thinking they were past all of that. Kya had been kidding herself when she wrote it. This was *exactly* like last time. They'd come full circle, only to land at the very spot where they'd started. She handed the note to Kya. She took it with shaking hands, then walked past her and locked herself in the bathroom. Quinn heard her running the tap, brushing her teeth.

Quinn left the bedroom for the safety of her studio. She dropped into her padded chair, suddenly excessively tired. She wanted to knock down the bathroom door and grab Kya. She wanted to tell her that no matter where she went, it would be fine. She could look for employment at the ends of the earth if she wanted. It would change nothing for her. She would be right here. Or she would follow. Or they would come to some hybrid arrangement. But she wouldn't do it. She could not reassure Kya any more than she'd already done. At some point, Kya would have to decide if they were worth saving. Quinn would wait, but that was all she was willing to do.

The next day, Quinn stuck to the routines that got her through the toughest times. She woke up early, slipped on gym clothes, grabbed her keys, filled a bottle with water, and headed to boot camp. It was her turn to sneak out and leave Kya, curled up at the furthest edge of the bed and fast asleep. Second to her home studio, this gym was her safe space. Only this morning, it was an emotional minefield. She walked past the smoothie bar where she and Kya had confronted each other on more than one occasion. She did not linger in the weights room where sometimes she ran into Adrian, and avoided the punching bag, Kya's spot. Plus, there was the car park where they'd once planned a spontaneous trip without any drama. They were a team, then. A proper couple. That was before Kya had decided to freeze her out.

Quinn was a fighter. But, sometimes, you had to learn when to give up the fight. If Kya needed distance to reshape her life, she would give her distance. If she needed a fresh start, then who was Quinn to stop her? No one could have talked her out of chasing her dreams. She'd left relationships behind, a home, a family, close friends; she'd sacrificed it all to fulfil her ambitions. She'd never been on the other side of that equation. She'd never been the one left behind. Well … that wasn't exactly true. Once or twice, she might have been dumped, but those guys didn't count. They'd never mattered to her, not like Kya mattered. They hadn't left a hole in her heart, like the one she had now, growing deeper by the minute. If she'd managed to outrun heartache her whole life, it was catching up with her now. It hurt so badly; she could hardly breathe. She would never wish this feeling on anyone.

Quinn skipped out of a Burn 'n' Sculpt class and retreated to the locker room. Even in the privacy of the shower stall, with steaming hot water raining down on her – the ideal place to melt down, if there ever was one – she couldn't bring herself to cry. She wouldn't allow it. She held herself together. This break-up wasn't going to break her. It would hurt for weeks, months, even years, but she'd get over it. Ivy had said something about a lunar eclipse imposing tough choices, forcing change. But, really, what choice did Quinn have but to take care of herself and survive?

CHAPTER FORTY-FIVE

Sam greeted her at Adrian's door, and announced her arrival. 'Hey, guys! Kya is here!'

The guys, Hugo and Roman, were carrying luggage down the hall and out to the garage. Adrian had already left for work. Sam was dressed for travel in her finest athleisure set, her face scrubbed clean and her hair in a bun.

'Come in,' she said. 'Did you come to say goodbye?'

'Yup!' Actually, she'd come to hide and avoid Quinn. Real mature.

They were off to Tobago where they'd stay at a resort for a couple of nights then at a cottage owned by Roman's grandfather. Sam had told them all this, in some detail, the night before. You'd never seen a girl look so tired, yet so luminous.

'Want coffee?' she asked. 'I'm so hungover. I don't know how you girls do it, night after night. I'd be dead, but I have no regrets. I had the best time. You should see the pictures! I know we said no pictures, still I took some. I'm dying to show Roman! It's torture because we share everything—'

Kya seized Sam by the elbow, marched her to Hugo's home office, and shut the door behind them.

'Oh! I get it!' Sam said, laughing. 'You want to see the photos!'

She was already pulling out her phone.

'No, I don't,' Kya said. She was sorry for the blunt tone, but they were short on time. 'I want you to tell me exactly how you did it. Like, for real. Step by step, how did you build your brand and business?'

She didn't want another inspirational pep talk. From one girl to another, she wanted the facts. How difficult was this undertaking? What were the odds of success? What obstacles would she be facing? How much would it cost, in time, in capital, and sweat equity? Seeing Sam, so radiant and happy, so *free*, on this terrible morning, Kya caught a glimpse of the person she wanted to be.

'Oh … That makes much more sense!' Sam tapped on her web browser instead of her photo app. 'Come. Show me your analytics and we'll work on a strategy to get from where you are to where you want to be.'

A solid twenty minutes later, when Hugo came tapping at the door, they had covered substantial ground. Kya walked her to the packed car. Sam renewed her promise to share the resources she'd gathered over the years. 'Just reach out. Hugo has my number, or hop onto our group chat.'

Adrian had told her all about that epic group chat, and Kya would not be joining. 'Thanks, and good luck,' she said. 'Let us know how it goes for you in Tobago, either way.'

Kya hugged her briefly, said goodbye to Roman, and then they were off to the airport.

The house was quiet when she took her bag to the bedroom. The original plan had been to collapse in bed and cry all day, but the idea no longer appealed to her. Now that she had a plan, she was feeling more like herself. Feeling like herself didn't stop her from feeling lonely.

Kya made her way to the kitchen, Lucky trailing happily at

her heels, her tail wagging. She filled the puppy's water bowl and poured herself a cup of coffee. She thumbed through the task list Sam had left her with while heating oat milk in the microwave. An email alert popped onto her phone's screen. A cry escaped her and ricocheted through the empty house.

From: Ron.Anderson@AIM.com
To: KReid@linkedin.com
Subject: Job Opportunity

Kya:

Hope this email finds you in good shape.

We've got a friend in common. Corinne Miller insists I hire you. I'm looking to expand my team; interviews are underway at HQ. If you're interested, let me know when you can come in, the sooner the better.

Sorry about the shakeup at Ex-Cell. It happens!

Ron

Ronald J. Anderson, Senior Design Officer
AI.M Technologies, San José
AI in Motion

Little Ronny Anderson? Of all people! He was a good four years her senior, but the old college nickname had stuck. They'd had friends in common back then, as well. Most recently, they spent a week in Austin hunting down barbecue between conferences at SXSW. The new dad was easy-going, passionate about his work, and liked his ribs coated in sauce. He was an ordinary guy who happened to lead an award-winning design team at AI.M, an artificial intelligence development company.

Dizzy, Kya pressed her forehead onto the cool refrigerator door. She should be happy, overjoyed! She should at the very least be grateful. She couldn't have asked for more. A job at AI.M would restore everything she'd lost, not the least her dignity. No one could laugh or look down at her then. No one could pity her. Artificial intelligence was the most dynamic field. Good or bad, it was the future. She could resume her blogging on her regular platform and be done with it. Why then was she having a panic attack? She stood with her forehead to the refrigerator, trying to regulate her breathing, until the milk boiled over in the microwave. She wiped up the mess and poured the milk down the drain. When she turned off the tap, the house was oddly still. Lucky was asleep in her bed in a sunny corner in the kitchen. The vintage analogue clock ticked the seconds. She knew what she had to do.

Within a half-hour, Kya had confirmed an interview on Friday with the understanding that it would be the first of many, as AI.M was notorious for its multistage hiring process. She did not care. Here, at last, was the lifeline she'd been waiting for. No matter how she felt, she would grab it and not let it go. Before she could talk herself out of it, she booked a flight home.

MIAMI TO SAN JOSE, TUESDAY 3:00PM, NON-STOP.

All that was left to do was inform her little circle. She sent a screenshot of her flight information to Adrian and Hugo. Got a job interview this week! Flying home on Tuesday to prepare.

Adrian replied right away. Wow! Congrats! Can't wait to hear all about it. We'll celebrate tonight.

A while later, Hugo responded with a thumbs-down emoji, followed by a winky-face emoji. Kya didn't like it. If there was one thing she knew about her brother-in-law, his first instincts were always right.

She paced around the kitchen wondering how best to break the news to Quinn. Should she call her? Would she answer?

Going for this job meant there would be no trips in their immediate future. She'd be too busy jumping through the hoops and hurdles of the interview process. She would have to stay focused. Once she got the job, she likely wouldn't have enough paid time off to take a trip for a while. Maybe Quinn could fly out west for a week or so. All this pointed to their great weakness. They had no fixed address, no permanent place to which they belonged. Quinn had a lucrative residency in Miami, and Kya's old life was calling. Vacation was over. It was time to pack and go.

She decided to break the news via text. **You won't believe this. Corinne Miller came through! I have a job interview at the end of the week. Flying home on Tuesday. This is just a heads up. Talk soon?**

Quinn didn't respond. Not one word, not a single emoji. As time passed, Kya realized that Quinn had no intention of responding – ever. She would keep calm and carry on. Yet, here Kya sat, like an idiot, staring at her phone, twisted in knots over this girl.

Kya's phone buzzed and she leaped for joy, only to come crashing down when she saw that it was Jon calling. And if she let one more of his calls go to voicemail, he would never speak to her again. She took the call.

'Hey,' Jon said. 'It's our last day here. I thought you might want to come and hang out. We could chill by the pool and talk.'

'Where did you say you were staying?'

'The Standard.'

That wasn't very far from the house. She could bike there. 'I'll be right over.'

'All right. Come through.'

Perfect. She had someplace to go and something to do – anything to keep her from obsessing over Quinn.

Jon met her at the hotel lobby. Liam had reserved their lounge chairs then left them alone to swim a few laps. They ordered iced coffees and settled back in the shade of umbrellas. It was a lovely set-up, the pool as blue as the sky above and the surrounding bay. Kya put her phone away and tried to soak it in.

'This is a chic hotel,' Kya said. 'We're unemployed. Shouldn't we be dialling it down?'

'Maybe, but I deserve it. Besides, YouTube keeps me afloat.'

'You have a YouTube channel?'

'Who doesn't?'

She raised her hand. 'Me!'

The wrinkle between his wispy brows creased deeper. 'I review tech. I thought you knew?'

'How would I know if you never told me?'

'I might've mentioned it during lunch.'

'Might have mentioned it? You should have sent me a link. Asked me to subscribe. Come on, Jon! I thought we were besties.'

'I'll be honest. I didn't want my co-workers to know.'

'I'm a random co-worker to you? You knew about my blog!'

'Your blog is noble and good. I give honest reviews on our products and our competitors' products. I think someone caught wind, and that's why I got cut. Who knows?'

They would never fully understand why they were fired, and not the others. They could spin a multitude of theories, but the best thing was to let it go.

'Actually, this is a great segue to what I wanted to talk to you about. Here's my pitch for GIRL DECODED. It's an app.'

Kya stirred her ice coffee with the straw. 'Not another goddamn app, Jon. Why would anyone download an app if you can't get a date or a deal on a designer bag?'

'I hear you,' he said. 'But we would add value. Your blog, for one thing. My reviews, for another. Maybe a social media component in the future. Essentially, it's a safe space for women to network, make friends, and get the information they need to make informed decisions. We pull together and make something new.'

Kya closed her eyes and tried to visualize it. For the first time, she could *see* it.

'For a strong launch, we'd have to pull in good numbers straight away.'

'A chunk of your followers would follow you. Plus, more than half of my YouTube followers are women.'

'Why? Because you're so cute?'

'Because I'm not an obnoxious tech bro with a God complex.'

'That'll do it,' Kya said. 'What are your numbers?'

'A half-million followers. Triple the views.'

'A half-million!'

Her sharp cry startled the woman sunbathing in a nearby chair and earned her a sharp side-eye.

Jon nudged her. 'I can't help it if people love me.'

'I guess not,' Kya said. 'What's the name of your channel? I'll look it up tonight.'

'The Queer Code.'

'I love it!'

'It's good, right?'

'So, why are you giving it up? Why should our app be just for the girls, not the gays?'

'The app can't be another tech review channel. You can get that information anywhere. We need your brand.'

'Hmm ...' Kya wasn't convinced. 'Let's revisit this when we're back on the West Coast. I'm booked on a flight out tomorrow.'

'What's the rush?' he asked. 'I'd stay, but Liam has to get back.'

She hadn't wanted to bring up the interview, but she couldn't lie to a possible future business partner. 'I have an interview with AI.M.'

'No shit? That's a big deal.'

'If I get it, sure.'

'You'll get it,' he said. 'Where does that leave us?'

'It changes nothing,' she assured him. 'I have to work, can't afford not to. But my future isn't tied to a corporation. I want to build something, too.'

Jon was silent for a while. Finally, he said, 'Too bad. Isn't Quinn headlining Bonus Track on Tuesday, the concert on the beach? Last year Idris Elba dropped in and played a while. It's always a vibe.'

This time when Kya closed her eyes it was to shut out all that awesome twinkling blue sea and sky. She felt too dark and ugly inside; it was too painful to gaze at. Kya had no doubt Quinn thought she'd booked the flight back to California on her last concert date on purpose, to drive home the point that she was moving on with her life. The interview wasn't until Friday; there truly was no rush. She could prepare just as well from Adrian's spare bedroom or Quinn's living room floor. No wonder she hadn't heard from her, and likely wouldn't anytime soon.

CHAPTER FORTY-SIX

Heads up? Quinn wanted someone's head on a spike, she was that furious. So suddenly, out of the blue, Kya secured a job interview? How likely was that? And if this was true, why hadn't she called with the news? Would she lie just to get away from her?

How could Kya be so careless with her feelings, with her heart? How could she fumble the bag so spectacularly? There was nothing Quinn could do to salvage this. Nothing more to do but wipe her hands of the entire situation. She'd loved and lost, that was just how it went sometimes. She wasn't the type to sit at home and wallow for a man or a woman or anyone. Yet, for a full hour that was exactly what she did. She circled the flat, trying to come up with a reply. Something cool, but clever, something witty. *Safe travels! Nice hanging out with you!* Or, *Bye, babe! Catch you next time!* Yes! That was it! It struck the right tone, detached but—

Quinn's phone rang in her hands. She nearly went blind with happiness until she realized it wasn't Kya calling. It was Amanda. She was off to the airport.

'Thought I'd swing by with Ivy to say goodbye.'

'You're leaving already?'

'I wish I could stay for your beach concert, but I have to go home. The fun is over, I'm afraid.'

Why did everyone keep saying that? *The fun is over. The party is over.* As if Quinn was only good for a good time, a welcome break from their hectic lives. Now they were all eager to get back to their routines, their commutes, their daily grind or whatever. As if her presence in their lives disrupted the natural order of things. It was insulting. Did anyone take a second to consider how it made her feel to be used like that? Were her relationships doomed to fail due to the nature of her work? Would she always be left behind?

'Q, are you still there?'

'I'm here,' she said. 'But, hey, why don't I ride with you to the airport?'

'You're not too busy?'

'Not for you!'

Amanda had come all this way for her, she could accompany her to the airport.

'We'll be right over.'

Quinn jumped into a pair of jeans and a plain T-shirt Kya had left behind. It still smelled of her skin. She was waiting in the lobby, chatting with Benny, when Amanda and Ivy pulled up. She squeezed into the back seat of Ivy's sports car and shared the tight space with odd pieces of Amanda's luggage, a vanity case from a posh British design house and last season's weekender bag from a trendy French designer. The perks of working for Harrods were on full display. 'I want that employee discount,' she reminded her.

'You'll get it,' Amanda said.

Ivy eased into the flow of traffic. 'Where's Kya?'

'We're done.'

Ivy hit the brakes and sent them all lurching forward. Amanda gripped the dashboard and cried, 'Don't kill us before I catch my flight!'

Don't kill us … That was such a Kya thing to say; it broke Quinn's heart.

Ivy sought her eyes in the rearview mirror. 'Are you *done* or on a break?'

'We're done. I was wasting my time with that girl.'

Amanda smoothed back her hair. 'Are you sure about that?'

'You two are a model couple,' Ivy said. 'You're open and communicative, and so supportive of each other. I've been taking notes.'

'Shred those notes,' Quinn said. 'They'll get you nowhere. I can't communicate worth a damn and Kya runs off whenever she gets scared.'

'We need details,' Amanda said. 'Where is she now? Where has she run off to?'

'To her brother's house for now, and she's booked her flight home. She says she has a job interview. I'm not sure I believe it.'

'Has she done this sort of thing before?' Amanda asked. 'Run off and hide, I mean. You make it sound like a pattern.'

'Once before, yes. It was a huge red flag, and I totally ignored it.'

'Sounds like a Victor move to me,' Ivy said, dryly.

'Kya is nothing like Victor,' Amanda said. 'And, since I'm headed to the airport and won't have to deal with any of the drama, I might as well say this: Victor isn't the villain in your story, Ivy. You are. You should have dumped him and moved on long ago. You kept hanging on even though it was clear as day the relationship was dead.'

Ivy gripped the steering wheel so hard, her knuckles turned white. 'I know it. I'm doing the work and can admit I kept the drama going.'

'We're proud of you, sweetie,' Amanda said. 'You've come so far.'

'It's a good thing you're heading home,' Ivy murmured. 'I wouldn't be good company tonight.'

Quinn and Amanda exchanged a glance and decided to steer the conversation in a different direction.

'Like I said,' Quinn continued. 'Kya booked her flight to California. She's running away.'

'That's not fair,' Amanda said. 'That's where she lives. What can she do? It's not like she can stay in Miami forever.'

'Why not? People live here, you know,' Ivy said. 'My family has lived here for generations.'

'All right, but it suits you, and your lifestyle.'

Quinn couldn't take it anymore. 'Just come out and say it. You think I'm a party girl, a silly little DJ, and Kya is too smart, too serious and important for me.'

Amanda opened wide eyes. 'My God, she's gone mad.'

'Listen, I get where you're coming from,' Ivy said. 'It's not easy working in the entertainment industry. People have their preconceived notions. They think you're erratic or unstable. If they're anything like my grandparents, they think you're too lazy to get a "real job". Why do you think I quit, and tried to transition to PR? But it changed nothing. So, screw it.'

'Nobody is handing out Nobel Prizes to fashion buyers, either,' Amanda said. 'I've been called everything from shallow to materialistic, and everything in between. Do you know what Brian said when I told him? He said I was thinking too small. I said, if you want to talk about small, let's talk about your small—'

'I hate to interrupt, because this is riveting, but your phone is buzzing non-stop,' Ivy said.

'Oh!' Amanda grabbed her phone off the centre deck charging station. As she reviewed her messages, the mood in the little car turned grim. Dark clouds gathered above. Fat drops of rain splattered onto the windshield. Ivy switched on the wipers.

'Bloody hell!' Amanda cried.

'What is it?' Quinn asked.

Amanda glared at her phone as if it had betrayed her. 'My flight is cancelled! It better not be the weather. It's just a little rain. This is a bright sunny day in London!'

It was a bright sunny day, here as well. The rain clouds would scatter eventually.

'Shit. It's not the weather. It's plain old incompetence. My flight is overbooked.'

'This happened to Kya the other week,' Quinn said. 'Her flight home was cancelled, and she decided to stay on.'

Amanda swivelled around to face her. 'Babe, God knows I love you and I really like Quinn, but let's make this crisis about me, okay? I have to get home. I need to report to HR, start training for the new job, and all that fun stuff.'

'That's fair,' Quinn said. 'Only one crisis at a time.'

Amanda started to tap on her phone screen in a frantic attempt to gather any information on the cancelled flight. Ivy reached out and lowered her phone. 'Never mind that. They're just going to put you on standby. I know a guy, a travel concierge. He'll help.'

'Who knows a travel concierge?' Quinn asked, bewildered.

'I do!' Ivy replied, smug.

'That's why you're my ride or die,' Amanda said.

Quinn took offence at that. 'What does that make me?'

'My one and only Q,' Amanda said with a cheeky smile.

'You're lucky I love you,' Quinn said. 'You're trying my last nerve today.'

Ivy got her concierge on the phone. He was a charming man named Oscar. She explained Amanda's predicament, and he promised to call back within the hour with an update. 'If I can get her on business class, would that work?'

'Sounds steep,' Ivy said.

'There's no cost,' he said. 'Consider this a professional courtesy. I hear you're on Trevor's shortlist.'

Ivy gasped. 'No, you didn't!'

'Yes, ma'am. Promise to remember me when you're handed the keys to the kingdom.'

'Oh, I will.'

She ended the call and all three of them gasped, screamed, drummed the dashboard, punched the air. The grim mood had lifted, and the dark clouds parted.

'It's happening!' Amanda cried. 'I can feel it.'

Ivy brushed away a tear. 'I feel it, too!'

'I love that Oscar. He's flirty,' Amanda said. 'Maybe you should look into it, Ivy.'

'Not now,' Ivy said. 'I'm focused on my career.'

'Spoken like a true rom-com heroine,' Quinn said.

'There's no point going to the airport, is there?' Amanda asked. 'Should we get a bite to eat? All this excitement has made me hungry.'

Quinn was up for it. She hadn't eaten all day. And a half-hour later, when Oscar called back with Amanda's flight confirmation number, they were at a fast-food drive-thru window, their takeaway order ready. Amanda had secured a window seat in business class on a direct flight to London, departing from

MIA in a few hours. That gave them a little time to kill before heading back to the airport.

To celebrate, they ordered extra crisps, and ate their lunch in the parked car.

'This is actually a good thing,' Amanda said. 'I was going to leave America without eating a proper greasy burger. That's ridiculous.'

'Now that we've got you sorted,' Quinn said. 'Could we focus on me, again? My crisis, my cancelled relationship? Is there a concierge for that?'

'We're here for you,' Ivy said. 'You don't need outside help.'

'Why not talk us through what happened?' Amanda suggested. 'Start from the beginning.'

'Sunday night took a toll on her,' Quinn said. 'When you think about it, we were all in high spirits, celebrating our wins, and it left her feeling like trash. I could see it happening in real time, and there was nothing I could do to stop it. She's insecure about getting fired, even after the way they treated her. Seeing us so happy brought all that up again. Now she's in a hurry to get back to the real world.'

Amanda pried open her hamburger and peeled off the lettuce. 'That's where some of us belong, sweetie.'

'And it doesn't mean you're over,' Ivy said. 'She's going back to Cali, not the International Space Station.'

'It's the way she minimized my work,' Quinn said. 'It's hurtful.'

'We were with her at Solstice,' Amanda said. 'I'm willing to bet good money on this: you could travel the world and never find a girl more devoted, more committed to your success, or prouder of your accomplishments than Kya Reid.'

'Period,' Ivy said. 'That girl is the president of your fan club. It used to be me, but I've passed the baton.'

'Q, you should've seen her face when you took the stage! My God! The girl was beaming!'

'Beaming!' Ivy echoed.

'Well, she wasn't beaming last night,' Quinn said. 'She was growling.'

'Like a mad dog?' Amanda asked.

'No … More like a wounded puppy.'

Ivy gulped her Diet Coke. 'That girl has feelings for you. She may growl like a puppy, but she's loyal.'

'Plus, we really like her, so could you please kiss and make up so we can all hang out together the next time I'm in town?' Amanda said.

Ivy checked the time. 'Speaking of travel. It's time to go.'

'Aw! But we were having so much fun!'

'Don't pout. Business class means you'll have access to the lounge.'

'Will there will be wings? Imagine leaving the States without eating buffalo wings. Tragic!'

Buffalo wings or no, their little interlude was over. They had to head back to the airport in order to ensure Amanda made her flight. Ivy wiped her greasy fingers on a napkin and started the car engine. They drove to the airport and, even though it was totally unnecessary, paid handsomely to park at the short-term car park. Ivy and Quinn each grabbed one of Amanda's suitcases and steered them to the airline gate.

'This is very sweet of you,' Amanda said, as she checked in. 'However, you two are going to have to cut the cord at some point.'

'But what will we do without you?' Quinn asked.

'You're grown up. It's time you made your way in the world, my little ducklings.'

She pulled them into a group hug so messy it drew looks from other travellers and the attention of a security guard who advised them to 'Keep it moving.'

Amanda left them with some parting words. 'I have every confidence you'll get that job, Ivy.'

'Fingers crossed,' Ivy said.

'As for you, Quinn, stop being so stubborn and go get that girl.'

Amanda was right about Ivy, yet she was wrong about this. 'I'm not the stubborn one! It's Kya! She's inflexible. She won't budge.'

'Then I guess you'll have to,' Amanda said. 'I don't see any other way out of this.'

'Tell her what you told us,' Ivy said. 'You're scared of losing her.'

'I never said that!'

'That's the takeaway, though, isn't it?' Amanda said.

'She's not like us,' Ivy said. 'Getting fired wouldn't get us down. We'd laugh it off, go day-drinking, and forget about the whole thing. Only, losing that job ripped her in half. She's going through a really tough time.'

I'm not like you. That's exactly what Kya had been trying to tell her, that she was different and had needs Quinn would never understand.

'And thank God she's not like us,' Amanda added. 'It's a good thing. Think how insufferable you two would be, two stars lighting up the sky.'

Quinn thought of her and Kya at home, eating takeaway on the floor, drinking tea and coffee on the balcony. When not off to gigs or girls' nights out, they were well-balanced, the cosiest couple you'd ever come across.

'You might have to trade in some pride, do a little grovelling, a grand romantic gesture, that sort of thing,' Amanda said. 'Are you up for it?'

'I won't grovel, but I'll return her text. Does that count as a romantic gesture?'

'Barely!' Ivy scoffed.

Good thing there wasn't time to dive into it. The security guard who'd advised them to keep it moving, now ordered them to clear out of the way. 'Ladies, either go through the checkpoint or get gone,' he said. 'You're blocking the flow.'

'All right, girls,' Amanda said. 'I should get going. Hugs and kisses, and *please* don't cry. I'll be back. I promise.'

They hugged. They kissed. They promised to keep in touch. To share photos and updates and generally keep each other in the loop. Then, arm in arm, Ivy and Quinn walked back to the car park, eyes wet with tears.

CHAPTER FORTY-SEVEN

Kya cut her visit with Jon short and headed out to Quinn's place. Only she wasn't home, Kya waited in the lobby, and passed the time chatting with Benny. After a while, even the warm, talkative doorman ran out of things to say. 'I'll call her,' Kya said, 'and ask when she'll be back.'

'Very well, miss,' he replied.

Kya stepped away and stared at her phone. She couldn't bring herself to dial the number. 'Actually,' she said to Benny. 'I have some errands to run. I'll take care of it and come back.'

'Very well,' he repeated, kindly.

Benny had seen it all. He knew all the telltale signs of a broken heart.

Head low and heavy, Kya walked to the nearby coffee shop. She must have looked like the loneliest woman alive, drawing pitying looks from the wait staff, sitting alone in a booth, waiting for her ride.

Only her precious Lucky was home to greet her when she got back. Kya poured herself a glass of water and sat at the kitchen table with the puppy on her lap. Hugo came home first. 'Hey, pretty girl!' he called out, dashing by. He explained that he was late for a conference call with the design magazine before locking himself in his office. Adrian arrived a moment later with bags of Chinese takeout, all her favourites. 'I was looking forward to this all day.'

'Me, too,' she replied, her voice thin.

He tossed her a fortune cookie. Kya unwrapped it, cracked it open, and teased out the strip of paper. YOU WILL LIVE AN ABUNDANT LIFE. It was as generic a fortune as anyone could expect. She read it, put it aside, and burst into tears. Sobs rattled through her. The silence amplified her sniffles and hiccups. Then suddenly, Adrian cried, 'I can't believe it!'

Startled, Kya looked up and questioned him with watery eyes.

'You and Quinn!' he cried. 'How could I be so dumb?'

Hugo entered the kitchen right then. 'My love, I was wondering the same thing,' he said. 'What took you so long?'

He confronted Hugo. 'Why didn't you tell me?'

'It was her news, not mine.'

'Fair enough.' He confronted Kya. 'Why didn't *you* tell me?'

'There's nothing to tell, Adrian,' Kya answered.

'You're crying over Quinn! Don't deny it.'

'I'm crying because it's over. We're done. End of story.'

Hugo ran a hand through his curls. 'You lose your job and your lover in the same month? How much grief can you take?'

Kya was wondering the same thing. Her karma must be in the trash to deserve all of this.

'I was too distracted with your career issues to pay attention.' Apparently, Adrian was more concerned with his failure to read a situation clearly than anything else. 'No wonder you didn't want to come home today. What went wrong with you two?'

'Everything went wrong,' she said, resigned. 'It's not the right time for us.'

That sounded infinitely better than what she knew to be true: she'd blown it. She'd escalated a minor issue until it drove a wedge between them. Quinn had not called or replied to her text message. After checking her phone all day, Kya had given up.

Hugo joined her at the table and picked up the fortune strip. 'Cheer up! You're gonna get some money, honey!'

She nudged him. 'Please! Give me a break.'

'You don't want to be sad *and* broke,' he said. 'That's tragic.'

'I don't want to be sad at all, yet here we are.'

'And you're sure you want to fly out tomorrow?' Adrian asked. 'There's a chance you could resolve this if you stayed.'

'I'm leaving. It's time to go.'

She had no regrets. Her extended stay in Miami wasn't wasted time. She'd met so many interesting people. Had she rushed back to California, she would have never considered starting her own company, even as a side hustle. Sam had only recently quit her day job; that seemed like the way to go.

Adrian came around and hugged her. 'You deserve to be happy.'

'You really do,' Hugo said.

'Thanks, guys.'

'It doesn't have to be like this,' Hugo said. 'You met someone wonderful, and you had a great time. There's no need for tears or a mental health crisis. Just say goodbye with love.'

Saying goodbye to Quinn would be difficult enough. Love would only make it ten times worse.

In the morning, her clothes were laundered and neatly folded in her luggage. She trusted Adrian to ship the laptop directly to Ex-Cell's headquarters; she would never step foot into that building again. Kya gathered her braids in a ponytail and slipped on her softest T-shirt and leggings. She was ready for the long trip back west. One last lunch on the patio, a final cuddle with Lucky, and it was time to head to the airport.

It was just the three of them, Hugo at the wheel, Adrian in the passenger seat, and Kya with the back seat to herself. She ignored the lump in her throat and the unbearable feeling that she was making a mistake. She ignored the voice that repeated: *Don't do this*. It seemed, the city itself did not want to let her go. Traffic piled up on the interstate. They advanced at a snail's pace. All the while, the guys did their best to cheer her up.

'Spend the holidays with us,' Adrian said. 'We'll have to do the family thing, visit Mom and Dad, but afterwards we'll come back to Miami to ring in the new year. It's always a blast. Right, H?'

'Always,' Hugo agreed. 'This is our first year in the new house, so you know we're going to throw down.'

'We'll see,' Kya said.

'If you're too busy over the holidays,' Adrian continued, 'come in the spring.'

'We're going to the Bahamas!' Hugo announced, 'come with!'

'Oh, cool,' Kya said with zero enthusiasm. 'I'll tag along with my big brother on a romantic getaway. I love that for me.'

'We're going with a bunch of friends,' Adrian said. 'You won't be the third wheel.'

'But it will be romantic,' Hugo insisted. 'That sunset does things to me. But who knows? You may meet someone.'

Kya wanted to scream. She *had* met someone. The cosmic piñata had been generous to her. She'd scooped up the possibility of a life with Quinn. A big, full, happy life, filled with music, fun, late nights out with the coolest girls you'd ever meet, and quiet nights in with wine, pasta, working through her collection of vinyl records, weekends at the beach, at the pool, spicy margaritas, watered-down cocktails, DJ battles, and so much drama. All of this had been dropped at her feet by forces unknown to her, and what had she done? She'd kicked it to the kerb.

Suddenly, the wide back seat was too small. Kya was close to suffocating. She took big laboured breaths. She would've toppled into a full-blown panic attack if her phone had not lit up with a text message.

Quinn: I'm still not scared.

'Stop this car! Stop right now!'

'What's wrong? Are you all right?' Adrian fired those questions, searching her face for signs of distress.

'I changed my mind. I'm not leaving.'

'What about your interview?'

'I'll leave tomorrow.'

Ever the pragmatist, Adrian was not willing to drop it. 'Kya, that doesn't make any sense. It's too late to cancel the flight. The airline won't refund you.'

'What does it matter?' Hugo asked Adrian. 'I once booked a first-class flight just to meet you in Hawaii, or don't you remember?'

'Guys, could we put your romance on the back burner a sec? I have to find Quinn and apologize. I have to do it right this second.'

Hugo flashed her a smile. 'What? Again?'

'You've done this before?' Adrian asked.

'Every eight to ten business days. Isn't that right, Kya?'

They could tease and laugh at her expense all they wanted, but Quinn had reached out, and for once, she had hope. 'If I don't go to her now, I'll lose the best thing that ever happened to me.'

'Good to see you're finally coming to your senses,' Adrian said. 'Better late than never, I suppose.'

'She's performing on the beach today. Take me home, and I'll ride over.'

'I know exactly where she's performing,' Hugo said. 'We'll take you there.'

Adrian slipped on his sunglasses. 'This is exciting.'

'You need to hang out with us more often,' Hugo replied, and veered off the nearest exit. A few crazy turns later, they were on their way back to Miami Beach.

They were late; the concert had started. They didn't have tickets, and their names weren't on a list. Hugo tapped his network and while they waited, the sun bored down on them. It was hot, and only getting hotter. Adrian decided he was not built for excitement. He wanted to go home and hydrate. As Kya listened to her brother complain and watched Hugo place call after call, she questioned the logic of her decision. Even if she got in, she'd have to fight to approach the stage. Even if she made it that far, it would be a struggle to catch Quinn's eye. Even if she managed to get her attention, she might not hold it for long. Her work meant everything to her. Maybe the smart thing to do was to go home and wait until the concert was over—

'You're in!' Hugo cried. 'I found a spare ticket, but only one. I'll forward it to you now. You're on your own.'

With that announcement, Kya's anxiety abated. Her body tingled with determination. If she had to fight her way through the crowd, she'd fight. Nothing would stop her. She had finally come to her senses, and it wasn't too late.

CHAPTER FORTY-EIGHT

BONUS TRACK

Quinn enquired about cancelling.

The event coordinator was a thin man with long hair the same colour as the sand. He did not take her inquiry well. 'I don't understand. You're our headline act. Are you sick?'

'I'm not ill,' Quinn replied. 'Something's come up. Something personal.'

'People are lining up in the sun for you!'

'I'm not your only act.'

'You're one of our hottest,' he replied. 'If you don't deliver, they'll want their money back. I'm sure of it.'

Quinn backed down. Above all, she was a professional. She had a job to do and a reputation to uphold. Besides, what was she going to do? Chase Kya down at the airport? That sort of thing only paid off in movies. Yesterday, she'd got a preview of the airport's tight security measures. They would likely have her detained if she stormed past security. That said, she had to do *something*. She couldn't let things end this way. It was a mistake; she could feel it. Quinn could always tell when her life was going off track, and this was one of those times. This morning, she woke up with a weight on her chest. Bonus Track was the last concert of the season. It was meant to be fun. How could it be without Kya?

Ivy and Amanda could skip it; that was fine with her. They were her friends, not her groupies. But Kya was her everything. Why hadn't she grovelled like Amanda suggested? She'd wasted time, too stubborn and proud to make the first move.

What could she do? The stage manager had already sent for her. The sound engineer checked the equipment while an assistant hooked her up to the mic. The spotlights were switched on and a disco ball hanging over the decks started to spin. What could she do in the short time remaining? Quinn hadn't replied to any of Kya's messages. Now was the time.

I'm still not scared.

For once, Quinn didn't intend to address the crowd; she would just get down to work. If she opened her mouth, her sadness would sail over the waters and tomorrow she'd read about it online; the trolls would make sure of it. On the topic of trolls, Nick was here, prowling about. She'd run into him backstage.

'Hey!' he said, casual. 'No hard feelings, right?'

'Oh, no!' Quinn replied. 'It's the opposite.'

Her feelings were as hard as lab-grown diamonds.

'Come on, Quinn. It wasn't personal,' he said. 'You know that.'

'Wrong again, mate!'

He coughed up a pathetic excuse for his behaviour. 'It was clickbait, pure and simple,' he said. 'You were always trending, more than Angelo, more than anyone. I could post anything about you, anything at all, and it would go viral. Your relationship with Kya was a gift. People were curious, and once the word was out, they couldn't get enough.'

'So, basically, you used us,' Quinn said.

'I didn't mean any harm.'

Unless they'd changed the definition of 'harm', how could she arrive at any other conclusion? It was too late to change the past. There was nothing else to do but wish him well … and tell him to sod off. Frankly, she had other things on her mind. Why concern herself with greedy men like Nick, when women like Kya existed, warm, generous, loving, smart, seductive women, who didn't exploit others for their own gain, but gave freely of themselves? The only way for her to crack on, do her job and fulfil the commitment of the day was to hold onto the belief that all was not lost. She'd wrap this up and fly out to California tonight. With some focus, she could play a solid set. Quinn could leave the venue knowing she hadn't let anyone down. This was the dream she'd sacrificed everything for. Yet, in that moment, it wasn't enough. A sea of people chanting her name wasn't enough.

Her gaze skimmed the crowd until she found her. Kya was struggling against the current, making her way to the stage. *I love her.* The thought paralysed her for a second, but only a second. She had to do something, somehow let her know that she was seen and loved and didn't have to struggle so hard. They would be together soon.

Quinn jumped and waved her arms, trying to get her attention. This only stirred up the crowd and pushed Kya further back. She couldn't go to her, couldn't reach out and pluck her from the mob. The concert was timed, and the stage manager gestured for her to begin. The crew was watching, questioning if something was wrong with the equipment or just with her. She would have to reach Kya in some other way, the best way she knew, through music.

Quinn exited her curated playlist and searched her catalogue until she found what she was looking for. When the lights dimmed, the disco ball whirled faster, and the chanting grew louder, Quinn slipped on her headphones and played Kya's song.

Kya had made it to the stage, but with no special bracelet or credentials to flash, she could not get any closer to Quinn. She didn't mind. She was exactly where she was meant to be. What better feeling than to know, for certain, that of all the possible paths, you'd chosen the correct one? Her mind was clear. She'd made work the priority, believing it was necessary to sort out her professional life *before* focusing on love. Really, it was the other way around. No matter what great job she got, no matter the salary, title, or benefits, her life would be empty without Quinn.

The set wrapped to raucous cheers. A moment later, Quinn charged down the side steps, pushed past security, and jumped Kya. They kissed frantically then broke away laughing. Kya led her away from a group who was gawking, and recording. When they were finally alone, she turned to her and cupped her heart-shaped face. 'You played my request.'

'Happy now?'

'It took you long enough. Was it really so hard?'

'You have no idea!'

'I love you for doing it.'

'I love you, too.'

Kya pulled away and studied her. The setting sun brought out her halo. There was no hint of fear in those sparkling brown eyes. 'You don't have to say that. It's enough that we're together.'

'You're wrong,' Quinn said, evenly. 'I love you, and I have to say it. Next time you try to walk away, you should know what you're leaving behind.'

'I will never leave you,' Kya said. 'I know where my heart is.'

Quinn leaned in and touched the tip of her nose to hers, a familiar gesture that always caused Kya's insides to melt. She whispered, 'Survivors always do.'

CHAPTER FORTY-NINE

LAST CALL

'Your attention, please! Guys, girls, gays! Everyone! Thank you for joining us at BLU on this gorgeous summer night! It's the last call, so you know what to do! Before we part ways, I'd like to give a shout-out to some special guests. With us tonight is the team of The Queer Code! Honourable mention goes to CEOs Jon Yi, man of the people, who passed on VIP to party in the crowd, and Kya Reid, a woman who needs no introduction, my heart, my treasure, the light of my life, the joy of my days, and a badass girl in tech! We are celebrating the one-year anniversary of an app that has helped many of you. If you feel like we feel, so proud, so hopeful, do me this small favour. Put your hands together and make some noise!'

ACKNOWLEDGEMENTS

I can't believe we're here again, celebrating my second book.

Thank you to everyone who read *Until I Met You*. It was so important to me to share a love story with characters who look and sound like me and like my friends from different backgrounds. To hear how much it has meant to you too has been so rewarding. You have made this second story possible.

This book is so close to my heart. It means a lot to me that I have had this opportunity to create a sapphic romance that is just as spicy, fun and romantic as all the books I know and love, but that also represents a lot more. I used to love reading when I was younger, but I never had the chance to read anything like this. There aren't enough romance stories out there that show lesbian or bisexual relationships, especially between Black women, and I'm so proud to be able to give young women like me the representation we never had growing up.

To Nadine, thank you once again for bringing my exact vision to life. I am so grateful that I get to work with you. You have a magical ability to take my characters and make them real.

Thank you to the HarperCollins and Mills & Boon teams for all their amazing work on this project. Your support, passion and endless positivity has made all of this possible.

Finally, thank you to all of you: to my supporters and followers who for the past five years have always believed in me. Without you, none of this would be possible. I hope you enjoy Kya's summer in Miami!

Amber

Enjoyed *One Summer in Miami*?

Read on for a taste of Amber Rose Gill's gorgeous, debut holiday romance, *Until I Met You*.

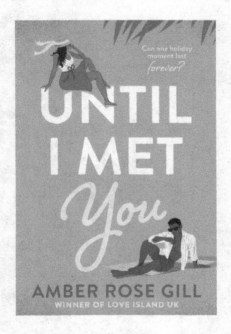

AVAILABLE NOW

Travel Blog

DRAFT ENTRY #1: GO IT ALONE

Attending a wedding alone. When a man does it, he's going stag. But if he plays it right, the odds of scoring that night are in his favour. What about women? Going doe is dull. But Hollywood loves the scenario. A single girl coercing or cajoling a random guy to avoid humiliation. Mind you, I'm not above these tactics, but such elaborate plots require time and/or money, both of which I'm fresh out of. The wedding is only days away and on my modest salary the most I could possibly offer a man is a free meal and a round of drinks. Besides, this isn't the sort of wedding you can take a stranger to. An intimate affair at a seaside resort in Tobago, the guest list is tighter than a steel drum.

Affirmation: I can do this. I can go it alone. I am whole and valuable all on my own.

CHAPTER ONE

'Ladies and gentlemen, this is the pre-boarding announcement for flight BA209 to Miami, Florida. At this time we ask passenger Samantha Roberts to proceed to the British Airways check-in desk. Passenger Samantha Roberts, please proceed to the check-in desk.'

The insistent monotone roused Samantha from her meditation. She hopped to her feet, grabbed the handle of her carry-on suitcase and made a beeline for the desk. Tall, curvy, with cinnamon brown skin and a head of wild corkscrew curls, she stood out in most crowds. But the Heathrow departure gate was packed. She had to elbow her way to the front of the line.

'Hello! I'm Samantha!' she called out. 'Is something wrong?'

The uniformed airline employee typed as he spoke. 'Ms Roberts?'

'Yes.' She handed over her British passport as proof.

'We see you're travelling alone with a window aisle all to yourself.'

Samantha blushed. *They know. They all know.* Every single person at Gate B12, every pasty, bleary-eyed traveller, knew that she was that sad, sorry girl on her way to a wedding without a date. Not only that, she'd had the nerve to take up an entire aisle just for herself. Before they judged her too harshly, perhaps

3

she should explain. Her ex-boyfriend had booked the seat next to hers. But at the very last minute he cancelled the trip, preferring to throw away an all-expenses-paid holiday in the Caribbean to travelling with her. What could she say? These things happened. Surely, they'd understand.

'We need to accommodate a couple travelling with a small child,' the attendant explained. 'If you'd be gracious enough to give up your window seat, we'll upgrade you to an aisle seat in our first class section. Is that all right?' It was clear he wasn't interested in her answer. Only a fool would pass up a free upgrade. He printed a new boarding pass and handed it to Samantha with a wink. 'Be ready to board when we call first class.'

Samantha returned to the waiting area and dropped into her seat. The upgrade took the sting out of her misery. The trip to Tobago was long and arduous. If she had to go it alone, might as well travel in style.

First stop was a one-night layover in Miami. There she would meet up with her friends, Hugo and Jasmine. All three would fly out to Tobago the next day. Why was she bemoaning her single status if she was travelling in such good company? The answer was simple: all her friends had someone. In fact, this destination wedding was shaping up as a couples' retreat. Jasmine was in a relationship with Jason, a Canadian corporate attorney. Hugo was married to Adrian, a plastic surgeon with such chiselled bone structure and gorgeous mocha skin tone he could have easily gone into modelling instead of medicine. The only other single girl on the guest list, as far as she knew, was Maya, the bride's teenage sister.

Samantha was actually looking forward to the short stay in Miami. She had never been to the city and her friends had a night out planned. Plus it was an opportunity to generate more content for her fledgling travel blog. It didn't change the fact that once she arrived – via first class transatlantic travel – there would be hell to pay.

★★★

In the spring, Samantha had RSVP'd for two for the event of the year: Naomi Reid's Caribbean nuptials. After a mere six months of courtship, Naomi was marrying her 'great love' Anthony Scott, aka 'Fit with Tony', a fitness trainer with an enviable online following. She'd helped choose the bridesmaids' dresses and Timothy, her boyfriend, had booked the flights. He'd been looking forward to it, talked nonstop about fishing and snorkelling. But people change, as seasons do. It was summer now. She and Timothy were through. He'd gone backpacking across Italy with friends, leaving Samantha agonizingly single and without a date for her best friend's wedding.

Samantha pulled out her phone and scrolled through old photos. Not the ones of her and Timothy, cheek-to-cheek, grinning stupidly into the camera – she'd long deleted those. The slightly blurred shots she was swiping through were of her and Naomi on their various trips. They'd grown up together, their identical homes standing side by side in a tidy suburb in Manchester. As girls they'd played with dolls and dreamed of travelling the world in a private jet like Barbie or Wonder Woman, depending on their mood. Although their paths had split after university, with Naomi moving to California to join a graphic design agency and Samantha staying close to home, they'd remained best friends.

Samantha didn't like to compare her life to others', but it was difficult not to draw some parallels. Her closest friend was getting married and settled. She on the other hand had been dumped. OK, fine. She hadn't been dumped exactly. It had been a mutual and cordial see-you-never type of break-up, only Samantha had not seen it coming.

She and Timothy (it was *Timothy*, never Tim or Timmy) had been dating for over two years. Her mother adored him and she'd met his parents. Her friends figured she would be first to go down the aisle. Samantha expected the same and took that responsibility seriously. For months, she hid a stash of bridal magazines under her bed. When Timothy suggested they take a moonlit walk one Sunday night after a light rain, she wasn't expecting him to propose. However, she could tell by his rigid posture that he was nervous and had something important to say. He slipped his hand in hers, mingled their fingers, and met her eyes. 'It's not working,' he said, 'and we both know it.'

Samantha had stared back at his glassy blue irises, wondering if she'd heard him right. Hours later, alone in bed, she replayed the scene in her mind. Every detail was as clear as day, from the shop windows stained with raindrops to the moonlight swirling on the pavement puddles. She heard Timothy's deep voice repeat the words: *It's not working, and we both know it*. She'd withdrawn her hand from his, feeling like a fool.

The man was direct; you had to give him props for that. Samantha sort of admired the straightforward manner in which he'd delivered the final blow. She could use some of that energy now.

Samantha was still actively dealing in half-truths. She hadn't broken the news to any of her friends, not even the bride.

When she turned up in Tobago alone, she'd get the full brunt of their loving concern. Naomi was going to flip. And before she even made her way to the Caribbean island, she had to face the dynamic duo: Hugo and Jasmine.

She should take a page from Timothy's book and deliver the news to them in a sanguine manner. If she broke the news now, they'd have plenty of time to recover from the shock before she arrived. A friendly heads-up text would take care of it.

Samantha closed the photo app and tapped on the WhatsApp icon. After a few swipes, she landed on the extended group chat saved under VEGAS SQUAD, in reference to the trip to Nevada nearly five years ago where she and Naomi had met Jasmine and Hugo. Her thumb hovered over the keyboard. She shouldn't be this nervous. These were her friends, after all. They adored her, but they had the doggedness of unjaded criminal investigators. They wouldn't stop until they got to the truth.

'We are now inviting first class passengers to board at this time.'

Samantha tucked away her phone, and proceeded to the gate. Breaking the news to her friends would certainly be easier while settled in a premium recliner with a warm towel and salted nuts to soothe her anxiety.

CHAPTER TWO

5 July, 7.15 a.m.

SAM'S PHONE TO VEGAS SQUAD (NAOMI, HUGO AND JASMINE)

Sam: This is to inform you that Timothy and I are no longer a couple. Please respect our privacy during this difficult time.

Hugo: What the hell is this?

Jasmine: Thought we banned drunk-texting in the group chat.

Hugo: It's 2 a.m. in Miami. I was dead asleep. This better not be a joke.

Sam: Sorry to wake you. I'm not drunk. This is not a joke.

Hugo: Why do you sound like Buckingham Palace's communication secretary?

Sam: Just trying to be frank.

Hugo: Stop.

Naomi: …

Jasmine: So this is real?

Hugo: OK! I'm up. What happened?

Jasmine: Can't sleep. Always get nervous before a big trip, so don't hold back. Tell us everything.

Sam: Nothing happened. Things fall apart.

Naomi: …

Hugo: Sure it's over, *gata*? Not just a rough patch. We all have bad days.

Jasmine: Couples fight, Sam. You get that, right? It doesn't mean anything.

Sam: Thanks for the insight, but there was no fight. It was a clean break. We both knew it wasn't working.

Hugo: Damn. You two were solid.

Sam: Not really.

Jasmine: What about the wedding? You're still coming, right?

Sam: Just boarded the plane. First class upgrade!!!

Jasmine: Nice!!!!

Hugo: Where were you and Timmy planning to spend the night in Miami?

Sam: At a hotel near the airport.

Hugo: Screw that. Jasmine is staying with Adrian and me. Join us.

Sam: No thanks. I'm fine!

Jasmine: Join us! It'll be fun.

Hugo: We'll take care of you.

Sam: All right. Why not!

Hugo: Good. It's settled! Text me the flight details. I'll meet you at the airport.

Naomi: Nothing is settled! Sam! Are you serious? The wedding is ten days out. TEN DAYS. I can't handle any drama right now!

Jasmine: That's … harsh.

Hugo: It's not like she arranged to get dumped just to give you a stress headache.

Sam: Who said anything about getting dumped?

Naomi: It was going to happen sooner or later. You two had lost your spark. But did it have to happen now? Couldn't you have waited until after the wedding? I gave the caterer a final headcount last week and Timothy was your plus one.

Sam: I was NOT dumped.

Naomi: Makes no difference. You're down a plus one.

Sam: I'm well aware!

Jasmine: Let it go! The food won't go to waste. Someone will eat it.

Naomi: OK … OK … Letting it go. Sorry about you and Timmy, sweetie. I love you like a sister. You know that, right?

Sam: Love you, too. Sorry I messed up your seating chart.

Naomi: No worries. I'll sort it out with the caterer. But no one else gets dumped in the next ten days. Got that?

Hugo: We'll do our best!

Jasmine: OMG

Naomi: Is that really too much to ask?

Sam: OK! Time to switch off mobile phones. Bye for now.

Hugo: See you soon! Going to dive into a bottle of Absolut.

Jasmine: I'm going to cry into a cup of matcha.

Naomi: I'm gutted. I don't know what I'm going to do.

Sam: Well, I'm going to order a mimosa. I could get used to travelling first class.

LET'S TALK
Romance

Follow us:

- Millsandboon
- @MillsandBoon
- @MillsandBoonUK
- @MillsandBoonUK

For all the latest titles and special offers, sign up to our newsletter:

Millsandboon.co.uk